# SWEENEY TODD

## The Demon Barber of Fleet Street

EDITED BY

ROBERT L. MACK

THOMAS PECKETT
PREST

**OXFORD**
UNIVERSITY PRESS

# OXFORD

### UNIVERSITY PRESS

Great Clarendon Street, Oxford ox2 6DP
Oxford University Press is a department of the University of Oxford.
It furthers the University's objective of excellence in research, scholarship,
and education by publishing worldwide in

Oxford  New York

Auckland  Cape Town  Dar es Salaam  Hong Kong  Karachi
Kuala Lumpur  Madrid  Melbourne  Mexico City  Nairobi
New Delhi  Shanghai  Taipei  Toronto

With offices in

Argentina  Austria  Brazil  Chile  Czech Republic  France  Greece
Guatemala  Hungary  Italy  Japan  Poland  Portugal  Singapore
South Korea  Switzerland  Thailand  Turkey  Ukraine  Vietnam

Oxford is a registered trade mark of Oxford University Press
in the UK and in certain other countries

Published in the United States
by Oxford University Press Inc., New York

British Library Cataloguing in Publication Data

Data available

Library of Congress Cataloging in Publication Data

Data available

Typeset in Miller
by Cepha Imaging Private Ltd., Bangalore, India
Printed in Great Britain by
Clays Ltd., St Ives plc.

ISBN 978-0-19-922933-8

1 3 5 7 9 10 8 6 4 2

# Contents

# Introduction

SWEENEY TODD—the 'demon barber' who is alleged to have slit the throats of his unsuspecting customers before dropping their bodies into a cellar that connected to a nearby pie shop—is one of the most famous Londoners of all time. Since he first entered the public scene in the mid-nineteenth century, his exploits have chilled and fascinated readers and audiences all the world over. Whether in print, on the stage, or in films, the name of Sweeney Todd has become so ubiquitous that it has entered the English dictionary.[1]

The general outline of his story, as it first appeared in the pages of nineteenth-century periodicals, and as it subsequently played itself out in a seemingly endless succession of melodramas on the Victorian stage, is straightforward enough. A prosperous London barber in the days when men were compelled regularly to bare their throats to be shaved by comparative (and often disreputable-looking) strangers, Todd routinely murders the unsuspecting patrons of his Fleet Street 'tonsorial parlour'. Making use of an ingeniously constructed barber's chair, he dramatically hurls his victims head over heels into the basement of his shop before robbing them. Occasionally, if the drop from the chair to the stone floor below has not already done the job for him, Todd is compelled to 'polish them off' with his razor. He then drags their bodies (via an ancient network of subterranean passageways) to the convenient cellar of the nearby premises of Mrs Margery Lovett, who transforms the fresh corpses into succulent meat pies. The clothes, walking sticks, hats, and other personal items belonging to Todd's unlucky customers are hidden in the barber's house; their otherwise 'unusable' remains are secreted within the mouldering and long-disused vaults beneath the neighbouring church of St Dunstan's. Todd's greed and increasing bloodlust inevitably gets the better of him, and his murderous activities spiral out of control. Thanks to the combined efforts of a well-known local magistrate, a team of Bow Street Runners, and an enterprising pair of star-crossed young lovers, the pair are eventually captured and brought to justice before the bar of the Old Bailey.

---

[1] See *OED*, s.v. 'Sweeney': 'a (nickname for a) barber'.

The relatively simple outline provided by this frankly ghoulish tale of terror has demonstrated itself to be peculiarly accommodating, however. Each generation has been compelled to make use of what might best be described as the 'mythic' elements inherent in the macabre story—its resonant themes of avarice, ambition, entrepreneurial capitalism, and cannibalism—effectively to mirror its own particular concerns. Todd's presence continues to haunt our storybooks, novels, plays, and our airwaves and works of musical theatre; his figure can often be found creeping, only barely disguised, through related collections of folklore and local legend. As the Chronology included in this edition makes clear, no sooner had Sweeney Todd made his first formal appearance on the stage of English fiction, than he appeared suddenly to be everywhere at once. The 'Demon Barber of Fleet Street' strode the boards of the late-Victorian and Edwardian theatre in the manner of a blood-splattered, razor-wielding colossus. The serendipitously named actor Tod Slaughter famously brought the character to life on cinema screens in 1936, although Slaughter's eye-rolling interpretation of the role was not the first 'Sweeney' to appear on film (nor, of course, was it to be the last). The twentieth century, quite apart from a seemingly unstoppable series of revisions of Todd's story as a stage melodrama, witnessed the re-emergence of the barber as a feature of popular musical-hall entertainments, as well as versions of his tale on radio, in elaborately illustrated graphic novels, and children's books. In 1959, the well-known composer Malcolm Arnold, with choreographer John Cranko, even reinterpreted the story as a Covent Garden ballet. The continued popularity of Todd's story well into the twenty-first century, as we shall see, owes a particularly great debt to the American composer Stephen Sondheim, whose spectacular 'musical thriller' based on the story premiered in 1979.

## Fine Young Cannibals: The Birth of Sweeney Todd

The story of the original, rip-roaring serial publication that first launched Todd's career is no less fascinating than the history of its many successors. Strikingly, the character of the demon barber made his first appearance in English in the pages of an eighteen-part serial that did not even bear his name in its title. The story that we today know as 'Sweeney Todd' originally appeared, rather, as

*The String of Pearls: A Romance* (the text that is reproduced in this edition). The serial was first included by the prolific publisher Edward Lloyd (1815–90) in his *The People's Periodical and Family Library*, where it ran from 21 November 1846 until 20 March 1847. The *People's Periodical* was one of several such papers published by the often unscrupulous Lloyd, whose London office at 12 Salisbury Square—just off Fleet Street—soon established itself as the informal centre of the 'penny blood' publishing industry.[2] (The terms 'penny bloods' or 'blood books' gained currency in the mid- to late-nineteenth century as shorthand colloquialisms to describe what were also known as 'blood-and-thunder books'—tales of the murderous exploits of outlaws, highwaymen, and thieves; the slightly later coinage 'penny dreadful' was also used to designate 'shockers' or crime stories 'written in a sensational or morbidly exciting style'.[3]) Lloyd had begun his career a decade earlier, publishing plagiarisms of the hugely popular works of Charles Dickens (his products included such audacious titles as *Oliver Twiss* (1838–9) and *Nikelas Nickelberry* (1838)). Yet even as early as 1836, when he had begun publishing works such as his *History and Lives of the Most Notorious Pirates* . . ., Lloyd had been alive to the potential market available to any publisher willing to provide the rapidly expanding audience of working-class readers with even cheaper and more 'sensational' reading material. Throughout the next few years, publications such as *Lloyd's Penny Atlas* (1842–5) and *Lloyd's Penny Weekly Miscellany* (1842–7) made a point of catering almost exclusively to this popular taste. Long-term technological progress (including the arrival of the new steam-powered printing press, the abolition of the stamp tax on newspapers, and the development of cheaper forms of paper made from Spanish esparto grass) had all worked in the publisher's favour. Lloyd's earliest productions were printed in the form of monthly 'chapbooks' or small pamphlets of anywhere from twenty-four to thirty-six pages. They typically sold for sixpence each. Lloyd later switched to the more rapidly produced and

[2] For an excellent summary of Lloyd's career as a publisher, see Rohan McWilliam on 'Edward Lloyd (1815–1890)', in *New Oxford Dictionary of National Biography* (Oxford University Press, 2004), 34, 118–19.

[3] See *OED*, s.v. 'dreadful'. See also C. B. Fry's anecdotal recollections of the usage of such terms in the 'Introduction' to E. S. Turner's *Boys Will Be Boys* (London: Michael Joseph, 1948), 7–12.

commercially viable format of the weekly magazine, each issue of
which provided readers with eight pages of any given serial narrative for only a penny. (By way of contrast, the original, individual
part numbers of Dickens's *Pickwick Papers*, beginning in March
1836, cost one shilling—or twelvepence each—with a final number
at two shillings; the earliest single-volume edition of the novel,
printed in November 1837, sold for twenty-one shillings.[4]) Lloyd's
penny bloods, in other words, although legitimately related to the
traditions of the Gothic novel, to the earliest work of writers such
as Dickens himself and to the so-called 'Newgate novels' of his
contemporaries (most notably William Harrison Ainsworth) and,
finally, to the hugely popular 'sensation' novels of authors a little
later in the century like M. E. Braddon, Wilkie Collins, and Ellen
Wood (Mrs Henry Wood), managed to embrace an entirely new
audience of readers—readers for whom even the part numbers of a
monthly serial would otherwise have remained financially just
beyond their reach.

Before the first appearance of Sweeney Todd in 1846, Lloyd
had already introduced what has been described as '[one] of the
most enduring icons of Victorian popular culture', when he published James Malcolm Rymer's *Varney the Vampyre, or, the Feast of
Blood* (1845).[5] The figure of Varney—a distant relation to John
Polidori's *The Vampyre* of 1819, and one of the progenitors of Bram
Stoker's much later *Dracula* (1897)—did much to establish the
figure of the 'aristocratic vampire' as a fixture in the public's imagination. Lloyd had even, in an 1844 issue of his *Penny Atlas* (vol. 2,
no. 97), already set about whetting the public's appetite for a tale
featuring a murderous barber. The anonymously authored 'Joddrel,
the Barber, or, Mystery unravelled' [*sic*] told the story of a London
barber whose neighbours begin to grow suspicious when many of
his customers seem mysteriously to disappear; their bodies are later
discovered hidden in a cupboard in Joddrel's Bishopsgate shop,
with wooden stakes driven through their heads. Although 'Joddrel,
the Barber' contains no references either to cavernous cellars or to
meat pies, the story nevertheless clearly anticipates the full-fledged

    [4] See James Kinsley, 'Introduction' to Charles Dickens, *The Pickwick Papers*
(Oxford: Clarendon Press, 1986), pp. xv–lxxxv.

    [5] See Louis James on 'James Malcolm Rymer *pseuds*. M. J. Errym, Malcolm J.
Merry (1803/4–1884)', in *New Oxford Dictionary of National Biography*, 48, 494–5.

narrative of Sweeney Todd as it was eventually to be presented in *The String of Pearls*.[6] Moreover, 'Joddrel' effected a further, important connection between the original 1846–7 serial and some even earlier, possible sources for the narrative. The most noteworthy of these precedents was a short, journalistic account that had first appeared in an 1824 publication called *The Tell-Tale*, under the eye-catching title 'A Terrific Story of the Rue de la Harpe, Paris'. Republished as recently as 1841, it told the story of a Parisian *peruquier* or barber and wig-maker, whose shop was visited by two 'incautious' visitors from the country. 'Whilst in the shop of this fiend', the item noted, the pair 'unhappily talked of the money they had about them, and the wretch, who was a robber and murderer by profession, as soon as the one turned his back, drew his razor across the throat of the other and plundered him'. 'The remainder of the story', the account relished, 'is almost too horrible for human ears, but is not upon that account the less credible':

[A] pastry-cook, whose shop was so remarkable for savoury patties that they were sent for to the Rue de la Harpe from the most distant parts of Paris, was the partner of this *peruquier*, and those who were murdered by the razor of the one were concealed by the knife of the other in those very identical patties, by which, independently of his partnership in those frequent robberies, he made a fortune.[7]

An even earlier item that first appeared in the *London Chronicle* of 2 December 1784 (soon republished in the *Annual Register* for 1784–5) told of 'a most remarkable murder' that was supposed to have been perpetrated 'by a journeyman barber . . . near Hyde Park Corner'.[8] Other sources traced the general story back even further, one of them insisting that the tale was based on an actual historical

[6] See Helen R. Smith, *New Light on Sweeney Todd, Thomas Peckett Prest, James Malcolm Rymer and Elizabeth Caroline Grey* (London: Jarndyce, 2002), 23. It was thanks to the diligent research of Smith that this vampiric variation on the Todd narrative was recovered; she further points out that the Joddrel story contains 'no cellars or pies', but effects a clear link between Todd's narrative and those of his earliest predecessors, generally.

[7] From *The Tell-Tale* (1824), cols. 509–12. The issue is noted to have been printed at the Caxton Press, by Henry Fisher, and published at 38 Newgate Street. The engraved frontispiece is dated 'Jan. 1 1824'. As noted, the 'Terrific story of the Rue de la Harpe' was reprinted in 1841; the account also appeared under the title 'The Murderous Barber' in a periodical entitled *The New Wonderful and Entertaining Magazine* (1825).

[8] *Annual Register* (1784–5), 208.

incident that had taken place in Venice some time in the mid-eighteenth century.[9]

Precedents of this sort are no doubt fascinating. Readers should always keep in mind, however, that the origins of Todd's story—a story that is essentially a nineteenth-century fable, the peculiar originality of which lies in its achievement of so spectacularly intertwining the narrative of a greedy, murderous barber, on the one hand, with that of a casually unprincipled and opportunistic baker of meat pies, on the other—lie much deeper than any of these more immediate textual 'cues' or sources. The underlying, cannibalistic obsessions of the atavistic Todd 'myth' can be traced back to sources as early as Homer's *Odyssey*, and are to be found everywhere in traditional fairy tales and folk narratives (e.g. 'Bluebeard', 'Captain Murder', 'Hansel and Gretel', 'Jack and the Beanstalk', etc.). The tale relies in a similar manner on a number of other related features of native and national mythologies (the fidelity of the hound Hector to his master, Lieutenant Thornhill, in the opening chapters of the novel, for example, is based upon the popular story of the 'Dog of Montargis', which in its own right furnished the plot for several popular melodramas in the mid-Victorian period).[10] Equally important literary and textual sources for the treatment of the themes of

[9] See Anthony Pasquin, *The Life of the Late Earl of Barrymore. Including a history of the Wargrave theatricals and original anecdotes of eminent persons. By Anthony Pasquin, esq. A new edition, corrected and much enlarged* (London: H. D. Symonds, 1793), 52–4. The story is recounted in this volume as an anecdote related to the author, Pasquin, by the Italian pantomimist Carlo Antonio Delpini (*c*.1740–1808).

[10] Those determined to find—if not any primary source for *Sweeney Todd*—then at least some of the more specific originating archetypes that inform his subsequent 'myth' have been prompted to point in turn to material as varied and as tenuously related to any 'final' version of Todd's story as the Ballad of the 'five Woemen-Barbers | That lived in Drewry-Lane' recalled so fondly by John Aubrey (1626–97) in his *Brief Lives*, or to Thomas Delonay's *Pleasant History of Thomas of Reading* (*c*.1602), an early example of a tradition of urban 'underworld' literature that includes the account of a murderous innkeeper and his wife; Delonay's narrative is remarkable for its detailed inclusion and description of a mechanical device remarkably similar to the barber's famous revolving chair. Sweeney's tale has been most often linked (although it is at best indebted only broadly and thematically) to the many narratives that surrounded 'Sawney Beane', the so-called 'Maneater of Midlothian', versions of whose supposedly true story were reprinted many times throughout the eighteenth century. Beane was alleged to have been an outlaw who raised an entire extended and incestuous 'family' of predatory cannibals who lived in a close-to-inaccessible cave on the shores of the county of Galloway; he was eventually to feature as a major character in his own right, in the Scottish novelist S. R. Crockett's 1876 novel, *The Grey Man of Auchinleck*.

greed, murder, guilt, and paranoia that are so memorably brought to life in *The String of Pearls* include the 'domestic' tragedies of George Lillo (particularly his hugely successful *The London Merchant* (1731), and his later *Fatal Curiosity* (1736)), as well as the enormously popular 'criminal biographies' by authors such as Henry Fielding (e.g. *Jonathan Wild* (1743)). Pamphlets detailing the lives, trials, confessions, and last days of the prisoners at Newgate—culminating in collections such as the *Newgate Calendar*, which began publication in the late-eighteenth century—had also catered to a reading public that was already well on its way to developing a taste for such fare as Mrs Lovett would have to offer.

## Fleshing Out the Story

Not that either Mrs Lovett or Sweeney Todd, we must again remind ourselves, would appear actually to have been intended to figure quite so centrally or spectacularly in the story with which they would later be so famously associated. The notorious 'Demon Barber of Fleet Street' is a character who from his very first appearance in English fiction is himself something of a cannibal—he is a character who takes over and devours what was intended to have been the tale of others. Sweeney Todd and Mrs Lovett are macabre, imaginative creations who even in their earliest incarnations suitably consume the narrative substance of what was meant primarily to be a romance (in this sense, Todd is reminiscent of another of his near-contemporaries in nineteenth-century fiction, Daniel Quilp, the malignant dwarf who effects a similar, imaginative co-option of narrative substance in Charles Dickens's *The Old Curiosity Shop* (1840–1)). As matters so turned out, *The String of Pearls* was a title that would within only a matter of months diminish in significance, and one that would eventually disappear altogether. Further complicating both the history of the barber's earliest appearance by name in fiction and the very notion of such narrative appropriation or cannibalism is the fact that even before the final number of Lloyd's story had appeared in print on 20 March 1847, a dramatized version of the tale, adapted for the stage by George Dibdin Pitt, was already being performed at the Britannia Theatre, Hoxton, since late February of that year performed, in other words, some three weeks *before* the 'original' narrative in *The People's Periodical* had even reached its own conclusion. So it was that the endings even of the earliest stage and prose versions of Todd's story were to differ from each other in several significant respects.

Rather than focusing with such relish on the activities that take place in Todd's Fleet Street barber shop, the particular story that self-consciously presented itself to its earliest readers as a 'romance' in Lloyd's original *The String of Pearls* was ostensibly the more conventional tale of a pair of young lovers. Their names in this first telling of the tale (as in many later versions) are Mark Ingestrie and Miss Johanna Oakley. For readers of mid-Victorian fiction, their dilemma would already have been a familiar one. Mark is described by his uncle early in the novel as a 'handsome, wild, harum-scarum, sort of fellow' who, rather than following the path of respectable convention and becoming a lawyer, as his guardian had planned, has opted rather to 'go abroad and make his fortune' at sea. Before sailing for the East Indies, Mark met and pledged his love to Johanna Oakley, the beautiful daughter of a successful City trades-man. Mark promised Johanna that in exactly two years' time he would either return to her or send her news of his whereabouts. 'If I heard nothing of him,' Johanna later confesses to her sympathetic father, 'I was to conclude he was no more.' When the novel opens in August 1785, the two-year anniversary of Mark's departure has arrived, and the distressed Johanna fears the worst. She is sur-prised when she is contacted not by Mark Ingestrie himself, but by one Colonel Jeffery. Jeffery informs her that the only individual who might have been able to tell her anything about her lover's fate—a fellow passenger of Mark's by the name of Lieutenant Thornhill, with whom Jeffery himself has only recently arrived in London—mysteriously disappeared shortly after alighting from their ship, at Temple Stairs. The eponymous 'string of pearls' appears to have been the only item of any real value in Thornhill's possession when he went missing. The privileged reader is informed in the novel's opening chapter that it had been the intention of Lieutenant Thornhill to pass these pearls on to Johanna in Mark's name; Thornhill, too, seems to believe that Johanna's lover is 'dead and gone, poor fellow, and the salt water washes over as brave a heart as ever beat'.

In such a manner are readers inducted into the mystery of the tale of Sweeney Todd. Like pioneer detectives we follow in the footsteps of Johanna and Colonel Jeffery in their search for Thornhill, who can in turn (they hope) provide them with some information regarding the fate or whereabouts of Mark Ingestrie. It soon becomes obvious to both Jeffery and Johanna that the trail of the recently arrived Thornhill goes cold from the moment he fatefully crossed the threshold of Todd's shop, which he seems to have entered simply with the intention of being shaved and making himself more presentable before seeking out Johanna. Only slowly are the several strands of the narrative that subsequently unfolds pulled together in the pages that follow, and only gradually do the ghoulish connections that link the repeated and increasingly suspicious disappearances of the customers of Todd's Fleet Street tonsorial parlour to Mrs Lovett's pie-shop in nearby Bell Yard become clear. Indeed, as was often the case with many of the hastily written stories that first appeared in publications such as Lloyd's penny bloods, some narrative strands are started only to be abandoned altogether as the interest of the writers or of the audience (or both) led them elsewhere; alternatively—as happens to be the case with some of the 'sub-plots' set up in the earliest chapters of *The String of Pearls*—such strands could be picked up, filled out, or otherwise exploited at much greater length in subsequent retellings of the story. (These could swell to enormous sizes, and in almost all cases the longer versions dilute rather than enhance their originals.) The primary intention of the writers of these 'bloods' was to hook their readers as quickly and as effectively as possible—something the author of *The String of Pearls* accomplishes with consummate ease. Within the space of just a few short pages, we are introduced to the spectacularly grotesque figure of Todd himself (characterized physically by his 'huge hands and feet', his bizarre hair, which is said to resemble 'a thickset hedge, in which a quantity of small wire had got entangled', and his 'immense mouth', out of which he spasmodically barks out his harsh and 'unmirthful' laugh). We look on in fascination, in the manner of unwilling yet hypnotized witnesses, as all the features of the larger mystery that soon emerge—the tantalizing details of which will titillate us in the weeks and months to come—are laid out for our consideration. The inexplicable disappearance of the patrons of Todd's shop; the curiously and suddenly 'vacant' barber's chair; the young apprentice terrified into submission by his master's all-too-believable threat to 'cut [his] throat from ear to ear' if he breathes a word to anyone of what passes inside the Fleet Street shop; the barber's inexplicably suspicious reaction to the same apprentice's innocent reference to 'the veal pies at [Mrs] Lovett's in Bell-yard'; the fatal admission, on the part of Todd's first customer, Lieutenant Thornhill, that he has only just returned from a voyage to the East Indies (a location redolent of the possibilities of untold wealth); the persistence of the faithful dog, Hector; the rueful recollection on the part of the barber's next patron, Mr Grant, of his missing nephew, Mark Ingestrie: we encounter all these narrative elements, remarkably, in little more than eight highly economical and tightly written pages. Strongly willed or pathologically incurious indeed would be those readers who could with any ease resign themselves never to learn anything more of just what it is that happens to any man so unfortunate as ever to set foot in the Fleet Street shop of Sweeney Todd!

### 'Polishing Him Off': Borrowed Seasonings

The name of the particular author (or authors) who actually sat down to write the earliest version of the story first published as *The String of Pearls* and later known as *Sweeney Todd* is likely forever to remain contested. Edward Lloyd employed a regular 'stable' of writers, and it was not uncommon for one 'hack' to begin a story, only to see the material then passed on to another member of the publisher's team for continuation, expansion, or completion. *The String of Pearls* as it first appeared in 1846–7 was for many years attributed vaguely to the prolific Thomas Peckett Prest, although Prest himself was in fact said to have taken up the tale only after the failing eyesight or generally poor health of its originating author, one George Macfarren, prevented him from working on it any further (this would also help to explain why several narrative strands begun in the earliest chapters of the novel are completely disregarded in the subsequent pages). But *The String of Pearls* is really not of a piece with Prest's other work (the quality of the writing is, in fact, arguably superior to most of his output). The most recent bibliographical scholarship on the writings of Prest and his peers argues convincingly that the narrative is far more likely to have been the work of James Malcolm Rymer, an author whose work was eventually to attract the favourable attention of Robert Louis Stevenson, and who, as the critic and 'bloods' bibliographer Helen R. Smith rightly asserts, 'now deserves proper reassessment as a writer'.[11]

Whoever it was that wrote the earliest version of the story, he was strongly under the influence of Charles Dickens at the time. Many commentators have noted a prominent cluster of references in Dickens's *Martin Chuzzlewit* (1843–4), all of which reveal the character of Tom Pinch, in that same novel, to be convinced that country visitors to London are regularly lured into unfamiliar quarters where they are 'made meat pies of or some horrible thing'.[12] Dickens writes that the guileless Pinch is grateful that his own 'evil genius did not lead him into the dens of any of those preparers of cannibalic pastry, who are represented in many standard country legends, as doing a lively retail business in the metropolis'.[13] Passages such as these clearly demonstrate Dickens's own familiarity with the prevalent rural fears regarding the increasingly voracious and appetitive dangers that were associated with the rapidly expanding urban environment. Insufficient attention has perhaps been paid to Dickens's very particular characterization of such stories as 'standard country legend[s]'. Many readers have assumed that the novelist's apparent allusions must only naturally have reflected his awareness—in some form or other—of the specific story of Sweeney Todd. In actual fact what is likely to have happened is that Dickens himself (albeit indirectly) is the one who unwittingly instigated the transformation of what had until then remained a vague and multifaceted rural myth into a more substantial and singular narrative reality. A collation of the major works that were being produced and published by Dickens in the early 1840s reveals the author of *The String of Pearls* to have been heavily and on occasion quite specifically indebted to the master novelist. Those strands of the Todd narrative that include the representation of the Oakley household on Fore Street—with the characters of the pompous and hypocritical preacher Mr Lupin, the shop-boy Mr Sam, and Johanna's protective uncle 'Big Ben'—have clearly been inspired by Dickens's description of the Varden family in the earliest chapters of *Barnaby Rudge* (13 February–27 November 1841); many of the details relating to

[11] See Smith, *New Light on Sweeney Todd*, 28.

[12] Charles Dickens, *Martin Chuzzlewit*, ed. Margaret Cardwell (Oxford: Clarendon Press, 1982), 495.

[13] Ibid. 496.

Todd's nocturnal journey to the lapidary in Moorfields in Chapter 7, and his unintentional visit to the 'thieves' den' in Chapter 8, appear likewise to have been taken from that same novel (particularly from the activities of the apprentice locksmith Sim Tappertit in the fourth weekly number of *Barnaby Rudge*). The central narrative that is based around Mark Ingestrie's attempts simultaneously to impress his uncle, Mr Grant, and to win the approval of Johanna's father by making his fortune in the East Indies, similarly bears a remarkably close resemblance to the earliest descriptions of Walter Gay, Sol Gills, and Captain Cuttle that had only just been offered to readers in the first monthly part of *Dombey and Son* in October 1846.

Yet as one might expect from Dickens's direct references to 'cannibalic pastries' in *Martin Chuzzlewit*, noted above, it was that same novel (published from January 1843 through to July 1844) that exerted the strongest influence on the author of *The String of Pearls*. In chapter 19 of *Martin Chuzzlewit* (which had been included in the monthly part for September 1843), the reader is first introduced to the character of Poll Sweedlepipe. Sweedlepipe is the landlord of the famous Sarah Gamp at Kingsgate Street in High Holborn, who 'was an easy shaver also, and a fashionable hair-dresser'.[14] His premises are noted as being 'next door but one to the celebrated mutton-pie shop, and directly opposite to the original cat's meat warehouse; the renown of which establishments was duly heralded on their respective fronts'.[15] (One of Hablot K. Browne's illustrations for the original number even features representations of both Sweedlepipe's shop—with a sign advertising 'Easy Shaving' in its window—as well as the neighbouring 'Mutton Pie Depot', the front of which is similarly ornamented with a signboard in the shape of a mutton pie.) It is not at all unlikely that the relatively straightforward notion of combining those long-standing, narrative traditions that told the story of a barber who cut the throats of his customers, on the one hand, with the rural legends that whispered of the bodies of slaughtered countrymen being disposed of in the form of succulent meat pies, on the other, may in this instance have been prompted by the simple contiguity of Dickens's description and Phiz's typically superb and economical

---

[14] Dickens, *Martin Chuzzlewit*, 265.
[15] Ibid. 266. 'Cat's meat', incidentally, was horse flesh that had been prepared and sold by street dealers as food for domestic cats.

Hablot K. Browne's ('Phiz') illustration for *Martin Chuzzlewit*,
with Poll Sweedlepipe's barber's shop and the 'Original Mutton Pie Depot'
in the background.

illustration in *Martin Chuzzlewit*. If anything, the conspicuous *absence* of any reference at all to Sweeney Todd or Mrs Lovett by name in Dickens's own writing suggests that, although the myths upon which their specific characters were to be based may have enjoyed a general circulation at the time, they had yet to coalesce into distinct and precisely named narrative figures.

It was perhaps inevitable, however, from the moment the simple premise of the story of Sweeney Todd was itself accepted as true, that readers would want to learn as much as they possibly could about the supposed 'facts' of the case. The historian Matthew Kilburn, in an entry on Todd rather oddly included in the *Oxford Dictionary of National Biography*, has emphasized that by as early as 1878 'it had become widely accepted that Sweeney Todd was a historical person'.[16] The reasons behind such easy acceptance are not hard to divine. At the very least, the specifics of the many spurious biographical narratives that have adhered to the figure of Todd from the late-nineteenth century onward could go some small way towards explaining just how such a monster could ever have come into being in the first place; they could help us to understand why an 'ordinary' barber such as Todd 'became' the creature that he did. More particularly, readers and audiences could comfort themselves with the knowledge that Sweeney Todd's adult crimes were rooted— as theatre programmes over the centuries have been compelled to insist—in such experiences as his mistreatment and abandonment as a child, in his appalling treatment as a young offender incarcerated amongst hardened criminals in Newgate, and in the justifiable (or explicable) resentment of a persecuted member of the working classes. Sweeney Todd had not been *born* a villain, the story of his 'life' looks to reassure us, he was himself the *victim* of a society that was guilty of treating an entire class of people as little more than a disposable source of cheap labour—of treating them as objects rather than as individuals. It cannot be emphasized too strongly that those accounts that insist, even today, on the historical 'truth' behind Todd's story are not only wrong-headed, but more often than not grossly and purposefully misleading. Such accounts routinely cite from 'first-hand documents' and sources that are supposed to

---

[16] Matthew Kilburn, 'Todd, Sweeney [*called* the Demon Barber of Fleet Street] (*supp. fl.* 1784)' in the *Oxford Dictionary of National Biography*, 54. 887–8.

have been included in otherwise reputable publications such as the *Gentleman's Magazine*, the *Newgate Calendar*, and the *Proceedings of the Old Bailey* (1674–1834); these sources and 'documents' simply do not exist. The only alternative for those who would wish to argue for the historical truth of Todd's story is for them to quote authoritatively from collections of London 'lore and legend'—collections that never, themselves, made any pretension to relate anything that was other than obviously and self-professedly fictional.[17]

However he came fully to be conceived—whoever it was that first gave to the constituent features of Todd's narrative a local habitation and a name—the Demon Barber is to some extent the product of the collective national psyche. Matthew Kilburn no doubt comes closest to the more nebulous 'truth' that lies behind the legend of Sweeney Todd when he asserts that the barber is 'perhaps best described as a personification of early nineteenth-century fears of the anonymity of urban life built around some recorded events and older fictional or legendary sources'.[18] The Demon Barber of Fleet Street is a particular manifestation of a legend that could perhaps lay claim to being as ancient as urban civilization itself. Sweeney Todd is arguably not so much an 'urban legend'—as that term is generally understood—as a *rural* legend. His tale is a sustained narrative expression of that peculiar, communal anxiety that manifests itself whenever an individual is surrendered to and swallowed by the greater cosmopolitan crowd; those people who chose to leave the safety and familiarity of their extended 'families' in smaller, close-knit rural communities are liable to 'disappear' in the big city. In *Sweeney Todd*, such individuals not only disappear, they are literally consumed; they are eaten up. What had once been metaphorical has become *real*. It is no mere accident of circumstance that Sweeney Todd himself emerges into life at the precise historical moment when the world city of London is perceived even by its most ardent champions to have swollen forever beyond the bounds of control—when it has become a metropolitan entity that is dangerous and non-negotiable. It is particularly striking, too, that although the original serial narratives and dramas

---

[17] See, e.g. George Walter Thornbury's *Haunted London* (London: Chatto & Windus, 1865), *Old Stories Retold* (London, 1869), and *Old and New London*, 2 vols. (London: Cassell & Co., 1875).

[18] Kilburn, 'Sweeney Todd', 888.

relating to Sweeney Todd quite clearly describe him as a late-eighteenth-century figure (the action in Lloyd's novel, again, is very explicitly set in August 1785), his status in the popular imagination is that of a conspicuously *Victorian* figure; time has transformed Todd into the natural companion, in fact, of 'Jack the Ripper' (*fl.* 1888–91).

## 'More Hot Pies': Stephen Sondheim's Sweeney

The fact that modern audiences continue to think of Sweeney Todd as one of the 'gaslight ghouls' of nineteenth-century London owes much to what has easily emerged as the most popular twentieth-century version of his narrative: the unlikely 'musical thriller' produced by the Broadway composer Stephen Sondheim. Sondheim first came across Todd's story during a working visit to London in 1973.[19] The playwright Christopher G. Bond's own reconception of Dibdin Pitt's original melodrama—a self-confessedly ambitious version of the story in which the author openly admitted to having 'cast [his] net wider than anyone else in "borrowing" from other authors' was then playing to a surprisingly responsive and enthusiastic audience at Joan Littlewood's Theatre Royal, Stratford East. Reviewing Bond's play as it was originally produced by the Theatre Workshop in pages of *The Times*, the critic Irving Wardle observed that 'the story is horrible partly because of the idea of queues in Fleet Street gorging themselves on human flesh, and partly because Sweeney [in Bond's version] is not a true villain. He starts with all the right on his side'.[20]

What Bond had done to Todd's story effectively turned the traditional dramatic narrative on its head. Rather than playing up the traditions of melodrama, or turning the play into a burlesque by playing them strictly for laughs, Bond embraced their relevance and enhanced their satiric possibilities. In earlier stage versions of the barber's career, Todd had invariably been portrayed as a dangerous and increasingly paranoid homicidal maniac. He murdered those of his customers who were unlikely to be traced to his shop

[19] Meryle Secrest, *Stephen Sondheim: A Life* (New York: Alfred Knopf, 1998), 289–90.

[20] Irving Wardle, rev. of *Sweeney Todd* (Theatre Workshop) in *The Times*, 3 May 1973, p. 7; issue 58772; col. G.

strictly for profit. His typical targets were farmers or drovers from the country who had sold their goods at market, or sailors who had only just returned from long stretches at sea. In a manner that was at once uncomplicated and yet at the same time terrifyingly *real*, Todd was quite simply revealed to be greedy. 'When I was a boy,' he confesses to the audience in one version of George Dibdin Pitt's frequently acted adaptation, 'the thirst of avarice was first awakened by the fair gift of a farthing; that farthing soon became a pound; the pound a hundred—so to a thousand, till I said to myself, I will possess a hundred thousand'.[21] In another passage in the drama, the apprentice Tobias denounces Todd as nothing more than a 'designing, cruel, and cold-blooded murderer'.[22] To make matters even less complicated and more melodramatic, the performances of those actors and actresses who specialized in the roles of Todd and Lovett both in the provinces and in London seemed to grow ever more hysterical and frenetic as the years wore on. Reviewing one particularly popular revival of the play at the Elephant and Castle Theatre in 1928, one commentator observed of the performance: 'No one minces his words, for this is not a puling naturalism, but the rhetoric of melodrama.' 'When Mark Ingestrie has been lured into Todd's shop', the notice continued,

and we, gazing outside from the frosted window-panes, see the shadow of the barber stoop over the shadow of the customer whom he is about to destroy, how necessary it is that the shadow of the razor should be a titanic menace! It is not a barber's implement in the naturalistic mode: it is a melodramatic symbol! It is larger than life . . . like the wickedness of . . . Lovett, and the wholesale homicide of Sweeney himself.[23]

Such high-flown forms of melodrama, however, tended to tread an increasingly thin line between tragedy and farce. 'There can be few audiences to which Todd could be played seriously today', one commentator wrote in response to a defence of the play by Montague Summers in the pages of the *Times Literary Supplement* in 1942,

[21] George Dibdin Pitt, *The String of Pearls (Sweeney Todd)*, in Michael Kilgariff (ed.), *The Golden Age of Melodrama: Twelve 19th-Century Melodramas* (London: Wolfe Publishing Ltd., 1974), 248.

[22] Ibid. 256.

[23] Unsigned notice in 'Entertainments': 'A Box at the Elephant' ('Sweeney Todd') in *The Times*, 6 Mar. 1928, p. 14; issue 44834; col. B.

'and to act it in any other spirit is not to act it at all.'[24] By the mid-twentieth century, Sweeney Todd was in danger of dwindling forever into the stuff of a two-dimensional burlesque.

Bond's 1973 revision of the drama changed all that. Although the earlier and spurious criminal 'biographies' purporting to tell Todd's life story had occasionally added some narrative details suggesting the barber's motives, Bond was the first dramatist to provide Todd with a convincing, well-thought-through, and fully integrated 'back story'. At the beginning of Bond's play, Todd's justifiable anger is far more focused; it is directed exclusively at the local judge and beadle who had together, many years earlier, destroyed his career, transported him for life as a convicted felon, and (he believes) killed his beloved wife. Todd's aim is revenge, pure and simple. Only after his initial attempts to do away with the judge and beadle are frustrated does he come to the conclusion that 'the work's its own reward', and decides that until he has another shot at his enemies he will be contented enough to spend his time 'in practice on less honoured throats'. 'For now I find I have a taste for blood', he cries to Mrs Lovett, 'and all the world's my meat.'[25] As one early director of Bond's play observed, 'Todd should be played as normally and sanely as possible within the context of [Bond's] play, and this interpretation [is] responsible for emphasizing the horror of the situation.'[26] In Sondheim's subsequent redaction of Bond's text, Todd's conclusion was to be even more stark and existential, as he experiences an astounding, climactic 'epiphany' in which he realizes that 'we *all* deserve to die!' 'The history of the world, my sweet,' as Sondheim's Todd succinctly explains to Mrs Lovett shortly after achieving this insight into the shared mortality of mankind (in which the members of the audience are, of course, themselves implicated), 'is who gets eaten and who gets to eat.'[27]

If Bond, in a preface to his printed theatre text, further reinforced the moral justice of Todd's righteous anger and vengeance by

[24] Unsigned notice in 'Editorials': 'Blood and Thunder' in *The Times*, 7 Apr. 1942, p. 5; issue 49203; col. D.

[25] Christopher G. Bond, *Sweeney Todd: The Demon Barber of Fleet Street* (London: Samuel French, 1974), 21.

[26] Director Maxwell Shaw, quoted ibid., p. iv.

[27] *Sweeney Todd: The Demon Barber of Fleet Street*. A Musical Thriller. Music and Lyrics by Stephen Sondheim. Book by Hugh Wheeler. Based on a Version of 'Sweeney Todd' by Christopher Bond (New York: Dodd, Mead, & Company, 1979), 94, 102.

pointing out parallels in the action of the play to Elizabethan and Jacobean 'revenge' tragedies and to works such as *The Count of Monte Cristo* (1844–6) by Alexandre Dumas, then the original production of his play revelled in the ghoulish inclusivity and tempered melodrama of the legend; Sondheim's agent, Flora Roberts, who accompanied him to Stratford that night, recalled that audience members were greeted as they stepped into the theatre by 'a piano player in the lobby and people drinking beer and eating meat pies'.[28] Sondheim himself later confessed that although he was immediately impressed by the vitality of the evening's performance, he only gradually awakened to the musical possibilities inherent in Bond's Todd. 'I had heard it was Grand Guignol,' he commented,

and it was something that just knocked me out. Bond's new version was a tiny play, still a melodrama, but also a legend, elegantly written, part in blank verse—which I didn't even recognize until I read the script. It had a weight to it, but I couldn't figure out how the language was so rich and thick without being fruity. . . . [Bond] was able to take all these disparate elements that had been in existence rather dully for a hundred and some-odd years and make them into a first-rate play. . . . It struck me as a piece that sings.[29]

Sondheim's reference to the traditions of the Grand Guignol suggests the theatrical characteristics that featured most prominently in Bond's *Sweeney Todd*, and that were eventually to figure no less prominently in his own adaptation. Ideally, audiences are brought physically close to the action of the drama, which is unapologetically presented as a grisly spectacle. As the composer later commented:

I was only worried about how the audience would take the murders, whether they'd think them silly or not. And then, when Mrs Lovett gets the idea of making the meat pies, what would the audience's reaction be? In America nobody's ever heard of Sweeney Todd . . . so they were seeing this wild plot for the first time, and there was a loud gasp at the first murder, which was staged very violently with a great swash of blood. Then when Mrs Lovett got the idea for the pies and the audiences realised what was up, there was a satisfying laugh, the likes of which I've rarely heard.[30]

[28] Flora Roberts, quoted in Craig Zadan, *Sondheim & Company* (1974; 2nd edn., updated, New York: De Capo Press, 1994), 243.

[29] Ibid. 243–4

[30] Secrest, *Stephen Sondheim*, 291.

Hugh Wheeler, who collaborated with Sondheim on the 'book'
for the musical, further observed of those changes that helped
to distinguish their version of the story from those that had
preceded it:

It's a wonderful story, and I thought Bond's version was slightly
better than the others, but from my point of view, even his version was
that absolutely unreal, old melodrama, where you boo the villain. . . .
[W]henever Sweeney came on the audience would hiss and throw hot
dogs. The version we wanted to do was a whole tone that was difficult to
get. We wanted to make it as nearly as we could into a sort of tragedy.
I wrote it as a play, but I encouraged [Sondheim] to cannibalise it and
make it nearly all music.[31]

Sondheim's version of _Sweeney Todd_, which finally premiered on
Broadway in March 1979 (and at the Theatre Royal Drury Lane, in
London's West End, the following year), also owed a considerable
debt to the Hollywood horror films of the 1940s and 1950s—
particularly to the work of Bernard Herrmann, whose score for the
1945 adaptation of Patrick Hamilton's _Hangover Square_ (1941) had
long haunted the composer's imagination. Some measure of the
success of Sondheim's adaptation can be located in the fact that,
having once settled into its Broadway run (and having been described
by New York theatre critics more typically hostile to the composer's
work as 'a musical . . . put together with unusual love, taste, and
style'), the production went on to win no fewer than eight out of the
nine Tony Awards for which it was nominated, including Best
Musical.[32] Even more tellingly, his _Sweeney Todd_ has become a fixture in the repertoires of opera houses all over the world, from New
York and London, to Sydney and Berlin. When the suitably Gothic
director Tim Burton decided once again to team up with actor
Johnny Depp in the twenty-first century to reintroduce an entire
generation to the story of the 'demon barber of Fleet Street', it was
inevitable that the particular version of the tale they would choose
to film would be Sondheim's.

To be fair, even had it never occurred to a composer such as
Sondheim to write a musical about a murderous barber and his
cannibalistic, pie-making accomplice, and even had Tim Burton's

---

[31] Zadan, _Sondheim & Company_, 246.
[32] Clive Barnes, quoted ibid. 258.

production never been green-lit by Hollywood producers understandably wary of selling such a film to Middle America's proverbial 'Mr and Mrs Front Porch', the seemingly slight and often spurious connections such as that which links the demon barber via cockney rhyming slang with members of the London Metropolitan Police Flying Squad (aka 'the Sweeny') would still have done much to keep the Fleet Street legend alive in English popular culture, at the very least.[33] Sweeney has always been hard at work somewhere within the British imagination, and (for all the truth of Sondheim's observation that until 1979 very few Americans 'had ever heard of Sweeney Todd'), the barber's influence can in fact clearly be traced in now classic American horror stories such as Stanley Ellin's chilling 'Speciality of the House' (1948), and Charles Beaumont's 'Free Dirt' (1955). In 1973 the popular British comic magazine *Shiver and Shake* first chronicled the adventures of one 'Sweeney Toddler' (continued in *Whoopee!*), and in 1996 the writer Frank Palmer produced the first of a series of detective thrillers featuring the character of one Phil 'Sweeney' Todd. The popular British comedy duo the Two Ronnies (Ronnie Barker and Ronnie Corbett) included a sketch featuring one 'Teeny Todd' (played by Corbett) in their *Sketchbook* series, airing first in March and April 2005. Modern purchasers of straight or 'cut throat' razors may be disconcerted to find such items not infrequently marketed as 'Sweeney Todd' blades, and there are even restaurants that carry Todd's name on their menus, and advertise a speciality in home-made meat pies. The modern novelist Neil Gaiman, who with artist Michael Zulli in the early 1990s contemplated an ambitious illustrated novel devoted to Todd's story, to be published as an ongoing 'work-in-progress', commented in a 1997 interview that he was at times baffled by these sorts of allusions, and by the many different versions of the myth that had been handed down to modern readers and audiences. 'I kept reading version after version of *Sweeney Todd*', Gaiman remarked of the more faithful references of the tale and its characters: 'here is a couple of Victorian plays, over here would be some

---

[33] See John Roberts Nash, *Dictionary of Crime* (London: Headline Books, 1992), s.v. 'Sweeny' [*sic*]. The reference is in actual fact more probably connected to John Sweeney, the Irishman who first organized the unit. The same slang would of course, in turn, provide the basis for the popular television drama series (1974–8) of the same name.

Penny Dreadfuls, here's something from the 1930s. There's always Mrs Lovett, there's always Sweeney Todd, there's always a judge. But after that it becomes so amazingly fluid, and I think that was what attracted me.'[34] However one chooses to define such an 'attraction', the simple fact remains that audiences and readers at the beginning of the twenty-first century are likely to greet the name of Sweeney Todd with a smile of recognition, and more than a passing familiarity with his gruesome story.

[34] Neil Gaiman and Michael Zulli, *Taboo 6 — The Sweeney Todd Penny Dreadful* (n.p., Spiderbaby Grafix and Publications, 1992).

# Note on the Text

THE narrative of Sweeney Todd was originally published as *The String of Pearls: A Romance* by Edward Lloyd in his *The People's Periodical and Family Library* in eighteen weekly instalments. The story appeared in the periodical's issues for the weeks ending Saturday, 21 November 1846 (issue 7) to Saturday, 20 March 1847 (issue 24).

From as early as 1847–8, Lloyd's original prose version of *The String of Pearls* was masively expanded and published in a penny-part serialization of 92 eight-page numbers. As was often the practice with such serial publications, nos. 2, 3, and 4 were given away 'free' with the first issue; consequently, the expanded version of the narrative appeared over a period of 89 weeks. A bound, single-volume edition of this version currently in the British Library and dated 1850 runs to 732 pages. The 1850 edition (like the many versions of the stage adaptations of George Dibdin Pitt, Frederick Hazleton, and others) vigorously protested the veracity of the story. Lloyd's 1850 volume is prefaced as follows:

THE ROMANCE OF THE STRING OF PEARLS having excited in the literary world an almost unprecedented interest, it behoves the author to say a few words to his readers upon the completion of his labours.

In answer to the many inquiries that have been, from time to time, made regarding the fact of whether there ever was such a person as Sweeney Todd in existence, we can unhesitatingly say, that there certainly was such a man; and the record of his crimes is still to be found in the chronicles of criminality of this country.

The house in Fleet Street, which was the scene of Todd's crimes, is no more. A fire, which destroyed some half-dozen buildings on that side of the way, involved Todd's in destruction; but the secret passage, although, no doubt, partially blocked up with the re-building of St. Dunstan's Church, connecting the vaults of that edifice with the cellars of what was Todd's house in Fleet Street, still remains.

From the great patronage which this work has received from the reading public, the author has to express his deep and earnest thanks; and he begs to state, that if anything more than another could stimulate him to renewed exertion to please his numerous patrons, it is the kind and liberal appreciation of his past labours.

Several other versions of Todd's story appeared throughout the middle and later decades of the nineteenth century. The most significant of these included those published by Charles Fox—*Sweeney Todd, The Demon Barber of Fleet Street*—which ran in *The Boys' Standard* magazine in 1878, and a much shorter version published by A. Ritchie of Red Lion Court in roughly the same period. The most popular dramatic versions of the story were the melodramas originally produced by George Dibdin Pitt (1847) and Frederick Hazleton (1862).

The present edition follows precisely that of the original 1846–7 text in Lloyd's *The People's Periodical and Family Library*, and has been taken from the copy currently in the British Library. The chapters have been correctly renumbered, and any irregular spellings that might otherwise have impeded the modern reader have been brought into conformity with the rest of the text. A number of internal inconsistencies in spelling, capitalization, and punctuation have been tactfully regularized. The end of each part issue has been marked with a short, centred rule in this edition. A single asterisk in the text signifies an editorial note at the back of the book.

# A Select Chronology

1846–7    (21 November–20 March) *The String of Pearls: A Romance* serialized in Edward Lloyd's *The People's Periodical and Family Library*. Published in eighteen weekly parts (issues nos. 7–24) and variously attributed to Edward P. Hingston, George Macfarren, Thomas Peckett Prest, James Malcolm Rymer, and Albert Richard Smith; the publication of the narrative marks the earliest appearance by name in English of the characters of Sweeney Todd, the barber, and his pie-maker accomplice, Margery Lovett.

1847    (February/March) *The String of Pearls*, written by George Dibdin Pitt, first produced and performed as a drama at the Britannia Theatre, Hoxton. Dibdin Pitt's stage version of Lloyd's story, significantly, premieres even before publication of the original serial has reached its completion. It is through the many later versions and variations of this original dramatic adaptation that the line most often associated with the barber—'I'll polish him off'—becomes Todd's 'catchphrase'.

1850    Bound, single-volume edition, running to a total of 732 pages, of an expanded version of the original 1846–7 tale published by Edward Lloyd. This lengthier (and much inferior) version of *The String of Pearls* (now for the first time subtitled 'The Barber of Fleet Street. A Domestic Romance') appears originally to have been published as a stand-alone penny-part serial, probably beginning some time in 1847–8. The part work ran for 92 eight-page numbers; as was then typically the practice, nos. 2, 3, and 4 were 'given away' with the first number. This 'penny blood' serial thus ran for a full 89 weeks. The British Library Catalogue suggests that the work was begun by George Macfarren and possibly completed by Thomas Peckett Prest (see 1846–7, above), although such an attribution is now considered unlikely.

c.1852–3    *Sweeney Todd: or the Ruffian Barber. A Tale of the Terror of the Seas and the Mysteries of the City* by 'Captain Merry' (pseudonym of American author Harry Hazel (1814–89)) published in New York by H. Long and Brother, Nassau Street. Hazel's work is often a rough and hastily written version (essentially a plagiarism) in thirty-six chapters of Lloyd's expanded text of 1850.

c.1865    *Sweeney Todd, the Barber of Fleet Street: or, the String of Pearls*, a new dramatic adaptation by Frederick Hazleton (*c*.1825–90) first performed at The Old Bower Saloon, Stangate Street, Lambeth. Hazleton was later alleged by some to have produced an alternative prose version or 'novelization' of the story at about the same time, although it is highly unlikely that such a prose version by Hazleton ever existed. A fraudulently edited and modernized 'version' of this 'novel' (essentially a redaction of Lloyd's 1846–7 text) was reprinted with an 'Introduction' by Peter Haining in 1980. A version of Hazleton's drama eventually appeared as vol. 102 (1875) of *Lacy's Acting Edition of Plays* (absorbed by Samuel French in 1872), a series originally intended to provide reliable acting play-texts of both 'classic' and popular dramas for provincial and amateur theatricals. Throughout the latter half of the nineteenth century, a number of other versions of *Sweeney Todd*—many based to some extent on the texts originally established by Dibdin Pitt and Hazleton—were advertised for performance both in London and in the provinces.

1866      First issue of Edward J. Brett's *The Boys of England*, a story paper designed to end the dominance of the 'penny bloods' by aiming at a distinctly juvenile readership with adventure stories that typically featured schoolboy heroes such as the popular 'Jack Harkaway', rather than criminal figures.

1873      First appearance of *The Link Boy of Old London* (attributed by some to Vane Ireton St John) in *Sons of Britannia*; the narrative, which also drew heavily on works such as Dickens's *Oliver Twist*, was to be republished in *The Boy's Standard*, nos. 78 (4 November 1882) to 91 (3 February 1883); Sweeney Todd features as a character in the serial, as does Mrs Lovett (under the name of 'the Widow Darkman').

c.1878–80 *Sweeney Todd, the Demon Barber of Fleet Street* published by Charles Fox and Co., of 4 Shoe Lane, near Fleet Street. This 48-part inferior and repetitive novelization—often based only very loosely on the original 1846–7 text—runs in total to 576 double-columned pages. This version of the story has plausibly been attributed to Charlton Lea, credited also with the version of *Spring-heel'd Jack: The Terror of London* (*c*.1878–9).

c.1880    George Dibdin Pitt's adaptation of *Sweeney Todd* published as one of 'John Dicks' Standard Plays' in a version substantially different from that first submitted to the Lord Chamberlain in 1847. This edition asserts that the play was first performed in 1842—a mistake of some consequence, insofar as it has resulted in the frequent attribution by later critics of the story itself to Dibdin Pitt, rather than to the anonymous author of the 1846–7 *People's Periodical* narrative published by Lloyd.

1885     Abridged version entitled *The String of Pearls, or Passages from the life of Sweeny [sic] Todd, the Demon Barber* published by Charles Fox in six instalments in *The Boy's Standard* (no. 213, NS 6 June–no. 218, 11 July). This edition appears to have been the first to promote itself to some extent on the basis of the 'Magnificent Large Coloured [Plate]' that was 'given away with Nos. 1 & 2'.

c.1892     *Sweeney Todd the Barber of Fleet Street. A Thrilling Story of the Old City of London. Founded on Facts* published in a shortened version of thirteen chapters by A. Ritchie of Red Lion Court, London.

1910     Publication by the Manchester-based Daisy Bank Press of a short version of the Sweeney Todd story, based on Edward Lloyd's original 1846–7 tale. Between 1910 and 1922 the press brought out some fifty illustrated publications, each of thirty-two pages, many of which reprinted familiar tales of crime and murder.

1926     The earliest film version of *Sweeney Todd* produced by New Era Productions as 'a comedy burlesque stage play' and filmed for the 'Kinematograph Society Garden Party'. The short film—now lost—was directed by British film pioneer George Dewhurst, and starred G. A. Baugham in the title role.

1928     Second (and earliest surviving) film version of *Sweeney Todd*, produced by Harry Rowson, directed by Walter West, and distributed by Ideal Films Limited. This film—which advertised itself as having been specifically 'adapted from the famous "Elephant and Castle" melodrama'—featured the well-known actor Moore Marriott as Todd.

    A self-described 'traditional' version of Dibdin Pitt's *Sweeney Todd*—with an introduction by Montagu Slater  published by John Lane (London).

1929     *Sweeney Todd, the Demon Barber* published by Pearson Press; the same 'edition' was to be republished by London's Mellifont Press c.1936. The text for this version of the story may have been written by Edwin T. Woodhall, a former police constable and agent who eventually contributed a number of other titles to Mellifont's 'Celebrated Crime Series', including *Jack the Ripper, or, When London Walked in Terror* (1937). Other possible authors, however, include most notably Hargrave L. Adam, or William and Leonard Townshend.

1935    Radio play by J. P. Quaine—*Sweeny* [*sic*] *Todd, The Demon Barber of Fleet Street* ('an entirely original version for the radio' and set 'in the Reign of George the Second')—printed in *The Collector's Miscellany*, NS nos. 11–14 (May–December 1935).

1936    Tod Slaughter stars in *Sweeney Todd, The Demon Barber*, directed by George King and released by Ambassador Pictures. Slaughter had already made a speciality of playing such villainous roles to great effect on the stage. The film—a much-simplified version of the story credited to Frederick Hayward and H. F. Maltby and notionally based on the earlier dramatizations of George Dibdin Pitt and Frederick Hazleton—also featured Stelle Rho in the part of Mrs Lovett, and Eve Lister as Johanna Oakley.

1948    Selections from Edward Lloyd's original version of *The String of Pearls* (1846–7) featured in E. S. Turner's *Boys Will Be Boys: The story of Sweeney Todd, Deadwood Dick, Sexton Blake, Billy Bunter, Dick Barton, et al.* (London: Michael Joseph). Turner's volume was among the first to argue for the value of the 'new mythology' of heroes and villains—e.g. Todd, Jack Sheppard, Spring-heeled Jack, Jack Harkaway, Sexton Blake, etc.—contained within the pages of the 'bloods' and 'penny dreadfuls'.

1956    'Sweeney Todd the Barber'—already a popular comic song by R. P. Weston (1906–34) in the tradition of the music hall monologue—recorded by the actor Stanley Holloway. Holloway's version of Weston's number (which began 'In Fleet Street, that's in London Town | When King Charlie wore the crown, | There lived a man of great renown | 'Twas Sweeney Todd the Barber') continued for some time to feature on the radio as a popular audience request.

1959    (10 December) world premiere of a one-act ballet adaptation—*Sweeney Todd*—with music by the well-known composer Malcolm Arnold (Op. 68a) and choreography by John Cranko at the Shakespeare Memorial Theatre, Stratford. The ballet's first London performance was to take place several months later at the Royal Opera House, Covent Garden, on 16 August 1960.

(10 December) premiere of *The Demon Barber* at the Lyric Theatre, Hammersmith, a musical version of the story with book and lyrics by Donald Cotton and music by Brian Burke; based on George Dibdin Pitt's original play and produced by Colin Graham. The musical starred Roy Godfrey as Sweeney Todd and Barbara Howitt as Mrs Lovett; the role of Jonas Fogg was played by Barry Humphries.

1962     (May) *The World of Sweeney Todd*, book and lyrics by William Scott and Ken Appleby (with additional lyrics by Alan Collins and Mike Burke, and music by Peter Satterfield; arranged by Alan Johnson) staged at the People's Theatre in Newcastle upon-Tyne. The production was revived in 1970, and again represented in April 1995 by the Redditch Operatic Society, at the Palace Theatre, Redditch.

(June) Brian Burton's *Sweeney Todd, The Barber. A Melodrama in four acts* adapted 'from George Dibdin Pitt's Victorian version of the legendary drama' first presented at the Crescent Theatre, Birmingham, on 16 June. Featuring Frank Jones as Sweeney Todd, and Frances Bull as Mrs Lovett.

1969     *Sweeney Todd: The Demon Barber of Fleet Street* (subtitled 'A Victorian Melodrama') by Austin Rosser performed at the Dundee Repertory Theatre, Scotland.

1970     *Bloodthirsty Butchers*, a film directed by Andy Milligan, and written by John Borske and Andy Milligan. An updated and— for its day—exceptionally violent and graphic retelling of the tale, starring Berwick Kaler, John Miranda, Jane Helay, and Annabella Wood.

1973     (May) *Sweeney Todd, The Demon Barber of Fleet Street* by Christopher G. Bond performed at the Theatre Royal, Stratford East (London). The text of Bond's play was to be published by Samuel French (London) in 1974; this version of the story was to serve as the primary source for Stephen Sondheim and Hugh Wheeler's 1979 'musical thriller' of the same name (see 1979, below).

*The True Life of Sweeney Todd: A Collage Novel* by Cozette de Charmoy published in London by the Gaberbocchus Press.

1974     Text of an original nineteenth-century version of George Dibdin Pitt's adaptation *The String of Pearls (Sweeney Todd)* included in Michael Kilgarrif's *Golden Age of Melodrama* (pp. 237–72); the volume also includes a valuable descriptive passage from Thomas W. Erle's 1880 *Letters From a Theatrical Scene-Painter* describing an actual nineteenth-century audience at a performance of Dibdin Pitt's drama at the Britannia Theatre, Hoxton.

1979     *Sweeney Todd, The Demon Barber of Fleet Street. A Musical Thriller*, with music and lyrics by Stephen Sondheim and a book by Hugh Wheeler, premieres on 1 March at the Uris Theatre in New York. The cast includes Len Cariou as Sweeney Todd, Angela Lansbury as Mrs Lovett, and Victor Garber as the young hero, Anthony Hope. Sondheim's musical is subsequently awarded the 1979 Tony, and the Drama Critics Circle Award for 'Best Musical'. The work initially attracted less attention when it was first staged at the Theatre Royal, Drury Lane, in London the following year. Sondheim's version would, however, be successfully revived by the New York City Opera as soon as October 1984 (having first been staged as an operatic production by the Houston Grand Opera in July of that same year).

1980     Publication of Peter Miller and Randall Lewton's *The Sweeney Todd Shock 'n' Roll Show*, an amateur musical adaptation loosely based on earlier dramatic versions of the story, and originally staged in Liverpool in January 1979.

1982     *The Dark Behind the Curtain*, written by Gillian Cross and illustrated by David Parkins. A novel for younger readers, the book takes as its premise the troubled production of a vaguely specified nineteenth-century dramatic version of *Sweeney Todd, the Demon Barber of Fleet Street* by a group of English schoolchildren.

1992     *Taboo 6—The Sweeney Todd Penny Dreadful* issued as a proposal for a limited edition, collaborative 'work in progress' uniting award-winning graphic novelist Neil Gaiman with artist Michael Zulli. Although promotional pamphlets for the project featuring 'A Brief Introduction', excerpts from earlier texts, as well as reproductions, pastiches, and original sketches and other artwork by Zulli were published, they did not receive a wide circulation, and neither Gaiman nor Zulli were able to follow through on the project.

1998     *The Tale of Sweeney Todd*, directed by John Schlesinger and featuring Ben Kingsley, Joanna Lumley, and Campbell Scott. The film was written by Peter Buckman with executive producer Peter Shaw (credited specifically with story adaptation). Originally produced for 'Showtime' and Third Row Center

Films as a made-for-television movie in America (first aired in the US on 19 April 1998).

2000     (4–6 May) Performance and recording of Sondheim's *Sweeney Todd 'Live in Concert'* by the New York Philharmonic at Lincoln Center, New York. Featuring George Hearn as Sweeney Todd and Patti LuPone as Mrs Lovett. This successful concert version of Sondheim's *Todd* was subsequently filmed by Ellen M. Krass Productions (in 2001), as performed by members of the same cast with the San Francisco Symphony. The filmed concert premiered on American television in October 2001.

2002     Director Francesca Joseph's made-for-television film *Tomorrow La Scala!*—in which a small opera company undertakes to mount a production of Sondheim's *Sweeney Todd* in a maximum security prison, and the premise of which is the featuring of criminals sentenced to life-imprisonment in the major roles—is premiered at the Cannes Film Festival. Starring Jessica Stevenson and Samantha Spiro, the critically acclaimed film was subsequently nominated for two BAFTA awards.

2003     Sondheim's *Sweeney Todd*—featuring Thomas Allen as Todd and Felicity Palmer as Mrs Lovett—receives its first staging at the Royal Opera House, Covent Garden, London. The production, by Neil Armfield, with designs by Brian Thomson, had in fact originated at the Lyric Opera in Chicago in 2002–3. (Sondheim's version of *Sweeney Todd* had first been staged in England specifically as an opera by director David McVicar for Opera North, in Leeds, in 1998.)

2004     Sondheim's *Sweeney Todd*—in a revival directed by John Doyle and originally staged as a chamber piece at the Watermill Theatre in Westbury, West Berkshire—transfers to London's West End and eventually (in 2005) to Broadway's Eugene O'Neill Theatre. Director John Doyle received a Tony award for the Broadway staging of the production in 2006.

2005     Ray Winstone, Essie Davis, and David Warner star in *Sweeney Todd*, an entirely new version of the story written for BBC 1 film productions by Joshua St Johnstone and directed by David Moore; originally aired on British television 3 January 2006.

2007     (February) Director Tim Burton begins production in England on the DreamWorks SKG production of the Stephen Sondheim musical *Sweeney Todd, The Demon Barber of Fleet Street*. The film stars actor Johnny Depp in the title role, and features Helena Bonham Carter as Mrs Lovett, and Alan Rickman as Judge Turpin.

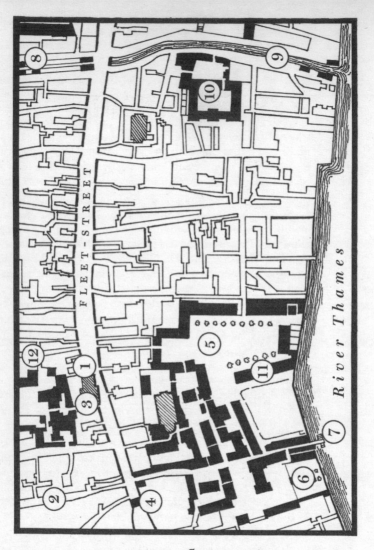

# SWEENEY TODD'S LONDON

## KEY

1. Sweeney Todd's barber shop (186 Fleet-street)
2. Mrs Lovett's Pie-shop (Bell-yard)
3. St Dunstan's church (St Dunstan in the West)
4. Temple-bar
5. The Temple
6. Temple-gardens
7. Temple-stairs
8. Fleet Market
9. Fleet Ditch
10. Bridewell Prison
11. Paper-buildings
12. Fetter-lane

# SWEENEY TODD

# THE
# PEOPLE'S PERIODICAL
### AND
## FAMILY LIBRARY.

### EDITED BY E. LLOYD.

No. 7. Vol. I.]      FOR THE WEEK ENDING NOVEMBER 21, 1846.      [Price One Penny

## THE STRING OF PEARLS.
### A ROMANCE.

#### CHAPTER I.

THE STRANGE CUSTOMER AT SWEENEY TODD'S.

BEFORE Fleet-street had reached its present importance, and when George the Third was young, and the two figures who used to strike the chimes at old St. Dunstan's church were in all their glory—being a great impediment to errand-boys on their progress, and a matter of gaping curiosity to country people—there stood close to the sacred edifice a small barber's shop, which was kept by a man of the name of Sweeney Todd.

How it was that he came by the name of Sweeney, as a Christian appellation, we are at a loss to conceive, but such was his name, as might be seen in extremely corpulent yellow letters over his shop window, by any one who chose there to look for it.

Barbers by that time in Fleet-street had not become fashionable, and no more dreamt of calling themselves artists than of taking the Tower by storm; moreover they were not, as they are now, constantly slaughtering fine fat bears, and yet somehow people had hair on their heads just the same as they have at present, without the aid of that unctuous auxiliary. Moreover Sweeney Todd, in common with his brethren in those really primitive sorts of times, did not think it at all necessary to have any waxen effigies of humanity in his window. There was no languishing young lady looking over the left shoulder in order that a profusion of auburn tresses might repose upon her lily neck, and great conquerors and great statesmen were not then, as they are now, held up to public ridicule with dabs of rouge upon their cheeks, a quantity of gunpowder scattered in for a beard, and some bristles sticking on end for eyebrows.

No. Sweeney Todd was a barber of the old school, and he never thought of glorifying himself on account of any extraneous circumstances. If he had lived in Henry the Eighth's palace, it would have been all the same to him as Henry the Eighth's dog-kennel, and he would scarcely have believed human nature to be so green as to pay an extra sixpence to be shaven and shorn in any particular locality.

A long pole painted white, with a red stripe curling spirally round it, projected into the street from his doorway, and on one of the panes of glass in his window was presented the following couplet :—

'Easy shaving for a penny,
As good as you will find any.'

We do not put these lines forth as a specimen of the poetry of the age; they may have been the production of some young Templer; but if they were a little wanting in poetic fire, that was amply made up by the clear and precise manner in which they set forth what they intended.

The barber himself was a long, low-jointed, ill-put-together sort of fellow, with an immense mouth, and such huge hands and feet, that he was, in his way, quite a natural curiosity; and, what was more wonderful, considering his trade, there never was seen such a head of hair as Sweeney Todd's. We know not what to compare it to: probably it came nearest to what one might suppose to be the appearance of a thick-set hedge, in which a quantity of small wire had got entangled. In truth, it was a most terrific head of hair; and as Sweeney Todd kept all his combs in it—some people said his scissors likewise—when he put his head out of the shop-door to see what sort of weather it was, he might have been mistaken for some Indian warrior with a very remarkable head-dress.

He had a short disagreeable kind of unmirthful laugh, which came in at all sorts of odd times when nobody else saw anything to laugh at at all, and which sometimes made people start again, especially when they were being shaved, and Sweeney Todd would stop short in that operation to indulge in one of these cachinnatory effusions. It was evident that the remembrance of some very strange and out-of-the-way joke must occasionally flit across him, and then he gave

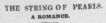

---

# 1

## *The Strange Customer at Sweeney Todd's*

BEFORE Fleet-street had reached its present importance, and when George the Third was young, and the two figures who used to strike the chimes at old St Dunstan's church were in all their glory—being a great impediment to errand-boys on their progress, and a matter of gaping curiosity to country people—there stood close to the sacred edifice a small barber's shop, which was kept by a man of the name of Sweeney Todd.*

How it was that he came by the name of Sweeney, as a Christian appellation, we are at a loss to conceive, but such was his name, as might be seen in extremely corpulent yellow letters over his shop window, by anyone who chose there to look for it.*

Barbers by that time in Fleet-street had not become fashionable, and no more dreamt of calling themselves artists than of taking the Tower by storm; moreover they were not, as they are now, constantly slaughtering fine fat bears, and yet somehow people had hair on their heads just the same as they have at present, without the aid of that unctuous auxiliary.* Moreover Sweeney Todd, in common with his brethren in those really primitive sorts of times, did not think it at all necessary to have any waxen effigies of humanity in his window. There was no languishing young lady looking over the left shoulder in order that a profusion of auburn tresses might repose upon her lily neck, and great conquerors and great statesmen were not then, as they are now, held up to public ridicule with dabs of rouge upon their cheeks, a quantity of gunpowder scattered in for a beard, and some bristles sticking on end for eyebrows.

No. Sweeney Todd was a barber of the old school, and he never thought of glorifying himself on account of any extraneous circumstance. If he had lived in Henry the Eighth's palace, it would have been all the same to him as Henry the Eighth's dog-kennel, and he would scarcely have believed human nature to be so green as to pay an extra sixpence to be shaven and shorn in any particular locality.

A long pole painted white, with a red stripe curling spirally round it, projected into the street from his doorway,* and on one of the panes of glass in his window was presented the following couplet:

> 'Easy shaving for a penny,
> As good as you will find any.'

We do not put these lines forth as a specimen of the poetry of the age; they may have been the production of some young Templer;* but if they were a little wanting in poetic fire, that was amply made up by the clear and precise manner in which they set forth what they intended.

The barber himself was a long, low-jointed, ill-put-together sort of fellow, with an immense mouth, and such huge hands and feet, that he was, in his way, quite a natural curiosity; and, what was more wonderful, considering his trade, there never was seen such a head of hair as Sweeney Todd's. We know not what to compare it to: probably it came nearest to what one might suppose to be the appearance of a thickset hedge, in which a quantity of small wire had got entangled. In truth, it was a most terrific head of hair; and as Sweeney Todd kept all his combs in it—some said his scissors likewise—when he put his head out of the shop-door to see what sort of weather it was, he might have been mistaken for some Indian warrior with a very remarkable head-dress.

He had a short disagreeable kind of unmirthful laugh, which came in at all sorts of odd times when nobody else saw anything to laugh at at all, and which sometimes made people start again, especially when they were being shaved, and Sweeney Todd would stop short in that operation to indulge in one those cacchinatory* effusions. It was evident that the remembrance of some very strange and out-of-the-way joke must occasionally flit across him, and then he gave his hyena-like laugh, but it was so short, so sudden, striking upon the ear for a moment, and then gone, that people have been known to look up to the ceiling, and on the floor, and all round them, to know from whence it had come, scarcely supposing it possible that it proceeded from mortal lips.

Mr Todd squinted a little to add to his charms; and so we think that by this time the reader may in his mind's eye see the individual whom we wish to present to him. Some thought him a careless enough harmless fellow, with not much sense in him, and at times they almost considered he was a little cracked; but there were others, again, who shook their heads when they spoke of him; and while they could say nothing to his prejudice, except that they certainly considered he was odd, yet, when they came to consider what a great crime and misdemeanour it really is in this world to be odd, we shall not be surprised at the ill-odour in which Sweeney Todd was held.

But for all that he did a most thriving business, and was considered by his neighbours to be a very well-to-do sort of man, and decidedly, in city phraseology, warm.*

It was so handy for the young students in the Temple to pop over to Sweeney Todd's to get their chins new rasped: so that from morning to night he drove a good business, and was evidently a thriving man.

There was only one thing that seemed in any way to detract from the great prudence of Sweeney Todd's character, and that was that he rented a large house, of which he occupied nothing but the shop and parlour, leaving the upper part entirely useless, and obstinately refusing to let it on any terms whatever.

Such was the state of things, AD 1785, as regarded Sweeney Todd.

The day is drawing to a close, and a small drizzling kind of rain is falling, so that there are not many passengers in the streets, and Sweeney Todd is sitting in his shop looking keenly in the face of a boy, who stands in an attitude of trembling subjection before him.

'You will remember,' said Sweeney Todd, and he gave his countenance a most horrible twist as he spoke, 'you will remember, Tobias Ragg, that you are now my apprentice,* that you have of me had board, washing, and lodging, with the exception that you don't sleep here, that you take your meals at home, and that your mother, Mrs Ragg, does your washing, which she may very well do, being a laundress* in the Temple, and making no end of money: as for lodging, you lodge here, you know, very comfortably in the shop all day. Now, are you not a happy dog?'

'Yes, sir,' said the boy timidly.

'You will acquire a first-rate profession, and quite as good as the law, which your mother tells me she would have put you to, only that a little weakness of the headpiece unqualified you. And now, Tobias, listen to me, and treasure up every word I say.'

'Yes, sir.'

'I'll cut your throat from ear to ear, if you repeat one word of what passes in this shop, or dare to make any supposition, or draw any conclusion from anything you may see, or hear, or fancy you see or hear. Now you understand me—I'll cut your throat from ear to ear—do you understand me?'

'Yes, sir, I won't say nothing. I wish, sir, as I may be made into veal pies at Lovett's in Bell-yard* if I as much as says a word.'

Sweeney Todd rose from his seat; and opening his huge mouth, he looked at the boy for a minute or two in silence, as if he fully intended swallowing him, but had not quite made up his mind where to begin.

'Very good,' he said at length, 'I am satisfied, I am quite satisfied; and mark me,—the shop, and the shop only, is your place.'

'Yes, sir.'

'And if any customer gives you a penny, you can keep it, so that if you get enough of them you will become a rich man; only I will take care of them for you, and when I think you want them I will let you have them. Run out and see what's o'clock by St Dunstan's.'

There was a small crowd collected opposite the church, for the figures were about to strike three-quarters past six; and among that crowd was one man who gazed with as much curiosity as anybody at the exhibition.

'Now for it!' he said, 'they are going to begin; well, that is ingenious. Look at the fellow lifting up his club, and down it comes bang upon the old bell.'

The three-quarters were struck by the figures; and then the people who had loitered to see it done, many of whom had day by day looked at the same exhibition for years past, walked away, with the exception of the man who seemed so deeply interested.

He remained, and crouching at his feet was a noble-looking dog, who looked likewise up at the figures; and who, observing his master's attention to be closely fixed upon them, endeavoured to show as great an appearance of interest as he possibly could.

'What do you think of that, Hector?' said the man.

The dog gave a short low whine, and then his master proceeded,—

'There is a barber's shop opposite, so before I go any farther, as I have got to see the ladies, although it's on a very melancholy errand, for I have got to tell them that poor Mark Ingestrie is no more, and Heaven knows what poor Johanna will say—I think I should know her by his description of her, poor fellow. It grieves me to think now how he used to talk about her in the long night-watches, when all was still, and not a breath of air touched a curl upon his cheek. I could almost think I saw her sometimes, as he used to tell me of her soft beaming eyes, her little gentle pouting lips, and the dimples that played about her mouth. Well, well, it's of no use grieving; he is dead and gone, poor fellow, and the salt water washes over as brave a heart as ever beat. His sweetheart, Johanna, though, shall have the string of pearls for all that; and if she cannot be Mark Ingestrie's wife in this world, she shall be rich and happy, poor young thing, while she stays in it, that is to say as happy as she can be; and she must just look forward to meeting him aloft, where there are no squalls or tempests.—And so I'll go and get shaved at once.'

He crossed the road towards Sweeney Todd's shop, and, stepping down the low doorway, he stood face to face with the odd-looking barber.

The dog gave a low growl and sniffed the air.

'Why, Hector,' said his master, 'what's the matter? Down, sir, down!'

'I have a mortal fear of dogs,' said Sweeney Todd. 'Would you mind him, sir, sitting outside the door and waiting for you, if it's all the same? Only look at him, he is going to fly at me!'

'Then you are the first person he ever touched without provocation,' said the man; 'but I suppose he don't like your looks, and I must confess I ain't much surprised at that. I have seen a few rum-looking guys in my time, but hang me if ever I saw such a figure-head as yours. What the devil noise was that?'

'It was only me,' said Sweeney Todd; 'I laughed.'

'Laughed! do you call that a laugh? I suppose you caught it of somebody who died of it. If that's your way of laughing, I beg you won't do it any more.'

'Stop the dog! stop the dog! I can't have dogs running into my back parlour.'

'Here, Hector, here!' cried his master; 'get out!'

Most unwillingly the dog left the shop, and crouched down close to the outer door, which the barber took care to close, muttering something about a draught of air coming in, and then, turning to the apprentice boy, who was screwed up in a corner, he said,—

'Tobias, my lad, go to Leadenhall-street, and bring a small bag of the thick biscuits from Mr Peterson's; say they are for me. Now, sir, I suppose you want to be shaved, and it is well you have come here, for there ain't a shaving-shop, although I say it, in the city of London that ever thinks of polishing anybody off as I do.'

'I tell you what it is, master barber: if you come that laugh again, I will get up and go. I don't like it, and there is an end of it.'

'Very good,' said Sweeney Todd, as he mixed up a lather. 'Who are you? where did you come from? and where are you going?'

'That's cool, at all events. Damn it! what do you mean by putting the brush in my mouth? Now, don't laugh; and since you are so fond of asking questions, just answer me one.'

'Oh, yes, of course: what is it, sir?'

'Do you know a Mr Oakley, who lives somewhere in London, and is a spectacle-maker?'

'Yes, to be sure I do—John Oakley, the spectacle-maker, in Fore-street, and he has got a daughter named Johanna, that the young bloods* call the Flower of Fore-street.'*

'Ah, poor thing! do they? Now, confound you! what are you laughing at now? What do you mean by it?'

'Didn't you say, "Ah, poor thing?" Just turn your head a little on one side; that will do. You have been to sea, sir?'

'Yes, I have, and have only now lately come up the river from an Indian voyage.'

'Indeed! where can my strop be? I had it this minute; I must have laid it down somewhere. What an odd thing that I can't see it! It's very extraordinary; what can have become of it? Oh, I recollect, I took it into the parlour. Sit still, sir. I shall not be gone a moment; sit still, sir, if you please. By the by, you can amuse yourself with the *Courier*,* sir, for a moment.'

Sweeney Todd walked into the back parlour and closed the door.

There was a strange sound suddenly compounded of a rushing noise and then a heavy blow, immediately after which Sweeney Todd emerged from his parlour, and, folding his arms, he looked upon *the vacant chair where his customer had been seated*, but the customer was gone, leaving not the slightest trace of his presence behind except his hat, and that Sweeney Todd immediately seized and thrust into a cupboard that was at one corner of the shop.

'What's that?' he said, 'what's that? I thought I heard a noise.'

The door was slowly opened, and Tobias made his appearance, saying, —

'If you please, sir, I have forgot the money, and have run all the way back from St Paul's churchyard.'

In two strides Todd reached him, and clutching him by the arm he dragged him into the farthest corner of the shop, and then he stood opposite to him glaring in his face with such a demoniac expression that the boy was frightfully terrified.

'Speak!' cried Todd, 'speak! and speak the truth, or your last hour is come! How long were you peeping through the door before you came in?'

'Peeping, sir?'

'Yes, peeping; don't repeat my words, but answer me at once, you will find it better for you in the end.'

'I wasn't peeping, sir, at all.'

Sweeney Todd drew a long breath as he then said, in a strange, shricking sort of manner, which he intended, no doubt, should be jocose, —

'Well, well, very well; if you did peep, what then? it's no matter; I only wanted to know, that's all; it was quite a joke, wasn't it— quite funny, though rather odd, eh? Why don't you laugh, you dog? Come, now, there is no harm done. Tell me what you thought about it at once, and we will be merry over it—very merry.'

'I don't know what you mean, sir,' said the boy, who was quite as much alarmed at Mr Todd's mirth as he was at his anger. 'I don't know what you mean, sir; I only just come back because I hadn't any money to pay for the biscuits at Peterson's.'

'I mean nothing at all,' said Todd, suddenly turning upon his heel; 'what's that scratching at the door?'

Tobias opened the shop-door, and there stood the dog, who looked wistfully round the place, and then gave a howl that seriously alarmed the barber.

'It's the gentleman's dog, sir,' said Tobias, 'it's the gentleman's dog, sir, that was looking at old St Dunstan's clock, and came in here to be shaved. It's funny, ain't it, sir, that the dog didn't go away with his master?'

'Why don't you laugh if it's funny? Turn out the dog, Tobias; we'll have no dogs here; I hate the sight of them; turn him out—turn him out.'

'I would, sir, in a minute; but I'm afraid he wouldn't let me, somehow. Only look, sir—look; see what he is at now! did you ever see such a violent fellow, sir? why he will have down the cupboard door.'

'Stop him—stop him! the devil is in the animal! stop him I say!'

The dog was certainly getting the door open, when Sweeney Todd rushed forward to stop him; but that he was soon admonished of the danger of doing, for the dog gave him a grip of the leg, which made him give such a howl, that he precipitately retreated, and left the animal to do its pleasure. This consisted in forcing open the cupboard door, and seizing upon the hat which Sweeney Todd had thrust therein, and dashing out of the shop with it in triumph.

'The devil's in the beast,' muttered Todd, 'he's off! Tobias, you said you saw the man who owned that fiend of a cur looking at St Dunstan's church.'

'Yes, sir, I did see him there. If you recollect, you sent me to see the time, and the figures were just going to strike three-quarters past six; and before I came away, I heard him say that Mark Ingestrie was dead, and Johanna should have the string of pearls. Then I came in, and then, if you recollect, sir, he came in, and the odd thing, you know, to me, sir, is that he didn't take his dog with him, because, you know, sir—'

'Because what?' shouted Todd.

'Because people generally do take their dogs with them, you know, sir; and may I be made into one of Lovett's pies, if I don't—'

'Hush! someone comes; it's old Mr Grant, from the Temple. How do you do, Mr Grant? glad to see you looking so well, sir. It does one's heart good to see a gentleman of your years looking so fresh and hearty. Sit down, sir; a little this way, if you please. Shaved, I suppose?'

'Yes, Todd, yes. Any news?'

'No, sir, nothing stirring. Everything very quiet, sir, except the high wind. They say it blew the king's hat off yesterday, sir, and he borrowed Lord North's.* Trade is dull, too, sir. I suppose people won't come out to be cleaned and dressed in a misling rain. We haven't had anybody in the shop for an hour and a half.'

'Lor! sir,' said Tobias, 'you forgot the seafaring gentleman with the dog, you know, sir.'

'Ah! so I do,' said Todd. 'He went away, and I saw him get into some disturbance, I think, just at the corner of the market.'

'I wonder I didn't meet him, sir,' said Tobias, 'for I came that way; and then it's so very odd leaving his dog behind him.'

'Yes very,' said Todd. 'Will you excuse me a moment, Mr Grant? Tobias, my lad, I just want you to lend me a hand in the parlour.'

Tobias followed Todd very unsuspectingly into the parlour; but when they got there and the door was closed, the barber sprang upon him like an enraged tiger, and, grappling him by the throat, he gave his head such a succession of knocks against the wainscot, that Mr Grant must have thought that some carpenter was at work. Then he tore a handful of his hair out, after which he twisted him round, and dealt him such a kick, that he was flung sprawling into a corner of the room, and then, without a word, the barber walked out again to his customer, and he bolted his parlour door on the outside, leaving Tobias to digest the usage he had received at his leisure, and in the best way he could.

When he came back to Mr Grant, he apologised for keeping him waiting by saying, —

'It became necessary, sir, to teach my new apprentice a little bit of his business. I have left him studying it now. There is nothing like teaching young folks at once.'

'Ah!' said Mr Grant, with a sigh, 'I know what it is to let young folks grow wild; for although I have neither chick nor child of my own, I had a sister's son to look to—a handsome, wild, harum-scarum sort of fellow, as like me as one pea is like another. I tried to make a lawyer of him, but it wouldn't do, and it's now more than two years ago he left me altogether; and yet there were some good traits about Mark.'

'Mark, sir! did you say Mark?'

'Yes, that was his name, Mark Ingestrie. God knows what's become of him.'

'Oh!' said Sweeney Todd; and he went on lathering the chin of Mr Grant.

## 2

## *The Spectacle-Maker's Daughter*

'JOHANNA, Johanna, my dear, do you know what time it is? Johanna, I say, my dear, are you going to get up? Here's your mother has trotted out to parson Lupin's and you know I have to go to Alderman Judd's house in Cripplegate* the first thing, and I haven't had a morsel of breakfast yet. Johanna, my dear, do you hear me?'

These observations were made by Mr Oakley, the spectacle-maker, at the door of his daughter Johanna's chamber, on the morning after the events we have just recorded at Sweeney Todd's; and presently a soft sweet voice answered him, saying, —

'I am coming, father, I am coming: in a moment, father, I shall be down.'

'Don't hurry yourself, my darling, I can wait.'

The little old spectacle-maker descended the staircase again and sat down in the parlour at the back of the shop where, in a few moments, he was joined by Johanna, his only and his much-loved child.

She was indeed a creature of the rarest grace and beauty. Her age was eighteen, but she looked rather younger, and upon her face she had that sweetness and intelligence of expression which almost bids defiance to the march of time. Her hair was of a glossy blackness, and what was rare in conjunction with such a feature, her eyes were of a deep and heavenly blue. There was nothing of the commanding or of the severe style of beauty about her, but the expression of her face was all grace and sweetness. It was one of those countenances which one could look at for a long summer's day, as upon the pages of some deeply interesting volume, which furnished the most abundant food for pleasant and delightful reflection.

There was a touch of sadness about her voice, which, perhaps, only tended to make it the more musical, although mournfully so, and which seemed to indicate that at the bottom of her heart there lay some grief which had not yet been spoken—some cherished aspiration of her pure soul, which looked hopeless as regards completion—some remembrance of a former joy, which had been turned to bitterness and grief: it was the cloud in the sunny sky—the shadow through which there still gleamed bright and beautiful sunshine, but which still proclaimed its presence.

'I have kept you waiting, father,' she said, as she flung her arms about the old man's neck. 'I have kept you waiting.'

'Never mind, my dear, never mind. Your mother is so taken up with Mr Lupin, that you know, this being Wednesday morning, she is off to his prayer meeting, and so I have had no breakfast; and really I think I must discharge Sam.'

'Indeed, father! what has he done?'

'Nothing at all, and that's the very reason. I had to take down the shutters myself this morning, and what do you think for? He had the coolness to tell me that he couldn't take down the shutter this morning, or sweep out the shop, because his aunt had the toothache.'

'A poor excuse, father,' said Johanna, as she bustled about and got the breakfast ready; 'a very poor excuse!'

'Poor indeed! but his month is up to-day, and I must get rid of him.* But I suppose I shall have no end of bother with your mother, because his aunt belongs to Mr Lupin's congregation;* but as sure as this is the 20th day of August—'*

'It is the 20th day of August,' said Johanna, as she sank into a chair and burst into tears. 'It is, it is! I thought I could have controlled this, but I cannot, father, I cannot. It was that which made me late. I knew mother was out; I knew that I ought to be down and attending upon you, and I was praying to Heaven for strength to do so because this was the 20th of August.'

Johanna spoke these words incoherently and amidst sobs, and when she had finished them she leant her sweet face upon her small hands and wept like a child.

The astonishment, not unmingled with positive dismay, of the old spectacle-maker, was vividly depicted on his countenance, and for some minutes he sat perfectly aghast, with his hands resting on his knees, and looking in the face of his beautiful child—that is to say, as much as he could see of it between those little taper fingers that were spread upon it—as if he were newly awakened from some dream.

'Good God, Johanna!' he said at length, 'what is this? my dear child, what has happened? Tell me, my dear, unless you wish to kill me with grief.'

'You shall know, father,' she said. 'I did not think to say a word about it, but considered I had strength enough of mind to keep my sorrows in my own breast, but the effort has been too much for me, and I have been compelled to yield. If you had not looked so kindly on me—if I did not know that you loved me as you do, I should easily have kept my secret, but knowing that much, I cannot.'

'My darling,' said the old man, 'you are right, there; I do love you. What would the world be to me now without you? There was a time, twenty years ago, when your mother made up much of my happiness, but of late, what with Mr Lupin, and psalm-singing, and tea-drinking, I see very little of her, and what little I do see is not very satisfactory. Tell me, my darling, what it is that vexes you, and I'll soon put it to rights. I don't belong to the City train-bands* for nothing.'

'Father, I know that your affection would do all for me that it is possible to do, but you cannot recall the dead to life; and if this day passes over and I see him not, or hear not from him, I know that, instead of finding a home for me whom he loved, he has in the effort to do so found a grave for himself. He said he would, he said he would.'

Here she wrung her hands, and wept again, and with such a bitterness of anguish that the old spectacle-maker was at his wit's end, and knew not what on earth to do or say.

'My dear, my dear!' he cried, 'who is he? I hope you don't mean—'

'Hush, father, hush! I know the name that is hovering on your lips, but something seems even now to whisper to me he is no more, and, being so, speak nothing of him, father, but that which is good.'

'You mean Mark Ingestrie.'

'I do, and if he had a thousand faults, he at least loved me. He loved me truly and most sincerely.'

'My dear,' said the old spectacle-maker, 'you know that I wouldn't for all the world say anything to vex you, nor will I; but tell me what it is that makes this day more than any other so gloomy to you.'

'I will, father; you shall hear. It was on this day two years ago that we last met; it was in the Temple-gardens,* and he had just had a stormy interview with his uncle, Mr Grant, and you will understand, father, that Mark Ingestrie was not to blame, because—'

'Well, well, my dear, you needn't say anything more upon that point. Girls very seldom admit their lovers are to blame, but there are two ways, you know, Johanna, of telling a story.'

'Yes; but, father, why should Mr Grant seek to force him to the study of a profession he disliked?'

'My dear, one would have thought that if Mark Ingestrie really loved you, and found that he might make you his wife, and acquire an honourable subsistence both for you and himself—it seems a very wonderful thing to me that he did not do so. You see, my dear, he should have liked you well enough to do something else that he did not like.'

'Yes, but, father, you know it is hard, when disagreements once arise, for a young ardent spirit to give in entirely; and so from one word, poor Mark, in his disputes with his uncle, got to another, when perhaps one touch of kindness or conciliation from Mr Grant would have made him quite pliant in his hands.'

'Yes, that's the way,' said Mr Oakley; 'there is no end of excuses: but go on, my dear, go on, and tell me exactly how this affair now stands.'

'I will, father. It was this day two years ago then that we met, and he told me that he and his uncle had at last quarrelled irreconcilably, and that nothing could possibly now patch up the difference between them. We had a long talk.'

'Ah! no doubt of that.'

'And at length he told me that he must go and seek his fortune— that fortune which he hoped to share with me. He said that he had an opportunity of undertaking a voyage to India, and that if he were successful he should have sufficient to return with and commence some pursuit in London, more congenial to his thoughts and habits than the law.'

'Ah, well! what next?'

'He told me that he loved me.'

'And you believed him?'

'Father, you would have believed him had you heard him speak. His tones were those of such deep sincerity that no actor who ever charmed an audience with an unreal existence could have reached them. There are times and seasons when we know that we are listening to the majestic voice of truth, and there are tones which sink at once into the heart, carrying with them a conviction of their sincerity which neither time nor circumstance can alter; and such were the tones in which Mark Ingestrie spoke to me.'

'And so you suppose, Johanna, that it is easy for a young man who has not patience or energy enough to be respectable at home, to go abroad and make his fortune. Is idleness so much in request in other countries, that it receives such a rich reward, my dear?'

'You judge him harshly, father; you do not know him.'

'Heaven forbid that I should judge anyone harshly! and I will freely admit that you may know more of his real character than I can, who of course have only seen its surface; but go on, my dear, and tell me all.'

'We made an agreement, father, that on that day two years he was to come to me or send me some news of his whereabouts; if I heard nothing of him I was to conclude he was no more, and I cannot help so concluding now.'

'But the day has not yet passed.'

'I know it has not, and yet I rest upon but a slender hope, father. Do you believe that dreams ever really shadow forth coming events?'

'I cannot say, my child; I am not disposed to yield credence to any supposed fact because I have dreamt it, but I confess to having heard some strange instances where these visions of the night have come strictly true.'

'Heaven knows but this may be one of them! I had a dream last night. I thought that I was sitting upon the sea-shore, and that all before me was nothing but a fathomless waste of waters. I heard the roar and the dash of the waves distinctly, and each moment the wind grew more furious and fierce, and I saw in the distance a ship—it was battling with the waves, which at one moment lifted it mountains high, and at another plunged it far down into such an abyss, that not a vestige of it could be seen but the topmost spars of the tall masts. And still the storm increased each moment in its fury, and ever and anon there came a strange sullen sound across the waters, and I saw a flash of fire, and knew that those in the ill-fated vessel were thus endeavouring to attract attention and some friendly aid. Father, from the first to the last I knew that Mark Ingestrie was there—my heart told me so: I was certain he was there, and I was helpless—utterly helpless, utterly and entirely unable to

lend the slightest aid. I could only gaze upon what was going forward as a silent and terrified spectator of the scene. And at last I
heard a cry come over the deep—a strange, loud, wailing cry—which
proclaimed to me the fate of the vessel. I saw its masts shiver for a
moment in the blackened air, and then all was still for a few seconds,
until there arose a strange, wild shriek, that I knew was the despairing
cry of those who sank, never to rise again, in that vessel. Oh! that
was a frightful sound—it was a sound to linger on the ears, and haunt
the memory of sleep—it was a sound never to be forgotten when
once heard, but such as might again and again be remembered with
horror and affright.'

'And all this was in your dream?'

'It was, father, it was.'

'And you were helpless?'

'I was—utterly and entirely helpless.'

'It was very sad.'

'It was, as you shall hear. The ship went down, and that cry that
I had heard was the last despairing one given by those who clung
to the wreck with scarce a hope, and yet because it was their only
refuge, for where else had they to look for the smallest ray of consolation? where else, save in the surging waters, were they to hunt
for safety? Nowhere! all was lost! all was despair! I tried to scream—
I tried to cry aloud to Heaven to have mercy upon those brave and
gallant souls who had trusted their dearest possession—life itself—
to the mercy of the deep; and while I so tried to render so inefficient
succour, I saw a small speck in the sea, and my straining eyes perceived that it was a man floating and clinging to a piece of the
wreck, and I knew it was Mark Ingestrie.'

'But, my dear, surely you are not annoyed at a dream?'

'It saddened me; I stretched out my arms to save him—I heard
him pronounce my name, and call upon me for help. 'Twas all in
vain; he battled with the waves as long as human nature could bat-
tle with them. He could do no more, and I saw him disappear
before my anxious eyes.'

'Don't say you saw him, my dear, say you fancy you saw him.'

'It was such a fancy as I shall not lose the remembrance of for
many a day.'

'Well, well, after all, my dear, it's only a dream; and it seems to
me, without at all adverting to anything that should give you pain

as regards Mark Ingestrie, that you made a very foolish bargain; for only consider how many difficulties might arise in the way of his keeping faith with you. You know I have your happiness so much at heart that, if Mark had been a worthy man and an industrious one, I should not have opposed myself to your union; but, believe me, my dear Johanna, that a young man with great facilities for spending money, and none whatever for earning any, is just about the worst husband you could choose, and such a man was Mark Ingestrie. But come, we will say nothing of this to your mother; let the secret, if we may call it such, rest with me; and if you can inform me in what capacity and in what vessel he left England, I will not carry my prejudice so far against him as to hesitate about making what enquiry I can concerning his fate.'

'I know nothing more, father; we parted, and never met again.'

'Well, well! dry your eyes, Johanna, and, as I go to Alderman Judd's, I'll think over the matter, which, after all, may not be so bad as you think. The lad is a good-enough-looking lad, and has, I believe, a good ability, if he would put it to some useful purpose; but if he goes scampering about the world in an unsettled manner, you are well rid of him, and as for his being dead, you must not conclude that by any means, for somehow or another, like a bad penny, these fellows always come back.'

There was more consolation in the kindly tone of the spectacle-maker than in the words he used; but, upon the whole, Johanna was well enough pleased that she had communicated the secret to her father, for now, at all events, she had someone to whom she could mention the name of Mark Ingestrie, without the necessity of concealing the sentiment with which she did so; and when her father had gone, she felt that, by the mere relation of it to him, some of the terrors of her dream had vanished.

She sat for some time in a pleasing reverie, till she was interrupted by Sam, the shop-boy, who came into the parlour and said, —

'Please, Miss Johanna, suppose I was to go down to the docks and try and find out for you Mr Mark Ingestrie. I say, suppose I was to do that. I heard it all, and if I do find him I'll soon settle him.'

'What do you mean?'

'I means that I won't stand it; didn't I tell you, more than three weeks ago, as you was the object of my infections? Didn't I tell you that when aunt died I should come in for the soap and candle business, and make you my missus?'

The only reply which Johanna gave to this was to rise and leave the room, for her heart was too full of grief and sad speculation to enable her to do now as she had often been in the habit of doing—viz., laugh at Sam's protestations of affection, so he was left to chew the cud of sweet and bitter fancy by himself.

'A thousand damns!' said he, when he entered the shop: 'I always suspected there was some other fellow, and now I know it I am ready to gnaw my head off that ever I consented to come here. Confound him! I hope he is at the bottom of the sea, and eat up by this time. Oh! I should like to smash everybody. If I had my way now I'd just walk into society at large, as they calls it, and let it know what one, two, three, slap in the eye, is—and down it would go.'

Mr Sam, in his rage, did upset a case of spectacles, which went down with a tremendous crash, and which, however good an imitation of the manner in which society at large was to be knocked down, was not likely to be at all pleasing to Mr Oakley.

'I have done it now,' he said; 'but never mind; I'll try the old dodge whenever I break anything; that is, I'll place it in old Oakley's way, and swear he did it. I never knew such an old goose; you may persuade him into anything; the idea, now, of his pulling down all the shutters this morning because I told him my aunt had the toothache; that was a go, to be sure. But I'll be revenged of that fellow who has took away, I consider, Johanna from me; I'll let him know what a blighted heart is capable of. He won't live long enough to want a pair of spectacles, I'll be bound, or else my name ain't Sam Bolt.'*

# 3

## *The Dog and the Hat*

THE earliest dawn of morning was glistening upon the masts, the cordage, and the sails of a fleet of vessels lying below Sheerness.*

The crews were rousing themselves from their night's repose, and to make their appearance on the decks of the vessels, from which the night-watch had just been relieved.

A man-of-war, which had been the convoy of the fleet of merchantmen through the channel, fired a gun as the first glimpse of the morning sun fell upon her tapering masts. Then from a battery in the neighbourhood came another booming report, and that was answered by another farther off, and then another, until the whole chain of batteries that girded the coast, for it was a time of war,* had proclaimed the dawn of another day.

The effect was very fine, in the stillness of the early morn, of these successions of reports; and as they died away in the distance like mimic thunder, some order was given on board the man-of-war, and, in a moment, the masts and cordage seemed perfectly alive with human beings clinging to them in various directions. Then, as if by magic, or as if the ship had been a living thing itself, and had possessed wings, which, at the mere instigation of a wish, could be spread far and wide, there fluttered out such sheets of canvas as was wonderful to see; and, as they caught the morning light, and the ship moved from the slight breeze that sprang up from the shore, she looked, indeed, as if she

Walk'd the waters like a thing of life.*

The various crews of the merchantmen stood upon the decks of their respective vessels, gazing after the ship-of-war, as she proceeded upon another mission similar to the one she had just performed in protecting the commerce of the country.

As she passed one vessel, which had been, in point of fact, actually rescued from the enemy, the crew, who had been saved from a foreign prison, cheered lustily.

There wanted but such an impulse as this, and then every merchant-vessel that the man-of-war passed took up the gladsome shout, and the crew of the huge vessel were not slow in their answer, for three deafening cheers—such as had frequently struck terror into the hearts of England's enemies—awakened many an echo from the shore.

It was a proud and a delightful sight—such a sight as none but an Englishman can thoroughly enjoy—to see that vessel so proudly stemming the waste of waters. We say none but an Englishman can enjoy it, because no other nation has ever attempted to achieve a great maritime existence without being most signally defeated, and leaving us still, as we shall ever be, masters of the seas.

These proceedings were amply sufficient to arouse the crews of all the vessels, and over the taffrail* of one in particular, a large-sized merchantman, which had been trading in the Indian seas, two men were leaning. One of them was the captain of the vessel, and the other a passenger, who intended leaving that morning. They were engaged in earnest conversation, and the captain, as he shaded his eyes with his hand, and looked along the surface of the river, said, in reply to some observation from his companion, —

'I'll order my boat the moment Lieutenant Thornhill comes on board; I call him Lieutenant, although I have no right to do so, because he has held that rank in the king's service, but when quite a young man was cashiered* for fighting a duel with his superior officer.'

'The service has lost a good officer,' said the other.

'It has indeed; a braver man never stepped, nor a better officer; but you see they have certain rules in the service and everything is sacrificed to maintain them. I can't think what keeps him; he went last night and said he would pull up to the Temple-stairs,* because he wanted to call upon somebody by the waterside, and after that he was going to the city to transact some business of his own, and that would have brought him nearer there, you see; and there are plenty of things coming down the river.'

'He's coming,' cried the other; 'don't be impatient; you will see him in a few minutes.'

'What makes you think that?'

'Because I see his dog—there, don't you see, swimming in the water, and coming direct towards the ship?'

'I cannot imagine—I can see the dog, certainly; but I can't see Thornhill, nor is there any boat at hand. I know not what to make of it. Do you know my mind misgives me that something has happened amiss? The dog seems exhausted. Lend a hand there to Mr Thornhill's dog, some of you. Why, it's a hat he has in his mouth.'

The dog made towards the vessel; but without the assistance of the seamen—with the whole of whom he was an immense favourite—he certainly could not have boarded the vessel; and when he reached the deck, he sank down upon it in a state of complete exhaustion, with the hat still in his grasp.

As the animal lay, panting, upon the deck, the sailors looked at each other in amazement, and there was but one opinion among them all now, and that was that something very serious had unquestionably happened to Mr Thornhill.

'I dread,' said the captain, 'an explanation of this occurrence. What on earth can it mean? That's Thornhill's hat, and here is Hector. Give the dog some drink and meat directly—he seems thoroughly exhausted.'

The dog ate sparingly of some food that was put before him; and then, seizing the hat again in his mouth, he stood by the side of the ship and howled piteously; then he put down the hat for a moment, and, walking up to the captain, he pulled him by the skirt of the coat.

'You understand him,' said the captain to the passenger; 'something has happened to Thornhill, I'll be bound; and you see the object of the dog is to get me to follow him to see what it's about.'

'Think you so? It is a warning, if it be such at all, that I should not be inclined to neglect; and if you will follow the dog, I will accompany you; there may be more in it than we think of, and we ought not to allow Mr Thornhill to be in want of any assistance that we can render him, when we consider what great assistance he has been to us. Look how anxious the poor beast is.'

The captain ordered a boat to be launched at once, and manned by four stout rowers. He then sprang into it, followed by the passenger, who was a Colonel Jeffery, of the Indian army,* and the dog immediately followed them, testifying by his manner great pleasure at the expedition they were undertaking, and carrying the hat with him, which he evidently showed an immense disinclination to part with.

––––––––––

The captain ordered the boat to proceed up the river towards the Temple-stairs, where Hector's master had expressed his intention of proceeding, and, when the faithful animal saw the direction in which they were going, he lay down in the bottom of the boat perfectly satisfied, and gave himself up to that repose, of which he was evidently so much in need.

It cannot be said that Colonel Jeffery suspected that anything of a very serious nature had happened; indeed, their principal anticipation, when they came to talk it over, consisted in the probability that Thornhill had, with an impetuosity of character they knew very well he possessed, interfered to redress what he considered some street grievance, and had got himself into the custody of the civil power in consequence.

'Of course,' said the captain, 'Master Hector would view that as a very serious affair, and finding himself denied access to his master, you see he has come off to us, which was certainly the most prudent thing he could do, and I should not be at all surprised if he takes us to the door of some watch-house,* where we shall find our friend snug enough.'

The tide was running up; and that Thornhill had not saved the turn of it, by dropping down earlier to the vessel, was one of the things that surprised the captain. However, they got up quickly, and as at that hour there was not much on the river to impede their progress, and as at that time the Thames was not a thoroughfare for little stinking steamboats, they soon reached the ancient Temple-stairs.

The dog, who had until then seemed to be asleep, suddenly sprung up, and seizing the hat again in his mouth, rushed again on shore, and was closely followed by the captain and colonel.

He led them through the Temple with great rapidity, pursuing with admirable tact the precise path his master had taken towards the entrance to the Temple in Fleet-street, opposite Chancery-lane.* Darting across the road then, he stopped with a low growl at the shop of Sweeney Todd—a proceeding which very much surprised those who followed him, and caused them to pause to hold a consultation ere they proceeded further. While this was proceeding Todd suddenly opened the door, and aimed a blow at the dog with an iron bar, but the latter dexterously avoided it, and, but that the door was suddenly closed again, he would have made Sweeney Todd regret such an interference.

'We must enquire into this,' said the captain; 'there seems to be mutual ill-will between that man and the dog.'

They both tried to enter the barber's shop, but it was fast on the inside; and after repeated knockings, Todd called from within, saying,—

'I won't open the door while that dog is there. He is mad, or has a spite against me—I don't know nor care which—it's a fact, that's all I am aware of.'

'I will undertake,' said the captain, 'that the dog shall do you no harm; but open the door, for in we must come, and will.'

'I will take your promise,' said Sweeney Todd; 'but mind you keep it, or I shall protect myself and take the creature's life; so, if you value it, you had better hold it fast.'

The captain pacified Hector as well as he could, and likewise tied one end of a silk handkerchief round his neck, and held the other firmly in his grasp; after which Todd, who seemed to have some means from within of seeing what was going on, opened his door and admitted his visitors.

'Well, gentlemen, shaved, or cut, or dressed, I am at your service; which shall I begin with?'

The dog never took his eye off Todd, but kept up a low growl from the first moment of his entrance.

'It's rather a remarkable circumstance,' said the captain, 'but this is a very sagacious dog, you see, and he belongs to a friend of ours, who has most unaccountably disappeared.'

'Has he, really?' said Todd. 'Tobias! Tobias!'

'Yes, sir.'

'Run to Mr Phillips's, in Cateaton-street, and get me six-penny-worth of preserved figs, and don't say that I don't give you the money this time when you go on a message. I think I did before, but you swallowed it; and when you come back, just please remember the insight into business I gave you yesterday.'

'Yes,' said the boy, with a shudder, for he had a great horror of Sweeney Todd, as well he might, after the severe discipline he had received at his hands, and away he went.

'Well, gentlemen,' said Todd, 'what is it you require of me?'

'We want to know if anyone having the appearance of an officer in the navy came to your house?'

'Yes—a rather good-looking man, weatherbeaten, with a bright blue eye, and rather fair hair.'

'Yes, yes! the same.'

'Oh! to be sure, he came here, and I shaved him and polished him off.'

'What do you mean by polishing him off?'

'Brushing him up a bit, and making him tidy: he said he had got somewhere to go in the city, and asked me the address of a Mr Oakley, a spectacle-maker. I gave it him, and then he went away; but as I was standing at my door about five minutes afterwards, it seemed to me, as well as I could see the distance, that he got into some row near the market.'

'Did this dog come with him?'

'A dog came with him, but whether it was that dog or not I don't know.'

'And that's all you know of him?'

'You never spoke a truer word in your life,' said Sweeney Todd, as he diligently stropped a razor upon his great, horny hand.

This seemed something like a complete fix; and the captain looked at Colonel Jeffery, and the colonel at the captain, for some moments, in complete silence. At length the latter said,—

'It's a very extraordinary thing that the dog should come here if he missed his master somewhere else. I never heard of such a thing.'

'Nor I either,' said Todd. 'It is extraordinary; so extraordinary that, if I had not seen it, I would not have believed. I dare say you will find him in the next watch-house.'

The dog had watched the countenance of all parties during this brief dialogue, and twice or thrice he had interrupted it by a strange howling cry.

'I'll tell you what it is,' said the barber; 'if that beast stays here, I'll be the death of him. I hate dogs—detest them; and I tell you, as I told you before, if you value him at all keep him away from me.'

'You say you directed the person you describe to us where to find a spectacle-maker named Oakley. We happen to know that he was going in search of such a person, and, as he had property of value about him, we will go there and ascertain if he reached his destination.'

'It is in Fore-street—a little shop with two windows; you cannot miss it.'

The dog, when he saw they were about to leave, grew furious; and it was with the greatest difficulty they succeeded, by main force, in getting him out of the shop, and dragging him some short distance with them, but then he contrived to get free of the handkerchief that held him, and darting back, he sat down at Sweeney Todd's door, howling most piteously.

They had no recourse but to leave him, intending fully to call as they came back from Mr Oakley's; and, as they looked behind them, they saw that Hector was collecting a crowd round the barber's door, and it was a singular thing to see a number of persons surrounding the dog, while he, to all appearance, appeared to be actually making efforts to explain something to the assemblage. They walked on until they reached the spectacle-maker's, and there they paused; for they all of a sudden recollected that the mission that Mr Thornhill had had to execute there was of a very delicate nature, and one by no means to be lightly executed, or even so much as mentioned, probably, in the hearing of Mr Oakley himself.

'We must not be so hasty,' said the colonel.

'But what am I to do? I sail tonight; at least I have got to go round to Liverpool with my vessel.'

'Do not then call at Mr Oakley's at all at present; but leave me to ascertain the fact quietly and secretly.'

'My anxiety for Thornhill will scarcely permit me to do so; but I suppose I must, and if you write me a letter to the Royal Oak Hotel, at Liverpool, it will be sure to reach me, that is to say, unless you find Mr Thornhill himself, in which case I need not by any means give you so much trouble.'

'You may depend upon me. My friendship for Mr Thornhill, and gratitude, as you know, for the great service he has rendered to us all, will induce me to do my utmost to discover him; and, but that I know he set his heart upon performing the message he had to deliver accurately and well, I should recommend that we at once go into this house of Mr Oakley's, only that the fear of compromising the young lady—who is in the case, and who will have quite enough to bear, poor thing! of her own grief—restrains me.'

After some more conversation of a similar nature, they decided that this should be the plan adopted. They made an unavailing call at the watch-house of the district, being informed there that no such person, nor anyone answering the description of Mr Thornhill had been engaged in any disturbance, or apprehended by any of the constables; and this only involved the thing in greater mystery than ever, so they went back to try and recover the dog, but that was a matter easier to be desired and determined upon than executed, for threats and persuasions were alike ineffectual.

Hector would not stir an inch from the barber's door. There he sat, with the hat by his side, a most melancholy and strange-looking spectacle, and a most efficient guard was he for that hat, and it was evident, that while he chose to exhibit the formidable row of teeth he did occasionally, when anybody showed a disposition to touch it, it would remain sacred. Some people, too, had thrown a few copper coins into the hat, so that Hector, if his mind had been that way inclined, was making a very good thing of it; but who shall describe the anger of Sweeney Todd, when he found that he was likely to be so beleaguered?

He doubted, if, upon the arrival of the first customer to his shop, the dog might dart in and take him by storm; but that apprehension went off at last, when a young gallant came from the Temple to have his hair dressed, and the dog allowed him to pass in and out unmolested, without making any attempt to follow him. This was something, at all events; but whether or not it insured Sweeney Todd's personal safety, when he should himself come out, was quite another matter.

It was an experiment, however, which he must try. It was quite out of the question that he should remain a prisoner much longer in his own place, so, after a time, he thought he might try the experiment, and that it would be best done when there were plenty of people there, because, if the dog assaulted him, he would have an excuse for any amount of violence he might think proper to use upon the occasion.

It took some time, however, to screw his courage to the sticking-place; but, at length, muttering deep curses between his clenched teeth, he made his way to the door, and carried in his hand a long knife, which he thought a more efficient weapon against the dog's teeth than the iron bludgeon he had formerly used.

'I hope he will attack me,' said Todd to himself, as he thought; but Tobias, who had come back from the place where they sold the preserved figs, heard him, and after devoutly in his own mind wishing that the dog would actually devour Sweeney, said aloud,—

'Oh dear, sir; you don't wish that, I'm sure!'

'Who told you what I wished, or what I did not? Remember, Tobias, and keep your own counsel, or it will be the worse for you, and your mother too—remember that.'

The boy shrunk back. How had Sweeney Todd terrified the boy about his mother! He must have done so, or Tobias would never have shrunk as he did.

Then that rascally barber, whom we begin to suspect of more crimes than fall ordinarily to the share of man, went cautiously out of his shop-door: we cannot pretend to account for why it was so, but, as faithful recorders of facts, we have to state that Hector did not fly at him, but with a melancholy and subdued expression of countenance he looked up in the face of Sweeney Todd; then he whined piteously, as if he would have said, 'Give me my master, and I will forgive you all that you have done; give me back my beloved master, and you shall see that I am neither revengeful nor ferocious.'

This kind of expression was as legibly written in the poor creature's countenance as if he had actually been endowed with speech, and uttered the words themselves.

This was what Sweeney Todd certainly did not expect, and, to tell the truth, it staggered and astonished him a little. He would have been glad of an excuse to commit some act of violence, but he had now none, and as he looked in the faces of the people who were around, he felt quite convinced that it would not be the most prudent thing in the world to interfere with the dog in any way that savoured of violence.

'Where's the dog's master?' said one.

'Ah, where indeed?' said Todd; 'I should not wonder if he had come to some foul end!'

'But I say, old soap-suds,' cried a boy; 'the dog says you did it.'

There was a general laugh, but the barber was no means disconcerted, and he shortly replied, —

'Does he? he is wrong then.'

Sweeney Todd had no desire to enter into anything like a controversy with the people, so he turned again and entered his own shop, in a distant corner of which he sat down, and folding his great gaunt-looking arms over his chest, he gave himself up to thought, and, if we might judge from the expression of his countenance, those thoughts were of a pleasant anticipatory character, for now and then he gave such a grim sort of smile as might well have sat upon the features of some ogre.

And now we will turn to another scene, of a widely different character.

# 4

## *The Pie-shop in Bell-yard*

HARK! twelve o'clock at mid-day is cheerily proclaimed by St Dunstan's church, and scarcely have the sounds done echoing throughout the neighbourhood, and scarcely has the clock of Lincoln's-inn done chiming in with its announcement of the same hour, when Bell-yard, Temple-bar,* becomes a scene of commotion.

What a scampering of feet is there, what a laughing and talking, what a jostling to be first; and what an immense number of man-ocuvres are resorted to by some of the throng to distance others!

And mostly from Lincoln's-inn* do these persons, young and old, but most certainly a majority of the former, come bustling and striving, although from the neighbouring legal establishments like-wise there come not a few; the Temple contributes its numbers, and from the more distant Gray's-inn* there come a goodly lot.

Now Bell-yard is almost choked up, and a stranger would wonder what could be the matter, and most probably stand in some doorway until the commotion was over.

Is it a fire? is it a fight? or anything else sufficiently alarming and extraordinary to excite the junior members of the legal profession to such a species of madness? No, it is none of these, nor is there a fat cause to be run for, which, in the hands of some clever practi-tioner, might become quite a vested interest. No, the enjoyment is purely one of a physical character, and all the pacing and racing—all this turmoil and trouble—all this pushing, jostling, laughing, and shouting, is to see who will get first to Lovett's pie-shop.

Yes, on the left-hand side of Bell-yard, going down from Carey-street, was, at the time we write of, one of the most celebrated shops for the sale of veal and pork pies that London ever produced. High and low, rich and poor, resorted to it; its fame had spread far and wide; and it was because the first batch of those pies came up at twelve o'clock that there was such a rush of the legal profession to obtain them.

Their fame had spread even to great distances, and many persons carried them to the suburbs of the city as quite a treat to friends and relations there residing. And well did they deserve their reputation, those delicious pies; there was about them a flavour never surpassed, and rarely equalled; the paste was of the most delicate construction, and impregnated with the aroma of a deli-cious gravy that defies description. Then the small portions of meat which they contained were so tender, and the fat and the lean so artistically mixed up, that to eat one of Lovett's pies was such a provocative to eat another, that many persons who came to lunch stayed to dine, wasting more than an hour, perhaps, of precious time, and endangering—who knows to the contrary?—the success of some law-suit thereby.

The counter in Lovett's pie-shop was in the shape of a horseshoe, and it was the custom of the young bloods from the Temple and Lincoln's-inn to sit in a row upon its edge while they partook of the delicious pies, and chatted gaily about one concern and another.

Many an appointment was made at Lovett's pie-shop, and many a piece of gossiping scandal was there first circulated. The din of tongues was prodigious. The ringing laugh of the boy who looked upon the quarter of an hour he spent at Lovett's as the brightest of the whole twenty-four, mingled gaily with the more boisterous mirth of his seniors; and oh! with what rapidity the pies disappeared!

They were brought up on large trays, each of which contained about a hundred, and from these trays they were so speedily transferred to the mouths of Mrs Lovett's customers that it looked like a work of magic.

And now we have let out some portion of the secret. There was a Mistress Lovett; but possibly our readers guessed as much, for what but a female hand, and that female buxom, young and good-looking, could have ventured upon the production of those pies. Yes, Mrs Lovett was all that; and every enamoured young scion of the law, as he devoured his pie, pleased himself with the idea that the charming Mrs Lovett had made that pie especially for him, and that fate or predestination had placed it in his hands.

And it was astonishing to see with what impartiality and with what tact the fair pastry cook bestowed her smiles upon her admirers, so that none could say he was neglected, while it was extremely difficult for anyone to say he was preferred.

This was pleasant, but at the same time it was provoking to all except Mrs Lovett, in whose favour it got up a sort of excitement that paid extraordinarily well, because some of the young fellows thought, and thought it with wisdom too, that he who consumed the most pies would be in the most likely way to receive the greatest number of smiles from the lady.

Acting upon this supposition, some of her more enthusiastic admirers went on consuming the pies until they were almost ready to burst. But there were others again, of a more philosophic turn of mind, who went for the pies only, and did not care one jot for Mrs Lovett.

These declared that her smile was cold and uncomfortable—that it was upon her lips, but had no place in her heart—that it was the set smile of a ballet-dancer, which is about one of the most unmirth-ful things in existence.

Then there were some who went even beyond this, and, while they admitted the excellence of the pies, and went every day to partake of them, swore that Mrs Lovett had quite a sinister aspect, and that they could see what a merely superficial affair her blandishments were, and that there was

'a lurking devil in her eye'*

that, if once roused, would be capable of achieving some serious things, and might not be so easily quelled again.

By five minutes past twelve Mrs Lovett's counter was full, and the savoury steam of the hot pies went out in fragrant clouds into Bell-yard, being sniffed up by many a poor wretch passing by who lacked the means of making one in the throng that were devouring the dainty morsels within.

'Why, Tobias Ragg,' said a young man, with his mouth full of pie, 'where have you been since you left Mr Snow's in Paper-buildings?* I have not seen you for some days.'

'No,' said Tobias, 'I have gone into another line: instead of being a lawyer, and helping to shave the clients, I am going to shave the lawyers now. A twopenny pork, if you please, Mrs Lovett. Ah! who would be an emperor, if he couldn't get pies like these—eh, Master Clift?'

'Well, they are good; of course we know that, Tobias; but do you mean to say you are going to be a barber?'

'Yes, I am with Sweeney Todd, the barber of Fleet-street, close to St Dunstan's.'

'The deuce you are! well, I am going to a party to-night, and I'll drop in and get dressed and shaved, and patronize your master.'

Tobias put his mouth close to the ear of the young lawyer, and in a fearful sort of whisper said the one word—'Don't.'

'Don't? what for?'

Tobias made no answer; and throwing down his two-pence, scampered out of the shop as fast as he could. He had only been sent a message by Sweeney Todd in the neighbourhood; but, as he heard the clock strike twelve, and two penny-pieces were lying at the bottom of his pocket, it was not in human nature to resist running into Lovett's and converting them into a pork pie.

'What an odd thing!' thought the young lawyer. 'I'll just drop in at Sweeney Todd's now on purpose, and ask Tobias what he means. I quite forgot, too, while he was here, to ask him what all that riot was about a dog at Todd's door.'

'A veal!' said a young man, rushing in; 'a two-penny veal, Mrs Lovett.' When he got it he consumed it with voracity, and then, noticing an acquaintance in the shop, he whispered to him, —

'I can't stand it any more. I have cut* the spectacle-maker—Johanna is faithless, and I know not what to do.'

'Have another pie.'

'But what's a pie to Johanna Oakley? You know, Dilki, that I only went there to be near the charmer. Damn the shutters and curse the spectacles! She loves another and I am a desperate individual! I should like to do some horrible and desperate act. Oh, Johanna, Johanna! you have driven me to the verge of what do you call it—I'll take another veal, if you please, Mrs Lovett.'

'Well, I was wondering how you got on,' said his friend Dilki, 'and thinking of calling upon you.'

'Oh! it was all right—it was all right at first: she smiled upon me.'

'You are quite sure she didn't laugh at you?'

'Sir! Mr Dilki!'

'I say, are you sure that instead of smiling upon you she was not laughing at you?'

'Am I sure? Do you wish to insult me, Mr Dilki? I look upon you as a puppy, sir—a horrid puppy.'

'Very good; now I am convinced that the girl has been having a bit of fun at your expense.—Are you not aware, Sam, that your nose turns up so much that it's enough to pitch you head over heels? How do you suppose that any girl under forty-five would waste a word upon you? Mind, I don't say this to offend you in any way, but just quietly, by way of asking a question.'

Sam looked daggers, and probably he might have attempted some desperate act in the pie-shop, if at the moment he had not caught the eye of Mrs Lovett, and he saw by the expression on that lady's face that anything in the shape of a riot would be speedily suppressed, so he darted out of the place at once to carry his sorrows and his bitterness elsewhere.

It was only between twelve and one o'clock that such a tremendous rush and influx of visitors came to the pie-shop, for, although there was a good custom the whole day, and the concern was a money-making one from morning till night, it was at that hour principally that the great consumption of pies took place.

Tobias knew from experience that Sweeney Todd was a skilful calculator of the time it ought to take to go to different places, and accordingly, since he had occupied some portion of that most valuable of all commodities at Mrs Lovett's, he arrived quite breathless at his master's shop.

There sat the mysterious dog with the hat, and Tobias lingered for a moment to speak to the animal. Dogs are great physiognomists; and as the creature looked into Tobias's face he seemed to draw a favourable conclusion regarding him, for he submitted to a caress.

'Poor fellow!' said Tobias. 'I wish I knew what had become of your master, but it made me shake like a leaf to wake up last night and ask myself the question. You shan't starve, though, if I can help it. I haven't much for myself, but you shall have some of it.'

As he spoke, Tobias took from his pocket some not very tempting cold meat, which was intended for his own dinner, and which he had wrapped up in not the cleanest of cloths. He gave a piece to the dog, who took it with a dejected air, and then crouched down at Sweeney Todd's door again.

Just then, as Tobias was about to enter the shop, he thought he heard from within a strange shrieking sort of sound. On the impulse of the moment he recoiled a step or two, and then, from some other impulse, he dashed forward at once, and entered the shop.

The first object that presented itself to his attention, lying upon a side table, was a hat with a handsome gold-headed walking-cane lying across it.

The armchair in which customers usually sat to be shaved, was vacant, and Sweeney Todd's face was just projected into the shop from the back parlour, and wearing a most singular and hideous expression.

'Well, Tobias,' he said, as he advanced, rubbing his great hands together, 'well, Tobias! so you could not resist the pie-shop?'

'How does he know?' thought Tobias. 'Yes, sir, I have been to the pie-shop, but I didn't stay a minute.'

'Hark ye, Tobias! the only thing I can excuse in the way of delay upon an errand is for you to get one of Mrs Lovett's pies: that I can look over, so think no more about it. Are they not delicious, Tobias?'

'Yes, sir, they are; but some gentleman seems to have left his hat and stick.'

'Yes,' said Sweeney Todd, 'he has'; and lifting the stick he struck Tobias a blow with it that felled him to the ground. 'Lesson the second to Tobias Ragg, which teaches him to make no remarks about what does not concern him. You may think what you like, Tobias Ragg, but you shall say only what I like.'

'I won't endure it,' cried the boy; 'I won't be knocked about in this way, I tell you, Sweeney Todd, I won't.'

'You won't! have you forgotten your mother?'

'You say you have a power over my mother; but I don't know what it is, and I cannot and will not believe it; I'll leave you, and, come of it what may, I'll go to sea or anywhere rather than stay in such a place as this.'

'Oh, you will, will you? then, Tobias, you and I must come to some explanation. I'll tell you what power I have over your mother, and then perhaps you will be satisfied. Last winter, when the frost had continued eighteen weeks, and you and your mother were starving, she was employed to clean out the chambers of a Mr King, in the Temple, a cold-hearted, severe man, who never forgave anything in all his life and never will.'

'I remember,' said Tobias: 'we were starving and owed a whole guinea for rent; but mother borrowed it and paid it, and after that got a situation where she now is.'

'Ah, you think so. The rent was paid; but, Tobias, my boy, a word in your ear—she took a silver candlestick from Mr King's chambers to pay it. I know it. I can prove it. Think of that, Tobias, and be discreet.'

'Have mercy upon us,' said the boy: 'they would take her life!'*

'Her life!' screamed Sweeney Todd; 'ay, to be sure they would: they would hang her—hang her, I say; and now mind, if you force me, by any conduct of your own, to mention this thing, you are your mother's executioner. I had better go and be deputy hangman at once, and turn her off.'

'Horrible! horrible!'

'Oh, you don't like that? indeed, that don't suit you, Master Tobias? Be discreet then, and you have nothing to fear. Do not force me to show a power which will be as complete as it is terrible.'

'I will say nothing—I will think nothing.'

' 'Tis well; now go and put that hat and stick in yonder cupboard. I shall be absent for a short time; and if anyone comes, tell them I am called out, and shall not return for an hour or perhaps longer, and mind you take good care of the shop.'

Sweeney Todd took off his apron, and put on an immense coat with huge lapels, and then, clapping a three-cornered hat on his head, and casting a strange withering kind of look at Tobias, he sallied forth into the street.

## 5

## *The Meeting in the Temple*

ALAS! poor Johanna Oakley—thy day has passed away and brought with it no tidings of him you love; and oh! what a weary day, full of fearful doubts and anxieties, has it been!

Tortured by doubts, hopes, and fears, that day was one of the most wretched that poor Johanna had ever passed. Not even two years before, when she had parted with her lover, had she felt such an exquisite pang of anguish as now filled her heart, when she saw the day gliding away and the evening creeping on apace, without word or token from Mark Ingestrie.

She did not herself know, until all the agony of disappointment had come across her, how much she had counted upon hearing something from him on that occasion; and when the evening deepened into night, and hope grew so slender that she could no longer rely upon it for the least support, she was compelled to proceed to her own chamber, and, feigning indisposition to avoid her mother's questions—for Mrs Oakley was at home, and making herself and everybody else as uncomfortable as possible—she flung herself on her humble couch and gave way to a perfect passion of tears.

'Oh, Mark, Mark!' she said, 'why do you thus desert me, when I have relied so abundantly upon your true affection? Oh, why have you not sent me some token of your existence, and of your continued love? the merest, slightest word would have been sufficient, and I should have been happy.'

She wept then such bitter tears as only such a heart as hers can know, when it feels the deep and bitter anguish of desertion, and when the rock upon which it supposed it had built its fondest hopes resolves itself to a mere quicksand, in which becomes engulphed all of good that this world can afford to the just and the beautiful.

Oh, it is heartrending to think that such a one as she, Johanna Oakley, a being so full of all those holy and gentle emotions which should constitute the truest felicity, should thus feel that life to her had lost its greatest charms, and that nothing but despair remained.

'I will wait until midnight,' she said; 'and even then it will be a mockery to seek repose, and tomorrow I must myself make some exertion to discover some tidings of him.'

Then she began to ask herself what that exertion could be, and in what manner a young and inexperienced girl, such as she was, could hope to succeed in her enquiries. And the midnight hour came at last, telling her that, giving the utmost latitude to the word day, it had gone at last, and she was left despairing.

She lay the whole of that night sobbing, and only at times dropping into an unquiet slumber, during which painful images were presented to her, all, however, having the same tendency, and pointing towards the presumed fact that Mark Ingestrie was no more.

But the weariest night to the weariest waker will pass away, and at length the soft and beautiful dawn stole into the chamber of Johanna Oakley, chasing away some of the more horrible visions of the night, but having little effect in subduing the sadness that had taken possession of her.

She felt that it would be better for her to make her appearance below than to hazard the remarks and conjectures that her not doing so would give rise to, so, all unfitted as she was to engage in the most ordinary intercourse, she crept down to the breakfast-parlour, looking more like the ghost of her former self than the bright and beautiful being we have represented her to the reader.

Her father understood what it was that robbed her cheek of its bloom: and although he saw it with much distress, yet he had fortified himself with what he considered were some substantial reasons for future hopefulness.

It had become part of his philosophy—it generally is a part of the philosophy of the old—to consider that those sensations of the

mind that arise from disappointed affections are of the most evanescent character; and that, although for a time they exhibit themselves with violence, they, like grief for the dead, soon pass away,
scarcely leaving a trace behind of their former existence.

And perhaps he was right as regards the greatest number of
those passions; but he was certainly wrong when he applied that
sort of worldly-wise knowledge to his daughter Johanna. She was
one of those rare beings whose hearts are not won by every gaudy
flatterer who may buzz the accents of admiration in their ears. No;
she was qualified, eminently qualified, to love once, but only once;
and, like the passion-flower, that blooms into abundant beauty
once and never afterwards puts forth a blossom, she allowed her
heart to expand to the soft influence of affection, which, when
crushed by adversity, was gone forever.

'Really, Johanna,' said Mrs Oakley, in the true conventicle twang,
'you look so pale and ill that I must positively speak to Mr Lupin
about you.'

'Mr Lupin, my dear,' said the spectacle-maker, 'may be all very
well in his way as a parson; but I don't see what he can do with
Johanna looking pale.'

'A pious man, Mr Oakley, has to do with everything and
everybody.'

'Then he must be the most intolerable bore in existence; and
I don't wonder at his being kicked out of some people's houses, as I
have heard Mr Lupin has been.'

'And if he has, Mr Oakley, I can tell you he glories in it. Mr Lupin
likes to suffer for the faith; and if he were to be made a martyr
to-morrow, I am quite certain it would give him a deal of pleasure.'

'My dear, I am quite sure it would not give him half the pleasure
it would me.'

'I understand your insinuation, Mr Oakley; you would like to
have him murdered on account of his holiness; but, though you say
these kind of things at your own breakfast-table, you won't say as
much when he comes to tea this afternoon.'

'To tea, Mrs Oakley! haven't I told you over and over again that I
will not have that man in my house!'

'And haven't I told you, Mr Oakley, twice that number of times that
he shall come to tea? and I have asked him now, and it can't be altered.'

'But, Mrs Oakley—'

'It's of no use, Mr Oakley, your talking. Mr Lupin is coming to tea, and come he shall; and if you don't like it, you can go out. There now, I am sure you can't complain, now you have actually the liberty of going out; but you are like the dog in the manger,* Mr Oakley, I know that well enough, and nothing will please you.'

'A fine liberty, indeed, the liberty of going out of my own house to let somebody else into it that I don't like!'

'Johanna, my dear,' said Mrs Oakley, 'I think my old complaint is coming on, the beating of the heart, and the hysterics. I know what produces it—it's your father's brutality; and just because Dr Fungus said over and over again that I was to be kept perfectly quiet, your father seizes upon the opportunity like a wild beast, or a raving maniac, to try and make me ill.'

Mr Oakley jumped up, stamped his feet upon the floor, and, uttering something about the probability of his becoming a maniac in a very short time, rushed into his shop, and set to polishing spectacles as if he were doing it for a wager.

This little affair between her father and her mother certainly had had the effect, for a time, of diverting attention from Johanna, and she was able to assume a cheerfulness she did not feel; but she had something of her father's spirit in her as regards Mr Lupin, and most decidedly objected to sitting down to any meal whatever with that individual, so that Mrs Oakley was left in a minority of one upon the occasion, which, perhaps, as she fully expected, was no great matter after all.

Johanna went upstairs to her own room, which commanded a view of the street. It was an old-fashioned house, with a balcony in front, and as she looked listlessly out into Fore-street, which was far then from being the thoroughfare it is now, she saw standing in a doorway on the opposite side of the way a stranger, who was looking intently at the house, and who, when he caught her eye, walked instantly across to it, and cast something into the balcony of the first floor. Then he touched his cap, and walked rapidly from the street.

The thought immediately occurred to Johanna that this might possibly be some messenger from him concerning whose existence and welfare she was so deeply anxious. It is not to be wondered at, therefore, that with the name of Mark Ingestrie upon her lips she should rush down to the balcony in intense anxiety to hear and see if such was really the case.

When she reached the balcony she found lying in it a scrap of paper, in which a stone was wrapped up, in order to give it weight, so that it might be cast with certainty into the balcony. With trembling eagerness she opened the paper, and read upon it the following words: —

'For news of Mark Ingestrie, come to the Temple-gardens one hour before sunset, and do not fear addressing a man who will be holding a white rose in his hand.'

'He lives! he lives!' she cried. 'He lives, and joy again becomes the inhabitant of my bosom! Oh, it is daylight now and sunshine compared to the black midnight of despair. Mark Ingestrie lives and I shall be happy yet.'

She placed the little scrap of paper in her bosom, and then, with clasped hands and a delighted expression of countenance, she repeated the brief but expressive words it contained, adding, —

'Yes, yes, I will be there; the white rose is an emblem of his purity and affection, his spotless love, and that is why his messenger carries it. I will be there. One hour before sunset, ay two hours before sunset, I will be there. Joy, joy! he lives, he lives! Mark Ingestrie lives! Perchance, too, successful in his object, he returns to tell me that he can make me his, and that no obstacle can now interfere to frustrate our union. Time, time, float onwards on your fleetest pinions!'

She went to her own apartment, but it was not, as she had last gone to it, to weep; on the contrary, it was to smile at her former fears, and to admit the philosophy of the assertion that we suffer much more from a dread of those things that never happen than we do for actual calamities which occur in their full force to us.

'Oh, that this messenger,' she said, 'had come but yesterday! what hours of anguish I should have been spared! But I will not complain; it shall not be said that I repine at present joy because it did not come before. I will be happy when I can; and, in the consciousness that I shall soon hear blissful tidings of Mark Ingestrie, I will banish every fear.'

The impatience which she now felt brought its pains and its penalties with it, and yet it was quite a different description of feeling to any she had formerly endured, and certainly far more desirable than the absolute anguish that had taken possession of her upon hearing nothing of Mark Ingestrie.

It was strange, very strange, that the thought never crossed her mind that the tidings she had to hear in the Temple-gardens from the stranger might be evil ones, but certainly such a thought did not occur to her, and she looked forward to a meeting which she certainly had no evidence to know might not be of the most disastrous character.

She asked herself over and over again if she should tell her father what had occurred, but as often as she thought of doing so she shrank from carrying out the mental suggestion, and all the natural disposition again to keep to herself the secret of her happiness returned to her with full force.

But yet she was not so unjust as not to feel that it was treating her father but slightingly to throw all her sorrows into his lap, as it were, and then to keep from him everything of joy appertaining to the same circumstances.

This was a thing that she was not likely to continue doing, and so she made up her mind to relieve her conscience from the pang it would otherwise have had, by determining to tell him, after the interview in the Temple-gardens, what was its result; but she could not make up her mind to do so beforehand; it was so pleasant and so delicious to keep the secret all to herself, and to feel that she alone knew that her lover had so closely kept faith with her as to be only one day behind his time in sending to her, and that day, perhaps, far from being his fault.

And so she reasoned to herself and tried to wile away the anxious hours, sometimes succeeding in forgetting how long it was still to sunset, and at others feeling as if each minute was perversely swelling itself out into ten times its usual proportion of time in order to become wearisome to her.

She had said she would be at the Temple-gardens two hours before sunset instead of one, and she kept her word, for, looking happier than she had done for weeks, she tripped down the stairs of her father's house, and was about to leave it by the private staircase when a strange gaunt-looking figure attracted her attention.

This was no other than the Rev Mr Lupin: he was a long strange-looking man, and upon this occasion he came upon what he called horseback, that is to say, he was mounted upon a very small pony, which seemed quite unequal to support his weight, and was so

short that, if the reverend gentleman had not poked his legs out at
an angle, they must inevitably have touched the ground.

'Praise the Lord!' he said: 'I have intercepted the evil one. Maiden,
I have come here at thy mother's bidding, and thou shalt remain
and partake of the mixture called tea.'

Johanna scarcely condescended to glance at him; but, drawing
her mantle close around her, which he actually had the impertin-
ence to endeavour to lay hold of, she walked on, so that the reverend gentleman was left to make the best he could of the matter.

'Stop!' he cried, 'stop! I can well perceive that the devil has a
strong hold of you: I can well perceive—the Lord have mercy upon
me! this animal hath some design against me as sure as fate.'

This last ejaculation arose from the fact that the pony had flung
up his heels behind in a most mysterious manner.

'I'm afraid, sir,' said a lad who was no other than our old acquaintance, Sam, 'I am afraid, sir, that there is something the matter with
the pony.'

Up went the pony's heels again in the same unaccustomed manner.

'God bless me!' said the reverend gentleman; 'he never did such a
thing before. I—there he goes again—murder! Young man, I pray you
help me to get down; I think I know you; you are the nephew of the
godly Mrs Pump—truly this animal wishes to be the death of me.'

At this moment the pony gave such a vigorous kick up behind
that Mr Lupin was fairly pitched upon his head, and made a complete somersault, alighting with his heels in the spectacle-maker's
passage; and it unfortunately happened that Mrs Oakley at that
moment, hearing the altercation, came rushing out, and the first
thing she did was to fall sprawling over Mr Lupin's feet.

Sam now felt it time to go; and as we dislike useless mysteries,
we may as well explain that these extraordinary circumstances
arose from the fact that Sam had bought himself from the haber-
dasher's opposite a halfpenny-worth of pins, and had amused himself by making a pincushion of the hind quarters of the Reverend
Lupin's pony, which, not being accustomed to that sort of thing,
had kicked out vigorously in opposition to the same, and produced
the results we have recorded.

Johanna Oakley was some distance upon her road before the
reverend gentleman was pitched into her father's house in the

manner we have described, so that she knew nothing of it, nor would she have cared if she had, for her mind was wholly bent upon the expedition she was proceeding on.

As she walked upon that side of the way of Fleet-street where Sweeney Todd's house and shop were situated, a feeling of curiosity prompted her to stop for a moment and look at the melancholy-looking dog that stood watching a hat at his door.

The appearance of grief upon the creature's face could not be mistaken, and, as she gazed, she saw the shop-door gently opened and a piece of meat thrown out.

'Those are kind people,' she said, 'be they who they may'; but when she saw the dog turn away from the meat with loathing, and herself observed that there was a white powder upon it, the idea that it was poisoned, and only intended for the poor creature's destruction, came instantly across her mind.

───────

And when she saw the horrible-looking face of Sweeney Todd glaring at her from the partially-opened door, she could not doubt any further the fact, for that face was quite enough to give a warrant for any amount of villainy whatever.

She passed on with a shudder, little suspecting, however, that that dog had anything to do with her fate, or the circumstances which made up the sum of her destiny.

It wanted a full hour to the appointed time of meeting when she reached the Temple-gardens, and, partly blaming herself that she was so soon, while at the same time she would not for worlds have been away, she sat down on one of the garden-seats to think over the past, and to recall to her memory, with all the vivid freshness of young Love's devotion, the many gentle words which, from time to time, had been spoken to her two summers since by him whose faith she had never doubted, and whose image was enshrined at the bottom of her heart.

# 6

## *The Conference, and the Fearful Narration in the Garden*

THE Temple clock struck the hour of meeting, and Johanna looked anxiously around her for anyone who should seem to bear the appearance of being such a person as she might suppose Mark Ingestrie would choose for his messenger.

She turned her eyes towards the gate, for she thought she heard it close, and then she saw a gentlemanly-looking man, attired in a cloak, and who was looking about him, apparently in search of someone.

When his eye fell upon her he immediately produced from beneath his cloak a white rose, and in another minute they met.

'I have the honour,' he said, 'of speaking to Miss Johanna Oakley?'

'Yes, sir; and you are Mark Ingestrie's messenger?'

'I am; that is to say, I am he who comes to bring you news of Mark Ingestrie, although I grieve to say I am not the messenger that was expressly deputed by him to do so.'

'Oh! sir, your looks are sad and serious, you seem as if you would announce that some misfortune had occurred. Tell me that it is not so; speak to me at once, or my heart will break!'

'Compose yourself, lady, I pray you.'

'I cannot—dare not do so, unless you tell me he lives. Tell me that Mark Ingestrie lives, and then I shall be all patience: tell me that, and you shall not hear a murmur from me. Speak the word at once—at once! It is cruel, believe me, to keep me in this suspense.'

'This is one of the saddest errands I ever came upon,' said the stranger, as he led Johanna to a seat. 'Recollect, lady, what creatures of accident and chance we are—recollect how the slightest circumstances will affect us, in driving us to the confines of despair, and remember by how frail a tenure the best of us hold existence.'

'No more—no more!' shrieked Johanna, as she clasped her hands—'I know all now and am desolate.'

She let her face drop upon her hands, and shook as with a convulsion of grief.

'Mark! Mark!' she cried, 'you have gone from me! I thought not this—I thought not this. Oh, Heaven why have I lived so long as to have the capacity to listen to such fearful tidings? Lost—lost—all lost! God of Heaven! what a wilderness the world is now to me!'

'Let me pray you, lady, to subdue this passion of grief, and listen truly to what I shall unfold to you. There is much to hear and much to speculate upon; and if, from all that I have learnt, I cannot, dare not tell you that Mark Ingestrie lives, I likewise shrink from telling you he is no more.'

'Speak again—say those words again! There is a hope, then—oh, there is a hope!'

'There is a hope; and better it is that your mind should receive the first shock of the probability of the death of him whom you have so anxiously expected and then afterwards, from what I shall relate to you, gather hope that it may not be so, than that from the first you should expect too much, and then have those expectations rudely destroyed.'

'It is so—it is so; this is kind of you, and if I cannot thank you as I ought, you will know that it is because I am in a state of too great affliction so to do, and not from want of will; you will understand that—I am sure you will understand that.'

'Make no excuses to me. Believe me. I can fully appreciate all that you would say, and all that you must feel. I ought to tell you who I am, that you may have confidence in what I have to relate to you. My name is Jeffery, and I am a colonel in the Indian army.'

'I am much beholden to you, sir; but you bring with you a passport to my confidence, in the name of Mark Ingestrie, which is at once sufficient. I live again in the hope that you have given me of his continued existence, and in that hope I will maintain a cheerful resignation that shall enable me to bear up against all you have to tell me, be that what it may, and with a feeling that through much suffering there may come joy at last. You shall find me very patient, ay, extremely patient—so patient that you shall scarcely see the havoc that grief has already made here.'

She pressed her hands on her breast as she spoke, and looked in his face with such an expression of tearful melancholy that it was quite heart-rending to witness it; and he, although not used to the melting-mood, was compelled to pause for a few moments ere he could proceed in the task which he had set himself.

'I will be as brief,' he said, 'as possible, consistent with stating all that is requisite for me to state, and I must commence by asking you if you are aware under what circumstances Mark Ingestrie went abroad?'

'I am aware of so much: that a quarrel with his uncle, Mr Grant, was the great cause, and that his main endeavour was to better his fortunes, so that we might be happy and independent of those who looked not with an eye of favour on our projected union.'

'Yes; but what I meant was, were you aware of the sort of adventure he embarked in to the Indian seas?'

'No, I know nothing further; we met here on this spot, we parted at yonder gate, and we have never met again.'

'Then I have something to tell you, in order to make the narrative clear and explicit.'

'I shall listen to you with an attention so profound that you shall see how my whole soul is wrapped up in what you say.'

They both sat upon the garden-seat; and while Johanna fixed her eyes upon her companion's face, expressive as it was of the most generous emotions and noble feelings, he commenced relating to her the incidents which never left her memory, and in which she took so deep an interest.

'You must know,' he said, 'that what it was which so much inflamed the imagination of Mark Ingestrie consisted in this. There came to London a man with a well-authenticated and extremely well put together report, that there had been discovered, in one of the small islands near the Indian seas, a river which deposited an enormous quantity of gold dust in its progress to the ocean.* He told his story so well, and seemed to be such a perfect master of all the circumstances connected with it, that there was scarcely room for a doubt upon the subject.

'The thing was kept quiet and secret; and a meeting was held of some influential men—influential on account of the money they possessed, among whom was one who had towards Mark Ingestrie most friendly feelings; so Mark attended the meeting with this friend of his, although he felt his utter incapacity, from want of resources, to take any part in the affair.

'But he was not aware of what his friend's generous intentions were in the matter until they were explained to him, and they consisted in this:—He, the friend, was to provide the necessary means for embarking in the adventure, so far as regarded taking a share in it, and he told Mark Ingestrie that, if he would go personally on the expedition, he would share in the proceeds with him, be they what they might.

'Now, to a young man like Ingestrie, totally destitute of personal resources, but of ardent and enthusiastic temperament, you can imagine how extremely tempting such an offer was likely to be. He embraced it at once with the greatest pleasure, and from that moment he took an interest in the affair of the closest and most powerful description. It seized completely hold of his imagination, presenting itself to him in the most tempting colours; and from the description that has been given me of his enthusiastic disposition, I can well imagine with what kindness and impetuosity he would enter into such an affair.'

'You know him well,' said Johanna, gently.

'No, I never saw him. All that I say concerning him is from the description of another who did know him well, and who sailed with him in the vessel that ultimately left the port of London on the vague and wild adventure I have mentioned.'

'That one, be he who he may, must have known Mark Ingestrie well, and have enjoyed much of his confidence to be able to describe him so accurately.'

'I believe that such was the case; and it is from the lips of that one, instead of mine, that you ought to have heard what I am now relating. That gentleman, whose name was Thornhill, ought to have made to you this communication; but by some strange accident it seems he has been prevented, or you would not be here listening to me upon a subject which would have come better from his lips.'

'And he was to have come yesterday to me?'

'He was.'

'Then Mark Ingestrie kept his word; and but for the adverse circumstances which delayed his messenger, I should have heard yesterday what you are now relating to me. I pray you go on, sir, and pardon the interruption.'

'I need not trouble you with all the negotiations, the trouble, and the difficulty that arose before the expedition could be started fairly—suffice it to say, that at length, after much annoyance and trouble, it was started, and a vessel was duly chartered and manned for the purpose of proceeding to the Indian seas in search of the treasure, which was reported to be there for the first adventurer who had the boldness to seek it.

'It was a gallant vessel. I saw it sail many a mile from England ere it sunk beneath the waves, never to rise again.'

'Sunk!'

'Yes; it was an ill-fated ship, and it did sink; but I must not anticipate—let me proceed in my narrative with regularity.

'The ship was called the Star; and if those who went with it looked upon it as the star of their destiny, they were correct enough, and it might be considered an evil star for them, in as much as nothing but disappointment and bitterness became their ultimate portion.

'And Mark Ingestrie, I am told, was the most hopeful man on board. Already in imagination he could fancy himself homeward-bound with the vessel, ballasted and crammed with the rich produce of that shining river.

'Already he fancied what he could do with his abundant wealth, and I have not a doubt but that, in common with many who went on that adventure, he enjoyed to the full the spending of the wealth he should obtain in imagination—perhaps, indeed, more than if he had obtained it in reality.

'Among the adventurers was one Thornhill, who had been a lieutenant in the Royal Navy, and between him and young Ingestrie there arose a remarkable friendship—a friendship so strong and powerful, that there can be no doubt they communicated to each other all their hopes and fears; and if anything could materially tend to beguile the tedium of such a weary voyage as those adventurers had undertaken, it certainly would be the free communication and confidential intercourse between two such kindred spirits as Thornhill and Mark Ingestrie.

'You will bear in mind, Miss Oakley, that in making this communication to you, I am putting together what I myself heard at different times, so as to make it for you a distinct narrative, which you can have no difficulty in comprehending, because, as I before stated, I never saw Mark Ingestrie, and it was only once, for about five minutes, that I saw the vessel in which he went upon his perilous adventure—for perilous it turned out to be   to the Indian seas. It was from Thornhill I got my information during the many weary and monotonous hours consumed in a homeward voyage from India.

'It appears that without accident or cross of any description the Star reached the Indian Ocean, and the supposed immediate locality of the spot where the treasure was to be found, and there she was spoken with by a vessel homeward-bound from India, called the Neptune

'It was evening, and the sun had sunk in the horizon with some appearance that betokened a storm. I was on board that Indian vessel; we did not expect anything serious, although we made every preparation for rough weather, and as it turned out, it was well indeed we did, for never, within the memory of the oldest seaman, had such a storm ravished the coast. A furious gale, which it was impossible to withstand, drove us southward; and but for the utmost precautions, aided by the courage and temerity on the part of the seamen, such as I have never before witnessed in the merchant-service, we escaped with trifling damage, but we were driven at least 200 miles out of our course; and instead of getting, as we ought to have done, to the Cape by a certain time, we were an immense distance east of it.

'It was just as the storm, which lasted three nights and two days, began to abate, that towards the horizon we saw a dull red light; and as it was not in a quarter of the sky where any such appearance might be imagined, nor were we in a latitude where electric phenomena might be expected, we steered towards it, surmising what turned out afterwards to be fully correct.'

'It was a ship on fire!' said Johanna.

'It was.'

'Alas! alas! I guessed it. A frightful suspicion from the first crossed my mind. It was a ship on fire, and that ship was—'

'The Star, still bound upon its adventurous course, although driven far out of it by adverse winds and waves. After about half an hour's sailing we came within sight distinctly of a blazing vessel.

'We could hear the roar of the flames, and through our glasses we could see them curling up the cordage and dancing from mast to mast, like fiery serpents, exulting in the destruction they were making. We made all sail, and strained every inch of canvas to reach the ill-fated vessel, for distances at sea that look small are in reality very great, and an hour's hard sailing in a fair wind with every stitch of canvas set, would not do more than enable us to reach that ill-fated bark; but fancy in an hour what ravages the flames might make!

"The vessel was doomed. The flat had gone forth that it was to be among the things that had been; and long before we could reach the spot upon which it floated idly on the now comparatively calm waters, we saw a bright shower of sparks rush up into the air. Then came a loud roaring sound over the surface of the deep, and all was still—the ship had disappeared, and the water had closed over her for ever.'

'But how knew you,' said Johanna, as she clasped her hands, and the pallid expression of her countenance betrayed the deep interest she took in the narration, 'how knew you that ship was the Star? might it not have been some other ill-fated vessel that met with so dreadful a fate?'

'I will tell you: although we had seen the ship go down, we kept on our course, straining every effort to reach the spot, with a hope of picking up some of the crew, who surely had made an effort by the boats to leave the burning vessel.

'The captain of the Indiaman kept his glass at his eye, and presently he said to me,—

"There is a floating piece of wreck, and something clinging to it; I know not if there be a man, but what I can perceive seems to me to be the head of a dog."

'I looked through the glass myself, and saw the same object; but as we neared it, we found that it was a large piece of the wreck, with a dog and a man supported by it, who were clinging with all the energy of desperation. In ten minutes more we had them on board the vessel—the man was the Lieutenant Thornhill I have before mentioned, and the dog belonged to him.

'He related to us that the ship we had seen burning was the Star; that it had never reached its destination, and that he believed all had perished but himself and the dog; for, although one of the boats had been launched, so desperate a rush was made into it by the crew that it had swamped, and all perished.

'Such was his own state of exhaustion, that, after he had made to us this short statement, it was some days before he left his hammock; but when he did, and began to mingle with us, we found an intelligent, cheerful companion—such a one, indeed, as we were glad to have on board, and in confidence he related to the captain and myself the object of the voyage of the Star, and the previous particulars with which I have made you acquainted.

'And then, during a night-watch, when the soft and beautiful moonlight was more than usually inviting, and he and I were on the deck, enjoying the coolness of the night, after the intense heat of the day in the tropics, he said to me, —

"I have a very sad mission to perform when I get to London. On board our vessel was a young man named Mark Ingestrie; and some time before the vessel in which we were went down, he begged of me to call upon a young lady named Johanna Oakley, the daughter of a spectacle-maker in London, providing I should be saved and he perish; and of the latter event, he felt so strong a presentiment that he gave me a string of pearls, which I was to present to her in his name; but where he got them I have not the least idea, for they are of immense value."

'Mr Thornhill showed me the pearls, which were of different sizes, roughly, strung together, but of great value; and when we reached the river Thames, which was only three days since, he left us with his dog, carrying his string of pearls with him, to find out where you reside.'

'Alas! he never came.'

'No; from all the enquiries we can make, and all the information we can learn, it seems that he disappeared somewhere about Fleet-street.'

'Disappeared!'

'Yes; we can trace him to the Temple-stairs, and from thence to a barber's shop, kept by a man named Sweeney Todd; but beyond there no information of him can be obtained.'

'Sweeney Todd!'

'Yes; and what makes the affair more extraordinary, is that neither force nor persuasion will induce Thornhill's dog to leave the place.'

'I saw it—I saw the creature, and it looked imploringly, but kindly, in my face; but little did I think, when I paused a moment to look upon that melancholy but faithful animal, that it held a part in my destiny. Oh! Mark Ingestrie, Mark Ingestrie, dare I hope that you live when all else have perished?'

'I have told you all that I can tell you, and according as your own judgement may dictate to you, you can encourage hope, or extinguish it for ever. I have kept back nothing from you which can make the affair worse or better—I have added nothing; but you have it simply as it was told to me.'

'He is lost—he is lost!'

'I am one, lady, who always thinks certainty of any sort preferable to suspense; and although, while there is no positive news of death, the continuance of life ought fairly to be assumed, yet you must perceive from a review of all the circumstances, upon how very slender a foundation all your hopes must rest.'

'I have no hope—I have no hope—he is lost to me for ever! It were madness to think he lived. Oh! Mark, Mark! and is this the end of all our fond affection? did I indeed look my last upon that face, when on this spot we parted?'

'The uncertainty,' said Colonel Jeffery, wishing to withdraw as much as possible from a consideration of her own sorrows, 'the uncertainty, too, that prevails with the regard to the fate of poor Mr Thornhill, is a sad thing. I much fear that those precious pearls he had have been seen by someone who has not scrupled to obtain possession of them by his death.'

'Yes, it would seem so indeed; but what are pearls to me? Oh! would that they had sunk to the bottom of that Indian sea, from whence they had been plucked. Alas, alas! it has been their thirst for gain that has produced all these evils. We might have been poor here, but we should have been happy. Rich we ought to have been, in contentment; but now all is lost, and the world to me can present nothing that is to be desired, but one small spot large enough to be my grave.'

She leant upon the arm of the garden-seat, and gave herself up to such a passion of tears that Colonel Jeffery felt he dared not interrupt her.

There is something exceedingly sacred about real grief, which awes the beholder, and it was with an involuntary feeling of respect that Colonel Jeffery stepped a few paces off, and waited until that burst of agony had passed away.

It was during those few brief moments that he overheard some words uttered by one who seemed likewise to be suffering from that prolific source of all affliction, disappointed affection. Seated at some short distance was a maiden, and one not young enough to be called a youth, but still not far enough advanced in existence to have had all his better feelings crushed by an admixture with the cold world, and he was listening while the maiden spoke.

'It is the neglect,' she said, 'which touched me to the heart. But one word spoken or written, one message of affection, to tell me that the memory of a love I thought would be eternal, still lingered in your heart, would have been a world of consolation; but it came not, and all was despair.'

'Listen to me,' said her companion, 'and if ever in this world you can believe that one who truly loves can be cruel to be kind, believe that I am that one. I yielded for a time to the fascination of a passion which should never have found a home within my heart; but yet it was far more of a sentiment than a passion, inasmuch as never for one moment did an evil thought mingle with its pure aspirations.

'It was a dream of joy, which for a time obliterated a remembrance that ought never to have been forgotten; but when I was rudely awakened to the fact that those whose opinions were of more importance to your welfare and your happiness knew nothing of love, but in its grossest aspect, it became necessary at once to crush a feeling, which, in its continuance, could shadow forth nothing but evil.

'You may not imagine, and you may never know, for I cannot tell the heart-pangs it has cost me to persevere in a line of conduct which I felt was due to you—whatever heart-pangs it might cost me. I have been content to imagine that your affection would turn to indifference, perchance to hatred; that a consciousness of being slighted would arouse in your defence all a woman's pride, and that thus you would be lifted above regret. Farewell for ever! I dare not love you honestly and truly; and better is it thus to part than to persevere in a delusive dream that can but terminate in degradation and sadness.'

'Do you hear those words?' whispered Colonel Jeffery to Johanna. 'You perceive that others suffer, and from the same cause, the perils of affection.'

'I do. I will go home, and pray for strength to maintain my heart against this sad affliction.'

'The course of true love never yet ran smooth;* wonder not, therefore, Johanna Oakley, that yours has suffered such a blight. It is the great curse of the highest and noblest feelings of which humanity is capable, that while, under felicitous circumstances, they produce an extraordinary amount of happiness, when anything adverse occurs, they are most prolific sources of misery. Shall I accompany you?'

Johanna felt grateful for the support of the colonel's arm towards her own home, and as they passed the barber's shop they were surprised to see that the dog and the hat were gone.

## 7

## *The Barber and the Lapidary*

IT is night; and a man, one of the most celebrated lapidaries* in London, but yet a man frugal withal, although rich, is putting up the shutters of his shop.

This lapidary is an old man; his scanty hair is white, and his hands shake as he secures the fastenings, and then, over and over again, feels and shakes each shutter, to be assured that his shop is well secured.

This shop of his is in Moorfields,* then a place very much frequented by dealers in bullion and precious stones. He was about entering his door, just having cast a satisfied look upon the fastenings of his shop, when a tall, ungainly-looking man stepped up to him. This man had a three-cornered hat, much too small for him, perched upon the top of his great, hideous-looking head, while the coat he wore had ample skirts enough to have made another of ordinary dimensions.

Our readers will have no difficulty in recognising Sweeney Todd, and well might the little old lapidary start as such a very unprepossessing-looking personage addressed him.

'You deal,' he said, 'in precious stones.'

'Yes, I do,' was the reply; 'but it's rather late. Do you want to buy or sell?'

'To sell.'

'Humph! Ah, I dare say it's something not in my line; the only order I get is for pearls, and they are not in the market.'

'And I have nothing but pearls to sell,' said Sweeney Todd; 'I mean to keep all my diamonds, my garnets, topazes, brilliants,* emeralds, and rubies.'

'The deuce you do! Why, you don't mean to say you have any of them? Be off with you! I am too old to joke with, and am waiting for my supper.'

'Will you look at the pearls I have?'

'Little seed-pearls, I suppose; they are of no value, and I don't want them; we have plenty of those. It's real, genuine, large pearls we want. Pearls worth thousands.'

'Will you look at mine?'

'No; good night!'

'Very good; then I will take them to Mr Coventry up the street. He will, perhaps, deal with me for them if you cannot.'

The lapidary hesitated. 'Stop,' he said; 'what's the use of going to Mr Coventry? he has not the means of purchasing what I can present cash for. Come in, come in; I will, at all events, look at what you have for sale.'

Thus encouraged, Sweeney Todd entered the little, low, dusky shop, and the lapidary having procured a light, and taken care to keep his customer outside the counter, put on his spectacles, and said, —

'Now, sir, where are your pearls?'

'There,' said Sweeney Todd, as he laid a string of twenty-four pearls before the lapidary.

The old man's eyes opened to an enormous width, and he pushed his spectacles right up upon his forehead, as he glared in the face of Sweeney Todd with undisguised astonishment. Then down he pulled his spectacles again, and taking up the string of pearls, he rapidly examined every one of them, after which he exclaimed, —

'Real, real, by Heaven! All real!'

Then he pushed his spectacles up again to the top of his head and took another long stare at Sweeney Todd.

'I know they are real,' said the latter. 'Will you deal with me or will you not?'

'Will I deal with you? Yes; I am quite sure that they are real. Let me look again. Oh, I see, counterfeits; but so well done, that really, for the curiosity of the thing, I will give £50 for them.'

'I am fond of curiosities,' said Sweeney Todd, 'and, as they are not real, I'll keep them; they will do for a present to some child or other.'

'What! give those to a child? you must be mad—that is to say, not mad, but certainly indiscreet. Come, now, at a word, I'll give you £100 for them.'

'Hark ye,' said Sweeney Todd, 'it neither suits my inclination nor my time to stand here chaffing* with you. I know the value of the pearls, and, as a matter of ordinary and every-day business, I will sell them to you so that you may get a handsome profit.'

'What do you call a handsome profit?'

'The pearls are worth £12,000, and I will let you have them for ten. What do you think of that for an offer?'

'What odd noise was that?'

'Oh, it was only I who laughed. Come, what do you say, at once; are we to do business or are we not?'

'Hark ye, my friend, since you do know the value of your pearls, and this is to be a downright business transaction, I think I can find a customer who will give £11,000 for them, and if so, I have no objection to give you £8,000.'

'Give me the £8,000,' said Sweeney Todd, 'and let me go. I hate bargaining.'

'Stop a bit; there are some rather important things to consider You must know, my friend, that a string of pearls of this value are not to be bought like a few ounces of old silver of anybody who might come with it. Such a string of pearls as these are like a house, or an estate, and when they change hands, the vendor of them must give every satisfaction as to how he came by them, and prove how he can give to the purchaser a good right and title to them.'

'Psha!' said Sweeney Todd, 'who will question you, who are well known to be in the trade, and to be continually dealing in such things?'

'That's all very fine; but I don't see why I should give you the full value of an article without evidence as to how you came by it.'

'In other words, you mean, you don't care how I came by them, provided I sell them to you at a thief's price, but if I want their value you mean to be particular.'

'My good sir, you may conclude what you like. Show me you have a right to dispose of the pearls, and you need go no further than my shop for a customer.'

'I am not disposed to take that trouble, so I shall bid you good-night, and when you want any pearls again, I would certainly advise you not to be so wonderfully particular where you get them.'

Sweeney Todd strode towards the door, but the lapidary was not going to part with him so easy, for springing over his counter with an agility one would not have expected from so old a man, he was at the door in a moment, and shouted at the top of his lungs, —

'Stop thief! Stop thief! Stop him! There he goes! The big fellow with the three-cornered hat! Stop thief! Stop thief!'

These cries, uttered with great vehemence, as they were, could not be totally ineffective, but they roused the whole neighbourhood, and before Sweeney Todd had proceeded many yards a man made an attempt to collar him, but was repulsed by such a terrific blow in his face, that another person, who had run half-way across the road with a similar object, turned and went back again, thinking it scarcely prudent to risk his own safety in apprehending a criminal for the good of the public.

Having thus got rid of one of his foes, Sweeney Todd, with an inward determination to come back someday and be the death of the old lapidary, looked anxiously about for some court down which he could plunge, and so get out of sight of the many pursuers who were sure to attack him in the public streets.

His ignorance of the locality, however, was a great bar to such a proceeding, for the great dread he had was, that he might get down some blind alley, and so be completely caged, and at the mercy of those who followed him.

He pelted on at a tremendous speed, but it was quite astonishing to see how the little old lapidary ran after him, falling down every now and then, and never stopping to pick himself up, as people say, but rolling on and getting on his feet in some miraculous manner, that was quite wonderful to behold, particularly in one so aged, and so apparently unable to undertake any active exertion.

There was one thing, however, he could not continue doing, and that was to cry 'stop thief!' for he had lost his wind, and was quite incapable of uttering a word. How long he would have continued the chase is doubtful, but his career was suddenly put an end to, as regards that, by tripping his foot over a projecting stone in the pavement, and shooting headlong down a cellar which was open.

But abler persons than the little old lapidary had taken up the chase, and Sweeney Todd was hard pressed; and, although he ran very fast, the provoking thing was, that in consequence of the cries and shouts of his pursuers, new people took up the chase, who were fresh and vigorous, and close to him.

There is something awful in seeing a human being thus hunted by his fellows; and although we can have no sympathy with a man such as Sweeney Todd, because, from all that has happened, we begin to have some very horrible suspicions concerning him, still, as a general principle, it does not decrease the fact that it is a dreadful thing to see a human being hunted through the streets.

On he flew at the top of his speed, striking down whoever opposed him, until at last many who could have outrun him gave up the chase, not liking to encounter the knock-down blow which such a hand as his seemed capable of inflicting.

His teeth were set, and his breathing came short and laborious, just as a man sprung out at a shop-door and succeeded in laying hold of him.

'I have got you, have I?' he said.

Sweeney Todd uttered not a word, but, putting forth an amount of strength that was perfectly prodigious, he seized the man by a great handful of his hair and by his clothes behind, and flung him through the shop-window, smashing glass, frame-work, and everything in his progress.

The man gave a shriek, for it was his own shop, and he was a dealer in fancy goods of the most flimsy texture, so that the smash with which he came down among his stock-in-trade, produced at once what the haberdashers are so delighted with in the present day, namely a ruinous sacrifice.

This occurrence had a great effect upon Sweeney Todd's pursuers; it taught them the practical wisdom of not interfering with a man possessed evidently of such tremendous powers of mischief, and consequently, as just about this period the defeat of the little lapidary took place, he got considerably the start of his pursuers.

But he was by no means yet safe. The cry of 'stop thief!' still sounded in his ears, and on he flew, panting with the exertion he made, until he heard a man behind him say, —

'Turn into the second court on your right and you will be safe. I'll follow you. They shan't nab you, if I can help it.'

Sweeney Todd had not much confidence in human nature—it was not likely he would; but, panting and exhausted as he was, the voice of anyone speaking in friendly accents was welcome, and, rather impulsively than from reflection, he darted down the second court to his right.

# 8

## *The Thieves' Home**

I N a very few minutes Sweeney Todd found that this court had no
thoroughfare, and therefore there was no outlet or escape; but
he immediately concluded that something more was to be found
than was at first sight to be seen, and, casting a furtive glance
beside him in the direction in which he had come, rested his hand
upon a door which stood close by.

The door gave way, and Sweeney Todd hearing, as he imagined,
a noise in the street, dashed in and closed the door, and then he,
heedless of all consequences, walked to the end of a long, dirty passage, and, pushing open a door, descended a short flight of steps, to
the bottom of which he had scarcely got, when the door which faced
him at the bottom of the steps opened by some hand, and he suddenly found himself in the presence of a number of men seated
round a large table.

In an instant all eyes were turned towards Sweeney Todd, who
was quite unprepared for such a scene, and for a minute he knew
not what to say; but, as indecision was not Sweeney Todd's characteristic, he at once advanced to the table and sat down.

There was some surprise evinced by the persons who were seated
in that room, of whom there were many more than a score, and
much talking was going on among them, which did not appear to
cease on his entrance.

Those who were near him looked hard at him, but nothing was
said for some minutes, and Sweeney Todd looked about to understand, if he could, how he was placed, though it could not be much
of a matter of doubt as to the character of the individuals present.

Their looks were often an index to their vocations, for all grades
of the worst of characters were there, and some of them were by no
means complimentary to human nature, for there were some of the
most desperate characters that were to be found in London.

They were dressed in various fashions, some after the manner of
the city—some more gay, and some half military, while not a few wore

the garb of country-men; but there was in all that an air of scampish, offhand behaviour, not unmixed with brutality.

'Friend,' said one, who sat near him, 'how came you here; are you known here?'

'I came here, because I found the door open, and I was told by someone to come here, as I was pursued.'

'Pursued!'

'Ay, some one running after me, you know.'

'I know what being pursued is,' replied the man, 'and yet I know nothing of you.'

'That is not at all astonishing,' said Sweeney, 'seeing that I never saw you before, nor you me; but that makes no difference. I'm in difficulties, and I suppose a man may do his best to escape the consequences.'

'Yes, he may, yet there is no reason why he should come here; this is the place for free friends, who know and aid one another.'

'And such I am willing to be; but at the same time I must have a beginning. I cannot be initiated without someone introducing me. I have sought protection, and I have found it; if there be any objection to my remaining here any longer, I will leave.'

'No, no,' said a tall man on the other side of the table, 'I have heard what you said, and we do not usually allow any such things; you have come here unasked, and now we must have a little explanation, our own safety may demand it; at all events we have our customs, and they must be complied with.'

'And what are your customs?' demanded Todd.

'This: you must answer the questions which we shall propound unto you; now answer truly what we shall ask of you.'

'Speak,' said Todd, 'and I will answer all that you proposed to me if possible.'

'We will not tax you too hardly, depend upon it: who are you?'

'Candidly, then,' said Todd, 'that's a question I do not like to answer, nor do I think it is one that you ought to ask. It is an inconvenient thing to name oneself—you must pass by *that* inquiry.'

'Shall we do so?' inquired the interrogator of those around him, and, gathering his cue from their looks, he after a brief pause continued,—

'Well, we will pass over that, seeing it is not necessary; but you must tell us what you are, cutpurse, footpad, or what not?'*

'I am neither.'

'Then tell us in your own words,' said the man, 'and be candid with us. What are you?'

'I am an artificial pearl-maker—or a sham pearl-maker, whichever way you please to call it.'

'A sham pearl-maker! that may be an honest trade for all we know, and that will hardly be your passport to our house, friend sham pearl-maker!'

'That may be as you say,' replied Todd, 'but I will challenge any man to equal me in my calling. I have made pearls that would pass with almost a lapidary, and which would pass with nearly all the nobility.'

'I begin to understand you, friend; but I would wish to have some proof of what you say: we may hear a very good tale, and yet none of it shall be true; we are not the men to be made dupes of, besides, there are enough to take vengeance, if we desire it.'

'Ay, to be sure there is,' said a gruff voice from the other end of the table, which was echoed from one to the other, till it came to the top of the table.

'Proof! proof! proof!' now resounded from one end of the room to the other.

'My friends,' said Sweeney Todd, rising up, and advancing to the table, and thrusting his hand into his bosom, and drawing out the string of twenty-four pearls, 'I challenge you or anyone to make a set of artificial pearls equal to these: they are my make, and I'll stand to it in any reasonable sum that you cannot bring a man who shall beat me in my calling.'

'Just hand them to me,' said the man who had made himself interrogator.

Sweeney Todd threw the pearls on the table carelessly, and then said,—

'There, look at them well, they'll bear it, and I reckon, though there may be some good judges 'mongst you, that you cannot any of you tell them from real pearls, if you had not been told so.'

'Oh, yes, we know pretty well,' said the man, 'what these things are: we have now and then a good string in our possession, and that helps us to judge of them. Well, this is certainly a good imitation.'

'Let me see it,' said a fat man; 'I was bred a jeweller, and I might say born, only I couldn't stick to it; nobody likes working for years upon little pay, and no fun with the gals. I say, hand it here!'

'Well,' said Todd, 'if you or anybody ever produced as good an imitation, I'll swallow the whole string; and, knowing there's poison in the composition, it would certainly not be a comfortable thing to think of.'

'Certainly not,' said the big man, 'certainly not; but hand them over, and I'll tell you all about it.'

The pearls were given into his hands; and Sweeney Todd felt some misgivings about his precious charge, and yet he showed it not, for he turned to the man, who sat beside him, saying, —

'If he can tell true pearls from them, he knows more than I think he does, for I am a maker, and have often had the true pearl in my hand.'

'And I suppose,' said the man, 'you have tried your hand at putting the one for the other, and so doing your confiding customers.'

'Yes, yes, that is the dodge, I can see very well,' said another man, winking at the first; 'and a good one too, I have known them do so with diamonds.'

'Yes, but never with pearls; however, there are some trades that it is desirable to know.'

'You're right.'

The fat man now carefully examined the pearls, and set them down on the table, and looked hard at them.

'There now, I told you I could bother you. You are not so good a judge that you would not have known, if you had not been told they were sham pearls, but what they were real.'

'I must say, you have produced the best imitations I have ever seen. Why, you ought to make your fortune in a few years—a handsome fortune!'

'So I should, but for one thing.'

'And what is that?'

'The difficulty,' said Todd, 'of getting rid of them; if you ask anything below their value, you are suspected, and you run the chance of being stopped and losing them at the least, and perhaps, entail a prosecution.'

'Very true; but there is risk in everything; we all run risks; but then the harvest!'

'That may be,' said Todd, 'but this is peculiarly dangerous. I have not the means of getting introductions to the nobility themselves, and if I had I should be doubted, for they would say a workman cannot come honestly by such valuable things, and then I must concoct a tale to escape the Mayor of London!'

'Ha! — ha! — ha!'

'Well, then, you can take them to a goldsmith.'

'There are not many of them who would do so; they would not deal in them; and, moreover, I have been to one or two of them; as for a lapidary, why, he is not so easily cheated.'

'Have you tried?'

'I did, and had to make the best of my way out, pursued as quickly as they could run, and I thought at one time I must have been stopped, but a few lucky turns brought me clear, when I was told to turn up this court, and I came in here.'

'Well,' said one man, who had been examining the pearls, 'and did the lapidary find out they were not real?'

'Yes, he did; and he wanted to stop me and the string altogether, for trying to impose upon him; however I made a rush at the door, which he tried to shut, but I was the stronger man, and here I am.'

'It has been a close chance for you,' said one.

'Yes, it just has,' replied Sweeney, taking up the string of pearls, which he replaced in his clothes, and continued to converse with some of those around him.

Things now subsided into their general course; and little notice was taken of Sweeney. There was some drink on the board, of which all partook. Sweeney had some, too, and took the precaution of emptying his pockets before them all, and gave a share of his money to pay his footing.

This was policy, and they all drank to his success, and were very good companions. Sweeney, however, was desirous of getting out as soon as he could, and more than once cast his eyes towards the door; but he saw there were eyes upon him, and dared not excite suspicion, for he might undo all that he had done.

To lose the precious treasure he possessed would be maddening; he had succeeded to admiration in inducing the belief that what he showed them was merely a counterfeit; but he knew so well that they were real, and that a latent feeling that they were humbugged might be hanging about; and that at the first suspicious movement he would be watched, and some desperate attempt would be made to make him give them up.

It was with no small violence to his own feelings that he listened to their conversation, and appeared to take an interest in their proceedings.

'Well,' said one, who sat next him, 'I'm just off for the north-road.'*

'Any fortune there?'

'Not much; and yet I mustn't complain: these last three weeks the best I have had has been two sixties.'*

'Well, that would do very well.'

'Yes, the last man I stopped was a regular looby* Londoner; he appeared like a don,* complete tip-top* man of fashion; but Lord! when I came to look over him, he hadn't as much as would carry me twenty-four miles on the road.'

'Indeed! don't you think he had any hidden about him? they do so now.'

---

'Ah, ah!' returned another, 'well said, old fellow; 'tis a true remark that we can't always judge a man from appearances. Lor! bless me, now, who'd a-thought your swell cove* proved to be out of luck! Well, I'm sorry for you; but you know 'tis a long lane that has no turning, as Mr Somebody says—so, perhaps, you'll be more fortunate another time. But come, cheer up, whilst I relate an adventure that occurred a little time ago; 'twas a slice of good luck, I assure you, for I had no difficulty in bouncing my victim out of a good swag of tin;* for you know farmers returning from market are not always too wary and careful, especially as the lots of wine they take at the market dinners make the cosy old boys ripe and mellow for sleep. Well, I met one of these jolly gentlemen, mounted on horseback, who declared he had nothing but a few paltry guineas about him; however, that would not do—I searched him, and found a hundred and four pounds secreted about his person.'

'Where did you find it?'

'About him. I tore his clothes to ribands. A pretty figure he looked upon horseback, I assure you. By Jove, I could hardly help laughing at him; in fact, I did laugh at him, which so enraged him, that he immediately threatened to horsewhip me, and yet he dared not defend his money; but I threatened to shoot him, and that soon brought him to his senses.'

'I should imagine so. Did you ever have a fight for it?' inquired Sweeney Todd.

'Yes, several times. Ah! it's by no means an easy life, you may depend. It is free, but dangerous. I have been fired at six or seven times.'

'So many?'

'Yes. I was near York once, when I stopped a gentleman; I thought him an easy conquest, but not so he turned out, for he was a regular devil.'

'Resisted you?'

'Yes, he did. I was coming along when I met him, and I demanded his money.

'"I can keep it myself," he said, "and do not want any assistance to take care of it."

'"But I want it," said I; "your money or your life."

'"You must have both, for we are not to be parted," he said, presenting his pistol at me; and then I had only time to escape from the effect of the shot. I struck the pistol up with my riding-whip, and the bullet passed by my temples, and almost stunned me.

'I cocked and fired; he did the same, but I hit him, and he fell. He fired, however, but missed me. I was down upon him; he begged hard for life.'

'Did you give it him?'

'Yes; I dragged him to one side of the road, and then left him.

'Having done so much I mounted my horse, and came away as fast as I could, and then I made for London, and spent a merry day or two there.'

'I can imagine you must enjoy your trips into the country, and then you must have still greater relish for the change when you come to London—the change is so great and so entire.'

'So it is; but have you never any run of luck in your line? I should think you must at times succeed in tricking the public.'

'Yes, yes,' said Todd, 'now and then we—but I tell you it is only now and then; and I have been afraid of doing too much. To small sums I have been a gainer; but I want to do something grand. I tried it on, but at the same time I have failed.'

'That is bad; but you may have more opportunities by-and-by. Luck is all chance.'

'Yes,' replied Todd, 'that is true, but the sooner the better, for I am growing impatient.'

Conversation now went on; each man speaking of his exploits, which were always some species of rascality and robbery accompanied by violence generally; some were midnight robbers and breakers into people's houses; in fact, all the crimes that could be imagined.

This place was, in fact, a complete home or rendezvous for thieves, cutpurses, highwaymen, footpads, and burglars of every grade and description—a formidable set of men of the most determined and desperate appearance.

Sweeney Todd knew hardly how to rise and leave the place, though it was now growing very late, and he was most anxious to get safe out of the den he was in; but how to do that was a problem yet to be solved.

'What is the time?' he muttered to the man next to him.

'Past midnight,' was the reply.

'Then I must leave here,' he answered, 'for I have work that I must be at in a very short time, and I shall not have too much time.'

So saying he watched his opportunity, and rising, walked up to the door, which he opened, and went out; after that he walked up the five steps that led to the passage, and this latter had hardly been gained when the street-door opened, and another man came in at the same moment, and met him face to face.

'What do you here?'

'I am going out,' said Sweeney Todd.

'You are going back: come back with me.'

'I will not,' said Todd. 'You must be a better man than I am, if you make me do my best to resist your attack, if you intend one.'

'That I do,' replied the man; and he made a determined rush upon Sweeney, who was scarcely prepared for such a sudden onslaught, and was pushed back till he came to the head of the stairs, where a struggle took place, and both rolled down the steps. The door was immediately thrown open, and everyone rushed out to see what was the matter, but it was some moments before they could make it out.

'What does he do here?' said the first, as soon as he could speak, and pointing to Sweeney Todd.

'It's all right.'

'All wrong, I say.'

'He's a sham pearl-maker, and has shown us a string of sham pearls that are beautiful.'

'Psha!'

'I will insist on seeing them; give them to me,' he said, 'or you do not leave this place.'

'I will not,' said Sweeney.

'You must. Here, help me—but I don't want help, I can do it by myself.'

As he spoke, he made a desperate attempt to collar Sweeney and pull him to the earth, but he had miscalculated his strength when he imagined that he was superior to Todd, who was by far the more powerful man of the two, and resisted the attack with success.

Suddenly, by an herculean effort, he caught his adversary below the waist, and lifting him up, he threw him upon the floor with great force; and then, not wishing to see how the gang would take this—whether they would take the part of their companion or of himself he knew not—he thought he had an advantage in the distance, and he rushed upstairs as fast as he could, and reached the door before they could overtake him to prevent him.

Indeed, for more than a minute they were irresolute what to do; but they were somehow prejudiced in favour of their companion, and they rushed up after Sweeney just as he got to the door.

He would have had time to escape them; but, by some means, the door became fast, and he could not open it, exert himself how he would.

There was no time to lose; they were coming to the head of the stairs, and Sweeney had hardly time to reach the stairs, to fly upwards, when he felt himself grasped by the throat.

This he soon released himself from; for he struck the man who seized him a heavy blow, and he fell backwards, and Todd found his way up to the first floor, but he was closely pursued.

Here was another struggle; and again Sweeney Todd was the victor, but he was hard pressed by those who followed him— fortunately for him there was a mop left in a pail of water, this he seized hold of, and, swinging it over his head, he brought it full on the head of the first man who came near him.

Dab it came, soft and wet, and splashed over some others who were close at hand.

It is astonishing what an effect a new weapon will sometimes have. There was not a man among them who would not have faced danger in more ways than one, that would not have rushed headlong upon deadly and destructive weapons, but who were quite awed when a heavy wet mop was dashed into their faces.

They were completely paralysed for a moment; indeed, they began to look upon it something between a joke and a serious matter, and either would have been taken just as they might be termed.

'Get the pearls!' shouted the man who had first stopped him; 'seize the spy! seize him—secure him—rush at him! You are men enough to hold one man!'

Sweeney Todd saw matters were growing serious, and he plied his mop most vigorously upon those who were ascending, but they had become somewhat used to the mop, and it had lost much of its novelty, and was by no means a dangerous weapon.

They rushed on, despite the heavy blows showered by Sweeney, and he was compelled to give way stair after stair.

The head of the mop came off, and then there remained but the handle, which formed an efficient weapon, and which made fearful havoc of the heads of the assailants; and despite all that their slouched hats could do in the way of protecting them, yet the staff came with a crushing effect.

The best fight in the world cannot last for ever; and Sweeney again found numbers were not to be resisted for long; indeed, he could not have physical energy enough to sustain his own efforts, supposing he had received no blows in return.

He turned and fled as he was forced back to the landing, and then came to the next stair-head, and again he made a desperate stand.

This went on for stair after stair, and continued for more than two or three hours.

There were moments of cessation when they all stood still and looked at each other.

'Fire upon him!' said one.

'No, no; we shall have the authorities down upon us, and then all will go wrong.'

'I think we had much better have let it alone in the first place, as he was in, for you may be sure this won't make him keep a secret; we shall all be split upon as sure as fate.'

'Well, then, rush upon him and down with him. Never let him out! On to him! Hurrah!'

Away they went, but they were resolutely met by the staff of Sweeney Todd, who had gained new strength by the short rest he had had.

'Down with the spy!'

This was shouted out by the men, but as each of them approached, they were struck down, and at length finding himself on the second floor landing, and being fearful that someone was descending from above, he rushed into one of the inner rooms.

In an instant he had locked the doors, which were strong and powerful.

'Now,' he muttered, 'for means to escape.'

He waited a moment to wipe the sweat from his brow, and then he crossed the floor to the windows, which were open.

They were the old-fashion bag-windows, with the heavy ornamental work which some houses possessed, and overhung the low doorways, and protected them from the weather.

'This will do,' he said, as he looked down to the pavement—'this will do. I will try this descent, if I fall.'

The people on the other side of the door were exerting all their force to break it open, and it had already given one or two ominous creaks, and a few minutes more would probably let them into the room.

The streets were clear—no human being was moving about, and there were faint signs of the approach of morning. He paused a moment to inhale the fresh air, and then he got outside of the window.

By means of the sound oaken ornaments, he contrived to get down to the drawing-room balcony, and then he soon got down into the street.

As he walked slowly away, he could hear the crash of the door, and a slight cheer, as they entered the room; and he could imagine to himself the appearance of the faces of those who entered, when they found the bird had flown, and the room was empty.

Sweeney Todd had not far to go; he soon turned into Fleet-street, and made for his own house. He looked about him, but there was none near him; he was tired and exhausted, and right glad was he when he found himself at his own door.

Then stealthily he put the key into the door, and slowly entered his house.

## 9

## Johanna at Home, and the Resolution

JOHANNA OAKLEY would not allow Colonel Jeffery to accompany her all the way home, and he, appreciating the scruples of the young girl, did not press his attention on her, but left her at the corner of Fore-street, after getting a half promise that she would meet him again on that day week, at the same hour, in the Temple-gardens.

'I ask this of you, Johanna Oakley,' he said, 'because I have resolved to make all the exertion in my power to discover what has become of Mr Thornhill, in whose fate I am sure I have succeeded in interesting you, although you care so little for the string of pearls, which he has in trust for you.'

'I do, indeed, care little for them,' said Johanna, 'so little, that it might be said to amount to nothing.'

'But still they are yours, and you ought to have the option of disposing of them as you please. It is not well to despise such gifts of fortune; for if you can yourself do nothing with them, there are surely some others whom you may know, upon whom they would bestow great happiness.'

'A string of pearls, great happiness?' said Johanna, inquiringly.

'Your mind is so occupied by your grief that you quite forget such strings are of great value. I have seen those pearls, Johanna, and can assure you that they are in themselves a fortune.'

'I suppose,' she said sadly, 'it is too much for human nature to expect two blessings at once. I had the fond, warm heart that loved me without the fortune, that would have enabled us to live in comfort and affluence; and now, when that is perchance within my grasp, the heart that was by far the most costly possession, and the richest jewel of them all, lies beneath the wave, with its bright influences, and its glorious and romantic aspirations, quenched for ever.'

'You will meet me then, as I request of you, to hear if I have any news for you?'

'I will endeavour so to do. I have all the will; but Heaven knows if I may have the power.'

'What mean you, Johanna?'

'I cannot tell what a week's anxiety may do; I know not but that a sick bed may be my resting-place, until I exchange it for the tomb. I feel even now my strength fail me, and I am scarcely able to totter to my home. Farewell, sir! I owe you my best thanks, as well for the trouble you have taken, as for the kindly manner in which you have detailed to me what has passed.'

'Remember!' said Colonel Jeffery, 'that I bid you adieu, with the hope of meeting you again.'

It was thus they parted, and Johanna proceeded to her father's house. Who now that had met her and chanced not to see that sweet face, which could never be forgotten, would have supposed her to be the once gay and sprightly Johanna Oakley? Her steps were sad and solemn, and all the juvenile elasticity of her frame seemed to be gone. She seemed like one prepared for death; and she hoped that she would be able to glide, silently and unobserved, to her own little bed-chamber—that chamber where she had slept since she was a little child, and on the little couch, on which she had so often laid down to sleep, that holy and calm slumber, which such hearts as hers can only know.

But she was doomed to be disappointed, for the Rev Mr Lupin was still there, and as Mrs Oakley had placed before that pious individual a great assortment of creature comforts, and among the rest some mulled wine, which seemed particularly to agree with him, he showed no disposition to depart.

It unfortunately happened that this wine, of which the reverend gentleman partook with such a holy relish, was kept in a cellar, and Mrs Oakley had had occasion twice to go down to procure a fresh supply, and it was on a third journey for the same purpose that she encountered poor Johanna, who had just let herself in at the private door.

'Oh! you have come home, have you?' said Mrs Oakley, 'I wonder where you have been to, gallivanting; but I suppose I may wonder long enough before you will tell me. Go into the parlour, I want to speak to you.'

Now poor Johanna had quite forgotten the very existence of Mr Lupin—so, rather than explain to her mother, which would beget more questions, she wished to go to bed at once, notwith-standing it was an hour before the usual time for so doing. She walked unsuspectingly into the parlour, and as Mr Lupin was sit-ting, the slightest movement of his chair closed the door, so she could not escape.

Under any other circumstances probably Johanna would have insisted upon leaving the apartment; but a glance at the counte-nance of the pious individual was quite sufficient to convince her he had been sacrificing sufficiently to Bacchus to be capable of any amount of effrontery, so that she dreaded passing him, more especially as he swayed his arms about like the sails of a windmill.

She thought at least that when her mother returned she would rescue her; but in that hope she was mistaken, and Johanna had no more idea of the extent to which religious fanaticism will carry its victim, than she had of the manners and customs of the inhabitants of the moon.

When Mrs Oakley did return, she had some difficulty in getting into the apartment, inasmuch as Mr Lupin's chair occupied so large a portion of it; but when she did obtain admission, and Johanna said, 'Mother, I beg of you to protect me against this man, and allow me a free passage from the apartment,' Mrs Oakley affected to lift up her hands in amazement as she said, —

'How dare you speak so disrespectfully of a chosen vessel. How dare you, I say, do such a thing—it's enough to drive anyone mad to see young girls now-a-days!'

'Don't snub her—don't snub the virgin,' said Mr Lupin; 'she don't know the honour yet that's intended her.'

'She don't deserve it,' said Mrs Oakley, 'she don't deserve it.'

'Never mind, madam—never mind; we—we—we don't get all what we deserve in this world.'

'Take a drop of something, Mr Lupin; you have got the hiccups.'

'Yes; I—I rather think I have a little. Isn't it a shame that anybody so intimate with the Lord should have the hiccups? What a lot of lights you have got burning, Mrs Oakley!'

'A lot of lights, Mr Lupin! Why, there is only one; but perhaps you allude to the lights of the gospel?'

'No; I—I don't, just at present; damn the lights of the gospel—that is, I mean damn all backsliders! But there is a lot of lights, and no mistake, Mrs Oakley. Give us a drop of something, I'm as dry as dust.'

'There is some more mulled wine, Mr Lupin; but I am surprised that you think there is more than one light.'

'It's a miracle, madam, in consequence of my great faith. I have faith in s–s–s–six lights, and here they are.'

'Do you see that, Johanna?' exclaimed Mrs Oakley, 'are you not convinced now of the holiness of Mr Lupin?'

'I am convinced of his drunkenness, mother, and entreat of you to let me leave the room at once.'

'Tell her of the honour,' said Mr Lupin—'tell her of the honour.'

'I don't know, Mr Lupin; but don't you think it would be better to take some other opportunity?'

'Very well, then, this is the opportunity.'

'If it's your pleasure, Mr Lupin, I will. You must know, then, Johanna, that Mr Lupin has been kind enough to consent to save my soul on condition that you marry him, and I am quite sure you can have no reasonable objection; indeed, I think it's the least you can do, whether you have any objection or not.'

'Well put,' said Mr Lupin, 'excellently well put.'

'Mother,' said Johanna, 'if you are so far gone in superstition as to believe this miserable drunkard ought to come between you and heaven, I am not so lost as not to be able to reject the offer with more scorn and contempt than ever I thought I could have entertained for any human being; but hypocrisy never, to my mind, wears so disgusting a garb as when it attires itself in the outward show of religion.'

'This conduct is unbearable,' cried Mrs Oakley; 'am I to have one of the Lord's saints insulted under my own roof?'

'If he were ten times a saint, mother, instead of being nothing but a miserable drunken profligate, it would be better that he should be insulted ten times over, than that you should permit your own child to have passed through the indignity of having to reject such a proposition as that which has just been made. I must claim the protection of my father; he will not suffer one, towards whom he has ever shown his affection, the remembrance of which sinks deep into my heart, to meet with so cruel an insult beneath his roof.'

'That's right, my dear,' cried Mr Oakley, at that moment pushing open the parlour-door. 'That's right, my dear; you never spoke truer words in your life.'

A faint scream came from Mrs Oakley, and the Rev Mr Lupin immediately seized upon the fresh jug of mulled wine, and finished it at a draught.

'Get behind me, Satan,' he said. 'Mr Oakley, you will be damned if you say a word to me.'

'It's all the same, then,' said Mr Oakley; 'for I'll be damned if I don't. Then, Ben, Ben, come—come in, Ben.'

'I'm a-coming,' said a deep voice, and a man about six feet four inches in height, and nearly two-thirds of that amount in width, entered the parlour. 'I'm a-coming, Oakley, my boy. Put on your blessed spectacles, and tell me which is the fellow.'

'I could have sworn it,' said Mrs Oakley, as she gave the table a knock, with her fist—'I could have sworn when you came in, Oakley— I could have sworn, you little snivelling, shrivelled-up wretch. You'd no more have dared to come into this parlour as never was with those words in your mouth than you'd have dared to have flown, if you hadn't had your cousin, Big Ben, the beef-eater from the Tower,* with you.'

'Take it easy, ma'am,' said Ben, as he sat down in a chair, which immediately broke all to pieces with his weight. 'Take it easy, ma'am; the devil—what's this?'

'Never mind, Ben,' said Mr Oakley; 'it's only a chair; get up.'

'A cheer,' said Ben; 'do you call that a cheer? but never mind— take it easy.'

'Why, you big, bullying, idle, swilling and guttling* ruffian!'

'Go on, ma'am, go on.'

'You good-for-nothing lump of carrion; a dog wears his own coat, but you wear your master's, you great stupid overgrown, lurking hound. You parish brought-up wild beast, go and mind your lions and elephants in the Tower,* and don't come into honest people's houses, you cut-throat, bullying, pickpocketing wretch.'

'Go on, ma'am, go on.'

This was a kind of dialogue that could not last, and Mrs Oakley sat down exhausted, and then Ben said,—

'I tell you what, ma'am, I considers you—I looks upon you, ma'am, as a female wariety of that ere animal as is very useful and saga-cious, ma'am.'

There was no mistake in this allusion, and Mrs Oakley was about to make some reply, when the Rev Mr Lupin rose from his chair, saying,—

'Bless you all! I think I'll go home.'

'Not yet, Mr Tulip,' said Ben; 'you had better sit down again—we've got something to say to you.'

'Young man, young man, let me pass. If you do not, you will endanger your soul.'

'I ain't got none,' said Ben; 'I'm only a beef-eater, and don't pretend to such luxuries.'

'The heathen!' exclaimed Mrs Oakley, 'the horrid heathen! but there's one consolation, and that is, that he will be fried in his own fat for everlasting.'

'Oh, that's nothing,' said Ben; 'I think I shall like it, especially if it's any pleasure to you. I suppose that's what you call a Christian consolation. Will you sit down, Mr Tulip?'

'My name ain't Tulip, but Lupin; but if you wish it, I don't mind sitting down, of course.'

The beef-eater, with a movement of his foot, kicked away the reverend gentleman's chair, and down he sat with a dab upon the floor.

'My dear,' said Mr Oakley to Johanna, 'you go to bed, and then your mother can't say you have anything to do with this affair. I intend to rid my house of this man. Good night, my dear, good night.'

Johanna kissed her father on the cheek, and then left the room, not at all sorry that so vigorous a movement was being made for the suppression of Mr Lupin.

When she was gone, Mrs Oakley spoke, saying, 'Mr Lupin, I bid you good night, and of course after the rough treatment of these wretches, I can hardly expect you to come again. Good night, Mr Lupin, good night.'

'That's all very well, ma'am,' said Ben, 'but before this ere wild beast of a parson goes away, I want to admonish him. He don't seem to be wide awake, and I must rouse him up.'

Ben took hold of the reverend gentleman's nose, and gave it such an awful pinch that when he took his finger and thumb away, it was perfectly blue.

'Murder, oh murder! my nose! my nose!' shrieked Mr Lupin, and at that moment Mrs Oakley, who was afraid to attack Ben, gave her husband such an open-handed whack on the side of his head, that the little man reeled again, and saw a great many more lights than the Rev Mr Lupin had done under the influence of the mulled wine.

'Very good,' said Ben, 'now we are getting into the thick of it.'

With this Ben took from his pocket a coil of rope, one end of which was a noose, and that he dexterously threw over Mrs Oakley's head.

'Murder!' she shrieked. 'Oakley, are you going to see me murdered before your eyes?'

'There is such a singing in my ears,' said Mr Oakley, 'that I can't see anything.'

'This is the way,' said Ben, 'we manages the wild beastesses when they shuts their ears to all sorts of argument. Now, ma'am, if you please, a little this way.'

Ben looked about until he found a strong hook in the wall, over which, in consequence of his great height, he was enabled to draw the rope, and then the other end of it he tied securely to the leg of a heavy secretaire that was in the room, so that Mrs Oakley was well secured.

'Murder!' she cried. 'Oakley, are you a man, that you stand by and see me treated in this way by a big brute?'

'I can't see anything,' said Mr Oakley; 'there is such a singing in my ears; I told you so before—I can't see anything.'

'Now, ma'am, you may just say what you like,' said Ben; 'it won't matter a bit, any more than the grumbling of a bear with a sore head; and as for your Mr Tulip, you'll just get down on your knees, and beg Mr Oakley's pardon for coming and drinking his tea without his leave, and having the internal impudence to speak to his daughter.'

'Don't do it, Mr Lupin,' cried Mrs Oakley—'don't do it.'

'You hear,' said Ben, 'what the lady advises. Now, I am quite different; I advise you to do it—for, if you don't, I shan't hurt you; but it strikes me I shall be obliged to fall on you and crush you.'

'I think I will,' said Mr Lupin; 'the saints were always forced to yield to the Philistines.'

'If you call me any names,' said Ben, 'I'll just wring your neck.'

'Young man, young man, let me exhort you. Allow me to go, and I will put up prayers for your conversion.'

'Confound your impudence! what do you suppose the beasts in the Tower would do, if I was converted? Why, that 'ere tiger we have had lately, would eat his own tail, to think I had turned out such an ass. Come, I can't waste any more of my precious time; and if you don't get down on your knees directly, we'll see what we can do.'

'I must,' said Mr Lupin, 'I must, I suppose'; and down he flopped on his knees.

'Very good; now repeat after me.—I am a wolf that stole sheep's clothing.'

'Yes; I am a wolf that stole sheep's clothing*—the Lord forgive me.'

'Perhaps he may, and perhaps he mayn't. Now go on—all that's wirtuous is my loathing.'

'Oh dear, yes—all that's wirtuous is my loathing.'

'Mr Oakley; I have offended.'

'Yes; I am a miserable sinner, Mr Oakley, I have offended.'

'And ask his pardon, on my bended—'

'Oh dear, yes—I asks his pardon on my bended—The Lord have mercy on us miserable sinners!'

'Knees—I won't do so no more.'

'Yes—knees, I won't do so no more.'

'As sure as I lies on this floor.'

'Yes—as sure as I lies on this floor.—Death and the devil, you've killed me!'

Ben took hold of the reverend gentleman by the back of the neck, and pressed his head down upon the floor, until his nose, which had before been such a sufferer, was nearly completely flattened with his face.

'Now you may go,' said Ben.

Mr Lupin scrambled to his feet; but Ben followed him into the passage, and did not yet let him go, until he had accelerated his movements by two hearty kicks. And then the victorious beef-eater returned to the parlour.

'Why, Ben,' said Mr Oakley, 'you are quite a poet.'

'I believe you, Oakley, my boy,' said Ben, 'and now let us be off, and have a pint round the corner.'

'What!' exclaimed Mrs Oakley, 'and leave me here, you wretches?'

'Yes,' said Ben, 'unless you promises never to be a female variety of the useful animal again, and begs pardon of Mr Oakley, for giving him all this trouble; as for me, I'll let you off cheap, you shall only have to give me a kiss, and say you loves me.'

'If I do, may I be—'

'Damned, you mean.'

'No, I don't; choked I was going to say.'

'Then you may be choked, for you have nothing to do but to let your legs go from under you, and you will be hung as comfortable as possible—come along; Oakley.'

'Mr Oakley—stop, stop—don't leave me here. I am sorry.'

'That's enough,' said Mr Oakley; 'and now, my dear, bear in mind one thing from me. I intend from this time forward to be master in my own house. If you and I are to live together, we must do so on very different terms to what we have been living, and if you won't make yourself agreeable, Lawyer Hutchins tells me that I can turn you out and give you a maintenance; and, in that case, I'll have home my sister Rachel to mind house for me; so now you know my determination, and what you have to expect.* If you wish to begin, well do so at once, by getting something nice and tasty for Ben's supper.'

Mrs Oakley made the required promise, and being released, she set about preparations for the supper in real earnest; but whether she was really subdued or not, we shall, in due time, see.

# 10

## *The Colonel and his Friend*

COLONEL JEFFERY was not at all satisfied with the state of affairs, as regarded the disappearance of Mr Thornhill, for whom he entertained a very sincere regard, both on account of the private estimation in which he held him, and on account of actual services rendered by Thornhill to him.

Not to detain Johanna Oakley in the Temple-gardens, he had stopped his narrative, completely at the point when what concerned her had ceased, and had said nothing of much danger which the ship Neptune and its crew and passengers has gone through, after Mr Thornhill had been taken on board with his dog.

The fact is, the storm which he had mentioned was only the first of a series of gales of wind that buffeted the ship for some weeks, doing it much damage, and enforcing almost the necessity of putting in somewhere for repairs.

But a glance at the map will be sufficient to show, that situated as the Neptune was, the nearest port at which they could at all expect assistance, was the British colony, at the Cape of Good Hope;*

but such was the contrary nature of the winds and waves, that just upon the evening of a tempestuous day, they found themselves bearing down close in shore, on the eastern coast of Madagascar.*

There was much apprehension that the vessel would strike on a rocky shore; but the water was deep, and the vessel rode well; there was a squall, and they let go both anchors to secure the vessel, as they were so close in shore, lest they should be driven in and stranded.

It was fortunate they had so secured themselves, for the gale while it lasted blew half a hurricane, and the ship lost some of her masts, and some other trifling damage, which, however, entailed upon them the necessity of remaining there a few days, to cut timber to repair their masts, and to obtain a few supplies.

There is but little to interest a general reader in the description of a gale. Order after order was given until the masts and spars went one by one, and then the orders for clearing the wreck were given.

There was much work to be done, and but little pleasure in doing it, for it was wet and miserable while it lasted, and there was the danger of being driven upon a lee shore,* and knocked to pieces úpon the rocks.

This danger was averted, and they anchored safe at a very short distance from the shore in comparative safety and security.

'We are safe now,' remarked the captain, as he gave his second in command charge of the deck, and approached Mr Thornhill and Colonel Jeffery.

'I am happy it is so,' replied Jeffery.

'Well, captain,' said Mr Thornhill, 'I am glad we have done with being knocked about; we are anchored, and the water here appears smooth enough.'

'It is so, and I dare say it will remain so; it is a beautiful basin of deep water—deep and good anchorage; but you see it is not large enough to make a fine harbour.'

'True; but it is rocky.'

'It is; and that may make it sometimes dangerous, though I don't know that it would be so in some gales. The sea may beat in at the opening, which is deep enough for anything to enter—even Noah's ark would enter there easily enough.'

'What will you do now?'

'Stay here for a day or so, and send boats ashore to cut some pine trees, to refit the ship with masts.'

'You have no staves, then?'

'Not enough for such a purpose; and we never do go out stored with such things.'

---

'You obtain them wherever you may go to.'

'Yes, any part of the world will furnish them in some shape or other.'

'When you send ashore, will you permit me to accompany the boat's crew?' said Jeffery.

'Certainly; but the natives of this country are violent and intractable, and, should you get into any row with them, there is every probability of your being captured, or some bodily injury done you.'

'But I will take care to avoid all that.'

'Very well, colonel, you shall be welcome to go.'

'I must beg the same permission,' said Mr Thornhill, 'for I should much like to see the country, as well as to have some acquaintance with the natives themselves.'

'By no means trust yourself alone with them,' said the captain, 'for if you live you will have cause to repent it—depend upon what I say.'

'I will,' said Thornhill; 'I will go nowhere but where the boat's company goes.'

'You will be safe then.'

'But do you apprehend any hostile attack from the natives?' inquired Colonel Jeffery.

'No, I do not expect it; but such things have happened before today, and I have seen them when least expected, though I have been on this coast before, and yet I have never met with any ill-treatment; but there have been many who have touched on this coast, who have had a brush with the natives and come off second best, the natives generally retiring when the ship's company muster strong in number, and calling out the chiefs, who come down in great force that we may not conquer them.'

\*    \*    \*    \*    \*

The next morning the boats were ordered out to go ashore with crews, prepared for cutting timber, and obtaining such staves as the ship was in want of.

With these boats old Thornhill and Colonel Jeffery went both of them on board, and after a short ride, they reached the shore of Madagascar.

It was a beautiful country, and one in which vegetables appeared abundant and luxuriant, and the party in search of timber, for ship-building purposes, soon came to some lordly monarchs of the forest, which would have made vessels of themselves.

But this was not what was wanted; but where the trees grew thicker and taller, they began to cut some tall pine trees down.

This was the wood they most desired; in fact it was exactly what they wanted; but they hardly got through a few such trees, when the natives came down upon them, apparently to reconnoitre.

At first they were quiet and tractable enough, but anxious to see and inspect everything, being very inquisitive and curious.

However, that was easily borne, but at length they became more numerous, and began to pilfer all they could lay their hands upon, which, of course, brought resentment, and after some time a blow or two was exchanged.

Colonel Jeffery was forward and endeavouring to prevent some violence being offered to one of the woodcutters; in fact, he was interposing himself between the two contending parties, and tried to restore order and peace, but several armed natives rushed suddenly upon him, secured him, and were hurrying him away to death before anyone could stir in his behalf.

His doom appeared certain, for, had they succeeded, they would have cruelly and brutally murdered him.

However, just at that moment aid was at hand, and Mr Thornhill, seeing how matters stood, seized a musket from one of the sailors, and rushed after the natives who had Colonel Jeffery.

There were three of them, two others had gone on to apprise, it was presumed, the chiefs. When Mr Thornhill arrived, they had thrown a blanket over the head of Jeffery; but Mr Thornhill in an instant hurled one with a blow from the butt-end of his musket, and the second met the same fate, as he turned to see what was the matter.

The third seeing the colonel free, and the musket levelled at his own head, immediately ran after the other two, to avoid any serious consequences to himself. 'Thornhill, you have saved my life,' said Colonel Jeffery, excitedly.

'Come away, don't stop here—to the ship!—to the ship!' And as he spoke, they hurried after the crew; and they succeeded in reaching the boats and the ship in safety; congratulating themselves not a little upon so lucky an escape from a people quite warlike enough to do mischief, but not civilised enough to distinguish when to do it.

When men are far away from home, and in foreign lands, with the skies of other climes above them, their hearts become more closely knit together in those ties of brotherhood which certainly ought to actuate the whole universe, but which as certainly do not do so, except in very narrow circumstances.

One of these instances, however, would probably be found in the conduct of Colonel Jeffery and Mr Thornhill, even under any circumstances, for they were most emphatically what might be termed kindred spirits; but when we come to unite to that fact the remarkable manner in which they had been thrown together, and the mutual services that they had had it in their power to render to each other, we should not be surprised at the almost romantic friendship that arose between them.

It was then that Thornhill made the colonel's breast the depository of all his thoughts and all his wishes, and a freedom of intercourse and a community of feeling ensued between them, which, when it does take place between persons of really congenial dispositions, produces the most delightful results of human companionship.

No one who has not endured the tedium of a sea voyage can at all be aware of what a pleasant thing it is to have someone on board in the rich stores of whose intellect and fancy one can find a never-ending amusement.

The winds might now whistle through the cordage, and the waves toss the great ship on their foaming crests; still Thornhill and Jeffery were together, finding, in the midst of danger, solace in each other's society, and each animating the other to the performance of deeds of daring that astonished the crew.

The whole voyage was one of the greatest peril, and some of the oldest seamen on board did not scruple, during the continuance of their night watches, to intimate to their companions that the ship, in their opinion, would never reach England, and that she would founder somewhere along the long stretch of the African coast.

The captain, of course, made every possible exertion to put a stop to such prophetic sayings, but when once they commenced, in short time there is no such thing as completely eradicating them; and they, of course, produced the most injurious effect, paralysing the exertions of the crew in times of danger, and making them believe that they are in a doomed ship, and, consequently, all they can do is useless.

Sailors are extremely superstitious on such matters, and there cannot be any reasonable doubt but that some of the disasters that befell the Neptune on her homeward voyage from India may be attributable to this feeling of fatality getting hold of the seamen, and inducing them to think that, let them try what they might, they could not save the ship.

It happened that after they had rounded the Cape, a dense fog came on, such as had not been known on that coast for many a year, although the western shore of Africa, at some seasons of the year, is subject to such a species of vaporous exhalation.

Every object was wrapped in the most profound gloom, and yet there was a strong eddy or current of the ocean, flowing parallel with the land, and as the captain hoped, rather off than on the shore.

In consequence of this fear, the greatest anxiety prevailed on board the vessel, and lights were left burning on all parts of the deck, while two men were continually engaged making soundings. It was about half-an-hour after midnight, as the barometer indicated a storm, that suddenly the men, who were on watch on the deck, raised a loud cry of alarm.

They had suddenly seen, close to the larboard bow, lights, which must belong to some vessel that, like the Neptune, was encompassed in the fog, and a collision was quite inevitable, for neither ship had time to put about.

The only doubt, which was a fearful and an agonising one to have solved, was whether the stronger vessel was of sufficient bulk and power to run them down, or they it; and that fearful question was one which a few moments must settle.

In fact, almost before the echo of that cry of horror, which had come from the men, had died away, the vessels met. There was a hideous crash—one shriek of dismay and horror, and then all was still. The Neptune, with considerable damage, and some of the bulwarks stove in, sailed on; but the other ship went with a surging sound, to the bottom of the sea.

Alas! nothing could be done. The fog was so dense, that, coupled, too, with the darkness of the night, there could be no hope of rescuing one of the ill-fated crew of the ship; and the officers and seamen of the Neptune, although they shouted for some time, and then listened, to hear if any of the survivors of the ship that had been run down were swimming, no answer came to them; and when, in about six hours more they sailed out of the fog into a clear sunshine, where there was not so much as a cloud to be seen, they looked at each other like men newly awakened from some strange and fearful dream.

They never discovered the name of the ship they had run down, and the whole affair remained a profound mystery. When the Neptune reached the port of London, the affair was repeated, and every exertion made to obtain some information concerning the ill-fated ship that had met with so fearful a doom.

Such were the circumstances which awakened all the liveliest feelings of gratitude on the part of Colonel Jeffery towards Mr Thornhill; and hence it was that he was in London, and had the necessary leisure so to do, to leave no stone unturned to discover what had become of him.

After deep and anxious thought, and feeling convinced that there was some mystery which it was beyond his power to discover, he resolved upon asking the opinion of a friend, likewise in the army, a Captain Rathbone, concerning the whole of the facts.

This gentleman, and a gentleman he was in the fullest acceptation of the term, was in London; in fact, he had retired from active service, and inhabited a small but pleasant house in the outskirts of the metropolis.

It was one of those old-fashioned cottage residences, with all sorts of odd places and corners about it, and a thriving garden full of fine old wood, such as are rather rare near to London, and which are daily becoming more rare, in consequence of the value of the land immediately contiguous to the metropolis not permitting large pieces to remain attached to small residences.

Captain Rathbone had an amiable family about him, such as he was and might well be proud of, and was living in as great a state of domestic felicity as this world could very well afford him.

It was to this gentleman, then, that Colonel Jeffery resolved upon going to lay all the circumstances before him concerning the possible and probable fate of poor Thornhill.

This distance was not so great but that he could walk it conveniently, and he did so, arriving towards the dusk of the evening, on the day following that which had witnessed his deeply interesting interview with Johanna Oakley in the Temple-gardens.

There is nothing on earth so delightfully refreshing, after a dusty and rather a long country walk, as to suddenly enter a well-kept and extremely verdant garden; and this was the case especially to the feelings of Colonel Jeffery, when he arrived at Lime Tree Lodge, the residence of Captain Rathbone.

He was met with a most cordial and frank welcome—a welcome which he expected, but which was none the less delightful on that account; and after sitting awhile with the family in the house, he and the captain strolled into the garden, and then Colonel Jeffery commenced with his revelation.

The captain, with very few interruptions, heard him to the end; and when he concluded by saying, 'And now I have come to ask your advice upon all these matters,' the captain immediately replied, in his warm, off-hand manner,—

'I'm afraid you won't find my advice of much importance; but I offer you my active co-operation in anything you think ought to be done or can be done in this affair, which, I assure you, deeply interests me, and gives me the greatest possible impulse to exertion. You have but to command me in the matter, and I am completely at your disposal.'

'I was quite certain you would say as much. But notwithstanding the manner in which you shrink from giving an opinion, I am anxious to know what you really think with regard to what are, you will allow, most extraordinary circumstances.'

'The most natural thing in the world,' said Captain Rathbone, 'at the first flush of the affair, seemed to be that we ought to look for your friend Thornhill at the point where he disappeared.'

'At the barber's in Fleet-street?'

'Precisely. Did he leave the barber, or did he not?'

'Sweeney Todd says that he left him, and proceeded down the street towards the city, in pursuance of a direction he had given to Mr Oakley, the spectacle-maker, and that he saw him get into some sort of disturbance at the end of the market; but to put against that, we have the fact of the dog remaining by the barber's door, and his refusing to leave it on any amount of solicitation. Now the very fact that a dog could act in such a way proclaims an amount of sagacity

that seems to tell loudly against the presumption that such a creature could make any mistake.'

'It does. What say you, now, to going into town tomorrow morning, and making a call at the barber's, without proclaiming we have
any special errand except to be shaved and dressed? Do you think
he would know you again?'

'Scarcely, in plain clothes; I was in my undress uniform when I
called with the captain of the Neptune, so that his impression of me
must be decidedly of a military character; and the probability is,
that he would not know me at all in the clothes of a civilian. I like
the idea of giving a call at the barber's.'

'Do you think your friend Thornhill was a man likely to talk
about the valuable pearls he had in his possession?'

'Certainly not.'

'I merely ask you, because they might have offered a great temptation; and if he has experienced any foul play at the hands of the
barber, the idea of becoming possessed of such a valuable treasure
might have been the inducement.'

'I do not think it probable, but it has struck me that, if we obtain
any information whatever of Thornhill, it will be in consequence of
these very pearls. They are of great value, and not likely to be overlooked; and yet, unless a customer be found for them, they are of no
value at all; and nobody buys jewels of that character but from the
personal vanity of making, of course, some public display of them.'

'That is true; and so, from hand to hand, we might trace those
pearls until we come to the individual who must have had them
from Thornhill himself, and who might be forced to account most
strictly for the manner in which they came into his possession.'

After some more desultory conversation upon the subject, it was
agreed that Colonel Jeffery should take a bed there for the night at
Lime Tree Lodge, and that, in the morning, they should both start
for London, and, disguising themselves as respectable citizens,
make some attempts, by talking about jewels and precious stones,
to draw out the barber into a confession that he had something of
the sort to dispose of; and, moreover, they fully intended to take away
the dog, with the care of which, Captain Rathbone charged himself.

We may pass over the pleasant, social evening which the colonel
passed with the amiable family of the Rathbones, and skipping
likewise a conversation of some strange and confused dreams

which Jeffery had during the night concerning his friend Thornhill, we will presume that both the colonel and the captain have break-fasted, and that they have proceeded to London and are at the shop of a clothier in the neighbourhood of the Strand, in order to pro-cure coats, wigs, and hats, that should disguise them for their visit to Sweeney Todd.

Then, arm-in-arm, they walked towards Fleet-street, and soon arrived opposite the little shop within which there appears to be so much mystery.

'The dog you perceive is not here,' said the colonel; 'I had my suspicions, however, when I passed with Johanna Oakley that something was amiss with him, and I have no doubt but that the rascally barber has fairly compassed his destruction.'

'If the barber be innocent,' said Captain Rathbone, 'you must admit that it would be one of the most confoundedly annoying things in the world to have a dog continually at his door assuming such an aspect of accusation, and in that case I can scarcely wonder at his putting the creature out of the way.'

'No, presuming upon his innocence, certainly; but we will say nothing about all that, and remember we must come in as perfect strangers, knowing nothing whatever of the affair of the dog, and presuming nothing about the disappearance of anyone in this locality.'

'Agreed, come on; if he should see us through the window, hanging about at all or hesitating, his suspicions will be at once awakened, and we shall do no good.'

They both entered the shop and found Sweeney Todd wearing an extraordinary singular appearance, for there was a black patch over one of his eyes, which was kept in its place by a green riband that went round his head, so that he looked more fierce and diabolical than ever; and having shaved off a small whisker that he used to wear, his countenance, although to the full as hideous as ever, cer-tainly had a different character of ugliness to that which had before characterised it, and attracted the attention of the colonel.

That gentleman would hardly have known him again anywhere but in his own shop, and when we come to consider Sweeney Todd's adventures of the preceding evening, we shall not feel surprised that he saw the necessity of endeavouring to make as much change in his appearance as possible for fear he should come across any of the parties who had chased him, and who, for all he knew to the contrary, might, quite unsuspectingly, drop in to be shaved in the course of the morning, perhaps to retail at that acknowledged mart for all sorts of gossip—a barber's shop—some of the very incidents which he was so well qualified himself to relate.

'Shaved and dressed, gentlemen,' said Sweeney Todd, as his customers made their appearance.

'Shaved only,' said Captain Rathbone, who had agreed to be the principal spokesman, in case Sweeney Todd should have any reminiscence of the colonel's voice, and so suspect him.

'Pray be seated,' said Sweeney Todd to Colonel Jeffery. 'I'll soon polish off your friend, sir, and then I'll begin upon you. Would you like to see the morning paper, sir? I was just looking myself, sir, at a most mysterious circumstance, if it's true, but you can't believe, you know, all that is put in the papers.'

'Thank you—thank you,' said the colonel.

Captain Rathbone sat down to be shaved, for he had purposely omitted that operation at home, in order that it should not appear a mere excuse to get into Sweeney Todd's shop.

'Why, sir,' continued Sweeney Todd, 'as I was saying, it is a most remarkable circumstance.'

'Indeed!'

'Yes, sir, an old gentleman of the name of Fidler had been to receive a sum of money at the west-end of the town, and has never been heard of since; that was only yesterday, sir, and there is a description of him in the papers of to-day.'

'"A snuff-coloured coat, and velvet smalls*—black velvet, I should have said—silk stockings, and silver shoe-buckles, and a golden-headed cane, with W. D. F. upon it, meaning William Dumpledown Fidler"—a most mysterious affair, gentlemen.'

A sort of groan came from the corner of the shop, and, on the impulse of the moment, Colonel Jeffery sprang to his feet, exclaiming,—

'What's that—what's that?'

'Oh, it's only my apprentice, Tobias Ragg. He has got a pain in his stomach from eating too many of Lovett's pork pies. Ain't that it, Tobias, my bud?'

'Yes, sir,' said Tobias, with another groan.

'Oh, indeed,' said the colonel, 'it ought to make him more careful for the future.'

'It's to be hoped it will, sir; Tobias, do you hear what the gentle-man says: it ought to make you more careful in future. I am too indulgent to you, that's the fact. Now, sir, I believe you are as clean shaved as ever you were in your life.'

'Why, yes,' said Captain Rathbone, 'I think that will do very well, and now, Mr Green,'—addressing the colonel by that assumed name—'and now, Mr Green, be quick, or we shall be too late for the duke, and so lose the sale of some of our jewels.'

'We shall indeed,' said the colonel, 'if we don't mind. We sat too long over our breakfast at the inn, and his grace is too rich and too good a customer to lose—he don't mind what price he gives for things that take his fancy, or the fancy of his duchess.'

'Jewel merchants, gentlemen, I presume,' said Sweeney Todd.

'Yes, we have been in that line for some time; and by one of us trading in one direction, and the other in another, we manage extremely well, because we exchange what suits our different customers, and keep up two distinct connexions.'

'A very good plan,' said Sweeney Todd. 'I'll be as quick as I can with you, sir. Dealing in jewels is better than shaving.'

'I dare say it is.'

'Of course it is, sir; here have I been slaving for some years in this shop, and not done much good—that is to say, when I talk of not having done much good, I admit I have made enough to retire upon, quietly and comfortably, and I mean to do so very shortly. There you are, sir, shaved with celerity you seldom meet with, and as clean as possible, for the small charge of one penny. Thank you, gentlemen—there's your change; good morning.'

They had no recourse but to leave the shop; and when they had gone, Sweeney Todd, as he stropped the razor he had been using upon his hand, gave a most diabolical grin, muttering,—

'Clever—very ingenious—but it wouldn't do. Oh dear no, not at all! I am not so easily taken in—diamond merchants, ah! ah! and no objection, of course, to deal in pearls—a good jest that, truly a capital jest. If I had been accustomed to be so defeated, I had not now been here a living man. Tobias, Tobias, I say!'

'Yes, sir,' said the lad, dejectedly.

'Have you forgotten your mother's danger in case you breathe a syllable of anything that has occurred here, or that you think has occurred here, or so much as dream of?'

'No,' said the boy, 'indeed I have not. I never can forget it, if I were to live a hundred years.'

'That's well, prudent, excellent, Tobias. Go out now, and if those two persons who were here last waylay you in the street, let them say what they will, and do you reply to them as shortly as possible; but be sure you come back to me quickly, and report what they do say. They turned to the left, towards the city—now be off with you.'

\* \* \* \* \*

'It's of no use,' said Colonel Jeffery to the captain; 'the barber is either too cunning for me, or he is really innocent of all participation in the disappearance of Thornhill.'

'And yet there are suspicious circumstances. I watched his countenance when the subject of jewels was mentioned, and I saw a sudden change come over it; it was but momentary, but still it gave me a suspicion that he knew something which caution alone kept within the recesses of his breast. The conduct of the boy, too, was strange; and then again, if he has the string of pearls, their value would give him all the power to do what he says he is about to do—viz., to retire from business with an independence.'

'Hush! there did you see the lad?'

'Yes; why it's the barber's boy.'

'It is the same lad he called Tobias—shall we speak to him?'

'Let's make a bolder push, and offer him an ample reward for any information he may give us.'

'Agreed, agreed.'

They both walked up to Tobias, who was listlessly walking along the streets, and when they reached him, they were both struck with the appearance of care and sadness that was upon the boy's face.

He looked perfectly haggard, and care-worn—an expression sad to see upon the face of one so young, and, when the colonel accosted him in a kindly tone he seemed so unnerved that tears immediately darted to his eyes, although at the same time he shrank back as if alarmed.

'My lad,' said the colonel, 'you reside, I think, with Sweeney Todd, the barber. Is he not a kind master to you that you seem so unhappy?'

'No, no, that is, I mean yes, I have nothing to tell. Let me pass on.'

'What is the meaning of this confusion?'

'Nothing, nothing.'

'I say, my lad, here is a guinea for you, if you will tell us what became of the man of a seafaring appearance, who came with a dog to your master's house, some days since to be shaved.'

'I cannot tell you,' said the boy, 'I cannot tell you, what I do not know.'

'But, you have some idea, probably. Come, we will make it worth your while, and thereby protect you from Sweeney Todd. We have the power to do so, and all the inclination; but you must be quite explicit with us, and tell us frankly what you think, and what you know concerning the man in whose fate we are interested.'

'I know nothing, I think nothing,' said Tobias. 'Let me go, I have nothing to say, except that he was shaved, and went away.'

'But how came he to leave his dog behind him?'

'I cannot tell. I know nothing.'

'It is evident that you do know something, but hesitate either from fear or some other motive to tell it; as you are inaccessible to fair means, we must resort to others, and you shall at once come before a magistrate, which will force you to speak out.'

'Do with me what you will,' said Tobias, 'I cannot help it. I have nothing to say to you, nothing whatever. Oh, my poor mother, if it were not for you—'

'What, then?'

'Nothing! nothing! nothing!'

It was but a threat of the colonel to take the boy before a magistrate, for he really had no grounds for so doing; and if the boy chose to keep a secret, if he had one, not all the magistrates in the world could force words from his lips that he felt not inclined to utter; and so, after one more effort, they felt that they must leave him.

'Boy,' said the colonel, 'you are young, and cannot well judge of the consequences of particular lines of conduct; you ought to weigh well what you are about, and hesitate long before you determine keeping dangerous secrets; we can convince you that we have the power of completely protecting you from all that Sweeney Todd could possibly attempt. Think again, for this is an opportunity of saving yourself perhaps from much future misery that may never arise again.'

'I have nothing to say,' said the boy, 'I have nothing to say.'

He uttered these words with such an agonised expression of countenance, that they were both convinced he had something to say, and that, too, of the first importance—a something which would be valuable to them in the way of information, extremely valuable probably, and yet which they felt the utter impossibility of wringing from him.

They were compelled to leave him, and likewise with the additional mortification, that, far from making any advance in the matter, they had placed themselves and their cause in a much worse position, in so far as they had awakened all Sweeney Todd's suspicions if he were guilty, and yet advanced not one step in the transaction.

And then to make matters all the more perplexing, there was still the possibility that they might be altogether upon a wrong scent, and that the barber of Fleet-street had no more to do with the disappearance of Mr Thornhill than they had themselves.

## 11

### *The Stranger at Lovett's*

TOWARDS the dusk of the evening in that day, after the last batch of pies at Lovett's had been disposed of, there walked into the shop a man most miserably clad, and who stood for a few moments staring with weakness and hunger at the counter before he spoke.

Mrs Lovett was there, but she had no smile for him, and instead of its usual bland expression, her countenance wore an aspect of anger, as she forestalled what the man had to say, by exclaiming, —

'Go away, we never give to beggars.'

There came a flush of colour, for a moment, across the features of the stranger, and then he replied, —

'Mistress Lovett, I do not come to ask alms of you, but to know if you can recommend me to any employment?'

'Recommend you! recommend a ragged wretch like you!'

'I am a ragged wretch, and, moreover, quite destitute. In better times I have sat at your counter, and paid cheerfully for what I have wanted, and then one of your softest smiles has been ever at my disposal. I do not say this as a reproach to you, because the cause of your smile was well-known to be a self-interested one, and when that cause has passed away, I can no longer expect it; but I am so situated that I am willing to do anything for a mere subsistence.'

'Oh, yes, and then when you have got into a better case again, I have no doubt but you have quite sufficient insolence to make you unbearable; besides, what employment can we have but pie-making, and we have a man already who suits us very well with the exception that he, as you would do if you were to exchange with him, has grown insolent, and fancies himself master of the place.'

'Well, well,' said the stranger, 'of course there is always sufficient argument against the poor and destitute to keep them so. If you will assert that my conduct would be of the nature you describe it, it is quite impossible for me to prove the contrary.'

He turned and was about to leave the shop, when Mrs Lovett called after him, saying—'Come in again in two hours.'

He paused a moment or two, and then, turning his emaciated countenance upon her, said,—'I will if my strength permits me—water from the pumps in the streets is but a poor thing for a man to subsist upon for twenty-four hours.'

'You may take one pie.'

The half-famished, miserable-looking man seized upon a pie, and devoured it in an instant.

'My name,' he said, 'is Jarvis Williams: I'll be here, never fear, Mrs Lovett, in two hours; and notwithstanding all you have said, you shall find no change in my behaviour because I may be well-kept and better clothed; but if I should feel dissatisfied with my situation, I will leave it and no harm done.'

So saying, he walked from the shop, and after he was gone, a strange expression came across the countenance of Mrs Lovett, and she said in a low tone to herself.—'He might suit for a few months, like the rest, and it is clear we must get rid of the one we have; I must think of it.'

\* \* \* \* \*

There is a cellar of vast extent, and of dim and sepulchral aspect— some rough red tiles are laid upon the floor, and pieces of flint and large jagged stones have been hammered into the earthen walls to strengthen them; while here and there rough huge pillars made by beams of timber rise perpendicularly from the floor, and prop large flat pieces of wood against the ceiling, to support it.

Here and there gleaming lights seem to be peeping out from furnaces, and there is a strange, hissing, simmering sound going on, while the whole air is impregnated with a rich and savoury vapour.

This is Lovett's pie manufactory beneath the pavement of Bell-yard, and at this time a night-batch of some thousands is being made for the purpose of being sent by carts the first thing in the morning all over the suburbs of London.

By the earliest dawn of the day a crowd of itinerant hawkers of pies would make their appearance, carrying off a large quantity to regular customers who had them daily, and no more thought of being without them than of forbidding the milkman or the baker to call at their residences.*

It will be seen and understood, therefore, that the retail part of Mrs Lovett's business, which took place principally between the hours of twelve and one, was by no means the most important or profitable portion of a concern which was really of immense magnitude, and which brought in a large yearly income.

To stand in the cellar when this immense manufacture of what, at first sight, would appear such a trivial article was carried on, and to look about as far as the eye could reach, was by no means to have a sufficient idea of the extent of the place; for there were as many doors in different directions, and singular low-arched entrances to different vaults, which all appeared as black as midnight, that one might almost suppose the inhabitants of all the surrounding neighbourhood had, by common consent, given up their cellars to Lovett's pie factory.

There is but one miserable light, except the occasional fitful glare that comes from the ovens where the pies are stewing, hissing, and spluttering in their own luscious gravy.

There is but one man, too, throughout all the place, and he is sitting on a low three-legged stool in one corner, with his head resting upon his hands, and gently rocking to and fro, as he utters scarcely audible moans.

He is but lightly clad; in fact, he seems to have but little on him except a shirt and a pair of loose canvas trousers. The sleeves of the former are turned up beyond his elbows, and on his head he has a white night-cap.

It seems astonishing that such a man, even with the assistance of Mrs Lovett, could make so many pies as are required in a day; but the system does wonders, and in those cellars there are various mechanical contrivances for kneading the dough, chopping up the meat, &c., which greatly reduce the labour.

But what a miserable object is this man—what a sad and soul-stricken wretch he looks! His face is pale and haggard, his eyes deeply sunken; and, as he removes his hands from before his visage, and looks about him, a more perfect picture of horror could not have been found.

'I must leave to-night,' he said, in coarse accents—'I must leave to-night. I know too much—my brain is full of horrors. I have not slept now for five nights, nor dare I eat anything but the raw flour. I will leave tonight if they do not watch me too closely. Oh! if I could but get into the streets—if I could but once again breathe the fresh air! Hush! what's that? I thought I heard a noise.'

He rose, and stood trembling and listening; but all was still, save the simmering and hissing of the pies, and then he resumed his seat with a deep sigh.

'All the doors fastened upon me,' he said, 'what can it mean? It's very horrible, and my heart dies within me. Six weeks only have I been here—only six weeks. I was starving before I came. Alas, alas! how much better to have starved! I should have been dead before now, and spared all this agony!'

'Skinner!' cried a voice, and it was a female one—'Skinner, how long will the ovens be?'

'A quarter of an hour,' he replied, 'a quarter of an hour, Mrs Lovett. God help me!'

'What is that you say?'

'I said, God help me! surely a man may say that without offence.'

A door slammed shut, and the miserable man was alone again.

'How strangely,' he said, 'on this night my thoughts go back to early days, and to what I once was. The pleasant scenes of my youth recur to me. I see again the ivy-mantled porch, and the pleasant green. I hear again the merry ringing laughter of my playmates, and there, in my mind's eye, appears to me, the bubbling stream, and the ancient mill, the old mansion-house, with its tall turrets, and its air of silent grandeur. I hear the music of the birds, and the winds making rough melody among the trees. 'Tis very strange that all these sights and sounds should come back to me at such a time as this, as if just to remind me what a wretch I am.'

He was silent for a few moments, during which he trembled with emotion; then he spoke again, saying, —

'Thus the forms of those whom I once knew, and many of whom have gone already to the silent tomb, appear to come thronging round me. They bend their eyes momentarily upon me, and, with settled expressions, show acutely the sympathy they feel for me.

'I see her, too, who first, in my bosom, lit up the flame of soft affection. I see her gliding past me like the dim vision of a dream, indistinct, but beautiful; no more than a shadow—and yet to me most palpable. What am I now—what am I now?'

He resumed his former position, with his head resting upon his hands; he rocked himself slowly to and fro, uttering those moans of a tortured spirit, which we have before noticed.

But see, one of the small arch doors opens, in the gloom of those vaults, and a man, in a stooping posture, creeps in—a half-mask is upon his face, and he wears a cloak; but both his hands are at liberty. In one of them he carries a double-headed hammer, with a powerful handle, of about ten inches in length.

He has probably come out of a darker place than the one into which he now so cautiously creeps, for he shades the light from his eyes, as if it was suddenly rather too much for him, and then he looks cautiously round the vault, until he sees the crouched-up figure of the man whose duty it is to attend to the ovens.

From that moment he looks at nothing else; but advances towards him, steadily and cautiously. It is evident that great secrecy is his object, for he is walking on his stocking soles only; and it is impossible to hear the slightest sound of his footsteps. Nearer and nearer he comes, so slowly, and yet so surely towards him, who still keeps up the low moaning sound, indicative of mental anguish. Now he is close to him, and he bends over him for a moment, with a look of fiendish malice. It is a look which, despite his mask, glances full from his eyes, and then, grasping the hammer tightly in both hands, he raises it slowly above his head, and gives it a swinging motion through the air.

There is no knowing what induced the man that was crouching upon the stool to rise at that moment; but he did so, and paced about with great quickness.

A sudden shriek burst from his lips, as he beheld so terrific an apparition before him; but, before he could repeat the word, the hammer descended, crushing into his skull, and he fell lifeless without a moan.

*     *     *     *     *

'And so Mr Jarvis Williams, you have kept your word,' said Mrs Lovett to the emaciated, care-worn stranger, who had solicited employment of her, 'and so Mr Jarvis Williams, you have kept your word, and come for employment.'

'I have, madam, and hope that you can give it to me: I frankly tell you that I would seek for something better, and more congenial to my disposition if I could; but who would employ one presenting such a wretched appearance as I do? You see that I am all in rags, and I have told you that I have been half starved, and therefore it is only some common and ordinary employment that I can hope to get, and that made me come to you.'

'Well, I don't see why we should not make a trial of you, at all events, so if you like to go down into the bakehouse, I will follow you, and show you what you have to do. You remember that you have to live entirely upon the pies, unless you like to purchase for yourself anything else, which you may do if you can get the money. We give none, and you must likewise agree never to leave the bake-house.'

'Never to leave it?'

'Never, unless you leave it for good, and for all; if upon those conditions you choose to accept the situation, you may, and if not you can go about your business at once, and leave it alone.'

'Alas, madam, I have no resource; but you spoke of having a man already.'

'Yes; but he has gone to some of his very oldest friends, who will be quite glad to see him, so now say the word:—Are you willing or are you not, to take the situation?'

'My poverty and my destitution consent, if my will be adverse,* Mrs Lovett; but, of course, I quite understand that I leave when I please.'

'Oh, of course, we never think of keeping anybody many hours after they begin to feel uncomfortable. If you are ready, follow me.'

'I am quite ready, and thankful for a shelter. All the brightest visions of my early life have long since faded away, and it matters little or, indeed, nothing what now becomes of me; I will follow you, madam, freely upon the condition you have mentioned.'

Mrs Lovett lifted up a portion of the counter which permitted him to pass behind it, and then he followed her into a small room, which was at the back of the shop. She then took a key from her pocket, and opened an old door which was in the wainscoting, and immediately behind which was a flight of stairs.

These she descended, and Jarvis Williams followed her, to a considerable depth, after which she took an iron bar from behind another door, and flung it open, showing to her new assistant the interior of that vault which we have already very briefly described.

'These,' she said, 'are the ovens, and I will proceed to show you how you can manufacture the pies, feed the furnaces, and make yourself generally useful. Flour will be always let down through a trap-door from the upper shop, as well as everything required for making the pies but the meat, and that you will always find ranged upon shelves either in lumps or steaks, in a small room through this door, but it is only at particular times you will find the door open; and whenever you do so, you had better always take out what meat you think you will require for the next batch.'

'I understand all that, madam,' said Williams, 'but how does it get there?'

'That's no business of yours; so long as you are supplied with it, that is sufficient for you; and now I will go through the process of making one pie, so that you may know how to proceed, and you will find with what amazing quickness they can be manufactured if you set about them in the proper manner.'

She then showed how a piece of meat thrown into a machine became finely minced up, by merely turning a handle; and then how flour and water and lard were mixed up together, to make the crusts of the pies, by another machine, which threw out the paste, thus manufactured, in small pieces, each just large enough for a pie.

Lastly, she showed him how a tray, which just held a hundred, could be filled, and, by turning a windlass, sent up to the shop, through a square trap-door, which went right up to the very counter.

'And now,' she said, 'I must leave you. As long as you are industrious, you will get on very well, but as soon as you begin to be idle, and neglect the orders that are sent to you by me, you will get a piece of information which will be useful, and which, if you are a prudent man, will enable you to know what you are about.'

'What is that? you may as well give it to me now.'

'No; we but seldom find there is occasion for it at first, but, after a time, when you get well fed, you are pretty sure to want it.'

So saying, she left the place, and he heard the door, by which he had entered, carefully barred after her. Suddenly then he heard her voice again, and so clearly and distinctly, too, that he thought she must have come back again; but, upon looking up at the door, he found that that arose from the fact of her speaking through a small grating at the upper part of it, to which her mouth was closely placed.

'Remember your duty,' she said, 'and I warn you that any attempt to leave here will be as futile as it will be dangerous.'

'Except with your consent, when I relinquish the situation.'

'Oh, certainly—certainly, you are quite right there, everybody who relinquishes the situation, goes to his old friends, whom he has not seen for many years, perhaps.'

'What a strange manner of talking she has!' said Jarvis Williams to himself, when he found he was alone. 'There seems to be some singular and hidden meaning in every word she utters. What can she mean by a communication being made to me, if I neglect my duty! It is very strange, and what a singular-looking place this is! I think it would be quite unbearable if it were not for the delicious odour of the pies, and they are indeed delicious—perhaps more delicious to me, who has been famished so long, and has gone through so much wretchedness; there is no one here but myself, and I am hungry now—frightfully hungry, and whether the pies are done or not, I'll have half a dozen of them at any rate, so here goes.'

He opened one of the ovens, and the fragrant steam that came out was perfectly delicious, and he sniffed it up with a satisfaction such as he had never felt before, as regarded anything that was eatable.

'Is it possible,' he said, 'that I shall be able to make such delicious pies? at all events one can't starve here, and if it is a kind of imprisonment, it's a pleasant one. Upon my soul, they are nice, even half-cooked—delicious! I'll have another half-dozen, there are lots of them—delightful! I can't keep the gravy from running out of the corners of my mouth. Upon my soul, Mrs Lovett, I don't know where you get your meat, but it's all as tender as young chickens, and the fat actually melts away in one's mouth. Ah, these are pies, something like pies!—they are positively fit for the gods!'

Mrs Lovett's new man ate twelve threepenny pies, and then he thought of leaving off. It was a little drawback not to have anything to wash them down with but cold water, but he reconciled himself to this. 'For,' as he said, 'after all it would be a pity to take the flavour of such pies out of one's mouth—indeed, it would be a thousand pities, so I won't think of it, but just put up with what I have got and not complain. I might have gone further and fared worse with a vengeance, and I cannot help looking upon it as a singular piece of good fortune that made me think of coming here in my deep distress to try and get something to do. I have no friends, and no money; she whom I loved is faithless, and here I am, master of as many pies as I like, and to all appearance monarch of all I survey; for there really seems to be no one to dispute my supremacy.

'To be sure, my kingdom is rather a gloomy one; but then I can abdicate it when I like, and when I am tired of those delicious pies, if such a thing be possible, which I really very much doubt, I can give up my situation and think of something else.

'If I do that I will leave England for ever; it's no place for me after the many disappointments I have had. No friend left me, my girl false, not a relation but who would turn his back upon me! I will go somewhere where I am unknown and can form new connections, and perhaps make new friendships of a more permanent and stable character than the old ones, which have all proved so false to me; and, in the meantime, I'll make and eat pies as fast as I can.'

## 12

## *The Resolution Come to by Johanna Oakley*

THE beautiful Johanna—when in obedience to the command of her father she left him, and begged him (the beef-eater) to manage matters with the Rev Mr Lupin—did not proceed directly upstairs to the apartment, but lingered on the staircase to hear what ensued; and if anything in her dejected state of mind could have given her amusement, it would certainly have been the way in which the beef-eater exacted a retribution from the reverend personage, who was not likely again to intrude himself into the house of the spectacle-maker.

But when he was gone, and she heard that a sort of peace had been patched up with her mother—a peace which, from her knowledge of the high-contracting parties, she conjectured would not last long—she returned to her room, and locked herself in; so that if any attempt was made to get her down to partake of the supper, it might be supposed she was asleep, for she felt herself totally unequal to the task of making one in any party, however much she might respect the individual members that composed it.

And she did respect Ben the beef-eater; for she had a lively recollection of much kindness from him during her early years, and she knew that he had never come to the house when she was a child without bringing her some token of his regard in the shape of a plaything, or some little article of doll's finery, which at that time was very precious.

———————

She was not wrong in her conjecture that Ben would make an attempt to get her downstairs, for her father came up at the beef-eater's request, and tapped at her door. She thought the best plan, as indeed it was, would be to make no answer, so that the old spectacle-maker concluded at once what she wished him to conclude, namely that she had gone to sleep; and he walked quietly down the stairs again, glad that he had not disturbed her, and told Ben as much.

Now feeling herself quite secure from interruption for the night, Johanna did not attempt to seek repose, but set herself seriously to reflect upon what had happened. She almost repeated to herself, word for word, what Colonel Jeffery had told her; and, as she revolved the matter over and over again in her brain, a strange thought took possession of her, which she could not banish, and which, when once it found a home within her breast, began to gather probability from every slight circumstance that was in any way connected with it. This thought, strange as it may appear, was that the Mr Thornhill, of whom Colonel Jeffery spoke in terms of such high eulogium, was no other than Mark Ingestrie himself.

It is astonishing, when once a thought occurs to the mind, that makes a strong impression, how, with immense rapidity, a rush of evidence will appear to come to support it. And thus it was with regard to this supposition of Johanna Oakley.

She immediately remembered a host of little things which favoured the idea, and among the rest, she fully recollected that Mark Ingestrie had told her he meant to change his name when he left England; for that he wished her and her only to know anything of him, or what had become of him; and that his intention was to baffle enquiry, in case it should be made, particularly by Mr Grant, towards whom he felt a far greater amount of indignation, than the circumstances at all warranted him in feeling.

Then she recollected all that Colonel Jeffery had said with regard to the gallant and noble conduct of this Mr Thornhill, and, girl-like, she thought that those high and noble qualities could surely belong to no one but her own lover, to such an extent; and that, therefore, Mr Thornhill and Mark Ingestrie must be one and the same person.

Over and over again, she regretted she had not asked Colonel Jeffery for a personal description of Mr Thornhill, for that would have settled all her doubts at once, and the idea that she had it still in her power to do so, in consequence of the appointment he had made with her for that day week, brought her some consolation.

'It must have been he,' she said. 'His anxiety to leave the ship, and get here by the day he mentions, proves it; besides, how improbable it is, that at the burning of the ill-fated vessel, Ingestrie should place in the hands of another what he intended for me, when that other was quite as likely, and perhaps more so, to meet with death as Mark himself.'

Thus she reasoned, forcing herself each moment into a stronger belief of the identity of Thornhill with Mark Ingestrie, and so certainly narrowing her anxieties to a consideration of the fate of one person instead of two.

'I will meet Colonel Jeffery,' she said, 'and ask him if his Mr Thornhill had fair hair, and a soft and pleasing expression about the eyes, that could not fail to be remembered. I will ask him how he spoke, and how he looked; and get him, if he can, to describe to me, even the very tones of his voice; and then I shall be sure, without the shadow of a doubt, that it is Mark. But then, oh! then comes the anxious question, of what has been his fate?'

When poor Johanna began to consider the multitude of things that might have happened to her lover during his progress from Sweeney Todd's, in Fleet-street, to her father's house, she became quite lost in a perfect maze of conjecture, and then her thoughts always painfully reverted back to the barber's shop where the dog had been stationed; and she trembled to reflect for a moment upon the frightful danger to which that string of pearls might have subjected him.

'Alas, alas!' she cried, 'I can well conceive that the man whom I saw attempting to poison the dog would be capable of any enormity. I saw his face but for a moment, and yet it was one never again to be forgotten. It was a face in which might be read cruelty and evil passions; besides, the man who would put an unoffending animal to a cruel death shows an absence of feeling, and a baseness of mind, which makes him capable of any crime he thinks he can commit with impunity. What can I do—oh! what can I do to unravel this mystery?'

No one could have been more tenderly and more gently brought up than Johanna Oakley, but yet, inhabitive of her heart was a spirit and a determination which few indeed could have given her credit for, by merely looking on the gentle and affectionate countenance which she ordinarily presented.

But it is no new phenomenon in the history of the human heart to find that some of the most gentle and loveliest of human creatures are capable of the highest efforts of perversion; and when Johanna Oakley told herself, which she did, she was determined to devote her existence to a discovery of the mystery that enveloped the fate of Mark Ingestrie, she likewise made up her mind that the most likely means for accomplishing that object should not be rejected by her on the score of danger, and she at once set to work considering what those means should be.

This seemed an endless task, but still she thought that if, by any means whatever, she could get admittance to the barber's house, she might be able to come to some conclusion as to whether or not it was there where Thornhill, whom she believed to be Ingestrie, had been stayed in his progress.

'Aid me Heaven,' she cried, 'in the adoption of some means of action on the occasion. Is there anyone with whom I dare advise? Alas! I fear not, for the only person in whom I have put my whole heart is my father, and his affection for me would prompt him at once to interpose every possible obstacle to my proceeding, for fear danger should come of it. To be sure, there is Arabella Wilmot, my old school fellow and bosom friend, she would advise me to the best of her ability, but I much fear she is too romantic and full of odd, strange notions, that she has taken from books, to be a good adviser; and yet what can I do? I must speak to someone, if it be but in case of any accident happening to me, my father may get news of it, and I know of no one else whom I can trust but Arabella.'

After some little more consideration, Johanna made up her mind that on the following morning she would go immediately to the house of her old school friend, which was in the immediate vicinity, and hold a conversation with her.

'I shall hear something,' she said, 'at least of a kindly and consoling character; for what Arabella may want in calm and steady judgement, she fully compensates for in actual feeling; and what is most of all, I know I can trust her word implicitly, and that my secret will remain as safely locked in her breast as if it were in my own.'

It was something to come to a conclusion to ask advice, and she felt that some portion of her anxiety was lifted from her mind by the mere fact that she had made so firm a mental resolution, that neither danger nor difficulty should deter her from seeking to know the fate of her lover.

She retired to rest now with a greater hope, and while she is courting repose, notwithstanding the chance of the discovered images that fancy may present to her in her slumbers, we will take a glance at the parlour below, and see how far Mrs Oakley is conveying out the pacific intention she had so tacitly expressed, and how the supper is going forward, which, with not the best grace in the world, she is preparing for her husband, who for the first time in his life had begun to assert his rights, and for Big Ben, the beefeater, whom she as cordially disliked as it was possible for any woman to detest any man.

Mrs Oakley by no means preserved her taciturn demeanour, for after a little while she spoke, saying—'There is nothing tasty in the house; suppose I run over the way to Waggarge's, and get some of those Epping sausages with the peculiar flavour.'

'Ah, do,' said Mr Oakley, 'they are beautiful, Ben, I can assure you.'

'Well, I don't know,' said Ben, the beef-eater, 'sausages are all very well in their way, but you need such a plagued lot of them; for if you only eat them one at a time, how soon will you get through a dozen or two?'

'A dozen or two,' said Mrs Oakley; 'why, there are only five to a pound.'

'Then,' said Ben, making a mental calculation, 'then, I think, ma'am, you ought not to get more than nine pounds of them, and that will be a matter of forty-five mouthfuls for us.'

'Get nine pounds of them,' said Mr Oakley, 'if they are wanted; I know Ben has an appetite.'

'Indeed,' said Ben, 'but I have fell off lately, and don't take to my wittals as I used; you can order, missus, if you please, a gallon of half-and-half as you go along. One must have a drain of drink of some sort; and mind you don't be going to any expense on my account, and getting anything but the little snack I have mentioned, for ten to one I shall take supper when I get to the Tower; only human nature is weak, you know, missus, and requires something to be a continually a-holding of it up.'

'Certainly,' said Mr Oakley, 'certainly have what you like, Ben; just say the word before Mrs Oakley goes out, is there anything else?'

'No, no,' said Ben, 'oh dear no, nothing to speak of; but if you should pass a shop where they sells fat bacon, about four or five pounds, cut into rashers, you'll find, missus, will help down the blessed sausages.'

'Gracious Providence,' said Mrs Oakley, 'who is to cook it?'

'Who is to cook it, ma'am? why, the kitchen fire, I suppose; but mind ye if the man ain't got any sausages, there's a shop where they sells biled beef at the corner, and I shall be quite satisfied if you brings in about ten or twelve pounds of that. You can make it up into about half a dozen sandwiches.'

'Go, my dear, go at once,' said Mr Oakley, 'and get Ben his supper. I am quite sure he wants it, and be as quick as you can.'

'Ah,' said Ben, when Mrs Oakley was gone, 'I didn't tell you how I was sarved last week at Mrs Harvey's. You know they are so precious genteel there that they won't speak above their blessed breaths for fear of wearing themselves out; and they sits down in a chair as if it was balanced only on one leg, and a little more one way or t'other would upset them. Then, if they sees a crumb a-laying on the floor they rings a bell, and a poor half-starved devil of a servant comes and says, "Did you ring, ma'am?" and then they says, "Yes, bring a dust shovel and a broom, there is a crumb a-laying there," and then says I—"Damn you all," says I, "bring a scavenger's cart, and a half-dozen birch brooms, there's a cinder just fell out of the fire."

'Then in course they gets shocked, and looks as blue as possible, and arter that when they sees as I ain't a-going, one of them says, "Mr Benjamin Blumergutts, would you like to take a glass of wine?" "I should think so," says I. Then he says, says he, "Which would you prefer, red or white?" says he.

' "White," says I, "while you are screwing up your courage to pull out the red," so out they pull it; and as soon as I got hold of the bottle, I knocked the neck of it off over the top of the fireplace, and then drank it all up.

' "Now, damn ye," says I, "you thinks as all this is mighty genteel and fine, but I don't, and consider you to be the blessedest set of humbugs ever I set eyes on; and, if you ever catch me here again, I'll be genteel too, and I can't say more than that. Go to the devil, all of ye." So out I went, only I met with a little accident in the hall, for they had got a sort of lamp hanging there, and, somehow or 'nother, my head went bang into it; and I carried it out round my neck; but, when I did get out, I took it off, and shied it slap in at the parlour window. You never heard such a smash in all your life. I dare say they all fainted away for about a week, the blessed humbugs.'

'Well, I should not wonder,' said Mr Oakley. 'I never go near them, because I don't like their foolish pomposity and pride, which, upon very slender resources, tries to ape what it don't at all under-stand; but here is Mrs Oakley with the sausages, and I hope you will make yourself comfortable, Ben.'

'Comfortable! I believe ye. I rather shall. I means it, and no mistake.'

'I have brought three pounds,' said Mrs Oakley, 'and told the man to call in a quarter of an hour, in case there is more wanted.'

'The devil you have; and the bacon, Mrs Oakley, the bacon!'

'I couldn't get any—the man had nothing but hams.'

'Lor', ma'am, I'd a put up with a ham, cut thick, and never have said a word about it. I am an angel of a temper, if you did but know it! Hilloa, look, is that the fellow with the half-and-half?'

'Yes, here it is—a pot.'

'A what!'

'A pot, to be sure.'

'Well, I never; you are getting genteel, Mrs Oakley. Then give us a hold of it.'

Ben took the pot, and emptied it at a draught, and then he gave a tap at the bottom of it with his knuckles, to signify he had accomplished that feat, and then he said, 'I tells you what, ma'am, if you takes me for a baby, it's a great mistake, and anyone would think you did, to see you offering me a pot merely; it's a insult, ma'am.'

'Fiddle-de-de,' said Mrs Oakley; 'it's a much greater insult to drink it all up, and give nobody a drop.'

'Is it? I wants to know how you are to stop it, ma'am, when you gets it to your mouth? that's what I axes you—how are you to stop it, ma'am? You didn't want me to spew it back again, did you, eh, ma'am?'

'You low, vile wretch.'

'Come, come, my dear,' said Mr Oakley, 'you know our cousin Ben don't live among the most refined society, and so you ought to be able to look over a little of—of—his—I may say, I am sure without offence, roughness, now and then;—come, come, there is no harm done, I'm sure. Forget and forgive, say I. That's my maxim; and always has been, and will always be.'

'Well,' said the beef-eater, 'it's a good one to get through the world with, and so there's an end of it. I forgives you, Mother Oakley.'

'You forgive—'

'Yes, to be sure. Though I am only a beef-eater, I supposes as I may forgive people for all that—eh, Cousin Oakley?'

'Oh, of course, Ben, of course. Come, come, wife, you know as well as I that Ben has many good qualities, and that take him for all in all as the man in the play says, we shan't in a hurry look upon his like again.'*

'And I'm sure I don't want to look upon his like again,' said Mrs Oakley; 'I'd rather by a good deal keep him a week than a fortnight. He's enough to breed a famine in the land, that he is.'

'Oh, bless you, no,' said Ben, 'that's amongst your little mistakes, ma'am, I can assure you. By-the-by, what a blessed long time that fellow is coming with the rest of the beer and the other sausages—why, what's the matter with you, Cousin Oakley—eh, old chap, you look out of sorts?'

'I don't feel just the thing, do you know, Ben.'

'Not—the thing—why—why now you come to mention it, I some-how feel as if all my blessed inside was on a turn and a twist. The devil—I—don't feel comfortable at all, I don't.'

'And I am getting very ill,' gasped Mr Oakley.

'And I'm getting iller,' said the beef-eater, manufacturing a word for the occasion. 'Bless my soul! there's something gone wrong in my inside. I know there's murder—there's a go—oh, Lord! it's a-doubling me up, it is.'

'I feel as if my last hour had come,' said Mr Oakley—'I'm a—a—dying, man—I am—oh, good gracious, there was a twinge!'

Mrs Oakley, with all the coolness in the world, took down her bonnet from behind the parlour-door where it hung, and, as she put it on, said,—

'I told you both that some judgement would come over you, and now you see it has. How do you like it? Providence is good, of course, to its own, and I have—'

'What—what—?'

'*Pisoned* the half-and-half.'

Big Ben, the beef-eater, fell off his chair with a deep groan, and poor Mr Oakley sat glaring at his wife, and shivering with appre-hension, quite unable to speak, while she placed a shawl over her shoulder, as she added, in the same tone of calmness she had made the terrific announcement concerning the poisoning,—

'Now, you wretches, you see what a woman can do when she makes up her mind for vengeance. As long as you all live, you'll recollect me; but if you don't, that won't much matter, for you won't live long, I can tell you, and now I'm going to my sister's, Mrs Tiddiblow.'

So saying, Mrs Oakley turned quickly round, and, with an insult-ing toss of her head, and not at all caring for the pangs and suffer-ings of her poor victims, she left the place, and proceeded to her sister's house, where she slept as comfortably as if she had not by any means committed two diabolical murders.

But has she done so, or shall we, for the honour of human nature, discover that she went to a neighbouring chemist's, and only pur-chased some dreadfully powerful medicinal compound, which she placed in the half-and-half, and which began to give those pangs to Big Ben, the beef-eater, and to Mr Oakley, concerning which they were so eloquent?

This must have been the case; for Mrs Oakley could not have been such a fiend in human guise as to laugh as she passed the chemist's shop. Oh no! she might not have felt remorse, but that is a very different thing, indeed, from laughing at the matter, unless it were really laughable and not serious, at all.

Big Ben and Mr Oakley must have at length found out how they had been hoaxed, and the most probable thing was that the before-mentioned chemist himself told them; for they sent for him in order to know if anything could be done to save their lives.

Ben from that day forthwith made a determination that he would not visit Mr Oakley, and the next time they met he said, —

'I tell you what it is, that old hag your wife is one too many for us, that's a fact; she gets the better of me altogether—so, whenever you feels a little inclined for a gossip about old times, just you come down to the Tower.'

'I will, Ben.'

'Do; we can always find you something to drink, and you can amuse yourself, too, by looking at the animals. Remember feeding time is two o'clock; so, now and then, I shall expect to see you, and, above all, be sure you let me know if that canting parson, Lupin, comes any more to your house.'

'I will, Ben.'

'Ah, do; and I'll give him another lesson if he should, and I'll tell you how I'll do it. I'll get a free admission to the wild *beastesses* in the Tower, and when he comes to see 'em, for them 'ere sort of fellows always goes everywhere they can go for nothing, I'll just manage to pop him into a cage along of some of the most *cantankerous* creatures as we have.'

'But would that not be dangerous?'

'Oh dear no! we has a laughing hyena as would frighten him out of his wits; but I don't think as he'd bite him much, do you know. He's as playful as a kitten, and very fond of standing on his head.'

'Well, then, Ben, I have, of course, no objection, although I do think that the lesson you have already given to the reverend gentleman will and ought to be fully sufficient for all purposes, and I don't expect we shall see him again.'

'But how does Mrs O. behave to you?' asked Ben.

'Well, Ben, I don't think there's much difference; sometimes she's a little civil, and sometimes she ain't; it's just as she takes into her head.'

'Ah! all that comes of marrying.'

'I have often wondered, though, Ben, that you never married.'

Ben gave a chuckle as he replied,—

'Have you, though, really? Well, Cousin Oakley, I don't mind telling you, but the real fact is, once I was very near being served out in that sort of way.'

'Indeed!'

'Yes. I'll tell you how it was: there was a girl called Angelina Day, and a nice-looking enough creature she was as you'd wish to see, and didn't seem as if she'd got any claws at all; leastways, she kept them in, like a cat at meal times.'

'Upon my word, Ben, you have a great knowledge of the world.'

'I believe you, I have! Haven't I been brought up among the wild beasts in the Tower all my life? That's the place to get a knowledge of the world in, my boy. I ought to know a thing or two, and in course I does.'

'Well, but how was it, Ben, that you did not marry this Angelina you speak of?'

'I'll tell you; she thought she had me as safe as a hare in a trap, and she was as amiable as a lump of cotton. You'd have thought, to look at her, that she did nothing but smile; and, to hear her, that she said nothing but nice, mild, pleasant things, and I really began to think as I had found the proper sort of animal.'

'But you were mistaken?'

'I believe you, I was. One day I'd been there to see her, I mean, at her father's house, and she'd been as amiable as she could be; I got up to go away, with a determination that the next time I got there I would ask her to say yes, and when I had got a little way out of the garden of the house where they lived—it was out of town some distance—I found I had left my little walking-cane behind me, so I goes back to get it, and when I got into the garden, I heard a voice.'

'Whose voice?'

'Why Angelina's to be sure; she was a-speaking to a poor little dab of a servant they had; and oh, my eye! how she did rap out, to be sure! Such a speech as I never heard in all my life. She went on for a matter of ten minutes without stopping, and every other word was some ill name or another, and her voice—oh, gracious! it was like a bundle of wire all of a tangle—it was.'

'And what did you do, then, upon making such a discovery as that in so very odd and unexpected a manner?'

'Do? What do you suppose I did?'

'I really cannot say, as you are rather an eccentric fellow.'

'Well then, I'll tell you. I went up to the house, and just popped in my head, and says I, "Angelina, I find out that all cats have claws after all; good-evening, and no more from your humble servant, who don't mind the job of taming a wild animal, but a woman;" and then off I walked, and I never heard of her afterwards.'

'Ah, Ben, it's true enough! You never know them beforehand; but, after a little time, as you say, then out come the claws.'

'They does—they does.'

'And I suppose you since then made up your mind to be a bachelor for the rest of your life, Ben?'

'Of course I did. After such experience as that I should have deserved all I got, and no mistake, I can tell you; and if you ever catches me paying any attention to a female woman, just put me in mind of Angelina Day, and you'll see how I shall be off at once like a shot.'

'Ah!' said Mr Oakley, with a sigh, 'everybody, Ben, ain't born with your good luck, I can tell you. You are a most fortunate man, Ben, and that's a fact. You must have been born under some lucky planet I think, Ben, or else you never would have had such a warning as you have had about the claws. I found 'em out, Ben, but it was a deal too late; so I had to put up with my fate, and put the best face I could upon the matter.'

'Yes, that's what learned folks call—what's its name—fill—fill—something.'

'Philosophy, I suppose you mean, Ben.'

'Ah, that's it—you must put up with what you can't help, it means, I take it. It's a fine name for saying you must grin and bear it.'

'I suppose that is about the truth, Ben.'

It cannot, however, be exactly said that the little incident connected with Mr Lupin had no good effect upon Mrs Oakley, for it certainly shook most alarmingly her confidence in that pious individual.

In the first place, it was quite clear that he shrank from the horrors of martyrdom; and, indeed, to escape any bodily inconvenience was perfectly willing to put up with any amount of degradation or humiliation that he could be subjected to; and that was, to the apprehension of Mrs Oakley, a great departure from what a saint ought to be.

Then again, her faith in the fact that Mr Lupin was such a chosen morsel as he had represented himself, was shaken from the circumstance that no miracle in the shape of a judgement had taken place to save him from the malevolence of Big Ben, the beef-eater; so that, taking one thing in connection with another, Mrs Oakley was not near so religious a character after that evening as she had been before it, and that was something gained.

Then circumstances soon occurred, of which the reader will very shortly be fully aware, which were calculated to awaken all the feelings of Mrs Oakley, if she really had any feelings to awaken, and to force her to make common cause with her husband in an affair that touched him to the very soul, and did succeed in awakening some feelings in her heart that had lain dormant for a long time, but which were still far from being completely destroyed.

These circumstances were closely connected with the fate of one in whom we hope that, by this time, the reader has taken a deep and kindly interest—we mean Johanna—that young and beautiful, and artless creature, who seemed to have been created to be so very happy, and yet whose fate had become so clouded by misfortune, and who appears now to be doomed through her best affections to suffer so great an amount of sorrow, and to go through so many sad difficulties.

Alas, poor Johanna Oakley! Better had you loved someone of less aspiring feelings, and of less ardent imagination, than him to whom you have given your heart's young affections.

It is true that Mark Ingestric possessed genius, and perhaps it was the glorious light that hovers around that fatal gift which prompted you to love him. But genius is not only a blight and a desolation to its possessor, but it is so to all who are bound to the gifted being by the ties of fond affection.

It brings with it that unhappy restlessness of intellect which is ever straining after the unattainable, and which is never content to know the end and ultimatum of earthly hopes and wishes; no, the whole life of such persons is spent in one long struggle for a fancied happiness, which like the *ignis-fatuus* of the swamp* glitters but to betray those who trust to its delusive and flickering beams.

# 13

## Johanna's Interview with Arabella Wilmot, and the Advice

ALAS! poor Johanna, thou hast chosen but an indifferent confidante in the person of that young and inexperienced girl to whom it seems good to thee to impart thy griefs.

Not for one moment do we mean to say, that the young creature to whom the spectacle-maker's daughter made up her mind to unbosom herself was not all that anyone could wish as regards honour, goodness, and friendship. But she was one of those creatures who yet look upon the world as a fresh green garden, and have not yet lost that romance of existence which the world and its ways soon banish from the breasts of all.

She was young, almost to girlhood, and having been the idol of her family circle, she knew just about as little of the great world as a child.

But while we cannot but to some extent regret that Johanna should have chosen such a confidante and admirer, we with feelings of great freshness and pleasure proceed to accompany her to that young girl's house.

Now, a visit from Johanna Oakley to the Wilmots was not so rare a thing, that it should excite any unusual surprise, but in this case it did excite unusual pleasure because she had not been there for some time.

And the reason she had not may well be found in the peculiar circumstances that had for a considerable period environed her. She had a secret to keep which, although it might not proclaim what it was most legibly upon her countenance, yet proclaimed that it had an existence, and as she had not made Arabella a confidante, she dreaded the other's friendly questions of the young creature.

It may seem surprising that Johanna Oakley had kept from one whom she so much esteemed, and with whom she had made such a friendship, the secret of her affections; but that must be accounted for by a difference of ages between them to a sufficient extent in that early period of life to show itself palpably.

That difference was not quite two years, but when we likewise state, that Arabella was of that small, delicate style of beauty which makes her look like a child, when even upon the verge of womanhood, we shall not be surprised that the girl of seventeen hesitated to confide a secret of the heart to what seemed but a beautiful child.

The last year, however, had made a great difference in the appearance of Arabella, for, although she still looked a year or so younger than she really was, a more staid and thoughtful expression had come over her face, and she no longer presented, except at times when she laughed, that child-like expression, which had been as remarkable in her as it was delightful.

She was as different looking from Johanna as she could be, for whereas Johanna's hair was of a rich and glossy brown, so nearly allied to black that it was commonly called such, the long waving ringlets that shaded the sweet countenance of Arabella Wilmot were like amber silk blended to a pale beauty.

Her eyes were really blue, and not that pale grey, which courtesy calls of that celestial colour, and their long, fringing lashes hung upon a cheek of the most delicate and exquisite hue that nature could produce.

Such was the young, lovable, and amiable creature who had made one of those girlish friendships with Johanna Oakley that, when they do endure beyond the period of almost mere childhood, endure for ever, and become one among the most dear and cherished sensations of the heart.

The acquaintance had commenced at school, and might have been of that evanescent character of so many school friendships, which, in after life, are scarcely so much remembered as the most dim visions of a dream; but it happened that they were congenial spirits, which, let them be thrown together under any circumstances whatever, would have come together with a perfect and a most endearing confidence in each other's affections.

That they were school companions was the mere accident that brought them together, and not the cause of their friendship.

Such, then, was the being to whom Johanna Oakley looked for counsel and assistance; and notwithstanding all that we have said respecting the likelihood of that counsel being of an inactive and girlish character, we cannot withhold our meed of approbation to Johanna that she had selected one so much in every way worthy of her honest esteem.

The hour at which she called was such as to insure Arabella being within, and the pleasure which showed itself upon the countenance of the young girl, as she welcomed her old playmate, was a feeling of the most delightful and unaffecting character.

'Why, Johanna,' she said, 'you so seldom call upon me now, that I suppose I must esteem it as a very special act of grace and favour to see you.'

'Arabella,' said Johanna, 'I do not know what you will say to me when I tell you that my present visit to you is because I am in a difficulty, and want your advice.'

'Then you could not have come to a better person, for I have read all the novels in London, and know all the difficulties that anybody can possibly get into, and, what is more important, I know all the means of getting out of them, let them be what they may.'

'And yet, Arabella, scarcely in your novel reading will you find anything so strange and so eventful as the circumstances, I grieve to say, it is in my power to record to you. Sit down, and listen to me, dear Arabella, and you shall know all.'

'You surprise and alarm me by the serious countenance, Johanna.'

'The subject is a serious one. I love.'

'Oh! is that all? So do I; there's young Captain Desbrook in the King's Guards. He comes here to buy his gloves; and if you did but hear him sigh as he leans over the counter, you would be astonished.'

'Ah! but, Arabella, I know you well. Yours is one of those fleeting passions that, like the forked lightning, appear for a moment, and ere you can say behold is gone again. Mine is deeper in my heart, so deep, that to divorce it from it would be to destroy its home for ever.'

'But why so serious, Johanna? You do not mean to tell me that it is possible for you to love any man without his loving you in return?'

'You are right there, Arabella. I do not come to speak to you of a hopeless passion—far from it; but you shall hear. Lend me, my dear friend, your serious attention, and you shall hear of such mysterious matters.'

'Mysterious? then I shall be in my very element. For know that I quite live and exult in mystery, and you could not possibly have come to anyone who would more welcomely receive such a commission from you; I am all impatience.'

Johanna then, with great earnestness, related to her friend the whole of the particulars connected with her deep and sincere attachment to Mark Ingestrie. She told her how, in spite of all circumstances which appeared to have a tendency to cast a shadow and a blight upon their young affection, they had loved and loved truly; how Ingestrie, disliking, both from principle and distaste, the study of the law, had quarrelled with his uncle, Mr Grant, and then how, as a bold adventurer, he had gone to seek his fortunes in the Indian seas, fortunes which promised to be splendid; but which might end in disappointment and defeat, and they had ended in such calamities most deeply and truly did she mourn to be compelled to state. And now she concluded by saying, —

'And now, Arabella, you know all I have to tell you. You know how truly I have loved, and how after teaching myself to expect happiness, I have met with nothing but despair; and you may judge for yourself, how sadly the fate of Mark Ingestrie must deeply affect me, and how lost my mind must be in all kinds of conjecture concerning him.'

The hilarity of spirits which had characterised Arabella, in the earlier part of their interview, entirely left her, as Johanna proceeded in her mournful narration, and by the time she had concluded, tears of the most genuine sympathy stood in her eyes.

She took the hands of Johanna in both her own, and said to her, —

'Why, my dear Johanna, I never expected to hear from your lips so sad a tale. This is most mournful, indeed very mournful; and although I was half inclined before to quarrel with you for this tardy confidence—for you must recollect that it is the first I have heard of this whole affair—but now the misfortunes that oppress you are quite sufficient, Heaven knows, without me adding to them by the shadow of a reproach.'

'They are indeed, Arabella, and believe me if the course of my love ran smoothly, instead of being, as it has been, full of misadventure, you should have had nothing to complain of on the score of want of confidence; but I will own I did hesitate to inflict upon you my miseries, for miseries they have been and alas! miseries they seem destined to remain.'

'Johanna, you could not have used an argument more delusive than that. It is not one which should have come from your lips to me.'

'But surely it was a good motive, to spare you pain?'

--------

'And did you think so lightly of my friendship that it was to be entrusted with nothing but what wore a pleasant aspect? True friendship is surely best shown in the encounter of difficulty and distress. I grieve, Johanna, indeed, that you have so much mistaken me.'

'Nay, now you do me an injustice: it was not that I doubted your friendship for one moment, but that I did indeed shrink from casting the shadow of my sorrows over what should be, and what I hope is, the sunshine of your heart. That was the respect which deterred me from making you aware of what I suppose I must call this ill-fated passion.'

'No, not ill-fated, Johanna. Let us believe that the time will come when it will be far otherwise than ill-fated.'

'But what do you think of all that I have told you? Can you gather from it any hope?'

'Abundance of hope, Johanna. You have no certainty of the death of Ingestrie.'

'I certainly have not, as far as regards the loss of him in the Indian sea; but, Arabella, there is one supposition which, from the moment it found a home in my breast, has been growing stronger and stronger, and that supposition is, that this Mr Thornhill was no other than Mark Ingestrie himself.'

'Indeed! Think you so? That would be a strange supposition. Have you any special reasons for such a thought?'

'None—further than a something which seemed ever to tell my heart from the first moment that such was the case, and a consideration of the improbability of the story related by Thornhill. Why should Mark Ingestrie have given him the string of pearls and the message to me, trusting to the preservation of this Thornhill, and assuming, for some strange reason, that he himself must fall?'

'There is good argument in that, Joanna.'

'And moreover Mark Ingestrie told me he intended altering his name upon the expedition.'

'It is strange; but now you mention such a supposition, it appears, do you know, Johanna, each moment more probable to me. Oh, that fatal string of pearls.'

'Fatal, indeed! for if Mark Ingestrie and Thornhill be one and the same person, the possession of those pearls has been the temptation to destroy him.'

'There cannot be a doubt upon that point, Johanna, and so you will find in all the tales of love and romance, that jealousy and wealth have been the sources of all the abundant evils which fond and attached hearts have from time to time suffered.'

'It is so; I believe, it is so, Arabella; but advise me what to do, for truly I am myself incapable of action. Tell me what you think it is possible to do, under these disastrous circumstances, for there is nothing which I will not dare attempt.'

'Why, my dear Johanna, you must perceive that all the evidence you have regarding this Thornhill follows him up to that barber's shop in Fleet-street, and no farther.'

'It does, indeed.'

'Can you not imagine, then, that there lies the mystery of his fate, and, from what you have yourself seen of that man, Todd, do you think he is one who would hesitate even at a murder?'

'Oh, horror! my own thoughts have taken that dreadful turn, but I dreaded to pronounce the word which would embody them. If, indeed, that fearful-looking man fancied that by any deed of blood he could become possessed of such a treasure as that which belonged to Mark Ingestrie, unchristian and illiberal as it may sound, the belief clings to me, that he would not hesitate to do it.'

'Do not, however, conclude, Johanna, that such is the case. It would appear, from all you have heard and seen of these circumstances, that there is some fearful mystery; but do not, Johanna, conclude hastily, that that mystery is one of death.'

'Be it so, or not,' said Johanna, 'I must solve it, or go distracted. Heaven have mercy upon me; for even now I feel a fever in my brain, that precludes almost the possibility of rational thought.'

'Be calm, be calm, we will think the matter over, calmly and seriously; and who knows but that, mere girls as we are, we may think of some adventitious mode of arriving at a knowledge of the truth; and now I am going to tell you something, which your narrative has recalled to my mind.'

'Say on, Arabella, I shall listen to you with deep attention.'

'A short time since, about six months, I think, an apprentice of my father, in the last week of his servitude, was sent to the west-end of the town to take a considerable sum of money; but he never came back with it, and from that day to this we have heard nothing of him, although from enquiry that my father made, he ascertained that he received the money, and that he met an acquaintance in the Strand, who parted from him at the corner of Milford-lane, and to whom he said he intended to call at Sweeney Todd, the barber's, in Fleet-street, to have his hair dressed, because there was to be a regatta on the Thames, and he was determined to go to it, whether my father liked or not.'

'And he was never heard of?'

'Never. Of course, my father made every enquiry upon the subject, and called upon Sweeney Todd for the purpose, but, as he declared that no such person had ever called at his shop, the inquiry there terminated.'

' 'Tis very strange.'

'And most mysterious; for the friends of the youth were indefatigable in their searches for him; and, by subscribing together for the purpose, they offered a large reward to anyone who could or would give them information regarding his fate.'

'And was it all in vain?'

'All; nothing could be learned whatever: not even the remotest clue was obtained, and there the affair has rested, in the most profound of mysteries.'

Johanna shuddered, and for some few moments the two young girls were silent. It was Johanna who broke that silence, by exclaiming, 'Arabella, assist me with what advice you can, so that I may go about what I purpose with the best prospect of success and the least danger; not that I shrink on my own account from risk; but if any misadventure were to occur to me, I might thereby be incapacitated from pursuing that object to which I will now devote the remainder of my life.'

'But what can you do, my dear Johanna? It was but a short time since there was a placard in the barber's window to say that he wanted a lad as an assistant in his business, but that has been removed, or we might have procured someone to take the situation, for the express purpose of playing the spy upon the barber's proceedings.'

'But, perchance, still there may be an opportunity of accomplishing something in that way, if you knew of anyone that would undertake the adventure.'

'There will be no difficulty, Johanna, in discovering one willing to do so, although we might be long in finding one of sufficient capacity that we could trust: but I am adventurous, Johanna, as you know, and I think I could have got my cousin Albert to personate the character, only that he's rather a giddy youth, and scarcely to be trusted with a mission of so much importance.'

'Yes, and a mission likewise, Arabella, which, by a single false step, might be made frightfully dangerous.'

'It might, indeed.'

'Then it would be unfair to place it upon anyone but those who feel most deeply for its success.'

'Johanna, the enthusiasm with which you speak awakens in me a thought which I shrank from expressing to you, and which, I fear, perhaps more originates from a certain feeling of romance, which, I believe, is a besetting sin, than from any other cause.'

'Name it, Arabella; name it.'

'It would be possible for you or I to accomplish the object, by going disguised to the barber's, and accepting such a situation, if it were vacant, for a period of about twenty-four hours, in order that during that time, some opportunity might be taken of searching in his house for some evidence upon the subject nearest to your heart.'

'It is a happy thought,' said Johanna, 'and why should I hesitate at encountering any risk or toil or difficulty for him who has risked so much for me? What is there to hinder me from carrying out such a resolution? At any moment, if great danger should beset me, I can rush into the street, and claim protection from the passers-by.'

'And, moreover, Johanna, if you went on with such a mission, remember you go with my knowledge, and that consequently I would bring you assistance, if you appeared not in the specified time for your return.'

'Each moment, Arabella, the plan assumes to my mind a better shape. If Sweeney Todd be innocent of contriving anything against the life and liberty of those who seek his shop, I have nothing to fear; but if, on the contrary he be guilty, danger to me would be the proof of such guilt, and that is a proof which I am willing to chance encountering for the sake of the great object I have in view; but how am I to provide myself with the necessary means?'

'Be at rest upon that score. My cousin Albert and you are as nearly of a size as possible. He will be staying here shortly, and I will secrete from his wardrobe a suit of clothes, which I am certain will answer your purpose. But let me implore you to wait until you have had your second interview with Colonel Jeffery.'

'That is well thought of. I will meet him, and question him closely as to the personal appearance of this Mr Thornhill; besides, I shall hear if he has any confirmed suspicion on the subject.'

'That is well, you will soon meet him, for the week is running on, and let me implore you, Johanna, to come to me the morning after you have met him, and then we will again consult upon this plan of operations, which appears to us feasible and desirable.'

Some more conversation of a similar character ensued between these young girls; and, upon the whole, Johanna Oakley felt much comforted by her visit, and more able to think calmly as well as seriously upon the subject which engrossed her whole thoughts and feelings; and when she returned to her own home, she found that much of the excitement of despair, which had formerly had possession of her, had given way to hope, and with that natural feeling of joyousness, and that elasticity of mind which belongs to the young, she began to build in her imagination some airy fabrics of future happiness.

Certainly, these suppositions went upon the fact that Mark Ingestrie was a prisoner, and not that his life had been taken by the mysterious barber; for although the possibility of his having been murdered had found a home in her imagination, still to her pure spirit it seemed by far too hideous to be true, and she scarcely could be said really and truly to entertain it as a matter which was likely to be true.

# 14

## *Tobias's Threat, and its Consequences*

PERHAPS one of the most pitiable objects now in our history is
poor Tobias, Sweeney Todd's boy, who certainly had his suspicions aroused in the most terrific manner, but who was terrified by
the threats of what the barber was capable of doing against his
mother, from making any disclosures.

The effect upon his personal appearance of this wear and tear of
his intellect was striking and manifest. The hue of youth and
health entirely departed from his cheeks, and he looked so sad
and care-worn, that it was quite a terrible thing to look upon a
young lad so, as it were, upon the threshold of existence, and in
whom anxious thoughts were making such war upon the physical
energies.

His cheeks were pale and sunken; his eyes had an unnatural
brightness about them, and, to look upon his lips, one would think
that they had never parted in a smile for many a day, so sadly were
they compressed together.

He seemed ever to be watching likewise for something fearful,
and even as he walked the streets, he would frequently turn, and
look enquiringly round him with a shudder, and in his brief interview with Colonel Jeffery and his friend the captain, we can have a
tolerably good impression of the state of his mind.

Oppressed with fears and all sorts of dreadful thoughts, panting
to give utterance to what he knew and to what he suspected, and
yet terrified into silence for his mother's sake, we cannot but view
him as signally entitled to the sympathy of the reader, and as, in all
respects, one sincerely to be pitied for the cruel circumstances in
which he was placed.

The sun is shining brightly, and even that busy region of trade
and commerce, Fleet-street, is looking gay and beautiful; but not
for that poor spirit-stricken lad are any of the sights and sounds
which used to make up the delight of his existence, reaching his
eyes or ears now with their accustomed force.

He sits moody and alone, and in the position which he always assumes when Sweeney Todd is from home—that is to say, with his head resting on his hands, and looking the picture of melancholy abstraction.

'What shall I do,' he said to himself, 'what will become of me! I think if I live here any longer, I shall go out of my senses. Sweeney Todd is a murderer—I am quite certain of it, and I wish to say so, but I dare not for my mother's sake. Alas! alas! the end of it will be that he will kill me, or that I shall go out of my senses, and then I shall die in some mad-house, and no one will care what I say.'

The boy wept bitterly after he had uttered these melancholy reflections, and he felt his tears something of a relief to him, so that he looked up after a little time, and glanced around him.

'What a strange thing,' he said, 'that people should come into this shop, to my certain knowledge, who never go out of it again, and yet what becomes of them I cannot tell.'

He looked with a shuddering anxiety towards the parlour, the door of which Sweeney Todd took care to lock always when he left the place, and he thought that he should like much to have a thorough examination of that room.

'I have been in it,' he said, 'and it seems full of cupboards and strange holes and corners, such as I never saw before, and there is an odd stench in it that I cannot make out at all; but it's out of the question thinking of ever being in it above a few minutes at a time, for Sweeney Todd takes good care of that.'

The boy rose, and opened a cupboard that was in the shop. It was perfectly empty.

'Now, that's strange,' he said; 'there was a walking-stick with an ivory top to it here just before he went out, and I could swear it belonged to a man who came in to be shaved. More than once—ah! and more than twice, too, when I have come in suddenly, I have seen people's hats, and Sweeney Todd would try and make me believe that people go away after being shaved and leave their hats behind them.'

He walked up to the shaving-chair, as it was called, which was a large old-fashioned piece of furniture, made of oak, and carved; and as the boy threw himself into it, he said, —

'What an odd thing it is that this chair is screwed so tight to the floor! Here is a complete fixture, and Sweeney Todd says that it is so because it's in the best possible light, and if he were not to make it fast in such a way, the customers would shift it about from place to place, so that he could not conveniently shave them; it may be true, but I don't know.'

'And you have your doubts,' said the voice of Sweeney Todd, as that individual, with a noiseless step, walked into the shop—'you have your doubts, Tobias? I shall have to cut your throat, that is quite clear.'

'No, no; have mercy upon me; I did not mean what I said.'

'Then it's uncommonly imprudent to say it, Tobias. Do you remember our last conversation? Do you remember that I can hang your mother when I please, because, if you do not, I beg to put you in mind of that pleasant little circumstance.'

'I cannot forget—I do not forget.'

''Tis well; and mark me, I will not have you assume such an aspect as you wear when I am not here. You don't look cheerful, Tobias; and notwithstanding your excellent situation, with little to do, and the number of Lovett's pies you eat, you fall away.'

'I cannot help it,' said Tobias. 'Since you told me what you did concerning my mother, I have been so anxious that I cannot help—'

'Why should you be so anxious? Her preservation depends upon yourself, and upon yourself wholly. You have but to keep silent, and she is safe; but if you utter one word that shall be displeasing to me about my affairs, mark me, Tobias, she comes to the scaffold; and if I cannot conveniently place you in the same mad-house where the last boy I had was placed, I shall certainly be under the troublesome necessity of cutting your throat.'

'I will be silent—I will say nothing, Mr Todd. I know I shall die soon, and then you will get rid of me altogether, and I don't care how soon that may be, for I am quite weary of my life—I shall be glad when it is over.'

'Very good,' said the barber; 'that's all a matter of taste. And now, Tobias, I desire that you look cheerful and smile, for a gentleman is outside feeling his chin with his hand, and thinking he may as well come in and be shaved. I may want you, Tobias, to go to Billingsgate, and bring me a pennyworth of shrimps.'

'Yes,' thought Tobias with a groan—'yes, while you murder him.'

## 15

## The Second Interview between Johanna and the Colonel in the Temple-gardens

Now that there was a great object to be gained by a second interview with Colonel Jeffery, the anxiety of Johanna Oakley to have it became extremely great, and she counted the very hours until the period should arrive when she could again proceed to the Temple-gardens with something like a certainty of finding him.

The object, of course, was to ask him for a description of Mr Thornhill, sufficiently accurate to enable her to come to something like a positive conclusion, as to whether she ought to call him to her own mind as Mark Ingestrie or not.

And Colonel Jeffery was not a bit the less anxious to see her, than she was to look upon him; for, although in diverse lands he had looked upon many a fair face, and heard many a voice that had sounded soft and musical to his ears, he had seen none that, to his mind, was so fair, and had heard no voice that he had considered really so musical and charming to listen to as Johanna Oakley's.

A man of more admirable and strict sense of honour than Colonel Jeffery could not have been found, and therefore it was that he allowed himself to admire the beautiful, under any circumstances, because he knew that his admiration was of no dangerous quality, but that, on the contrary, it was one of those feelings which might exist in a bosom such as his, quite undebased by a meaner influence.

We think it necessary, however, before he has his second interview with Johanna Oakley, to give such an explanation of his thoughts and feelings, as is in our power.

When first he met her, the purity of her mind, and the genuine and beautiful candour of all she said, struck him most forcibly, as well as her great beauty, which could not fail to be extremely manifest.

After that he began to reason with himself as to what ought to be his feelings with regard to her—namely, what portion of these ought to be suppressed, and what ought to be encouraged.

If Mark Ingestrie were dead, there was not a shadow of interference or dishonour in him, Colonel Jeffery, loving the beautiful girl, who was surely not to be shut out of the pale of all affections, because the first person to whom her heart had warmed, with a pure and holy passion, was no more.

'It may be,' he thought, 'that she is incapable of feeling a sentiment which can at all approach that which once she felt; but still she may be happy and serene, and may pass many joyous hours as the wife of another.'

He did not positively make these reflections, as applicable to himself, although they had a tendency that way, and he was fast verging on a state of mind which might induce him to give them a more actual application.

He did not tell himself that he loved her—no, the word 'admiration' took the place of the more powerful term; but then, can we not doubt that, at this time, the germ of a very pure and holy affection was lighted up in the heart of Colonel Jeffery, for the beautiful creature, who had suffered the pangs of so much disappointment, and who loved one so well, who, we almost fear, if he was living, was scarcely the sort of person fully to requite such an affection.

But we know so little of Mark Ingestrie, and there appears to be so much doubt as to whether he be alive or dead, that we should not prejudge him upon such very insufficient evidence.

Johanna Oakley did think of taking Arabella Wilmot with her to this meeting with Colonel Jeffery, but she abandoned the idea, because it really looked as if she was either afraid of him, or afraid of herself, so she resolved to go alone; and when the hour of appointment came, she was there walking upon that broad, gravelled path, which has been trodden by some of the best, and some of the most eminent, as well as some of the worst of human beings.

It was not likely that with the feelings of Colonel Jeffery towards her, he should keep her waiting. Indeed, he was there a good hour before the time, and his only great dread was, that she might not come.

He had some reason for this dread, because it will be readily recollected by the reader, that she had not positively promised to come; so that all he had was a hope that way tending and nothing further.

As minute after minute had passed away, she came not, although the time had not really arrived; his apprehension that she would not give him the meeting, had grown in his mind, almost to a certainty, when he saw her timidly advancing along the garden walk.

He rose to meet her at once, and for a few moments after he had greeted her with kind civility she could do nothing but look enquiringly in his face, to know if he had any news to tell her of the object of her anxious solicitude.

'I have heard nothing, Miss Oakley,' he said, 'that can give you any satisfaction, concerning the fate of Mr Thornhill, but we have much suspicion—I say we, because I have taken a friend into my confidence—that something serious must have happened to him, and that the barber, Sweeney Todd, in Fleet-street, at whose door the dog so mysteriously took his post, knows something of that circumstance, be it what it may.'

He led her to a seat as he spoke, and when she had recovered sufficiently the agitation of her feelings to speak, she said in a timid, hesitating voice, —

'Had Mr Thornhill fair hair, and large, clear, grey eyes?'

'Yes, he had such; and, I think, his smile was the most singularly beautiful I ever beheld in a man.'

'Heaven help me!' said Johanna.

'Have you any reason for asking that question regarding Thornhill?'

'God grant, I had not; but alas! I have indeed. I feel that, in Thornhill, I must recognise Mark Ingestrie himself.'

'You astonish me.'

'It must be so, it must be so; you have described him to me, and I cannot doubt it; Mark Ingestrie and Thornhill are one; I knew that he was going to change his name when he went upon that wild adventure to the Indian sea. I was well aware of that fact.'

'I cannot think, Miss Oakley, that you are correct in that supposition. There are many things which induce me to think otherwise; and the first and foremost of them is, that the ingenuous character of Mr Thornhill forbids the likelihood of such a thing occurring. You may depend it is not—cannot be, as you suppose.'

'The proofs are too strong for me, and I find I dare not doubt them. It is so, Colonel Jeffery, as time, perchance, may show; it is sad, very sad, to think that it is so, but I dare not doubt it, now that you have described him to me exactly as he lived.'

'I must own, that in giving an opinion on such a point to you, I may be accused of arrogance and assumption, for I have had no description of Mark Ingestrie, and never saw him; and although you never saw certainly Mr Thornhill, yet I have described him to you, and therefore you are able to judge from that description something of him.'

'I am indeed, and I cannot—dare not doubt. It is horrible to be positive on this point to me, because I do fear with you that something dreadful has occurred, and that the barber in Fleet-street could unravel a frightful secret, if he chose, connected with Mark Ingestrie's fate.'

'I do sincerely hope from my heart that you are wrong; I hope it, because I tell you frankly, dim and obscure as is the hope that Mark Ingestrie may have been picked up from the wreck of his vessel, it is yet stronger than the supposition that Thornhill has escaped the murderous hands of Sweeney Todd, the barber.'

Johanna looked in his face so imploringly, and with such an expression of hopelessness, that it was most sad indeed to see her, and quite involuntarily he exclaimed,—

'If the sacrifice of my life would be to you a relief, and save you from the pangs you suffer, believe me, it should be made.'

She started as she said, 'No, no; Heaven knows enough has been sacrificed already—more than enough, much more than enough. But do not suppose that I am ungrateful for the generous interest you have taken in me. Do not suppose that I think any the less of the generosity and nobility of soul that would offer a sacrifice, because it is one I would hesitate to accept. No, believe me, Colonel Jeffery, that among the few names that are enrolled in my breast—and such to me will ever be honoured—remember yours will be found while I live, but that will not be long—but that will not be long.'

'Nay, do not speak so despairingly.'

'Have I not cause for despair?'

'Cause have you for great grief, but yet scarcely for despair. You are young yet, and let me entertain a hope that even if a feeling of regret may mingle with your future thoughts, time will achieve something in tempering your sorrow, and if not great happiness, you may know great serenity.'

'I dare not hope it, but I know your words are kindly spoken, and most kindly meant.'

'You may well assure yourself that they are so.'

'I will ascertain his fate, or perish.'

'You alarm me by those words, as well as by your manner of uttering them. Let me implore you, Miss Oakley, to attempt nothing rash; remember how weak and inefficient must be the exertions of a young girl like yourself, one who knows so little of the world, and can really understand so little of its wickedness.'

'Affection conquers all obstacles, and the weakest and most inefficient girl that ever stepped, if she have strong within her that love which, in all its sacred intensity, knows no fear, shall indeed accomplish much. I feel that in such a cause, I could shake off all girlish terrors and ordinary alarms; and if there be danger, I would ask, what is life to me without all that could adorn it, and make it beautiful?'

'This, indeed, is the very enthusiasm of affection, when believe me, it will lead you to some excess—to some romantic exercise of feeling, such as will bring great danger in its train, to the unhappiness of those who love you.'

'Those who love me—who is there to love me now?'

'Johanna Oakley, I dare not and will not utter words that come thronging to my lips, but which I fear might be unwelcome to your ears; I will not say that I can answer the questions you have asked, because it would sound ungenerous at such a time as this, when you have met me to talk of the fate of another. Oh! forgive me, that hurried away by the feeling of a moment, I have uttered these words, for I meant not to utter them.'

Johanna looked at him in silence, and it might be that there was the slightest possible tinge of reproach in her look, but it was very slight, for one glance at that ingenuous countenance would be sufficient to convince the most sceptical of the truth and singlemindedness of its owner: of this, there could be no doubt whatever, and if anything in the shape of a reproach was upon the point of coming from her lips, she forbore to utter it.

'May I hope,' he added, 'that I have not lowered myself in your esteem, Miss Oakley, by what I have said?'

'I hope,' she said gently, 'you will continue to be my friend.'

She laid an emphasis on the word 'friend', and he fully understood what she meant to imply thereby, and after a moment's pause said,—

'Heaven forbid, that ever by word, or by action, Johanna, I should do aught to deprive myself of that privilege. Let me be your friend, since—'

He left the sentence unfinished, but if he had added the words—'since I can do no more', he could not have made it more evident to Johanna that those were the words he intended to utter.

'And now,' he added, 'that I hope and trust we understand each other better than we did, and you are willing to call me by the name of friend, let me once more ask you, by the privilege of such a title, to be careful of yourself, and not to risk much in order that you may perhaps have some remote chance of achieving very little.'

'But can I endure this dreadful suspense?'

'It is, alas! too common an affliction on human nature, Johanna. Pardon me for addressing you as Johanna.'

'Nay, it requires no excuse. I am accustomed so to be addressed by all who feel a kindly interest for me. Call me Johanna if you will, and I shall feel a greater assurance of your friendship and your esteem.'

'I will then avail myself of that permission, and again and again I will entreat you to leave to me the task of making what attempts may be made to discover the fate of Mr Thornhill. There must be danger even in enquiring for him, if he has met with any foul play, and therefore I ask you to let that danger be mine.'

Johanna asked herself if she should or not tell him of the scheme of operations that had been suggested by Arabella Wilmot, but, somehow or another, she shrank most wonderfully from so doing, both on account of the censure which she concluded he would be likely to cast upon it, and the romantic, strange nature of the plan itself, so she said, gently and quickly,—

'I will attempt nothing that shall not have some possibility of success attending it. I will be careful, you may depend, for many considerations. My father, I know, centres all his affections in me, and for his sake I will be careful.'

'I shall be content then, and now may I hope that this day week I may see you here again, in order that I may tell you if I have made any discovery, and that you may tell me the same; for my interest in Thornhill is that of a sincere friend, to say nothing of the deep interest in your happiness which I feel, and which has now become an element in the transaction of the highest value.'

'I will come,' said Johanna, 'if I can come.'

'You do not doubt?'

'No, no. I will come, and I hope to bring you some news of him in whom you are so much interested. It shall be no fault of mine if I come not.'

He walked with her from the gardens, and together they passed the shop of Sweeney Todd, but the door was close shut, and they saw nothing of the barber, or that of the poor boy, his apprentice, who was so much to be pitied.

He parted with Johanna near to her father's house, and he walked slowly away with his mind so fully impressed with the excellence and beauty of the spectacle-maker's daughter, that it was quite clear, as long as he lived, he would not be able to rid himself of the favourable impression she had made upon him.

'I love her,' he said; 'I love her, but she seems in no respect willing to enchain her affections. Alas! how sad it is for me that the being whom, above all others, I could wish to call my own, instead of being a joy to me, I have only encountered that she might impart a pang to my heart. Beautiful and excellent Johanna, I love you, but I can see that your own affections are withered for ever.'

## 16

## *The Barber Makes Another Attempt to Sell the String of Pearls*

I T would seem as if Sweeney Todd, after his adventure in trying to dispose of the string of pearls which he possessed, began to feel a little doubtful about his chances of success in that matter, for he waited patiently for a considerable period, before he again made the attempt, and then he made it after a totally different fashion.

Towards the close of night on that same evening when Johanna Oakley had met Colonel Jeffery for the second time, in the Temple-gardens, and while Tobias sat alone in the shop in his usual deep dejection, a stranger entered the place, with a large blue bag in his hand, and looked enquiringly about him.

'Hilloa, my lad!' said he. 'Is this Mr Todd's?'

'Yes,' said Tobias; 'but he is not at home. What do you want?'

'Well, I'll be hanged,' said the man, 'if this don't beat everything; you don't mean to tell me he is a barber, do you?'

'Indeed I do; don't you see?'

'Yes, I see, to be sure; but I'll be shot if I thought of it beforehand. What do you think he has been doing?'

'Doing,' said Tobias, with animation; 'do you think he will be hung?'

'Why, no, I don't say it is a hanging matter, although you seem as if you wished it was; but I'll just tell you now we are artists at the west-end of the town.'

'Artists! Do you mean to say you draw pictures?'

'No, no, we make clothes; but we call ourselves artists now, because tailors are out of fashion.'

'Oh, that's it, is it?'

'Yes, that's it; and you would scarcely believe it, but he came to our shop actually, and ordered a suit of clothes, which were to come to no less a sum than thirty pounds, and told us to make them up in such a style that they were to do for any nobleman, and he gave his name and address, as Mr Todd, at this number in Fleet-street, but I hadn't the least idea that he was a barber; if I had, I am quite certain that the clothes would not have been finished in the style they are, but quite the reverse.'

'Well,' said Tobias, 'I can't think what he wants such clothing for, but I suppose it's all right. Was he a tall, ugly-looking fellow?'

'As ugly as the very devil. I'll just show you the things, as he is not at home. The coat is of the finest velvet, lined with silk, and trimmed with lace. Did you ever, in all your life, see such a coat for a barber?'

'Indeed, I never did; but it is some scheme of his, of course. It is a superb coat.'

'Yes, and all the rest of the dress is of the same style; what on earth can he be going to do with it I can't think, for it's only fit to go to court in.'

'Oh, well, I know nothing about it,' said Tobias, with a sigh, 'you can leave it or not as you like, it is all one to me.'

'Well, you seem to be the most melancholy wretch ever I came near; what's the matter with you?'

'The matter with me? Oh, nothing. Of course, I am as happy as I can be. Ain't I Sweeney Todd's apprentice, and ain't that enough to make anybody sing all day long?'

'It may be for all I know, but certainly you don't seem to be in a singing humour; but, however, we artists cannot waste our time, so just be so good as to take care of the clothes, and be sure you give them to your master; and so I wash my hands of the transaction.'

'Very good, he shall have them; but, do you mean to leave such valuable clothes without getting the money for them?'

'Not exactly, for they are paid for.'

'Oh! that makes all the difference—he shall have them.'

Scarcely had this tailor left the place, when a boy arrived with a parcel, and, looking around him with undisguised astonishment, said,—'Isn't there some other Mr Todd in Fleet-street?'

'Not that I know of,' said Tobias. 'What have you got there?'

'Silk stockings, gloves, lace, cravats, ruffles, and so on.'

'The deuce you have; I dare say it's all right.'

'I shall leave them; they are paid for. This is the name, and this is the number.'

'Now, stupid!'

This last exclamation arose from the fact that this boy, in going out, ran up against another who was coming in.

'Can't you see where you're going?' said the new arrival.

'What's that to you? I have a good mind to punch your head.'

'Do it, and then come down to our court, and see what a licking I'll give you.'

'Will you? Why don't you? Only let me catch you, that's all.'

They stood for some moments so close together that their noses very nearly touched; and then after mutual assertions of what they would do if they caught each other—although, in either case, to stretch out an arm would have been quite sufficient to have accomplished that object—they separated, and the last comer said to Tobias, in a tone of irritation, probably consequent upon the misunderstanding he had just had with the hosier's boy,—

'You can tell Mr Todd that the carriage will be ready at half-past seven precisely.'

And then he went away, leaving Tobias in a state of great bewilderment as to what Sweeney Todd could possibly be about with such an amount of finery as that which was evidently coming home for him.

'I can't make it out,' he said. 'It's some villainy of course, but I can't make out what it is; I wish I knew; I might thwart him in it. He is a villain, and neither could nor would project anything good; but what can I do? I am quite helpless in this, and will just let it take its course. I can only wish for a power of action I will never possess. Alas, alas! I am very sad, and know not what will become of me. I wish that I was in my grave, and there I am sure I shall be soon, unless something happens to turn the tide of all this wretched evil fortune that has come upon me.'

It was in vain for Tobias to think of vexing himself with conjectures as to what Sweeney Todd was about to do with so much finery, for he had not the remotest foundation to go upon in the matter, and could not for the life of him imagine any possible contingency or chance which should make it necessary for the barber to deck himself in such gaudy apparel.

All he could do was to lay down in his own mind a general principle as regarded Sweeney Todd's conduct, and that consisted in the fact, that whatever might be his plans, and whatever might be his objects, they were for no good purpose; but, on the contrary, were most certainly intended for the accomplishment of some great evil which that most villainous person intended to perpetrate.

'I will observe all I can,' thought Tobias to himself, 'and do what I can to put a stop to his mischiefs; but I fear it will be very little he will allow me to observe, and perhaps still less that he will allow me to do; but I can but try, and do my best.'

Poor Tobias's best, as regarded achieving anything against Sweeney Todd, we may well suppose would be little indeed, for that individual was not the man to give anybody an opportunity of doing much; and possessed as he was of the most consummate art, as well as the greatest possible amount of unscrupulousness, there can be very little doubt but that any attempt poor Tobias might make would recoil upon himself.

In about another half hour the barber returned, and his first question was, 'Have any things been left for me?'

'Yes, sir,' said Tobias, 'here are two parcels, and a boy has been to say that the carriage will be ready at half-past seven precisely.'

' 'Tis well,' said the barber, 'that will do; and Tobias, you will be careful, whilst I am gone, of the shop. I shall be back in half an hour, mind you, and not later; and be sure I find you here at your post.

But you may say, if anyone comes here on business, that there will be neither shaving nor dressing tonight. You understand me?'

'Yes, sir, certainly.'

Sweeney Todd then took the bundles which contained the costly apparel, and retired into the parlour with them; and, as it was then seven o'clock, Tobias correctly enough supposed that he had gone to dress himself, and he waited with a considerable amount of curiosity to see what sort of an appearance the barber would cut in his fine apparel.

Tobias had not to control his impatience long, for in less than twenty minutes out came Sweeney Todd, attired in the very height of fashion for the period. His waistcoat was something positively gorgeous, and his fingers were loaded with such costly rings that they quite dazzled the sight of Tobias to look upon; then, moreover, he wore a sword with a jewelled hilt, but it was one which Tobias really thought he had seen before, for he had a recollection that a gentleman had come in to have his hair dressed, and had taken it off, and laid just such a sword across his hat during the operation.

'Remember,' said Sweeney Todd, 'remember your instructions; obey them to the letter, and no doubt you will ultimately become happy and independent.'

With these words, Sweeney Todd left the place, and poor Tobias looked after him with a groan, as he repeated the words 'happy and independent. Alas! what a mockery it is of this man to speak to me in such a way—I only wish that I were dead!'

But we will leave Tobias to his own reflections, and follow the more interesting progress of Sweeney Todd, who, for some reason best known to himself, was then playing so grand a part, and casting away so large a sum of money. He made his way to a livery-stables in the immediate neighbourhood, and there, sure enough, the horses were being placed to a handsome carriage; and all being very soon in readiness, Sweeney Todd gave some whispered directions to the driver, and the vehicle started off westward.

At that time Hyde Park Corner was very nearly out of town,* and it looked as if you were getting a glimpse of the country, and actually seeing something of the peasantry of England, when you got another couple of miles off, and that was the direction in which Sweeney Todd went; and as he goes, we may as well introduce to the reader the sort of individual whom he was going to visit in so much state, and for whom he thought it necessary to go to such great expense.

At that period the follies and vices of the nobility were somewhere about as great as they are now, and consequently extravagance induced on many occasions troublesome sacrifice of money, and it was found extremely convenient to apply to a man of the name of John Mundel, an exceedingly wealthy person, a Dutchman by extraction, who was reported to make immense sums of money by lending to the nobility and others what they required on emergencies, at enormous rates of interest.*

But it must not be supposed that John Mundel was so confiding as to lend his money without security. It was quite the reverse, for he took care to have the jewels, some costly plate, or the title deeds of an estate, perchance, as security, before he would part with a single shilling of his cash.

In point of fact, John Mundel was nothing more than a pawnbroker on a very extensive scale, and, although he had an office in town, he usually received his more aristocratic customers at his private residence, which was about two miles off, on the Uxbridge Road.*

After this explanation, it can very easily be imagined what was the scheme of Sweeney Todd, and that he considered if he borrowed from John Mundel a sum equal in amount to half the real value of the pearls he should be well rid of a property which he certainly could not sufficiently well account for the possession of, to enable him to dispose of it openly to the highest bidder.

We give Sweeney Todd great credit for the scheme he proposes. It was eminently calculated to succeed, and one which in the way he undertook it was certainly set about in the best possible style.

During his ride, he revolved in his mind exactly what he should say to John Mundel, and from what we know of him we may be well convinced that Sweeney Todd was not likely to fail from any amount of bashfulness in the transaction; but that, on the contrary, he was just the man to succeed in any scheme which required great assurance to carry it through; for he was certainly master of great assurance, and possessed of a kind of diplomatic skill, which, had fortune placed him in a more elevated position of life, would no doubt have made a great man of him, and gained him great political reputation.

John Mundel's villa, which was called, by-the-by, Mundel House, was a large, handsome, and modern structure, surrounded by a few acres of pleasure gardens, which however the money-lender never looked at, for his whole soul was too much engrossed by his love for cash to enable him to do so; and, if he derived any satisfaction at all from it, that satisfaction must have been entirely owing to the fact that he had wrung mansion, grounds, and all the costly furnishing of the former from an improvident debtor, who had been forced to fly the country, and leave his property wholly in the hands of the money-lender and usurer.

It was but a short drive with the really handsome horses that Sweeney Todd had succeeded in hiring for the occasion, and he soon found himself opposite the entrance gates of Mundel House.

---

His great object now was that the usurer should see the equipage which he had brought down; and he accordingly desired the footman, who had accompanied him, at once to ring the bell at the entrance-gate, and to say that a gentleman was waiting in his carriage to see Mr Mundel.

This was done; and when the money-lender's servant reported to him that the equipage was a costly one, and that, in his opinion, the visitor must be some nobleman of great rank, John Mundel made no difficulty about the matter, but walked down to the gate at once, where he immediately mentally subscribed to the opinion of his servant, by admitting to himself that the equipage was faultless, and presumed at once that it did belong to some person of great rank.

He was proportionally humble, as such men always are, and advancing to the side of the carriage, he begged to know what commands his lordship—for so he called him at once—had for him.

'I wish to know,' said Sweeney Todd, 'Mr Mundel, if you are inclined to lay under an obligation a rather illustrious lady, by helping her out of a little pecuniary difficulty.'

John Mundel glanced again at the equipage, and he likewise saw something of the rich dress of his visitor, who had not disputed the title which had been applied to him, of lord; and he made up his mind accordingly, that it was just one of the transactions that would suit him, provided the security that would be offered was of a tangible nature. That was the only point upon which John Mundel had the remotest doubt, but, at all events, he urgently pressed his visitor to alight, and walk in.

## 17

## *The Great Change in the Prospects of Sweeney Todd*

As Sweeney Todd's object, as far as the money-lender having seen the carriage, was fully answered, he had no objection to enter the house, which he accordingly did at once, being preceded by John Mundel, who became each moment more and more impressed with the fact, as he considered it, that his guest was some person of very great rank and importance in society.

He ushered him into a splendidly-furnished apartment, and after offering him refreshments, which Sweeney Todd politely declined, he waited with no small degree of impatience for his visitor to be explicit with regard to the object of his visit.

'I should,' said Sweeney Todd, 'have myself accommodated the illustrious lady with the sum of money she requires, but as I could not do so without encumbering some estates, she positively forbade me to think of it.'

'Certainly,' said Mr Mundel, 'she is a very illustrious lady, I presume?'

'Very illustrious indeed, but it must be a condition of this transaction, if you at all enter into it, that you are not to enquire precisely who she is, nor are you to enquire precisely who I am.'

'It's not my usual way of conducting business, but if everything else be satisfactory, I shall not cavil at that.'

'Very good; by everything else being satisfactory I presume you mean the security offered?'

'Why, yes, that is of great importance, my lord.'

'I informed the illustrious lady that as the affair was to be wrapped up in something of a mystery, the security must be extremely ample.'

'That's a very proper view to take of the matter, my lord.'

'I wonder,' thought John Mundel, 'if he is a duke; I'll call him your grace next time and see if he objects to it.'*

'Therefore,' continued Sweeney Todd, 'the illustrious lady placed in my hands security to a third greater amount than she required.'

'Certainly, certainly, a very proper arrangement, your grace; may I ask the nature of the proffered security?'

'Jewels.'

'Highly satisfactory and unexceptionable security; they go into a small space, and do not deteriorate in value.'

'And if they do,' said the barber, 'deteriorate in value, it would make no difference to you, for the illustrious person's honour will be committed to their redemption.'

'I don't doubt that, your grace, in the least; I merely made the remark incidentally, quite incidentally.'

'Of course, of course; and I trust, before going further, that you are quite in a position to enter into this subject.'

'Certainly I am, and, I am proud to say, to any amount. Show me the money's worth, your grace, and I will show you the money— that's my way of doing business; and no one can say that John Mundel ever shrunk from a matter that was brought fairly before him, and that he considered worth his going into.'

'It was by hearing such a character of you that I was induced to come to you. What do you think of that?'

Sweeney Todd took from his pocket, with a careless air, the string of pearls, and cast them down before the eyes of the money-lender, who took them up and ran them rapidly through his fingers for a few seconds before he said,—

'I thought there was but one string like this in the kingdom, and that those belonged to the Queen.'

'Well!' said Sweeney Todd.

'I humbly beg your grace's pardon. How much money does your grace require on these pearls?'

'Twelve thousand pounds is their current value, if a sale of them was enforced; eight thousand are required of you on their security.'

'Eight thousand is a large sum. As a general thing I lend but half the value upon anything; but in this case, to oblige your grace and the illustrious personage, I do not of course hesitate for one moment, but shall for one month lend the required amount.'

'That will do,' said Sweeney Todd, scarcely concealing the exultation he felt at getting so much more from John Mundel than he expected, and which he certainly would not have got if the money-lender had not been most fully and completely impressed with the idea that the pearls belonged to the Queen, and that he had actually at length majesty itself for a customer.

He did not suppose for one moment that it was the Queen who wanted the money; but his view of the case was, that she had lent the pearls to this nobleman to meet some exigency of his own, and that of course they would be redeemed very shortly.

Altogether a more pleasant transaction for John Mundel could not have been imagined. It was just the sort of thing he would have looked out for, and had the greatest satisfaction in bringing to a conclusion, and he considered it was opening the door to the highest class of business in his way that he was capable of doing.

'In what name, your grace,' he said, 'shall I draw a check upon my banker?'

'In the name of Colonel George.'

'Certainly, certainly; and if your grace will give me an acknowledgement for £8,000, and please to understand that at the end of a month from this time the transaction will be renewed if necessary, I will give you a check for £7,500.'

'Why £7,500 only, when you mentioned £8,000?'

'The £500 is my little commission upon the transaction. Your grace will perceive that I appreciate highly the honour of your grace's custom, and consequently charge the lowest possible price. I can assure your grace I could get more for my money by a great deal, but the pleasure of being able to meet your grace's views is so great, that I am willing to make a sacrifice, and therefore it is that I say £500, when really I ought to say £1,000, taking into consideration the great scarcity of money at the present juncture; and I can assure your grace that—'

'Peace, peace,' said Sweeney Todd; 'give me the money, and if it be not convenient to redeem the jewels at the end of a month from this time, you will hear from me most assuredly.'

'I am quite satisfied of that,' said John Mundel, and he accordingly drew a check for £7,500, which he handed to Sweeney Todd, who put it in his pocket, not a little delighted that at last he had got rid of his pearls, even at a price so far beneath their real value.

'I need scarcely urge upon you, Mr Mundel,' he said, 'the propriety of keeping this affair profoundly secret.'

'Indeed, you need not, your grace, for it is part of my business to be discreet and cautious. I should very soon have nothing to do in my line, your grace may depend, if I were to talk about it. No, this transaction will for ever remain locked up in my own breast, and no living soul but your grace and I need know what has occurred.'

With this, John Mundel showed Sweeney Todd to his carriage, with abundance of respect, and in two minutes more he was travelling along towards town with what might be considered a small fortune in his pocket.

We should have noticed earlier that Sweeney Todd had, upon the occasion of his going to sell the pearls to the lapidary, in the city, made some great alterations in his appearance, so that it was not likely he should be recognised again to a positive certainty. For example,—having no whiskers whatever of his own, he had put on a large black pair of false ones, as well as moustachios, and he had given some colour to his cheeks likewise, which had so completely altered his appearance, that those who were most intimate with him would not have known him except by his voice, and that he took great care to alter in his intercourse with John Mundel, so that it should not become a future means of detection.

'I thought that this would succeed,' he muttered to himself, as he went towards town, 'and I have not been deceived. For three months longer, and only three, I will carry on the business in Fleet-street, so that any sudden alteration in my fortunes may not give rise to suspicion.'

He was then silent for some minutes, during which he appeared to be revolving some very knotty question in his brain, and then he said, suddenly,—

'Well, well, as regards Tobias, I think it will be safer, unquestionably, to put him out of the way by taking his life than to try to dispose of him in a mad-house, and I think there are one or two more persons whom it will be highly necessary to prevent being mischievous, at all events at present. I must think—I must think.'

When such a man as Sweeney Todd set about thinking, there could be no possible doubt but that some serious mischief was meditated, and anyone who could have watched his face during that ride home from the money-lender's would have seen by its expression that the thoughts which agitated him were of a dark and a desperate character, and such as anybody but himself would have shrunk from, aghast.

But he was not a man to shrink from anything, and, on the contrary, the more a set of circumstances presented themselves in a gloomy and a terrific aspect, the better they seemed to suit him, and the peculiar constitution of his mind.

There can be no doubt but that the love of money was the predominant feeling in Sweeney Todd's intellectual organisation and that, by the amount it would bring him, or the amount it would deprive him of, he measured everything.

With such a man, then, no question of morality or ordinary feeling could arise, and there can be no doubt but that he would quite willingly have sacrificed the whole human race, if, by doing so, he could have achieved any of the objects of his ambition.

And so on his road homeward, he probably made up his mind to plunge still deeper into criminality; and perchance to indulge in acts that a man not already so deeply versed in iniquity would have shrunk from with the most positive terror.

And by a strange style of reasoning, such men as Sweeney Todd reconcile themselves to the most heinous crimes upon the ground of what they call policy.

That is to say, that having committed some serious offence, they are compelled to commit a great number more for the purpose of endeavouring to avoid the consequences of the first lot; and hence the continuance of criminality becomes a matter necessary to self-defence, and an essential ingredient in their consideration of self-preservation.

Probably Sweeney Todd had been, for the greater part of his life, aiming at the possession of extensive pecuniary resources, and, no doubt, by the aid of a superior intellect, and a mind full of craft and design, he had managed to make others subservient to his views, and now that those views were answered, and that his underlings and accomplices were no longer required, they became positively dangerous.

He was well aware of that cold-blooded policy which teaches that it is far safer to destroy than to cast away the tools, by which a man carves his way to power and fortune.

'They shall die,' said Sweeney Todd, 'dead men tell no tales, nor women nor boys either, and they shall all die, after which there will, I think, be a serious fire in Fleet-street. Ha! ha! it may spread to what mischief it likes, always provided it stops not short of the entire destruction of my house and premises.

'Rare sport—rare sport will it be to me, for then I will at once commence a new career, in which the barber will be forgotten, and the man of fashion only seen and remembered, for with this last addition to my means, I am fully capable of vying with the highest and the noblest, let them be who they may.'

This seemed a pleasant train of reflections to Sweeney Todd, and as the coach entered Fleet-street, there sat such a grim smile upon his countenance that he looked like some fiend in human shape, who had just completed the destruction of a human soul.

When he reached the livery stables to which he directed them to drive, instead of to his own shop, he rewarded all who had gone with him most liberally, so that the coachman and footman who were both servants out of place, would have had no objection for Sweeney Todd every day to have gone on some such an expedition, so that they should receive as liberal wages for the small part they enacted in it as they did upon that occasion.

He then walked from the stables towards his own house, but upon reaching there, a little disappointment awaited him, for he found to his surprise that no light was burning; and when he placed his hand upon the shop-door, it opened, but there was no trace of Tobias, although he, Sweeney Todd, called loudly upon him the moment he set foot within the shop.

Then a feeling of great apprehension crept across the barber, and he groped anxiously about for some matches, by the aid of which he hoped to procure a light, and then an explanation of the mysterious absence of Tobias.

But in order that we may in its proper form relate how it was that Tobias had had the daring, thus in open contradiction of his master, to be away from the shop, we must devote to Tobias a chapter which will plead his extenuation.

## 18

### *Tobias's Adventures during the Absence of Sweeney Todd*

TOBIAS guessed, and guessed rightly, too, that when Sweeney Todd said he would be away half an hour, he only mentioned that short period of time, in order to keep the lad's vigilance on the

alert, and to prevent him from taking advantage of a more pro-
tracted absence.

The very style and manner in which he had gone out precluded
the likelihood of it being for so short a period of time; and that circumstance set Tobias seriously thinking over a situation which was
becoming more intolerable every day.

The lad had the sense to feel that he could not go on much longer
as he was going on, and that in a short time such a life would
destroy him.

'It is beyond endurance,' he said, 'and I know not what to do; and
since Sweeney Todd has told me that the boy he had before went
out of his senses, and is now in the cell of a mad-house, I feel that
such will be my fate, and that I, too, shall come to that dreadful
end, and then no one will believe a word I utter, but consider everything to be mere raving.'

After a time, as the darkness increased, he lit the lamp which
hung in the shop, and which, until it was closed for the night, usually shed a dim ray from the window. Then he sat down to think
again, and he said to himself,—

'If I could but summon courage to ask my mother about this robbery which Sweeney Todd imputes to her, she might assure me it
was false, and that she never did such a deed; but then it is dreadful
for me to ask her such a question, because it may be true; and then
how shocking it would be for her to be forced to confess to me, her
own son, such a circumstance.'

These were the honourable feelings which prevented Tobias from
questioning his mother as regarded Todd's accusation of her—an
accusation too dreadful to believe implicitly, and yet sufficiently
probable for him to have a strong suspicion that it might be true
after all.

It is to be deeply regretted that Tobias's philosophy did not carry
him a little further, and make him see, the moment the charge was
made, that he ought unquestionably to investigate it to the very
utmost.

But, still, we could hardly expect from a mere boy that acute reasoning and power of action, which depends so much on the knowledge of the world, and an extensive practice in the usages of society.

It was sufficient if he felt correctly—we could scarcely expect him
to reason so. But upon this occasion above all other, he seemed

completely overcome by the circumstances which surrounded him; and from his excited manner, one might almost have imagined that the insanity he himself predicted at the close of his career was really not far off.

He wrung his hands, and he wept, every now and then, in sad speech, bitterly bemoaning his situation, until at length, with a sudden resolution, he sprang to his feet, exclaiming, —

'This night shall end it. I can endure it no more. I will fly from this place, and seek my fortune elsewhere. Any amount of distress, danger, or death itself even, is preferable to the dreadful life I lead.'

He walked some paces towards the door, and then he paused, as he said to himself in a low tone, —

'Todd will surely not be home yet for awhile, and why should I then neglect the only opportunity I may ever have of searching this house to satisfy my mind as regards any of the mysteries it contains.'

He paused over this thought, and considered well its danger, for dangerous indeed it was to no small extent, but he was desperate; and with a resolution that scarcely could have been expected from him, he determined upon taking that first step above all others, which Todd was almost certain to punish with death.

He closed the shop door, and bolted it upon the inside, so that he could not be suddenly interrupted, and then he looked round him carefully for some weapon by the aid of which he should be able to break his way into the parlour, which the barber always kept closed and locked in his absence. A weapon that would answer the purpose of breaking any lock, if Tobias chose to proceed so roughly to work, was close at hand in the iron bar, which, when the place was closed at night, secured a shutter to the door.

Wrought up as he was to almost frenzy, Tobias seized this bar, and advancing towards the parlour-door, he with one blow smashed the lock to atoms, and the door soon yielded.

The moment it did so, there was a crash of glass, and when Tobias entered the room he saw that upon its threshold lay a wine-glass shattered to atoms, and he felt certain it had been placed in some artful position by Sweeney Todd as a detector, when he should return, of any attempt that had been made upon the door of the parlour.

And now Tobias felt that he was so far committed that he might as well go on with his work, and accordingly he lit a candle, which he found upon the parlour table, and then proceeded to make what discoveries he could.

Several of the cupboards in the room yielded at once to his hands, and in them he found nothing remarkable, but there was one that he could not open; so, without a moment's hesitation, he had recourse to the bar of iron again, and broke its lock, when the door swung open, and to his astonishment there tumbled out of this cupboard such a volley of hats of all sorts and descriptions, some looped with silver, some three-cornered, and some square, that they formed quite a museum of that article of attire, and excited the greatest surprise in the mind of Tobias, at the same time that they tended very greatly to confirm some other thoughts and feelings which he had concerning Sweeney Todd.

This was the only cupboard which was fast, although there was another door which looked as if it opened into one; but when Tobias broke that down with the bar of iron, he found it was the door which led to the staircase conducting to the upper part of the house, that upper part which Sweeney Todd with all his avarice would never let, and of which the shutters were kept continually closed, so that the opposite neighbours never caught a glimpse into any of the apartments.

With cautious and slow steps, which he adopted instantaneously, although he knew that there was no one in the house but himself, Tobias ascended the staircase.

'I will go to the very top rooms first,' he said to himself, 'and so examine them all as I come down, and then if Todd should return suddenly, I shall have a better chance of hearing him than if I began below and went upwards.'

Acting upon this prudent scheme, he went up to the attics, all the doors of which were swinging open, and there was nothing in any one of them whatever.

He descended to the second floor with the like result, and a feeling of great disappointment began to creep over him at the thought that, after all, the barber's house might not repay the trouble of examination.

But when he reached the first floor he soon found abundant reason to alter his opinion. The doors were fast, and he had to burst them open; and, when he got in, he found that those rooms were partially furnished, and that they contained a great quantity of miscellaneous property of all kinds and descriptions.

In one corner was an enormous quantity of walking-sticks, some of which were of a very costly and expensive character, with gold and silver chased tops to them, and in another corner was a great number of umbrellas—in fact at least a hundred of them.

Then there were boots and shoes, lying upon the floor, partially covered up, as if to keep them from dirt; there were thirty or forty swords of different styles and patterns, many of them appearing to be very firm blades, and in one or two cases the scabbards were richly ornamented.*

At one end of the front and larger of the two rooms was an old-fashioned-looking bureau of great size, and with as much wood-work in it as seemed required to make at least a couple of such articles of furniture.

This was very securely locked, and presented more difficulties in the way of opening it, than any of the doors had done, for the lock was of great strength and apparent durability. Moreover it was not so easily got at, but at length by using the bar as a sort of lever, instead of as a mere machine to strike with, Tobias succeeded in forcing this bureau open, and then his eyes were perfectly dazzled with the amount of jewellery and trinkets of all kinds and descriptions that were exhibited to his gaze.

There was a great number of watches, gold chains, silver and gold snuff-boxes, and a large assortment of rings, shoe-buckles, and brooches.

These articles must have been of great value, and Tobias could not help exclaiming aloud,—

'How could Sweeney Todd come by these articles, except by the murder of their owners?'

This, indeed, seemed but too probable a supposition, and the more especially so, as in a further part of this bureau a great quantity of apparel was found by Tobias.

He stood with a candle in his hand, looking upon these various objects for more than a quarter of an hour, and then as a sudden and a natural thought came across him of how completely a few of them even would satisfy his wants and his mother's for a long time to come, he stretched forth his hand towards the glittering mass, but he drew it back again with a shudder, saying,—

'No, no, these things are the plunder of the dead. Let Sweeney Todd keep them to himself, and look upon them if he can with the eyes of enjoyment. I will have none of them: they would bring misfortune along with every guinea that they might be turned into.'

As he spoke, he heard St Dunstan's clock strike nine, and he started at the sound, for it let him know that already Sweeney Todd had been away an hour beyond the time he said he would be absent, so that there was a probability of his quick return now, and it would scarcely be safe to linger longer in his home.

'I must be gone, I must be gone, I should like to look upon my mother's face once more before I leave London for ever perhaps. I may tell her of the danger she is in from Todd's knowledge of her secret; no, no, I cannot speak to her of that, I must go, and leave her to those chances which I hope and trust will work favourable for her.'

Flinging down the iron bar which had done him such good service, Tobias stopped not to close any of those receptacles which contained the plunder that Sweeney Todd had taken most probably from murdered persons, but he rushed downstairs into the parlour again, where the boots that had fallen out of the cupboard still lay upon the floor in wild disorder.

It was a strange and sudden whim that took him, rather than a matter of reflection, that induced him instead of his own hat to take one of those which were lying so indiscriminately at his feet; and he did so.

By mere accident it turned out to be an exceedingly handsome hat, of rich workmanship and material, and then Tobias, feeling terrified lest Sweeney Todd should return before he could leave the place, paid no attention to anything, but turned from the shop, merely pulling the door after him, and then darting over the road towards the Temple like a hunted hare; for his great wish was to see his mother, and then he had an undefined notion that his best plan for escaping the clutches of Sweeney Todd would be to go to sea.

In common with all boys of his age, who know nothing whatever of the life of a sailor, it presented itself in the most fascinating colours.

A sailor ashore and a sailor afloat are about as two different things as the world can present; but, to the imagination of Tobias Ragg, a sailor was somebody who was always dancing hornpipes, spending money, and telling wonderful stories. No wonder, then, that the profession presented itself under such fascinating colours to all such persons as Tobias; and, as it seemed, and seems still, to be a sort of general understanding that the real condition of a sailor should be mystified in every possible way and shape both by novelist and dramatist, it is no wonder that it requires actual experience to enable those parties who are in the habit of being carried away by just what they hear, to come to a correct conclusion.

'I will go to sea!' ejaculated Tobias. 'Yes, I will go to sea!'

As he spoke those words, he passed out of the gate of the Temple, leading into Whitefriars,* in which ancient vicinity his mother dwelt, endeavouring to eke out a living as best she might.

She was very much surprised (for she happened to be at home) at the unexpected visit of her son Tobias, and uttered a faint scream as she let fall a flat-iron very nearly upon his toe.

'Mother,' he said, 'I cannot stay with Sweeney Todd any longer, so do not ask me.'

'Not stay with such a respectable man?'

'A respectable man, mother! Alas, alas, how little you know of him! But what am I saying? I dare not speak! Oh, that fatal, fatal candlestick!'

'But how are you to live, and what do you mean by a fatal candlestick?'

'Forgive me—I did not mean to say that! Farewell, mother! I am going to sea.'

'To see what, my dear?' said Mrs Ragg, who was much more difficult to talk to than even Hamlet's grave-digger.* 'You don't know how much I am obliged to Sweeney Todd.'

'Yes, I do. And that's what drives me mad to think of. Farewell, mother, perhaps for ever! If I can, of course, I will communicate with you, but now I dare not stay.'

'Oh! what have you done, Tobias—what have you done?'

'Nothing—nothing! but Sweeney Todd is—'

'What—what?'

'No matter—no matter! Nothing—nothing! And yet at this last moment I am almost tempted to ask you concerning a candlestick.'

'Don't mention that,' said Mrs Ragg; 'I don't want to hear anything said about it.'

'It is true, then?'

'Yes; but did Mr Todd tell you?'

'He did—he did. I have now asked the question I never thought could have passed my lips. Farewell, mother, for ever farewell!'

Tobias rushed out of the place, leaving old Mrs Ragg astonished at his behaviour, and with a strong suspicion that some accession of insanity had come over him.

'The Lord have mercy upon us!' she said, 'what shall I do? I am astonished at Mr Todd telling him about the candlestick; it's true enough, though, for all that. I recollect it as well as if it were yesterday; it was a very hard winter, and I was minding a set of chambers, when Todd came to shave the gentleman, and I saw him with my own eyes put a silver candlestick in his pocket. Then I went over to his shop and reasoned with him about it, and he gave it me back, and I brought it to the chambers, and laid it down exactly on the spot where he took it from.

'To be sure,' said Mrs Ragg, after a pause of a few moments, 'to be sure he has been a very good friend to me ever since, but that I suppose is for fear I should tell, and get him hung or transported. But, however, we must take the good with the bad, and when Tobias comes to think of it, he will go back again to his work, I dare say, for, after all, it's a very foolish thing for him to trouble his head whether Mr Todd stole a silver candlestick or not.'

# 19

## *The Strange Odour in Old St Dunstan's Church*

ABOUT this time and while these incidents of our most strange and eventful narrative were taking place, the pious frequenters of old St Dunstan's church began to perceive a strange and most abominable odour throughout that sacred edifice.

It was in vain that old women who came to hear the sermons, although they were too deaf to catch a third part of them, brought smelling-bottles, and other means of stifling their noses; still that dreadful charnel-house sort of smell would make itself most painfully and most disagreeably apparent.

And the Rev Joseph Stillingport, who was the regular preacher, smelt it in the pulpit; and had been seen to sneeze in the midst of a most pious discourse indeed, and to hold to his pious mouth a handkerchief, in which was some strong and pungent essence, for the purpose of trying to overcome the horrible effluvia.

The organ-blower and the organ-player were both nearly stifled, for the horrible odour seemed to ascend to the upper part of the church; although those who sat in what may be called the pit by no means escaped it.

The churchwardens looked at each other in their pews with contorted countenances, and were almost afraid to breathe; and the only person who did not complain bitterly of the dreadful odour in St Dunstan's church, was an old woman who had been a pew-opener for many years; but then she had lost the faculties of her nose, which, perhaps, accounted satisfactorily for that circumstance.

At length, however, the nuisance became so intolerable, that the beadle, whose duty it was in the morning to open the church-doors, used to come up to them with the massive key in one hand, and a cloth soaked in vinegar in the other, just as the people used to do in the time of the great plague of London; and when he had opened the doors, he used to run over to the other side of the way.

'Ah, Mr Blunt!' he used to say to the bookseller, who lived opposite—'ah, Mr Blunt! I is obligated to cut over here, leastways, till the *atymonspheric* air is mixed up all along with the *stinkifications*\* which come from the church.'

By this, it will be seen that the beadle was rather a learned man, and no doubt went to some mechanics' institution of those days, where he learned something of everything but what was calculated to be of some service to him.\*

As might be supposed from the fact that this sort of thing had gone on for a few months, it began to excite some attention with a view to a remedy; for, in the great city of London, a nuisance of any sort of description requires to become venerable by age before anyone thinks of removing it; and after that, it is quite clear that that becomes a good argument against removing it at all.

But at last, the churchwardens began to have a fear that some pestilential disease would be the result, if they for any longer period of time put up with the horrible stench; and that they might be among its first victims, so they began to ask each other what could be done to obviate it.

Probably, if this frightful stench, being suggestive, as it was, of all sorts of horrors, had been graciously pleased to confine itself to some poor locality, nothing would have been heard of it; but when it became actually offensive to a gentleman in a metropolitan pulpit, and when it began to make itself perceptible to the sleepy faculties of the churchwardens of St Dunstan's church, in Fleet-street, so as to prevent them even from dozing through the after-noon sermon, it became a very serious matter indeed.

But what it was, what could it be, and what was to be done to get rid of it—these were the anxious questions that were asked right and left, as regarded the serious nuisance, without the nuisance acceding any reply.

But yet one thing seemed to be generally agreed, and that was, that it did come, and must come, somehow or other, out of the vaults from beneath the church.

But then, as the pious and hypocritical Mr Batterwick, who lived opposite, said,—

'How could that be, when it was satisfactorily proved by the present books that nobody had been buried in the vault for some time, and therefore it was a very odd thing that dead people, after leaving off smelling and being disagreeable, should all of a sudden burst out again in that line, and be twice as bad as ever they were at first.'

And on Wednesdays sometimes, too, when pious people were not satisfied with the Sunday's devotion, but began again in the middle of the week, the stench was positively terrific.

Indeed so bad was it, that some of the congregation were forced to leave, and have been seen to slink into Bell-yard, where Lovett's pie-shop was situated, and then and there relieve themselves with a pork or a veal pie, in order that their mouths and noses should be full of a delightful and agreeable flavour, instead of one most pecu-liarly and decidedly the reverse.

At last there was a confirmation to be held at St Dunstan's church, and so great a concourse of persons assembled, for a sermon was to be preached by the bishop, after the confirmation; and a very great fuss indeed was to be made about really nobody knew what."

Preparations, as newspapers say, upon an extensive scale, and regardless of expense, were made for the purpose of adding lustre to the ceremony, and surprising the bishop when he came with a good idea that the authorities of St Dunstan's church were some-bodies and really worth confirming.

The confirmation was to take place at twelve o'clock, and the bells ushered in the morning with their most pious tones, for it was not every day that the authorities of St Dunstan's succeeded in catching a bishop, and when they did so, they were determined to make the most of him.

And the numerous authorities, including churchwardens, and even the very beadle, were in an uncommon fluster, and running about and impeding each other, as authorities always do upon public occasions.

But of those who only look to the surface of things, and who come to admire what was grand and magnificent in the preparations, the beadle certainly carried away the palm, for that functionary was attired in a completely new cocked hat and coat, and certainly looked very splendid and showy upon the occasion. Moreover, the beadle had been well and judiciously selected, and the parish authorities made no secret of it, when there was an election for beadle, that they threw all their influence into the scale of that candidate who happened to be the biggest, and, consequently, who was calculated to wear the official costume with an air that no smaller man could possibly have aspired to on any account.*

---

At half-past eleven o'clock the bishop made his gracious appearance, and was duly ushered into the vestry, where there was a comfortable fire, and on the table in which, likewise, were certain cold chickens and bottles of rare wines; for confirming a number of people, and preaching a sermon besides, was considered no joke, and might, for all they knew, be provocative of a great appetite in the bishop.

And with a bland and courtly air the bishop smiled as he ascended the steps of St Dunstan's church. How affable he was to the churchwardens, and he actually smiled upon a poor, miserable charity boy, who, his eyes glaring wide open, and his muffin cap in his hand,* was taking his first stare at a real live bishop.

To be sure, the beadle knocked him down directly the bishop had passed, for having the presumption to look at such a great personage, but then that was to be expected fully and completely, and only proved that the proverb which permits a cat to look at a king, is not equally applicable to charity boys and bishops.

When the bishop got to the vestry, some very complimentary words were uttered to him by the usual officiating clergyman, but, somehow or another, the bland smile had left the lips of the great personage, and, interrupting the vicar in the midst of a fine flowing period, he said,—

'That's all very well, but what a terrible stink there is here!'

The churchwardens gave a groan, for they had flattered themselves, that perhaps the bishop would not notice the dreadful smell, or that, if he did, he would think it was accidental and say nothing about it; but now, when he really did mention it, they found all their hopes scattered to the winds, and that it was necessary to say something.

'Is this horrid charnel-house sort of smell always here?'

'I am afraid it is,' said one of the churchwardens.

'Afraid!' said the bishop, 'surely you know; you seem to me to have a nose.'

'Yes,' said the churchwarden, in great confusion, 'I have that honour, and I have the pleasure of informing you, my lord bishop—I mean I have the honour of informing you, that this smell is always here.'

The bishop sniffed several times, and then he said,—

'It is very dreadful; and I hope that by the next time I come to St Dunstan's you will have the pleasure and the honour, both, of informing me that it has gone away.'

The churchwarden bowed, and got into an extreme corner, saying to himself,—

'This is the bishop's last visit here, and I don't wonder at it, for as if out of pure spite, the smell is ten times worse than ever to-day.'

And so it was, for it seemed to come up through all the crevices of the flooring of the church with a power and perseverance that was positively dreadful.

'Isn't it dreadful?—did you ever before know the smell in St Dunstan's so bad before?' and everybody agreed that they had never known it anything like so bad, for that it was positively awful—and so indeed it was.

The anxiety of the bishop to get away was quite manifest, and if he could decently have taken his departure without confirming anybody at all, there is no doubt but that he would have willingly done so, and left all the congregation to die and be—something or another.

But this he could not do, but he could cut it short, and he did so. The people found themselves confirmed before they almost knew where they were, and the bishop would not go into the vestry again on any account, but hurried down the steps of the church and into his carriage, with the greatest precipitation in the world, thus proving that holiness is no proof against a most abominable stench.

As may be well supposed, after this, the subject assumed a much more serious aspect, and on the following day a solemn meeting was held of all the church authorities, at which it was determined that men should be employed to make a thorough and searching examination of all the vaults of St Dunstan's, with the view of discovering, if possible, from whence particularly the abominable stench emanated.

And then it was decided that the stench was to be put down, and that the bishop was to be apprised it was put down, and that he might visit the church in perfect safety.

## 20

*Sweeney Todd's Proceedings Consequent upon
the Departure of Tobias*

WE left the barber in his own shop, much wondering that Tobias had not responded to the call which he had made upon him, but yet scarcely believing it possible that he could have ventured upon the height of iniquity, which we know Tobias had really been guilty of.

He paused for a few moments, and held up the light which he had procured, and gazed around him with enquiring eyes, for he could, indeed, scarcely believe it possible that Tobias had sufficiently cast off his dread of him, Sweeney Todd, to be enabled to achieve any act for his liberation. But when he saw that the lock of the parlour-door was open, positive rage obtained precedence over every other feeling.

'The villain!' he cried, 'has he dared really to consummate an act I thought he could not have dreamt of for a moment? Is it possible that he can have presumed so far as to have searched the house?'

That Tobias, however, had presumed so far, the barber soon discovered, and when he went into his parlour and saw what had actually occurred, and that likewise the door which led to the staircase and the upper part of the house had not escaped, he got perfectly furious, and it was some time before he could sufficiently calm himself to reflect upon the probable and possible amount of danger he might run in consequence of these proceedings.

When he did, his active mind at once told him that there was not much to be dreaded immediately, for that, most probably, Tobias, still having the fear before his eyes of what he might do as regarded his mother, had actually run away; and, 'In all likelihood,' muttered the barber, 'he has taken with him something which would allow me to fix upon him the stigma of robbery: but that I must see to.'

Having fastened the shop-door securely, he took the light in his hands, and ascended to the upper part of his house—that is to say, to the first floor, where alone anything was to be found.

He saw at once the open bureau with all its glittering display of jewels, and as he gazed upon the heap he muttered, —

'I have not so accurate a knowledge of what is here, as to be able to say if anything be extracted or not, but I know the amount of money, if I do not know the precise number of jewels which this bureau contains.'

He opened a small drawer which had entirely evaded the scrutiny of Tobias, and proceeded to count a large number of guineas which were there.

'These are correct,' he said, when he had finished his examination, — 'these are correct, and he has touched none of them.'

He then opened another drawer, in which were a great many packets of silver done up in paper, and these likewise he carefully counted and was satisfied they were right.

'It is strange,' he said, 'that he has taken nothing, but yet perhaps it is better that it should be so, inasmuch as it shows a wholesome fear of me. The slightest examination would have shown him these hoards of money; and since he has not made that slight examination, nor discovered any of them, it seems to my mind decisive upon the subject, that he has taken nothing, and perchance I shall discover him easier than I imagine.'

He repaired to the parlour again and carefully divested himself of everything which had enabled him so successfully to impose upon John Mundel, and replaced them by his ordinary costume, after which he fastened up his house and sallied forth, taking his way direct to Mrs Ragg's humble home, in the expectation that there he would hear something of Tobias, which would give him a clue where to search for him, for to search for him he fully intended; but what were his precise intentions perhaps he could hardly have told himself, until he actually found him.

When he reached Mrs Ragg's house, and made his appearance abruptly before that lady, who seemed somehow or another always to be ironing and always to drop the iron when anyone came in very near their toes, he said,—'Where did your son Tobias go after he left you to-night?'

'Lor! Mr Todd, is it you? you are as good as a conjurer, sir, for he was here; but bless you, sir, I know no more where he is gone to than the man in the moon. He said he was going to sea, but I am sure I should not have thought it, *that* I should not.'

'To sea! then the probability is that he would go down to the docks, but surely not to-night. Do you not expect him back here to sleep?'

'Well, sir, that's a very good thought of yours, and he may come back here to sleep, for all I know to the contrary.'

'But you do not know it for a fact.'

'He didn't say so; but he may come, you know, for all that.'

'Did he tell you his reason for leaving me?'

'Indeed no, sir; he really did not, and he seemed to me to be a little bit out of his senses.'

'Ah! Mrs Ragg,' said Sweeney Todd, 'there you have it. From the first moment that he came into my service, I knew and felt confident that he was out of his senses. There was a strangeness of behaviour about him, which soon convinced me of that fact, and I am only anxious about him, in order that some effort may be made to cure him of such a malady, for it is a serious, and a dreadful one, and one which, unless taken in time, will yet be the death of Tobias.'

These words were spoken with such solemn seriousness, that they had a wonderful effect upon Mrs Ragg, who, like most ignorant persons, began immediately to confirm that which she most dreaded.

'Oh, it's too true,' she said, 'it's too true. He did say some extraordinary things to-night, Mr Todd, and he said he had something to tell which was too horrid to speak of. Now the idea, you know, Mr Todd, of anybody having anything at all to tell, and not telling it at once, is quite singular.'

'It is; and I am sure that his conduct is such as you never would be guilty of, Mrs Ragg; but hark! what's that?'

'It's a knock, Mr Todd.'

'Hush, stop a moment, what if it be Tobias?'

'Goodness gracious! it can't be him, for he would have come in at once.'

'No; I slipped the bolt of the door, because I wished to talk to you without observation; so it may be Tobias you perceive, after all; but let me hide somewhere, so that I may hear what he says, and be able to judge how his mind is affected. I will not hesitate to do something for him, let it cost me what it may.'

'There's the cupboard, Mr Todd. To be sure there is some dirty saucepans and a frying-pan in it, and of course it ain't a fit place to ask you to go into.'

'Never mind that—never mind that; only you be careful, for the sake of Tobias's very life, to keep secret that I am here.'

The knocking at the door increased each moment in vehemence, and just as Sweeney Todd had succeeded in getting into the cupboard along with Mrs Ragg's pots and pans, and thoroughly concealing himself, she opened the door; and, sure enough, Tobias, heated, tired, and looking ghastly pale, staggered into the room.

'Mother,' he said, 'I have taken a new thought, and have come back to you.'

'Well, I thought you would, Tobias; and a very good thing it is that you have.'

'Listen to me: I thought of flying from England for ever, and of never setting foot upon its shores, but I have altered that determination completely, and I feel now that it is my duty to do something else.'

'To do what, Tobias?'

'To tell all I know—to make a clean breast, mother, and, let the consequences be what they may, to let justice take its course.'

'What do you mean, Tobias?'

'Mother, I have come to a conclusion that what I have to tell is of such vast importance, compared with any consequences that might arise from the petty robbery of the candlestick, which you know of, that I ought not to hesitate a moment in revealing everything.'

'But, my dear Tobias, remember that is a dreadful secret, and one that must be kept.'

'It cannot matter—it cannot matter; and, besides, it is more than probable that by revealing what I actually know, and which is of such great magnitude, I may, mother, in a manner of speaking, perchance completely exonerate you from the consequences of that transaction. Besides, it was long ago, and the prosecutor may have mercy; but be that how it may, and be the consequences what they may, I must and will tell what I now know.'

'But what is it, Tobias, that you know?'

'Something too dreadful for me to utter to you alone. Go into the Temple, mother, to some of the gentlemen whose chambers you attend to, and ask them to come to me, and listen to what I have got to say. They will be amply repaid for their trouble, for they will hear that which may, perhaps, save their own lives.'

'He is quite gone,' thought Mrs Ragg, 'and Mr Todd is correct; poor Tobias is as mad as he can be! Alas, alas, Tobias, why don't you try to reason yourself into a better state of mind! You don't know a bit what you are saying any more than the man in the moon.'

'I know I am half mad, mother, but yet I know what I am saying well; so do not fancy that it is not to be relied upon, but go and fetch someone at once to listen to what I have to relate.'

'Perhaps,' thought Mrs Ragg, 'if I were to pretend to humour him, it would be as well, and while I am gone, Mr Todd can speak to him.'

This was a bright idea of Mrs Ragg's, and she forthwith proceeded to carry it into execution, saying,—

'Well, my dear, if it must be, it must be; and I will go; but I hope while I have gone, somebody will speak to you, and convince you that you ought to try to quiet yourself.'

These words Mrs Ragg uttered aloud, for the special benefit of Sweeney Todd, who, she considered, would have been there, to take the hint accordingly.

It is needless to say he did hear them, and how far he profited by them, we shall quickly perceive.

As for poor Tobias, he had not the remotest idea of the close proximity of his arch enemy; if he had, he would quickly have left that spot, where he ought well to conjecture so much danger awaited him; for although Sweeney Todd under the circumstances probably felt, that he dare not take Tobias's life, still he might exchange something that could place it in his power to do so shortly, without the least personal danger to himself.

The door closed after the retreating form of Mrs Ragg, and as considering the mission she was gone upon, it was very clear some minutes must elapse before she could return, Sweeney Todd did not feel there was any very particular hurry in the transaction.

'What shall I do?' he said to himself. 'Shall I await his mother's coming again, and get her to aid me, or shall I of myself adopt some means which will put an end to trouble on this boy's account?'

Sweeney Todd was a man tolerably rapid in thought, and he contrived to make up his mind that the best plan unquestionably would be to lay hold on poor Tobias at once, and so prevent the possibility of any appeal to his mother becoming effective.

Tobias, when his mother left the place, as he imagined, for the purpose of procuring someone to listen to what he considered to be Sweeney Todd's delinquencies, rested his face upon his hands, and gave himself up to painful and deep thought.

He felt that he had arrived at quite a crisis in his history, and that the next few hours cannot but surely be very important to him in their results; and so they were indeed, but not certainly exactly in the way that he had all along anticipated, for he thought of nothing but of the arrest and discomfiture of Todd, little expecting how close was his proximity to that formidable personage.

'Surely,' thought Tobias, 'I shall by disclosing all that I know about Todd, gain some consideration for my mother, and after all she may not be prosecuted for the robbery of the candlestick; for how very trifling is that affair compared to the much more dreadful things which I more than suspect Sweeney Todd to be guilty of. He is, and must be, from all that I have seen, and heard, a murderer— although how he disposes of his victims is involved in the most complete mystery; and it is to me a matter past all human power of comprehension. I have no idea even upon that subject whatever.'

This, indeed, was a great mystery, for even admitting that Sweeney Todd was a murderer, and it must be allowed that as yet we have only circumstantial evidence of that fact, we can form no conclusion from such evidence as to how he perpetrated the deed, or how afterwards he disposed of the body of his victim.

This grand and principal difficulty in the way of committing murder with impunity—namely, the disposal of a corpse, certainly did not seem at all to have any effect on Sweeney Todd; for if he made corpses, he had some means of getting rid of them with the most wonderful expedition as well as secrecy.

'He is a murderer,' thought Tobias. 'I know he is, although I have never seen him do the deed, or seen any appearance in the shop of a deed of blood having been committed. Yet, why is it that occasionally when a better dressed person than usual comes into the shop he sends me out on some errand to a distant part of the town?'

Tobias did not forget, too, that on more than one occasion he had come back quicker doubtless than he had been expected, and that he had caught Sweeney Todd in some little confusion, and seen the hat, the stick, or perhaps the umbrella of the last customer quietly waiting there, although the customer had gone; and, even if the glaring improbability of a man leaving his hat behind him in a barber's shop was got over, why did he not come back for it?

This was a circumstance which was entitled to all the weight which Tobias during his mental cogitation could give to it, and there could be but one possible explanation of a man not coming back for his hat, and that was that he had not the power to do so.

'His house will be searched,' thought Tobias, 'and all those things which must of course have belonged to so many different people will be found, and then they will be identified, and he will be required to say how he came by them, which, I think, will be a difficult task indeed for Sweeney Todd to accomplish. What a relief it will be to me, to be sure, when he is hanged, as I think he is tolerably sure to be!'

'What a relief!' muttered Sweeney Todd, as he slowly opened the cupboard-door unseen by Tobias—'what a relief it will be to me when this boy is in his grave, as he really will be soon, or else I have forgotten all my moral learning, and turned chicken-hearted—neither of them very likely circumstances.'

# 21

## *The Misadventure of Tobias.—The Mad-House on Peckham Rye*

SWEENEY TODD paused for a moment at the cupboard-door, before he made up his mind as to whether he should pounce on poor Tobias at once, or adopt a more creeping, cautious mode of operation.

The latter course was by far the more congenial to him, and so he adopted it in another moment or so, and stole quietly from his place of concealment, and with so little noise, that Tobias could not have the least suspicion anyone was in the room but himself.

Treading as if each step might involve some fearful consequences, he thus at length got completely behind the chair on which Tobias was sitting, and stood with folded arms, and such a hideous smile upon his face, that they together formed no inept representation of the Mephistopheles of the German drama.*

'I shall at length,' murmured Tobias, 'be free from my present dreadful state of mind by thus accusing Todd. He is a murderer—of that I have no doubt; it is but a duty of mine to stand forward as his accuser.'

Sweeney Todd stretched out his two brawny hands, and clutched Tobias by the head, which he turned round till the boy could see him, and then he said,—

'Indeed, Tobias, and did it never strike you that Todd was not so easily to be overcome as you would wish him, eh, Tobias?'

The shock of this astonishing and sudden appearance of Sweeney Todd was so great, that for a few moments Tobias was deprived of all power of speech or action, and with his head so strangely twisted as to seem to threaten the destruction of his neck, he glared in the triumphant and malignant countenance of his persecutor, as he would into that of the arch enemy of all mankind, which probably he now began to think the barber really was.

If aught more than another was calculated to delight such a man as Todd, it certainly was to perceive what a dreadful effect his presence had upon Tobias, who remained about a minute and a half in this state before he ventured upon uttering a shriek, which, however, when it did come almost frightened Todd himself.

It was one of those cries which can only come from a heart in its utmost agony—a cry which might have heralded the spirit to another world, and proclaimed as it very nearly did, the destruction of the intellect for ever.

The barber staggered back a pace or two as he heard it, for it was too terrific even for him, but it was for a very brief period that it had that stunning effect upon him, and then, with a full consciousness of the danger to which it subjected him, he sprang upon poor Tobias as a tiger might be supposed to do upon a lamb, and clutched him by the throat, exclaiming,—

'Such another cry, and it is the last you ever live to utter, although it cover me with difficulties to escape the charge of killing you. Peace! I say, peace!'

This exhortation was quite needless, for Tobias could not have uttered a word, had he been ever so much inclined to do so; the barber held his throat with such an iron clutch, as if it had been in a vice.

'Villain,' growled Todd, 'villain, so this is the way in which you have dared to disregard my injunctions. But no matter, no matter! you shall have plenty of leisure to reflect upon what you have done for yourself. Fool to think that you could cope with me, Sweeney Todd. Ha! ha!'

He burst into a laugh, so much more hideous, more than his ordinary efforts in that way, that, had Tobias heard it—which he did not, for his head had dropped upon his breast, and he had become insensible—it would have terrified him almost as much as Sweeney Todd's sudden appearance had done.

'So,' muttered the barber, 'he has fainted, has he? Dull child, that is all the better—for once in a way, Tobias, I will carry you, not to oblige you, but to oblige myself—by all that's damnable it was a lively thought that brought me here tonight, or else I might, by the dawn of the morning, have had some very troublesome inquiries made of me.'

He took Tobias up as easily as if he had been an infant, and strode from the chambers with him, leaving Mrs Ragg to draw whatever inference she chose from his absence, but feeling convinced that she was too much under his control to take any steps of a nature to give him the smallest amount of uneasiness.

'The woman,' he muttered to himself, 'is a double distilled ass, and can be made to believe anything, so that I have no fear whatever of her. I dare not kill Tobias, because it is necessary, in case of the matter being at any other period mentioned, that his mother shall be in a position to swear that she saw him after this night alive and well.'

The barber strode through the Temple, carrying the boy, who seemed not at all in a hurry to recover from the nervous and partial state of suffocation into which he had fallen.

As they passed through the gate, opening into Fleet-street, the porter, who knew the barber well by sight, said, —

'Hilloa, Mr Todd, is that you? Why, who are you carrying?'

'Yes, it's I,' said Todd, 'and I am carrying my apprentice boy, Tobias Ragg, poor fellow.'

'Poor fellow! why, what's the matter with him?'

'I can hardly tell you, but he seems to me and to his mother to have gone out of his senses. Good-night to you, good-night. I'm looking for a coach.'

'Good-night, Mr Todd; I don't think you'll get one nearer than the market—what a kind thing now of him to carry the boy! It ain't every master would do that; but we must not judge of people by their looks, and even Sweeney Todd, though he has a face that one would not like to meet in a lonely place on a dark night, may be a kind-hearted man.'

Sweeney Todd walked rapidly down Fleet-street, towards old Fleet Market,* which was then in all its glory, if that could be called glory which consisted in all sorts of filth enough to produce a pestilence within the city of London.

When there he addressed a large bundle of great coats, in the middle of which was supposed to be a hackney coachman of the regular old school, and who was lounging over his vehicle, which was as long and lumbering as a city barge.

'Jarvey,'* he said, 'what will you take me to Peckham Rye* for?'

'Peckham Rye—you and the boy—there ain't any more of you waiting round the corner are there, 'cos, you know, that won't be fair.'

'No, no, no.'

'Well, don't be in a passion, master, I only asked, you know, so you need not be put out about it; I will take you for twelve shillings, and that's what I call remarkable cheap, all things considered.'

'I'll give you half the amount,' said Sweeney Todd, 'and you may consider yourself well paid.'

'Half, master! that is cutting it low; but howsoever, I suppose I must put up with it, and take you. Get in, I must try and make it up by some better fare out of somebody else.'

The barber paid no heed to these renewed remonstrances of the coachman, but got into the vehicle, carrying Tobias with him, apparently with great care and consideration; but when the coach door closed, and no one was observing him, he flung him down among the straw that was at the bottom of the vehicle, and resting his immense feet upon him, he gave one of his disagreeable laughs, as he said,—

'Well, I think I have you now, Master Tobias; your troubles will soon be over. I am really very much afraid that you will die suddenly, and then there will be an end of you altogether, which will be a very sad thing, although I don't think I shall go into mourning, because I have an opinion that that only keeps alive the bitterness of regret, and that it's a great deal better done without, Master Tobias.'

The hackney coach swung about from side to side in the proper approved manner of hackney coaches in the olden times, when they used to be called bone shakers, and to be thought wonderful if they made a progress of three miles and a half an hour.

This was the sort of vehicle then in which poor Tobias, still perfectly insensible, was rumbled over Blackfriars-bridge, and so on towards Peckham, which Sweeney Todd announced to be his place of destination.

Going at the rate they did, it was nearly two hours before they arrived upon Peckham Rye; and any one acquainted with that locality is well aware that there are two roads, the one to the left, and the other to the right, both of which are pleasantly enough studded with villa residences. Sweeney Todd directed the coachman to take the road to the left, which he accordingly did, and they pursued it for a distance of about a mile and a half.*

It must not be supposed that this pleasant district of country was then in the state it is now, as regards inhabitants or cultivation.

On the contrary, it was rather a wild spot, on which now and then a serious robbery had been committed; and which had witnessed some of the exploits of those highwaymen, whose adventures, in the present day, if one may judge from the public patronage they may receive, are viewed with a great amount of interest.

There was a lonely, large, rambling old-looking house by the wayside, on the left. A high wall surrounded it, which only allowed the topmost portion of it to be visible, and that presented great symptoms of decay, in the dilapidated character of the chimney-pots, and the general appearance of discomfort which pervaded it.

Then Sweeney Todd directed the coachman to stop, and when the vehicle, after swinging to and fro for several minutes, did indeed at last resolve itself into a state of repose, Sweeney Todd got out himself, and rang a bell, the handle of which hung invitingly at the gate.

He had to wait several minutes before an answer was given to this summons, but at length a noise proceeded from within, as if several bars and bolts were being withdrawn; and presently the door was opened, and a huge, rough-looking man made his appearance on the threshold.

'Well! what is it now?' he cried.

'I have a patient for Mr Fogg,' said Sweeney Todd. 'I want to see him immediately.'

'Oh! well, the more the merrier; it don't matter to me a bit. Have you got him with you and is he tolerably quiet?'

'It's a mere boy, and he is not violently mad, but very decidedly so as regards what he says.'

'Oh! that's it, is it? He can say what he likes here, it can make no difference in the world to us. Bring him in—Mr Fogg is in his own room.'

'I know the way: you take charge of the lad, and I will go and speak to Mr Fogg about him. But stay, give the coachman these six shillings, and discharge him.'

The doorkeeper of the lunatic asylum, for such it was, went out to obey the injunctions of Sweeney Todd, while that rascally individual himself walked along a wide passage to a door which was at the further extremity of it.

## 22

## The Mad-House Cell

WHEN the porter of the mad-house went out to the coach, his first impression was that the boy, who was said to be insane, was dead; for not even the jolting ride to Peckham had been sufficient to arouse him to a consciousness of how he was situated; and there he lay still at the bottom of the coach alike insensible to joy or sorrow.

'Is he dead?' said the man to the coachman.

'How should I know?' was the reply; 'he may be or he may not, but I want to know how long I am to wait here for my fare.'

'There is your money, be off with you. I can see now that the boy is all right, for he breathes, although it's after an odd fashion that he does so. I should rather think he has had a knock on the head, or something of that kind.'

As he spoke, he conveyed Tobias within the building, and the coachman, since he had no further interest in the matter, drove away at once, and paid no more attention to it whatever.

When Sweeney Todd reached the door at the end of the passage, he tapped at it with his knuckles, and a voice cried, —

'Who knocks — who knocks? Curses on you all, who knocks?'

Sweeney Todd did not make any verbal reply to this polite request, but opening the door he walked into the apartment, which is one that really deserves some description.

It was a large room with a vaulted roof, and in the centre was a superior oaken table, at which sat a man considerably advanced in years, as was proclaimed by his grizzled locks that graced the sides of his head, but whose herculean frame and robust constitution had otherwise successfully resisted the assaults of time.

A lamp swung from the ceiling, which had a shade over the top of it, so that it kept a tolerably bright glow upon the table below, which was covered with books and papers, as well as glasses and bottles of different kinds, which showed that the mad-house keeper was, at all events, as far as he himself was concerned, not at all indifferent to personal comfort.

The walls, however, presented the most curious aspect, for they were hung with a variety of tools and implements, which would have puzzled anyone not initiated into the matter even to guess at their uses.

These were, however, in point of fact, specimens of the different kinds of machinery which were used for the purpose of coercing the unhappy persons whose evil destiny made them members of that establishment.

Those were what is called the good old times, when all sorts of abuses flourished in perfection, and when the unhappy insane were actually punished, as if they were guilty of some great offence. Yes, and worse than that were they punished, for a criminal who might have injustice done to him by any who were in authority over him, could complain, and if he got hold of a person of higher power, his complaints might be listened to, but no one heeded what was said by the poor maniac, whose bitterest accusations of his keepers, let their conduct have been to him what it might, was only listened to and set down as a further proof of his mental disorder.*

This was indeed a most awful and sad state of things, and, to the disgrace of this country, it was a social evil allowed until very late years to continue in full force.

Mr Fogg, the mad-house keeper, fixed his keen eyes, from beneath his shaggy brows, upon Sweeney Todd, as the latter entered his apartment, and then he said, —

'Mr Todd, I think, unless my memory deceives me.'

'The same,' said the barber, making a hideous face. 'I believe I am not easily forgotten.'

'True,' said Mr Fogg, as he reached for a book, the edges of which were cut into a lot of little slips, on each of which was a capital letter, in the order of the alphabet—'True, you are not easily forgotten, Mr Todd.'

He then opened the book at the letter T, and read from it: —

'Mr Sweeney Todd, Fleet-street, London, paid one year's keep and burial of Thomas Simkins, aged 13, found dead in his bed, after a residence in the asylum of 14 months and 4 days. I think, Mr Todd, that was our last little transaction: what can I do now for you, sir?'

'I am rather unfortunate,' said Todd, 'with my boys. I have got another here, who has shown such decided symptoms of insanity, that it has become absolutely necessary to place him under your care.'

'Indeed! does he rave?'

'Why, yes, he does, and it's the most absurd nonsense in the world he raves about; for, to hear him, one would really think that, instead of being one of the most humane of men, I was in point of fact an absolute murderer.'

'A murderer, Mr Todd!'

'Yes, a murderer—a murderer to all intents and purposes; could anything be more absurd than such an accusation?—I, that have the milk of human kindness flowing in every vein, and whose very appearance ought to be sufficient to convince anybody at once of my kindness of disposition.'

Sweeney Todd finished his speech by making such a hideous face, that the mad-house keeper could not for the life of him tell what to say to it; and then there came one of those short, disagreeable laughs which Todd was such an adept in, and which, somehow or another, never appeared exactly to come from his mouth, but always made people look up at the walls and ceiling of the apartment in which they were, in great doubt as to whence the remarkable sound came.

'For how long,' said the mad-house keeper, 'do you think this malady will continue?'

'I will pay,' said Sweeney Todd, as he leaned over the table, and looked into the face of his questioner, 'I will pay for twelve months; but I don't think, between you and I, that the case will last anything like so long—I think he will die suddenly.'

'I shouldn't wonder if he did. Some of our patients do die very suddenly, and somehow or another, we never know exactly how it happens; but it must be some sort of fit, for they are found dead in the morning in their beds, and then we bury them privately and quietly, without troubling anybody about it at all, which is decidedly the best way, because it saves a great annoyance to friends and relations, as well as prevents any extra expenses which otherwise might be foolishly gone to.'

'You are wonderfully correct and considerate,' said Todd, 'and it's no more than what I expected from you, or what anyone might expect from a person of your great experience, knowledge, and acquirements. I must confess I am quite delighted to hear you talk in so elevated a strain.'

'Why,' said Mr Fogg, with a strange leer upon his face, 'we are forced to make ourselves useful, like the rest of the community; and we could not expect people to send their mad friends and relatives here, unless we took good care that their ends and views were answered by so doing. We make no remarks, and we ask no questions. Those are the principles upon which we have conducted business so successfully and so long; those are the principles upon which we shall continue to conduct it, and to merit, we hope, the patronage of the British public.'

'Unquestionably, most unquestionably.'

'You may as well introduce me to your patient at once, Mr Todd, for I suppose, by this time, he has been brought into this house.'

'Certainly, certainly, I shall have great pleasure in showing him to you.'

The mad-house keeper rose, and so did Mr Todd, and the former, pointing to the bottles and glasses on the table, said, 'When this business is settled, we can have a friendly glass together.'

To this proposition Sweeney Todd assented with a nod and then they both proceeded to what was called a reception-room in the asylum, and where poor Tobias had been conveyed and laid upon a table, when he showed slight symptoms of recovering from the state of insensibility into which he had fallen, and a man was sluicing water on his face by the assistance of a hearth broom, occasionally dipped into a pailful of that fluid.

'Quite young,' said the mad-house keeper, as he looked upon the pale and interesting face of Tobias.

'Yes,' said Sweeney Todd, 'he is young—more's the pity—and, of course, we deeply regret his present situation.'

'Oh, of course, of course; but see, he opens his eyes, and will speak directly.'

'Rave, you mean, rave!' said Todd; 'don't call it speaking, it is not entitled to the name. Hush,—listen to him.'

'Where am I?' said Tobias, 'where am I—Todd is a murderer. I denounce him.'

'You hear—you hear,' said Todd.

'Mad indeed,' said the keeper.

'Oh, save me from him,—save me from him,' said Tobias, fixing his eyes upon Mr Fogg. 'Save me from him, it is my life he seeks, because I know his secrets—he is a murderer—and many a person comes into his shop who never leaves it again in life, if at all.'

'You hear him,' said Todd, 'was there anybody so mad?'

'Desperately mad,' said the keeper. 'Come, come, young fellow, we shall be under the necessity of putting you in a straight waistcoat, if you go on in that way. We must do it, for there is no help in such cases if we don't.'

Todd slunk back into the darkness of the apartment, so that he was not seen, and Tobias continued, in an imploring tone.

'I do not know who you are, sir, or where I am; but let me beg of you to cause the house of Sweeney Todd, the barber, in Fleet-street, near St Dunstan's church, to be searched, and there you will find that he is a murderer. There are at least a hundred hats, quantities of walking-sticks, umbrellas, watches and rings, all belonging to unfortunate persons who, from time to time, have met with their deaths through him.'

'How uncommonly mad!' said Fogg.

'No, no,' said Tobias, 'I am not mad; why call me mad, when the truth or falsehood of what I say can be ascertained so easily? Search his house, and if those things be not found there, say that I am mad, and have but dreamed of them. I do not know how he kills the people. That is a great mystery to me yet, but that he does kill them I have no doubt—I cannot have a doubt.'

'Watson,' cried the mad-house keeper, 'hilloa! here, Watson.'

'I am here, sir,' said the man, who had been dashing water upon poor Tobias's face.

'You will take this lad, Watson, as he seems extremely feverish and unsettled. You will take him, and shave his head, Watson, and put a straight waistcoat upon him, and let him be put in one of the dark, damp cells. We must be careful of him, and too much light encourages delirium and fever.'

'Oh! no, no!' cried Tobias; 'what have I done that I should be subjected to such cruel treatment? What have I done that I should be placed in a cell? If this be a mad-house, I am not mad. Oh, have mercy upon me, have mercy upon me!'

'You will give him nothing but bread and water, Watson, and the first symptoms of his recovery, which will produce better treatment, will be his exonerating his master from what he has said about him, for he must be mad so long as he continues to accuse such a gentleman as Mr Todd of such things; nobody but a mad man or a mad boy would think of it.'

'Then,' said Tobias, 'I shall continue mad, for if it be madness to know and to aver that Sweeney Todd, the barber, of Fleet-street, is a murderer, mad am I, for I know it, and aver it. It is true, it is true.'

'Take him away, Watson, and do as I desired you. I begin to find that the boy is a very dangerous character, and more viciously mad than anybody we have had here for a considerable time.'

The man named Watson seized upon Tobias, who again uttered a shriek something similar to the one which had come from his lips when Sweeney Todd clutched hold of him in his mother's room. But they were used to such things at that mad-house, and cared little for them, so no one heeded the cry in the least, but poor Tobias was carried to the door half maddened in reality by the horrors that surrounded him.

Just as he was being conveyed out, Sweeney Todd stepped up to him, and putting his mouth close to his ear, he whispered, —

'Ha! ha! Tobias! how do you feel now? Do you think Sweeney Todd will be hung, or will you die in the cell of a mad-house?'

## 23

### *The New Cook to Mrs Lovett Gets Tired of his Situation*

FROM what we have already had occasion to record about Mrs Lovett's new cook, who ate so voraciously in the cellar, our readers will no doubt be induced to believe that he was a gentleman likely enough soon to tire of his situation.

To a starving man, and one who seemed completely abandoned even by hope, Lovett's bake-house, with an unlimited leave to eat as much as possible, must of course present itself in the most desirable and lively colours; and no wonder, therefore, that banishing all scruple, a man so pleased, would take the situation with very little inquiry.

But people will tire of good things; and it is a remarkably well-authenticated fact that human nature is prone to be discontented.

And those persons who are well acquainted with the human mind, and who know well how little value people soon set upon things which they possess, while those which they are pursuing, and which seem to be beyond their reach, assume the liveliest colours imaginable, adopt various means of turning this to account.

Napoleon took good care that the meanest of his soldiers should see in perspective the possibility of grasping a marshal's baton.

Confectioners at the present day, when they take a new apprentice, tell him to eat as much as he likes of those tempting tarts and sweetmeats, one or two of which before had been a most delicious treat.

The soldier goes on fighting away, and never gets the marshal's baton. The confectioner's boy crams himself with Banbury cakes,* gets dreadfully sick, and never touches one afterwards.

And now, to revert to our friend in Mrs Lovett's bake-house.

At first everything was delightful, and, by the aid of the machinery, he found that it was no difficult matter to keep up the supply of pies by really a very small amount of manual labour. And that labour was such a labour of love, for the pies were delicious; there could be no mistake about that. He tasted them half cooked, he tasted them wholly cooked, and he tasted them overdone; hot and cold, pork and veal with seasoning, and without seasoning, until at last he had had them in every possible way and shape; and when the fourth day came after his arrival in the cellar, he might have been seen sitting in rather a contemplative attitude with a pie before him.

It was twelve o'clock: he heard that sound come from the shop. Yes, it was twelve o'clock, and he had eaten nothing yet; but he kept his eyes fixed upon the pie that lay untouched before him.

'The pies are all very well,' he said, 'in fact of course they are capital pies; and now that I see how they are made, and know that there is nothing wrong in them, I of course relish them more than ever, but one can't live always upon pies; it's quite impossible one can subsist upon pies from one end of the year to the other, if they were the finest pies the world ever saw, or ever will see. I don't say anything against the pies—I know they are made of the finest flour, the best possible butter, and that the meat, which comes from God knows where, is the most delicate-looking and tender I ever ate in my life.'

He stretched out his hand and broke a small portion of the crust from the pie that was before him, and he tried to eat it.

He certainly did succeed, but it was a great effort; and when he had done, he shook his head, saying, —

'No, no! damn it, I cannot eat it, and that's the fact—one cannot be continually eating pie; it is out of the question, quite out of the question, and all I have to remark is, damn the pies! I really don't think I shall be able to let another one pass my lips.'

He rose and paced with rapid strides the place in which he was, and then suddenly he heard a noise, and, looking up, he saw a trap-door in the roof open, and a sack of flour begin gradually to come down.

'Hilloa, hilloa!' he cried, 'Mrs Lovett, Mrs Lovett!'

Down came the flour, and the trap-door was closed.

'Oh, I can't stand this sort of thing,' he exclaimed. 'I cannot be made into a mere machine for the manufacture of pies. I cannot, and will not endure it—it is past all bearing.'

For the first time almost since his incarceration, for such it really was, he began to think that he would take an accurate survey of the place where this tempting manufacture was carried on.

---

The fact was, his mind had been so intensively occupied during the time he had been there in providing merely for his physical wants, that he had scarcely had time to think or reason upon the probabilities of an uncomfortable termination of his career; but now, when he had become quite surfeited with the pies, and tired of the darkness and gloom of the place, many unknown fears began to creep across him, and he really trembled, as he asked himself what was to be the end of all.

It was with such a feeling as this that he now set about taking a careful and accurate survey of the place, and, taking a little lamp in his hand, he resolved to peer into every corner of it, with a hope that surely he should find some means by which he should effect an escape from what otherwise threatened to be an intolerable imprisonment.

The vault in which the ovens were situated was the largest; and although a number of smaller ones communicated with it, containing the different mechanical contrivances for the pie-making, he could not from any one of them discover an outlet.

But it was to the vault where the meat was deposited upon stone shelves, that he paid the greatest share of attention, for to that vault he felt convinced there must be some hidden and secret means of ingress, and therefore of egress likewise, or else how came the shelves always so well stocked with meat as they were?

This vault was larger than any of the other subsidiary ones, and the roof was very high, and, come into it when he would, it always happened that he found meat enough upon the shelves, cut into large lumps and sometimes into slices, to make a batch of pies with.

When it got there was not so much a mystery to him as how it got there; for of course, as he must sleep sometimes, he concluded, naturally enough, that it was brought in by some means during the period that he devoted to repose.

He stood in the centre of this vault with the lamp in his hand, and he turned slowly round, surveying the walls and the ceiling with the most critical and marked attention, but not the smallest appearance of an outlet was observable.

In fact, the walls were so entirely filled up with the stone shelves, that there was no space left for a door; and, as for the ceiling, it seemed to be perfectly entire.

Then the floor was of earth; so that the idea of a trap-door opening in it was out of the question, because there was no one on his side of it to place the earth again over it, and give it its compact and usual appearance.

'This is most mysterious,' he said; 'and if ever I could have been brought to believe that anyone had the assistance of the devil himself in conducting human affairs, I should say that by some means Mrs Lovett had made it worth the while of that elderly individual to assist her; for, unless the meat gets here by some supernatural agency, I really cannot see how it can get here at all. And yet here it is, so fresh, and pure, and white-looking, although I never could tell the pork from the veal myself, for they seemed to me both alike.'

He now made a still narrower examination of this vault, but he gained nothing by that. He found that the walls at the backs of the shelves were composed of flat pieces of stone, which, no doubt, were necessary for the support of the shelves themselves; but beyond that he made no further discovery, and he was about leaving the place, when he fancied he saw some writing on the inner side of the door.

A closer inspection convinced him that there were a number of lines written with lead pencil, and after some difficulty he deciphered them as follows: —

'Whatever unhappy wretch reads these lines may bid adieu to the world and all hope, for he is a doomed man! He will never emerge from these vaults with life, for there is a hideous secret connected with them so awful and so hideous, that to write it makes one's blood curdle, and the flesh to creep upon my bones. That secret is this—and you may be assured, whoever is reading these lines, that I write the truth, and that it is as impossible to make that awful truth worse by any exaggeration, as it would be by a candle at midday to attempt to add lustre to the sunbeams.'

Here, most unfortunately, the writing broke off, and our friend, who, up to this point, had perused the lines with the most intense interest, felt great bitterness of disappointment, from the fact that enough should have been written to stimulate his curiosity to the highest possible point, but not enough to gratify it.

'This is, indeed, most provoking,' he exclaimed; 'what can this most dreadful secret be, which it is impossible to exaggerate? I cannot, for a moment, divine to what it can allude.'

In vain he searched over the door for some more writing—there was none to be found, and from the long straggling pencil mark which followed the last word, it seemed as if he who had been then writing had been interrupted, and possibly met the fate that he had predicted, and was about to explain the reason of.

'This is worse than no information. I had better have remained in ignorance than have so indistinct a warning; but they shall not find me an easy victim, and, besides, what power on earth can force me to make pies unless I like, I should wish to know.'

As he stepped out of the place in which the meat was kept into the large vault where the ovens were, he trod upon a piece of paper that was lying upon the ground, and which he was quite certain he had not observed before. It was fresh and white, and clean too, so that it could not have been long there, and he picked it up with some curiosity.

That curiosity was, however, soon turned to dismay when he saw what was written upon it, which was to the following effect, and well calculated to produce a considerable amount of alarm in the breast of anyone situated as he was, so entirely friendless and so entirely hopeless of any extraneous aid in those dismal vaults, which he began, with a shudder, to suspect would be his tomb: —

'You are getting dissatisfied, and therefore it becomes necessary to explain to you your real position, which is simply this: —you are a prisoner, and were such from the first moment that you set foot where you now are; and you will find that, unless you are resolved upon sacrificing your life, your best plan will be to quietly give in to the circumstances in which you find yourself placed. Without going into any argument or details upon the subject, it is sufficient to inform you that so long as you continue to make the pies, you will be safe; but if you refuse, then the first time you are caught sleeping your throat will be cut.'

This document was so much to the purpose, and really had so little of verbosity about it, that it was extremely difficult to doubt its sincerity.

It dropped from the half-paralysed hands of that man who, in the depth of his distress, and urged on by great necessity, had accepted a situation that he would have given worlds to escape from, had he been possessed of them.

'Gracious Heaven!' he exclaimed, 'and am I then indeed condemned to such a slavery? Is it possible that even in the very heart of London I am a prisoner, and without the means of resisting the most frightful threats that are uttered against me? Surely, surely, this must all be a dream! It is too terrific to be true!'

He sat down upon that low stool where his predecessor had sat before, receiving his death wound from the assassin who had glided in behind him, and dealt him that terrific crashing blow, whose only mercy was that it at once deprived the victim of existence.

He could have wept bitterly, wept as he there sat, for he thought over days long passed away, of opportunities let go by with the heedless laugh of youth; he thought over all the chances and misfortunes of his life, and now to find himself the miserable inhabitant of a cellar, condemned to a mean and troublesome employment, without even the liberty of leaving that to starve if he chose, upon pain of death—a frightful death which had been threatened him—was indeed torment!

No wonder that at times he felt himself unnerved, and that a child might have conquered him, while at other moments such a feeling of despair would come across him, that he called aloud to his enemies to make their appearance, and give him at least the chance of a struggle for his life.

'If I am to die,' he cried, 'let me die with some weapon in my hand, as a brave man ought, and I will not complain, for there is little indeed in life now which should induce me to cling to it; but I will not be murdered in the dark.'

He sprang to his feet, and running up to the door, which opened from the house into the vaults, he made a violent and desperate effort to shake it.

But such a contingency as this had surely been looked forward to and provided against, for the door was of amazing strength, and most effectually resisted all his efforts, so that the result of his endeavours was but to exhaust himself, and he staggered back, panting and despairing, to the seat he had so recently left.

Then he heard a voice, and upon looking up he saw that the small square opening in the upper part of the door, through which he had been before addressed, was open, and a face there appeared, but it was not the face of Mrs Lovett.

On the contrary, it was a large and hideous male physiognomy, and the voice that came from it was croaking and harsh, sounding most unmusically upon the ears of the unfortunate man, who was then made a victim to Mrs Lovett's pies' popularity.

'Continue at your work,' said the voice, 'or death will be your portion as soon as sleep overcomes you, and you sink exhausted to that repose which you will never awaken from, except to feel the pangs of death, and to be conscious that you are weltering in your blood.

'Continue at your work and you will escape all this—neglect it and your doom is sealed.'

'What have I done that I should be made such a victim of? Let me go, and I will swear never to divulge the fact that I have been in these vaults, so I cannot disclose any of their secrets, even if I knew them.'

'Make pies,' said the voice, 'eat them and be happy. How many a man would envy your position—withdrawn from all the struggles of existence, amply provided with board and lodging, and engaged in a pleasant and delightful occupation. It is astonishing how you can be dissatisfied!'

Bang! went the little square orifice at the top of the door, and the voice was heard no more. The jeering mockery of those tones, however, still lingered upon the ear of the unhappy prisoner, and he clasped his head in his hands with a fearful impression upon his brain that he surely must be going mad.

'He will drive me to insanity,' he cried; 'already I feel a sort of slumber stealing over me for want of exercise, and the confined air of these vaults hinders me from taking regular repose; but now, if I close an eye, I shall expect to find the assassin's knife at my throat.'

He sat for some time longer, and not even the dread he had of sleep could prevent a drowsiness creeping over his faculties, and this weariness would not be shaken off by any ordinary means, until at length he sprang to his feet, and shaking himself roughly like one determined to be wide awake, he said to himself mournfully, —

'I must do their bidding or die; hope may be a delusion here, but I cannot altogether abandon it, and not until its faintest image has departed from my breast can I lie down to sleep and say—Let death come in any shape it may, it is welcome.'

With a desperate and despairing energy he set about replenishing the furnaces of the oven, and when he had got them all in a good state he commenced manufacturing a batch of one hundred pies, which, when he had finished and placed upon the tray and set the machine in motion which conducted them up to the shop, he considered to be a sort of price paid for his continued existence, and flinging himself upon the ground, he fell into a deep slumber.

## 24

## *The Night at the Mad-House*

WHEN Sweeney Todd had with such diabolical want of feeling whispered the few words of mockery which we have recorded in Tobias's ear, when he was carried out of Mr Fogg's reception-room to be taken to a cell, the villainous barber drew back and indulged in rather a longer laugh than usual.

'Mr Todd,' said Fogg, 'I find that you still retain your habit of merriment, but yours ain't the most comfortable laugh in the world, and we seldom hear anything to equal it, even from one of our cells.'

'No!' said Sweeney Todd, 'I don't suppose you do, and for my part I never heard of a cell laughing yet.'

'Oh! you know what I mean, Mr Todd, well enough.'

'That may be,' said Todd, 'but it would be just as well to say it for all that. I think, however, as I came in, you said something about refreshment?'

'I certainly did; and if you will honour me by stepping back to my room, I think I can offer you, Mr Todd, a glass of as nice wine as the king himself could put on his table, if he were any judge of that commodity, which I am inclined to think he is not.'

'What do you expect,' said Sweeney Todd, 'that such an idiot should be a judge of; but I shall have great pleasure in tasting your wine, for I have no hesitation in saying that my work to-night has made me thirsty.'

At this moment a shriek was heard, and Sweeney Todd shrank away from the door.

'Oh! it's nothing, it's nothing,' said Mr Fogg: 'if you had resided here as long as I have, you would get accustomed to hearing a slight noise. The worst of it is, when half a dozen of the mad fellows get shrieking against each other in the middle of the night. Then, I grant, it is a little annoying.'

'What do you do with them?'

'We send in one of the keepers with the lash, and soon put a stop to that. We are forced to keep the upper hand of them, or else we should have no rest. Hark! do you hear that fellow now? he is generally pretty quiet, but he has taken it into his head to be outrageous today; but one of my men will soon put a stop to that. This way, Mr Todd, if you please, and as we don't often meet, I think when we do we ought to have a social glass.'

Sweeney Todd made several horrible faces as he followed the mad-house keeper, and he looked as if it would have given him quite as much pleasure, and no doubt it would, to brain that individual, as to drink his wine, although probably he would have preferred doing the latter process first, and executing the former afterwards, and at his leisure.

They soon reached the room which was devoted to the use of Mr Fogg and his friends, and which contained the many little curiosities in the way of mad-house discipline, that were in that age considered indispensable in such establishments.

Mr Fogg moved away with his hands a great number of the books and papers which were on the table, so as to leave a vacant space, and then drawing the cork of a bottle he filled himself a large glass of its contents, and invited Sweeney Todd to do the same, who was by no means slow in following his example.

While these two villains are carousing, and caring nothing for the scene of misery with which they are surrounded, poor Tobias, in conformity with the orders that had been issued with regard to him, was conveyed along a number of winding passages and down several staircases towards the cells of the establishment.

In vain he struggled to get free from his captor—as well might a hare have struggled in the fangs of a wolf—nor were his cries at all heeded; although, now and then, the shriek he uttered was terrible to hear, and enough to fill anyone with dismay.

'I am not mad,' said he, 'indeed I am not mad—let me go, and I will say nothing—not one word shall ever pass my lips regarding Mr Todd—let me go, oh, let me go, and I will pray for you as long as I live.'

Mr Watson whistled a lively tune.

'If I promise—if I swear to tell nothing, Mr Todd will not wish me kept here—all he wants is my silence, and I will take any oath he likes. Speak to him for me, I implore you, and let me go.'

Mr Watson commenced the second part of his lively tune, and by that time he reached a door, which he unlocked, and then, setting down Tobias upon the threshold, he gave him a violent kick, which flung him down two steps on to the stone floor of a miserable cell, from the roof of which continual moisture was dripping, the only accommodation it possessed being a truss of damp straw flung into one corner.

'There,' said Mr Watson, 'my lad, you can stay there and make yourself comfortable till somebody comes to shave your head, and after that you will find yourself quite a gentleman.'

'Mercy! mercy—have mercy on me!'

'Mercy! what the devil do you mean by mercy? Well, that's a good joke; but I can tell you, you have come to the wrong shop for that, we don't keep it in stock here, and if we wanted ever so little of it, we should have to go somewhere else for it.'

Mr Watson laughed so much at his own joke, that he felt quite amiable, and told Tobias that if he were perfectly quiet, and said 'thank you' for everything, he wouldn't put him in the straight waistcoat, although Mr Fogg had ordered it; 'for,' added Mr Watson, 'so far as that goes, I don't care a straw what Mr Fogg says or what he does; he can't do without me, damn him! because I know too many of his secrets.'

Tobias made no answer to this promise, but he lay upon his back on the floor of his cell wringing his hands despairingly, and feeling that almost the very atmosphere of the place seemed pregnant with insanity, and giving himself up for lost entirely.

'I shall never—never,' he said, 'look upon the bright sky and the green fields again. I shall be murdered here, because I know too much; what can save me now? Oh, what an evil chance it was that brought me back again to my mother, when I ought to have been far, far away by this time, instead of being, as I know I am, condemned to death in this frightful place. Despair seizes upon me! What noise is that—a shriek? Yes, yes, there is some other blighted heart beside mine in this dreadful house. Oh, Heaven! what will become of me? I feel already stifled and sick, and faint with the air of this dreadful cell. Help, help, help! have mercy upon me, and I will do anything, promise anything, swear anything!'

If poor Tobias had uttered his complaints on the most desolate shore that ever a shipwrecked mariner was cast upon, they could not have been more unheeded than they were in that house of terror.

He screamed and shrieked for aid. He called upon all the friends he had ever known in early life, and at that moment he seemed to remember the name of everyone who had ever uttered a kind word to him; and to those persons who, alas! could not hear him, but were far enough removed away from his cell, he called for aid in that hour of his deep distress.

At length, faint, wearied and exhausted, he lay a mere living wreck in that damp, unwholesome cell, and felt almost willing that death should come and relieve him, at least from the pang of constantly expecting it!

His cries, however, had had the effect of summoning up all the wild spirits in that building; and, as he now lay in the quiet of absolute exhaustion, he heard from far and near smothered cries and shrieks and groans, such as one might expect would fill the air of the infernal regions with dismal echoes.

A cold and clammy perspiration broke out upon him, as these sounds each moment more plainly fell upon his ear, and as he gazed upon the profound darkness of the cell, his excited fancy began to people it with strange, unearthly beings, and he could suppose that he saw hideous faces grinning at him, and huge misshapen creatures crawling on the walls, and floating in the damp, pestiferous atmosphere of the wretched cell.

In vain he covered his eyes with his hands; these creatures of his imagination were not to be shut out from the mind, and he saw them, if possible, more vividly than before, and presenting themselves with more frightfully tangible shapes. Truly, if such visions should continue to haunt him, poor Tobias was likely enough to follow the fate of many others who had been held in that establishment perfectly sane, but in a short time exhibited in it as raving lunatics.

\*        \*        \*        \*        \*

'A nice clear cool glass of wine,' said Sweeney Todd, as he held up his glass between him and the light, 'and pleasant drinking; so soft and mild in the mouth, and yet gliding down the throat with a pleasant strength of flavour!'

'Yes,' said Mr Fogg, 'it might be worse. You see, some patients, who are low and melancholy mad, require stimulants, and their friends send them wine. This is some that was so sent.'

'I should certainly, Mr Fogg, not expect such an act of indiscretion from you, knowing you as I do to be quite a man of the world.'

'Thank you for the compliment. This wine, now, was sent for an old gentleman who had turned so melancholy, that he not only would not take food enough to keep life and soul together, but he really terrified his friends so by threatening suicide that they sent him here for a few months; and, as stimulants were recommended for him, they sent this wine, you see; but I stimulated him without it quite as well, for I drink the wine myself and give him such an infernal good kick or two every day, and that stimulates him, for it puts him in such a devil of a passion that I am quite sure he doesn't want any wine.'

'A good plan,' said Sweeney Todd, 'but I wonder you don't contrive that your own private room should be free from the annoyance of hearing such sounds as those that have been coming upon my ears for the last five or ten minutes.'

'It's impossible; you cannot get out of the way if you live in the house at all; and you see, as regards these mad fellows, they are quite like a pack of wolves, and when once one of them begins howling and shouting, the others are sure to chime in, in full chorus, and make no end of a disturbance till we stop them, as I have already told you we do, with a strong hand.'

'While I think of it,' said Sweeney Todd, as he drew from his pocket a leathern bag, 'while I think of it, I may as well pay you the year's money, for the lad I have brought you; you see, I have not forgot the excellent rule you have of being paid in advance. There is the amount.'

'Ah, Mr Todd,' said the mad-house keeper, as he counted the money, and then placed it in his pocket, 'it's a pleasure to do business with a thorough business man like yourself. The bottle stands with you, Mr Todd, and I beg you will not spare it. Do you know, Mr Todd, this is a line of life which I have often thought would have suited you; I am certain you have a genius for such things.'

'Not equal to you,' said Todd; 'but as I am fond, certainly, of what is strange and out of the way, some of the scenes and characters you come across would, I have no doubt, be highly entertaining to me.'

'Scenes and characters, I believe you! During the course of a business like ours, we come across all sorts of strange things; and if I chose to do it, which, of course, I don't, I could tell a few tales which would make some people shake in their shoes; but I have no right to tell them, for I have been paid, and what the deuce is it to me?'

'Oh, nothing, of course, nothing. But just while we are sipping our wine, now, couldn't you tell me something that would not be betraying anybody else's confidence?'

'I could, I could; I don't mean to say that I could not, and I don't much care if I do to you.'

# 25

## Mr Fogg's Story at the Mad-House to Sweeney Todd

AFTER a short pause, during which Mr Fogg appeared to be referring to the cells of memory, with the view of being refreshed in a matter that had long since been a bygone, but which he desired to place as clearly before his listener as he could, in fact, to make if possible that relation real to him, and to omit nothing during its progress that should be told; or possibly that amiable individual was engaged in considering if there were any salient points that might incriminate himself, or give even a friend a handle to make use of against him, but apparently there was nothing of the kind, for, after a loud 'hem!' he filled the glasses, saying,—

'Well, now, as you are a friend, I don't mind telling you how we do business here—things that have been done, you know, by others; but I have had my share as well as others—I have known a thing or two, Mr Todd, and I may say I have done a thing or two, too.'

'Well, we must live and let live,' said Sweeney Todd, 'there's no going against that, you know; if all I have done could speak, why—but no matter, I am listening to you—however, if deeds could speak, one or two clever things would come out, rather, I think.'

'Ay, 'tis well they don't,' said Mr Fogg, with much solemnity, 'if they did, they would constantly be speaking at times when it would be very inconvenient to hear them, and dangerous besides.'

'So it would,' said Sweeney, 'a still tongue makes a wise head—but, then the silent system would bring no grist to the mill, and we must speak when we know we are right and among friends.'

'Of course,' said Fogg, 'of course, that's the right use of speech, and one may as well be without it as to have it and not use it; but come—drink, and fill again before I begin, and then to my tale. But we may as well have sentiment. Sentiment, you know,' continued Fogg, 'is the very soul of friendship. What do you say to "The heart that can feel for another"?'

'With all my soul,' said Sweeney Todd; 'it's very touching—very touching indeed. "The heart that can feel for another!"' and as he spoke, he emptied the glass, which he pushed towards Fogg to refill.

'Well,' said Fogg, as he complied, 'we have had the sentiment, we may as well have the exemplification.'

'Ha! ha! ha!' said Todd, 'very good, very good indeed; pray go on, that will do capitally.'

'I may as well tell you the whole matter, as it occurred; I will then let you know all I know, and in the same manner. None of the parties are now living, or, at least, they are not in this country, which is just the same thing, so far as I am concerned.'

'Then that is an affair settled and done with,' remarked Sweeney Todd parenthetically.

'Yes, quite:—Well, it was one night—such a one as this, and pretty well about the same hour, perhaps somewhat earlier than this. However, it doesn't signify a straw about the hour; but it was quite night, a dark and wet night too, when a knock came at the street door—a sharp double knock—it was. I was sitting alone, as I might have been now, drinking a glass or two of wine; I was startled, for I was thinking about an affair I had on hand at that very moment, of which there was a little stir.

'However, I went to the door, and peeped through a grating that I had there, and saw only a man; he had drawn his horse inside the gate, and secured him; he wore a large Whitney riding-coat with a cape that would have thrown off a deluge.*

'I fancied, or I thought I could tell, that he meant no mischief; so I opened the door at once and saw a tall gentlemanly man, but wrapped up so, that you could not tell who or what he was; but my eyes are sharp, you know, Mr Todd: we haven't seen so much of the world without learning to distinguish what kind of person one has to deal with.'

'I should think not,' said Todd.

'"Well," said I, "what is your pleasure, sir?"

'The stranger paused a moment or two before he made any reply to me.

'"Is your name Fogg?" he said.

'"Yes, it is," said I, "my name is Fogg,—what is your pleasure, sir?"

'"Why," said he, after another pause, during which he fixed his eye very hard upon me—"why, I wish to have a little private conversation with you, if you can spare so much time, upon a very important matter which I have in hand."

'"Walk in, sir," said I, as soon as I heard what it was he wanted, and he followed me in. "It is a very unpleasant night, and it's coming on to rain harder: I think it is fortunate you have got housed."

'He came into this very parlour, and took a seat before the fire, with his back to the light, so that I couldn't see his face very well.

'However, I was determined that I would be satisfied in these particulars, and so, when he had taken off his hat, I stirred up the fire, and made a blaze that illuminated the whole room, and which showed me the sharp, thin visage of my visitor, who was a dark man with keen grey eyes that were very restless,—

'"Will you have a glass of wine?" said I; "the night is cold as well as wet."

'"Yes, I will," he replied; "I am cold with riding. You have a lonely place about here; your house, I see, stands alone too. You have not many neighbours."

'"No, sir," said I; "we hadn't need, for when any of the poor things set to screaming, it would make them feel very uncomfortable indeed."

'"So it would; there is an advantage in that both to yourself as well as to them. It would be disagreeable to you to know that you were disturbing your neighbours, and they would feel equally uncomfortable in being disturbed, and yet you must do your duty."

'"Ay! to be sure," said I; "I must do my duty, and people won't pay me for letting madmen go, though they may for keeping them; and besides that, I think some on 'em would get their throats cut if I did."

'"You are right—quite right," said he; "I am glad to find you of that mind, for I came to you about an affair that requires some delicacy about it, since it is a female patient."

'"Ah!" said I, "I always pay a great attention, very great attention, and I don't recollect a case, however violent it may be, but what I can overcome. I always make 'em acknowledge me, and there's much art in that."

'"To be sure, there must be."

'"And moreover, they wouldn't so soon crouch and shrink away from me, and do what I tell 'em, if I did not treat them with kindness, that is, as far as is consistent with one's duty, for I mustn't forget that."

"'Exactly," he replied; "those are my sentiments, exactly."

"'And now, sir, will you inform me in what way I can serve you?"

"'Why, I have a relative—a female relative, who is unhappily affected with a brain disease; we have tried all we can do, without any effect. Do what we will, it comes to the same thing in the end."

"'Ah!" said I; "poor thing—what a dreadful thing it must be to you or any of her friends, who have the charge of her, to see her day by day an incurable maniac. Why, it is just as bad as when a friend or relative was dead, and you were obliged to have the dead body constantly in your house before your eyes."

"'Exactly, my friend," replied the stranger, "exactly, you are a man of discernment, Mr Fogg. I see that is truly the state of the case. You may then guess at the state of our feelings, when we have to part with one beloved by us."

'As he spoke, he turned right round, and faced me, looking very hard into my face.

"'Well," said I, "yours is a hard case; but to have one afflicted about you in the manner the young lady is, is truly distressing: it is like having a perpetual lumbago in your back."

"'Exactly," said the stranger. "I tell you what, you are the very man to do this thing for me."

"'I am sure of it," said I.

"'Then we understand each other, eh?" said the stranger. "I must say I like your appearance; it is not often such people as you and I meet."

"'I hope it will be to our mutual advantage," said I, "because such people don't meet every day, and we oughtn't to meet to no purpose; so, in anything delicate and confidential, you may command me."

"'I see you are a clever man," said he; "well, well, I must pay you in proportion to your talents. How do you do business—by the job, or by the year?"

"'Well," said I, "where it's a matter of some nicety it may be both—but it entirely depends upon circumstances. I had better know exactly what it is I have to do."

"'Why, you see, it is a young female about eighteen, and she is somewhat troublesome, takes to screaming and all that kind of thing. I want her taken care of, though you must be very careful she neither runs away, nor suddenly commits any mischief, as her madness does not appear to me to have any particular form, and would, at times, completely deceive the best of us, and then suddenly she will break out violently, and snap or fly at anybody with her teeth."

"'Is she so bad as that?'"

"'Yes, quite. So, it is quite impossible to keep her at home; and I expect it will be a devil of a job to get her here. I tell you what you shall have; I'll pay you your yearly charge for board and care, and you'll come and assist me in securing her, and bringing her down. It will take some trouble."

"'Very well,' said I, "that will do; but you must double the note and make it twenty, if you please; it will cost something to come and do the job well."

"'I see—very well—we won't disagree about a ten-pound note; but you'll know how to dispose of her if she comes here."

"'Oh, yes—very healthy place.'"

"'But I don't know that health is a very great blessing to anyone under such circumstances; indeed, who would begrudge an early grave to one severely afflicted?'"

"'Nobody ought,' said I; "if they know what mad people went through, they would not, I'm sure."

"'That is very true again, but the fact is, they don't, and they only look at one side of the picture; for my own part, I think that it ought to be so ordained, that when people are so afflicted, nature ought to sink under the affliction, and so insensibly to revert to the former state of nonentity."

---

"'Well,' said I, "that may be as you please, I don't understand all that; but I tell you what, I hope if she were to die much sooner than you expect, you would not think it too much trouble to afford me some compensation for my loss."

"'Oh dear no! and to show you that I shall entertain no such illiberal feeling, I will give you two hundred pounds, when the certificate of her burial can be produced. You understand me?'"

"'Certainly.'"

"'Her death will be of little value to me, without the legal proof,' said the stranger; "so she must die at her own pleasure, or live while she can."

"'Certainly,' said I.

"'But what terrifies me,' said the stranger, "most is, her terror-stricken countenance, always staring us in our faces; and it arose from her being terrified; indeed, I think if she were thoroughly frightened, she would fall dead. I am sure, if any wickedly disposed person were to do so, death would no doubt result.'

"'Ah!' said I, 'it would be a bad job; now tell me where I am to see you, and how about the particulars.'

"'Oh, I will tell you; now, can you be at the corner of Grosvenor-street, near Park-lane*?'

"'Yes,' I replied, 'I will.'

"'With a coach, too. I wish you to have a coach, and one that you can depend upon, because there may be a little noise. I will try to avoid it, if possible, but we cannot always do what we desire; but you must have good horses.'

"'Now, I tell you what is my plan; that is, if you don't mind the damages, if any happen.'

"'What are they?'

"'This—suppose a horse falls, and is hurt, or an upset,—would you stand the racket?'

"'I would, of course.'

"'Then listen to me; I have had more of these affairs than you have, no doubt. Well, then, I have had experience which you have not. Now, I'll get a trotting-horse, and a covered cart or chaise—one that will go along well at ten miles an hour, and no mistake about it.'

"'But will it hold enough?'

"'Yes, four or five or six, and upon a push, I have known eight to cram in it; but then you know we were not particular how we were placed; but still it will hold as many as a hackney coach, only not so conveniently; but then we have nobody in the affair to drive us, and there can't be too few.'

"'Well, that is perhaps best; but have you a man on whom you can depend, because if you could, why, I would not be in the affair at all.'

"'You must,' said I; 'in the first place, I can depend upon one man best; him I must leave here to mind the place; so if you can manage the girl, I will drive, and know the road as well as the way to my own mouth; I would rather have as few in it as possible.'

'"Your precaution is very good, and I think I will try and manage it, that there shall be only you and I acquainted with the transaction; at all events, should it become necessary, it will be time enough to let some other person into the secret at the moment their services are required. That, I think, will be the best arrangement that I can come to; what do you say?"

'"That will do very well—when we get her here, and when I have seen her a few days, I can tell you what to do with her."

'"Exactly; and now, goodnight—there is the money I promised, and now again, good-night! I shall see you at the appointed time."

'"You will," said I—"one glass more, it will do you good, and keep the rain out."

'He took off a glass of wine, and then pulled his hat over his face, and left the house.

'It was a dark, wet night, and the wind blew, and we heard the sound of his horse's hoofs for some time; however, I shut the door and went in, thinking over in my own mind what would be the gain of my own exertions.

\*    \*    \*    \*    \*

'Well, at the appointed hour, I borrowed a chaise cart, a covered one, with what you call a head to it, and I trotted to town in it. At the appointed time, I was at the corner of Grosvenor-street; it was late, and yet I waited there an hour or more before I saw any one.

'I walked into a little house to get a glass of spirits to keep up the warmth of the body, and when I came out again, I saw someone standing at my horse's head. I immediately went up.

'"Oh, you are here," he said.

'"Yes, I am," said I, "I have been here the Lord knows how long. Are you ready?"

'"Yes, I am come," said he, as he got into the cart, "come to the place I shall tell you—I shall only get her into the cart, and you must do the rest."

'"You'll come back with me: I shall want help on the road, and I have no one with me."

'"Yes, I will come with you, and manage the girl, but you must drive, and take all the casualties of the road, for I shall have enough to do to hold her, and keep her from screaming, when she does awake."

"'What! is she asleep?'

"'I have given her a small dose of laudanum,* which will cause her to sleep comfortably for an hour or two, but the cold air and disturbance will most probably awaken her first.'

"'Throw something over her, and keep her warm, and have something ready to thrust into her mouth, in case she takes to screaming, and then you are all right.'

"'Good,' he replied: 'now wait here. I am going to yon house. When I've entered, and disappeared several minutes, you may quietly drive up, and take your station on the other side of the lamp-post.'

'As he spoke he got out, and walked to a large house which he entered softly, and left the door ajar; and after he had gone in, I walked the horse quietly up to the lamp-post, and as I placed it, the horse and front of the cart were completely in the dark.

'I had scarcely got up to the spot, when the door opened, and he looked out to see if anybody was passing. I gave him the word, and out he came, leaving the door, and came with what looked like a bundle of clothes, but which was the young girl and some clothes he had brought with him.

"'Give her to me,' said I, 'and jump up and take the reins; go on as quickly as you can.'

'I took the girl in my arms, and handed her into the back part of the chaise, while he jumped up, and drove away. I placed the young girl in an easy position upon some hay, and stuffed the clothes under her, so as to prevent the jolting from hurting her.

"'Well,' said I, 'you may as well come back here, and sit beside her: she is all right. You seem rather in a stew.'

"'Why, I have run with her in my arms, and altogether it has flurried me.'

"'You had better have some brandy,' said I.

"'No, no! don't stop.'

"'Pooh, pooh!' I replied, pulling up, 'here is the last house we shall come to, to have a good stiff tumbler of hot brandy-and-water. Come, have you any change, about a sovereign will do, because I shall want change on the road? Come, be quick.'

'He handed me a sovereign, saying,—

"'Don't you think it's dangerous to stop—we may be watched, or she may wake.'

'"Not a bit of it. She snores too loudly to wake just yet, and you'll faint without the cordial; so keep a good look-out upon the wench, and you will recover your nerves again."

'As I spoke, I jumped out, and got two glasses of brandy and water, hot, strong, and sweet. I had in about two minutes made out of the house.

'"Here," said I, "drink—drink it all up—it will bring the eyes out of your head."

'I spoke the truth, for what with my recommendation and his nervousness and haste, he drank about half of it at a gulp.

'I shall never forget his countenance. Ha! ha! ha! I can't keep my mirth to myself. Just imagine the girl inside a covered cart, all dark, so dark that you could hardly see the outlines of the shadow of a man—and then imagine, if you can, a pair of keen eyes, that shone in the dark like cat's eyes, suddenly give out a flash of light, and then turn round in their sockets, showing the whites awfully, and then listen to the fall of the glass, and see him grasp his throat with one hand, and thrust the other hand into his stomach.

'There was a queer kind of voice came from his throat, and then something like a curse and a groan escaped him.

'"Damn it," said I; "what is the matter now—you've supped all the liquor—you are very nervous—you had better have another dose."

'"No more—no more," he said, faintly and huskily, "no more, for God's sake no more. I am almost choked, my throat is scalded, and my entrails on fire."

'"I told you it was hot," said I.

'"Yes, hot, boiling—go on. I'm mad with pain—push on."

'"Will you have any water or anything to cool your throat?" said I.

'"No, no—go on."

'"Yes," said I, "but the brandy-and-water is hot; however, it's going down very fast now—very fast indeed, here is the last mouthful"; and as I said so, I gulped it down, returned with the one glass, and then paid for the damage.

'This did not occupy five minutes, and away we came along the road at a devil of a pace, and we were all right enough; my friend behind me got over his scald, though he had a very sore gullet, and his intestines were in a very uncomfortable state; but he was better.

'Away we rattled, the ground rattling to the horse's hoofs and the wheels of the vehicle, the young girl still remaining in the same state of insensibility in which she had first been brought out.

'No doubt she had taken a stronger dose of the opium than she was willing to admit. That was nothing to me, but made it all the better, because she gave the less trouble, and made it safer.

'We got here easy enough, drove slap up to the door, which was opened in an instant, jumped out, took the girl, and carried her in.

'When once these doors are shut upon anyone, they may rest assured that it is quite a settled thing, and they don't get out very easy, save in a wooden surtout;* indeed, I never lost a boarder by any other means; we always keep one connection, and they are usually so well satisfied, that they never take anyone away from us.

'Well, well! I carried her indoors, and left her in a room by herself on a bed. She was a nice girl—a handsome girl, I suppose people would call her, and had a low, sweet and plaintive voice. But enough of this!

'"She's all right," said I, when I returned to this room. "It's all right—I have left her."

'"She isn't dead?" he enquired, with much terror.

'"Oh! no, no!—she is only asleep, and has not woke up yet from the effects of the laudanum. Will you now give me one year's pay in advance?"

'"Yes," he replied, as he handed the money, and the remainder of the bonds. "Now, how am I to do about getting back to London to-night?"

'"You had better remain here."

'"Oh, no! I should go mad too, if I were to remain here; I must leave here soon."

'"Well, will you go to the village inn?"

'"How far is that off?"

'"About a mile—you'll reach it easy enough; I'll drive you over for the matter of that, and leave you there. I shall take the cart there."

'"Very well, let it be so; I will go. Well, well, I am glad it is all over, and the sooner it is over for ever, the better. I am truly sorry for her, but it cannot be helped. It will kill her, I have no doubt; but that is all the better; she will escape the misery consequent upon her departure, and release us from a weight of care."

'"So it will," said I, "but come, we must go at once, if going you are."

'"Yes, yes," he said hurriedly.

'"Well, then, come along; the horse is not yet unharnessed, and if we do not make haste, we shall be too late to obtain a lodging for the night."

'"That is very good," he said, somewhat wildly; "I am quite ready— quite."

'We left the house, and trotted off to the inn at a good rate, where we arrived in about ten minutes or less, and then I put up the horse, and saw him in the inn, and came back as quick as I could on foot. "Well, well," I thought, "this will do, I have had a good day of it—paid well for business, and haven't wanted for sport on the road."

'Well, I came to the conclusion that if the whole affair was to speedily end, it would be more in my pocket than if she were living, and she would be far happier in heaven than here, Mr Todd.'

'Undoubtedly,' said Mr Sweeney Todd, 'undoubtedly that is a very just observation of yours.'

'Well, then I set to work to find out how the matter could be managed, and I watched her until she awoke. She looked around her, and seemed much surprised, and confused, and did not seem to understand her position, while I remained near at hand.

'She sighed deeply, and put her hand to her head, and appeared for a time quite unable to comprehend what had happened to her, or where she was.

'I sent some tea to her, as I was not prepared to execute my purpose, and she seemed to recover, and asked some questions, but my man was dumb for the occasion, and would not speak, and the result was, she was very much frightened. I left her so for a week or two, and then, one day, I went into her cell. She had greatly altered in appearance, and looked very pale.

'"Well," said I, "how do you find yourself now?"

'She looked up into my face, and shuddered; but she said in a calm voice, looking round her,—

'"Where am I?"

'"You are here!" said I, "and you'll be very comfortable if you only take on kindly, but you will have a straight waistcoat put on you if you do not."

'"Good God!" she exclaimed, clasping her hands, "have they put me here—in—in—"

'She could not finish the sentence, and I supplied the word which she did not utter, until I had done so, and then she screamed loudly,—

———

"*A mad-house!*"

"'Come,' said I, 'this will never do; you must learn to be quiet, or you'll have fearful consequences.'

"'Oh, mercy, mercy! I will do no wrong! What have I done that I should be brought here—what have I done? They may have all I have if they will let me live in freedom. I care not where or how poor I may be. Oh! Henry, Henry!—if you knew where I was, would you not fly to my rescue? Yes, you would, you would!'

"'Ah,' said I, 'there is no Henry here, and you must be content to do without one.'

"'I could not have believed that my brother would have acted such a base part. I did not think him wicked; although I knew him to be selfish, mean and stern, yet I did not think he intended such wickedness; but he thinks to rob me of all my property—yes, that is the object he has in sending me here.'

"'No doubt,' said I.

"'Shall I ever get out?' she enquired in a pitiful tone; 'do not say my life is to be spent here.'

"'Indeed it is,' said I; 'while he lives, you'll never leave these walls.'

"'He shall not attain his end, for I have deeds about me that he will never be able to obtain; indeed he may kill me, but he cannot benefit by my death.'

"'Well,' said I, 'it serves him right. And how did you manage that matter—how did you contrive to get the deeds away?'

"'Never mind that; it is a small deed, and I have secured it. I did not think he would have done this thing, but he may yet relent. Will you aid me? I shall be rich, and can pay you well.'

"'But your brother?' said I.

"'Oh, he is rich without mine, but he is over-avaricious; but say you will help me—only help me to get out, and you shall be no loser by the affair.'

"'Very well,' said I. 'Will you give me this deed as a security that you will keep your word?'

'"Yes," she replied, drawing forth the deed—a small parchment— from her bosom. "Take it, and now let me out; you shall be handsomely rewarded."

'"Ah!" said I, "but you must allow me first to settle this matter with my employers. You must really be mad. We do not hear of young ladies carrying deeds and parchments about them when they are in their senses."

'"You do not mean to betray me?" she said, springing up wildly, and running towards the deed, which I carefully placed in my breast-coat-pocket.

'"Oh dear no! but I shall retain the deed, and speak to your brother about this matter."

'"My God! my God!" she exclaimed, and then she sank back on her bed, and in another moment she was covered with blood. She had burst a blood vessel.

'I sent for a surgeon and physician, and they both gave it as their opinion that she could not be saved, and that a few hours would see the last of her.

'That was the fact. She was dead before another half hour, and then I sent to the authorities for the purpose of burial; and, producing the certificate of the medical men, I had no difficulty, and she was buried all comfortably without any trouble.'

\*　　\*　　\*　　\*　　\*

'"Well," thought I, "this is a very comfortable affair, but it will be more profitable than I had any idea of, and I must get my first reward first; and if there should be any difficulty, I have the deed to fall back upon."

'He came down next day, and appeared with rather a long face.

'"Well," said he, "how do matters go on here?"

'"Very well," said I; "how is your throat?"

'I thought he cast a malicious look at me, as much as to imply he laid it all to my charge.

'"Pretty well," he replied; "but I was ill for three days. How is the patient?"

'"As well as you could possibly wish," said I.

'"She takes it kindly, eh? Well, I hardly expected it—but no matter. She'll be a long while on hand, I perceive. You haven't tried the frightening system yet, then?"

"'Hadn't any need," I replied, putting the certificate of her burial in his hand, and he jumped as if he had been stung by an adder, and turned pale; but he soon recovered, and smiled complaisantly as he said, —

"Ah! well, I see you have been diligent; but I should have liked to have seen her, to have asked her about a missing deed, but no matter."

"'Now, about the two hundred pounds," said I.

"'Why," said he, "I think one will do when you come to consider what you have received, and the short space of time and all: you have had a year's board in advance."

"'I know I had; but because I have done more than you expected, and in a shorter time, instead of giving me more, you have the conscience to offer me less."

"'No, no, not the—the—what did you call it? —we'll have nothing said about that—but here is a hundred pounds, and you are well paid."

"'Well," said I, taking the money, "I must have £500 at any rate, and unless you give it me, I will tell other parties where a certain deed is to be found."

"'What deed?"

"'The one you were alluding to. Give me £400 more, and you shall have the deed."

'After much conversation and trouble he gave it to me, and I gave him the deed, with which he was well pleased, but looked hard at the money, and seemed to grieve at it very much.

'Since that time I have heard that he was challenged by his sister's lover, and they went out to fight a duel, and he fell—and died. The lover went to the continent, where he has since lived.'

'Ah,' said Sweeney Todd, 'you had decidedly the best of this affair: nobody gained anything but you.'

'Nobody at all that I know of, save distant relations, and I did very well; but then you know I can't live upon nothing: it costs me something to keep my house and cellar, but I stick to business, and so I shall as long as business sticks to me.'

## 26

## Colonel Jeffery Makes Another Effort to Come at Sweeney Todd's Secret

I F we were to say that Colonel Jeffery was satisfied with the state of affairs as regarded the disappearance of his friend Thornhill, or that he had made up his mind now contentedly to wait until chance, or the mere progress of time, blew something of a more defined nature in his way, we should be doing that gentleman a very great injustice indeed.

On the contrary, he was one of those chivalrous persons who, when they do commence anything, take the most ample means to bring it to a conclusion, and are not satisfied that they have made one great effort, which, having failed, is sufficient to satisfy them.

Far from this, he was a man who, when he commenced any enterprise, looked forward to but one circumstance that could possibly end it, and that was its full and complete accomplishment in every respect; so that in this affair of Mr Thornhill, he certainly did not intend by any means to abandon it.

But he was not precipitate. His habits of military discipline, and the long life he had led in camps, where anything in the shape of hurry and confusion is much reprobated, made him pause before he decided upon any particular course of action; and this pause was not one contingent upon a belief, or even a surmise, in the danger of the course that suggested itself, for such a consideration had no effect whatever upon him; and if some other mode had suddenly suggested itself, which, while it placed his life in the most imminent peril, would have seemed more likely to accomplish his object, it would have been at once most gladly welcomed.

And now, therefore, he set about thinking deeply over what could possibly be done in a matter that as yet appeared to be involved in the most profound of possible mysteries.

That the barber's boy, who had been addressed by him, and by his friend, the captain, knew something of an extraordinary character, which fear prevented him from disclosing, he had no doubt, and, as the colonel remarked, —

'If fear keeps that lad silent upon the subject, fear may make him speak; and I do not see why we should not endeavour to make ourselves a match for Sweeney Todd in such a matter.'

'What do you propose, then?' said the captain.

'I should say that the best plan would be, to watch the barber's shop, and take possession of the boy, as we may find an opportunity of so doing.'

'Carry him off!'

'Yes, certainly; and as in all likelihood his fear of the barber is but a visionary affair, after all, it can really, when we have him to ourselves, be dispelled; and then when he finds that we can and will protect him, we shall hear all he has to say.'

After some further conversation, the plan was resolved upon; and the captain and the colonel, after making a careful *reconnaissance*, as they called it,\* of Fleet-street, found that by taking up a station at the window of a tavern, which was very nearly opposite to the barber's shop, they should be able to take such effectual notice of whoever went in and came out, that they would be sure to see the boy sometime during the course of the day.

This plan of operations would no doubt have been greatly successful, and Tobias would have fallen into their hands, had he not, alas! for him, poor fellow, already been treated by Sweeney Todd, as we have described, by being incarcerated in that fearful mad-house on Peckham Rye, which was kept by so unscrupulous a personage as Fogg.

And we cannot but consider that it was most unfortunate, for the happiness of all those persons in whose fate we take so deep an interest, and in whom we hope, as regards the reader, we have likewise awakened a feeling of great sympathy—if Tobias had not been so infatuated as to make the search he did of the barber's house, but had waited even for twenty-four hours before doing so, in that case, not only would he have escaped the dreadful doom which awaited him, but Johanna Oakley would have been saved from much danger, which afterwards befell her.

But we must not anticipate; and the fearful adventures which it was her doom to pass through, before she met with the reward of her great virtue, and her noble perseverance will speak for themselves, trumpet-tongued indeed.

It was at a very early hour in the morning that the two friends took up their station at the public house so nearly opposite to Sweeney Todd's, in Fleet-street; and then, having made an arrangement with the landlord of the house, that they were to have undisturbed possession of the room for as long as they liked, they both sat at the window, and kept an eye upon Todd's house.

It was during the period of time there spent, that Colonel Jeffery first made the captain acquainted with the fact of his great affection for Johanna, and that, in her he thought he had at last fixed his wandering fancy, and found, really, the only being with whom he thought he could, in this world, taste the sweets of domestic life, and know no regret.

'She is all,' he said, 'in beauty that the warmest imagination can possibly picture, and along with these personal charms, which certainly are most peerless, I have seen enough of her to feel convinced that she has a mind of the purest order that ever belonged to any human being in the world.'

'With such sentiments and feelings towards her, the wonder would be,' said the captain, 'if you did not love her, as you now avow you do.'

'I could not be insensible to her attractions. But, understand me, my dear friend, I do not on account of my own suddenly-conceived partiality for this young and beautiful creature, intend to commit the injustice of not trying might and main, and with heart and hand, to discover, if she supposes it be true, that Thornhill and Mark Ingestrie be one and the same person; and when I tell you that I love her with a depth and a sincerity of affection that makes her happiness of greater importance to me than my own—you know, I think, enough of me to feel convinced that I am speaking only what I really feel.'

'I can,' said the captain; 'and I do give you credit for the greatest possible amount of sincerity, and I feel sufficiently interested myself in the future fate of this fair young creature to wish that she may be convinced her lover is no more, and may so much better herself as I am quite certain she would, by becoming your wife; for all we can hear of this Ingestrie seems to prove that he is not the most stable-minded of individuals the world ever produced, and perhaps not exactly the sort of man to make such a girl as Johanna Oakley happy; however, of course she may think to the contrary, and he may in all sincerity think likewise.'

'I thank you for the kind feeling towards me, my friend, which has dictated that speech, but—'

'Hush!' said the captain, suddenly, 'hush! look at the barber!'

'The barber? Sweeney Todd?'

'Yes, yes, there he is; do you not see him? There he is, and he looks as if he had come off a long journey. What can he have been about, I wonder? He is draggled in mud.'

Yes, there was Sweeney Todd, opening his shop from the outside with a key that, after a vast amount of fumbling, he took from his pocket; and, as the captain said, he did indeed look as if he had come off a long journey, for he was draggled with mud, and his appearance altogether was such as to convince anyone that he must have fallen during the early part of the morning upon London and its suburbs.

And this was just the fact, for after staying with the mad-house keeper in the hope that the bad weather which had set in would be alleviated, he had been compelled to give up all chance of such a thing, and as no conveyance of any description was to be had, he enjoyed the pleasure, if it could be called such, of walking home up to his knees in the mud of that dirty neighbourhood.

It was, however, some satisfaction to him to feel that he had got rid of Tobias, who, from what he had done as regarded the examination of the house, had become extremely troublesome indeed, and perhaps the most serious enemy that Sweeney Todd had ever had.

'Ha!' he said, as he came within sight of his shop in Fleet-street, — 'ha! Master Tobias is safe enough; he will give me no more trouble, that is quite clear. What a wonderfully convenient thing it is to have such a friend as Fogg, who for a consideration will do so much towards ridding one of an uncomfortable encumbrance. It is possible enough that that boy might have compassed my destruction. I wish I dared, with the means I now have from the string of pearls, joined to my other resources, to leave the business, and so not be obliged to run the risk and have the trouble of another boy.'

Yes, Sweeney Todd would have been glad now to shut up his shop in Fleet-street at once and for ever, but he dreaded that when John Mundel found that his customer did not come back to him to redeem the pearls, that he, John Mundel, would proceed to sell them, and that then their beauty, and their great worth would excite much attention, and someone might come forward who knew much more about their early history than he did.

'I must keep quiet,' he thought, 'I must keep quiet; for although I think I was pretty well disguised, and it is not at all likely that anyone—no, not even the acute John Mundel himself—would recognise in Sweeney Todd, the poor barber of Fleet-street, the nobleman who came from the Queen to borrow £8,000 upon a string of pearls, yet there is a remote possibility of danger, and should there be a disturbance about the precious stones, it is better that I should remain in obscurity until that disturbance is completely over.'

This was no doubt admirable policy on the part of Todd, who, although he found himself a rich man, had not, as many people do when they make that most gratifying and interesting discovery, forgotten all the prudence and tact that had made him one of that most envied class of personages.

He was some few minutes before he could get the key to turn in the lock of his street-door, but at length he effected that object and disappeared from before the eyes of the colonel and his friend into his own house, and the door was instantly again closed upon him.

'Well,' said Colonel Jeffery, 'what do you think of that?'

'I don't know what to think, further than that your friend Todd has been out of town, as the state of his boots abundantly testifies.'

'They do indeed; and he has the appearance of having been a considerable distance, for the mud that is upon his boots is not London mud.'

'Certainly not; it is of quite a different character altogether. But see, he is coming out again.'

Sweeney Todd strode out of his house, bare-headed now, and proceeded to take down the shutters of his shop, which, there being but three, he accomplished in a few seconds of time, and walked in again with them in his hand, along with the iron bar which had secured them, and which he had released from the inside.

This was all the ceremony that took place at the opening of Sweeney Todd's shop, and the only surprise our friends, who were at the public house window, had upon the subject was, that having a boy, he, Todd, should condescend to make himself so useful as to open his own shop. And nothing could be seen of the lad, although the hour, surely, for his attendance must have arrived; and Todd, equally surely, was not the sort of man to be so indulgent to a boy, whom he employed to make himself generally useful, as to allow him to come when all the dirty work of the early morning was over.

But yet such to all appearances would seem to be the case, for presently Todd appeared with a broom in his hand, sweeping out his shop with a rapidity and a vengeance which seemed to say, that he did not perform that operation with the very best grace in the world.

'Where can the boy be!' said the captain. 'Do you know, little reason as I may really appear to have for such a supposition, I cannot help in my own mind connecting Todd's having been out of town, somehow, with the fact of that boy's non-appearance this morning.'

'Indeed! the coincidence is curious, for such was my own thought likewise upon the occasion, and the more I think of it the more I feel convinced that such must be the case, and that our watch will be a fruitless one completely. Is it likely—for possible enough it is—that the villain has found out that we have been asking questions of the boy, and has thought proper to take his life?'

'Do not let us go too far,' said the captain, 'in mere conjecture; recollect that as yet, let us suspect what we may, we know nothing, and that the mere fact of our not being able to trace Thornhill beyond the shop of this man will not be sufficient to found an accusation upon.'

'I know all that, and I feel how very cautious we must be; and yet to my mind the whole of the circumstances have been day by day assuming a most hideous air of probability, and I look upon Todd as a murderer already.'

'Shall we continue our watch?'

'I scarcely see its utility. Perchance we may see some proceedings which may interest us; but I have a powerful impression that we certainly shall not see the boy we want. But, at all events, the barber, you perceive, has a customer already.'

As they looked across the way, they saw a well-dressed-looking man, who, from a certain air and manner which he had, could be detected not to be a Londoner. He had rather resembled some substantial yeoman,* who had come to town to pay or receive money, and, as he came near to Sweeney Todd's shop, he might have been observed to stroke his chin, as if debating in his mind the necessity or otherwise of a shave.

The debate, if it were taking place in his mind, ended by the ayes having it, for he walked into Todd's shop, being most unquestionably the first customer which he had had that morning.

Situated as the colonel and his friend were, they could not see into Todd's shop, even if the door had been opened, but they saw that after the customer had been in for a few moments, it was closed, so that, had they been close to it, all the interior of the shaving establishment would have been concealed.

They felt no great degree of interest in this man, who was a commonplace personage enough, who had entered Sweeney Todd's shop; but when an unreasonable time had elapsed, and he did not come out, they did begin to feel a little uneasy. And when another man went in and was only about five minutes before he emerged shaved, and yet the first man did not come, they knew not what to make of it, and looked at each other for some moments in silence. At length the colonel spoke—saying,—

'My friend, have we waited here for nothing now? What can have become of that man whom we saw go into the barber's shop; but who, I suppose we feel ourselves to be in a condition to take our oaths never came out?'

'I could take my oath; and what conclusion can we come to?'

'None, but that he has met his death there; and that, let his fate be what it may, is the same which poor Thornhill has suffered. I can endure this no longer. Do you stay here, and let me go alone.'

---

'Not for worlds—you would rush into an unknown danger: you cannot know what may be the powers of mischief that man possesses. You shall not go alone, colonel, you shall not indeed; but something must be done.'

'Agreed; and yet that something surely need not be of the desperate character you meditate.'

'Desperate emergencies require desperate remedies.'

'Yes, as a general principle I will agree with you there, too, colonel; and yet I think that in this case everything is to be lost by precipitation, and nothing is to be gained. We have to do with one who to all appearance is keen and subtle, and if anything is to be accomplished contrary to his wishes, it is not to be done by that open career which for its own sake, under ordinary circumstances, both you and I would gladly embrace.'

'Well, well,' said the colonel, 'I do not and will not say but what you are right.'

'I know I am—I am certain I am; and now hear me: I think we have gone quite far enough unaided in this transaction, and that it is time we drew some others into the plot.'

'I do not understand what you mean.'

'I will soon explain. I mean, that if in the pursuit of this enterprise, which grows each moment to my mind more serious, anything should happen to you and me, it is absolutely frightful to think that there would then be an end of it.'

'True, true; and as for poor Johanna and her friend Arabella, what could they do?'

'Nothing, but expose themselves to great danger. Come, come now, colonel, I am glad to see that we understand each other better about this business; you have heard, of course, of Sir Richard Blunt?'

'Sir Richard Blunt—Blunt—oh, you mean the magistrate?'

'I do; and what I propose is, that we have a private and confidential interview with him about the matter—that we make him possessed of all the circumstances, and take his advice what to do. The result of placing the affair in such hands will at all events be, that, if, in anything we may attempt, we may be by force or fraud overpowered, we shall not fall wholly unavenged.'

'Reason backs your proposition.'

'I knew it would, when you came to reflect. Oh, Colonel Jeffery, you are too much a creature of impulse.'

'Well,' said the colonel, half jestingly, 'I must say that I do not think the accusation comes well from you, for I have certainly seen you do some rather impulsive things, I think.'

'We won't dispute about that; but since you think with me upon the matter, you will have no objection to accompany me at once to Sir Richard Blunt's?'

'None in the least; on the contrary, if anything is to be done at all, for Heaven's sake let it be done quickly. I am quite convinced that some fearful tragedy is in progress, and that, if we are not most prompt in our measures, we shall be too late to counteract its dire influence upon the fortunes of those in whom we have become deeply interested.'

'Agreed, agreed! Come this way, and let us now for a brief space, at all events, leave Mr Todd and his shop to take care of each other, while we take an effectual means of circumventing him. Why do you linger?'

'I do linger. Some mysterious influence seems to chain me to the spot.'

'Some mysterious fiddlestick! Why, you are getting superstitious, colonel.'

'No, no! Well, I suppose I must come along with you. Lead the way, lead the way; and believe me that it requires all my reason to induce me to give up a hope of making some important discovery by going to Sweeney Todd's shop.'

'Yes, you might make an important discovery, and only suppose that the discovery you did make was that he murdered some of his customers. If he does so, you may depend that such a man takes good care to do the deed effectually, and you might make the discovery just a little too late. You understand that?'

'I do, I do. Come along, for I positively declare that if we see anybody else going into the barber's, I shall not be able to resist rushing forward at once, and giving an alarm.'

It was certainly a good thing that the colonel's friend was not quite as enthusiastic as he was, or from what we happen actually to know of Sweeney Todd, and from what we suspect, the greatest amount of danger might have befallen Jeffery, and instead of being in a position to help others in unravelling the mysteries connected with Sweeney Todd's establishment, he might be himself past all help, and most absolutely one of the mysteries.

But such was not to be.

### 27

## Tobias Makes an Attempt to Escape from the Mad-House

W E cannot find it in our hearts to force upon the mind of the reader the terrible condition of poor Tobias.

No one, certainly, of all the *dramatis personæ* of our tale, is suffering so much as he; and, consequently, we feel it to be a sort of duty to come to a consideration of his thoughts and feelings as he lay in that dismal cell, in the mad-house at Peckham Rye.

Certainly Tobias Ragg was as sane as any ordinary Christian need wish to be, when the scoundrel, Sweeney Todd, put him in the coach, to take him to Mr Fogg's establishment; but if by any ingenious process the human intellect can be toppled from its throne, certainly that process must consist in putting a sane person into a lunatic asylum.

To the imagination of a boy, too, and that boy one of vivid imagination, as was poor Tobias, a mad-house must be invested with a world of terrors. That enlarged experience which enables persons of more advanced age to shake off much of the unreal, which seemed so strangely to take up its abode in the mind of the young Tobias, had not reached him; and no wonder, therefore, that to him his present situation was one of acute and horrible misery and suffering.

\*     \*     \*     \*     \*

He lay for a long time in the gloomy dungeon-like cell, into which he had been thrust, in a kind of stupor, which might or might not be the actual precursor of insanity, although, certainly, the chances were all in favour of its being so. For many hours he moved neither hand nor foot, and as it was a part of the policy of Mr Fogg to leave well alone, as he said, he never interfered, by any intrusive offers of refreshment, with the quiet or the repose of his patients.

Tobias, therefore, if he had chosen to remain as still as an Indian fakir, might have died in one position, without any remonstrances from anyone.

It would be quite a matter of impossibility to describe the strange visionary thoughts and scenes that passed through the mind of Tobias during this period. It seemed as if his intellect was engulphed in the charmed waters of some whirlpool, and that all the different scenes and actions which, under ordinary circumstances, would have been clear and distinct, were mingled together in inextricable confusion.

In the midst of all this, at length he began to be conscious of one particular impression or feeling, and that was, that someone was singing in a low, soft voice, very near to him.

This feeling, strange as it was in such a place, momentarily increased in volume, until at length it began, in its intensity, to absorb almost every other; and he gradually awakened from the sort of stupor that had come over him. Yes, someone was singing. It was a female voice, he was sure of that; and as his mind became more occupied with that one subject of thought, and his perceptive faculties became properly exercised, his intellect altogether assumed a healthier tone.

He could not distinguish the words that were sung, but the voice itself was very sweet and musical; as Tobias listened, he felt as if the fever of his blood was abating, and that healthier thoughts were taking the place of those disordered fancies that had held sway within the chambers of his brain.

'What sweet sounds!' he said. 'Oh! I do hope that singing will go on. I feel happier to hear it; I do so hope it will continue. What sweet music! Oh, mother, mother, if you could but see me now!'

He pressed his hands over his eyes, but he could not stop the gush of tears that came from them, and which would trickle through his fingers. Tobias did not wish to weep, but those tears, after all the horrors of the night, did him a world of good, and he felt wonderfully better after they had been shed. Moreover, the voice continued singing without intermission.

'Who can it be,' thought Tobias, 'that don't tire with so much of it?'

Still the singer continued; but now and then Tobias felt certain that a very wild note or two was mingled with the ordinary melody; and that bred a suspicion in his mind, which gave him a shudder to think of, namely, that the singer was mad.

'It must be so,' said he. 'No one in their senses could or would continue to sing for so long a period of time such strange snatches of song. Alas! alas, it is someone who is really mad, and confined for life in this dreadful place; for life do I say, and am I not too confined for life here? Oh! help, help, help!'

Tobias called out in so loud a tone, that the singer of the sweet strains that had for a time lulled him to composure, heard him, and the strains which had before been redolent of the softest and sweetest melody, suddenly changed to the most terrific shrieks that can be imagined.

In vain did Tobias place his hands over his ears to shut out the horrible sounds. They would not be shut out, but ran, as it were, into every crevice of his brain, nearly driving him distracted by their vehemence.

But hoarser tones came upon his ears, and he heard the loud, rough voice of a man say, —

'What, do you want the whip so early this morning? The whip, do you understand that?'

These words were followed by the lashing of what must have been a heavy carter's whip, and then the shrieks died away in deep groans, every one of which went to the heart of poor Tobias.

'I can never live amid all these horrors,' he said. 'Oh, why don't they kill me at once? It would be much better, and much more merciful. I can never live long here. Help, help, help!'

When he shouted this word 'help', it was certainly not with the most distant idea of getting any help, but it was a word that came at once uppermost to his tongue; and so he called it out with all his might, that he should attract the attention of someone, for the solitude, and the almost total darkness of the place he was in, were beginning to fill him with new dismay.

There was a faint light in the cell, which made him know the difference between day and night; but where that faint light came from, he could not tell, for he could see no grating or opening whatever; but yet that was in consequence of his eyes not being fully accustomed to the obscurity of the place; otherwise he would have seen that close up to the roof there was a narrow aperture, certainly not larger than anyone could have passed a hand through, although of some four or five feet in length; and from a passage beyond that, there came the dim borrowed light, which made darkness visible in Tobias's cell.

With a kind of desperation, heedless of what might be the result, Tobias continued to call aloud for help, and after about a quarter of an hour he heard the sound of a heavy footstep.

Some one was coming; yes, surely someone was coming, and he was not to be left to starve to death. Oh, how intently he now listened to every sound, indicative of the nearer approach of whoever it was who was coming to his prison-house.

Now he heard the lock move, and a heavy bar of iron was let down with a clanging sound.

'Help, help!' he cried again, 'help, help!' for he feared that whoever it was might even yet go away again, after making so much progress to get at him.

The cell door was flung open, and the first intimation that poor Tobias got of the fact of his cries having been heard, consisted in a lash with a whip which, if it had struck him as fully as it was intended to do, would have done him serious injury.

'So, do you want it already?' said the same voice he had before heard.

'Oh, no, mercy, mercy,' said Tobias.

'Oh, that's it now, is it? I tell you what it is, if we have any more disturbance here, this is the persuader to silence that we always use: what do you think of that as an argument, eh?'

As he spoke, the man gave the whip a loud smack in the air, and confirmed the truth of the argument by reducing poor Tobias to absolute silence; indeed the boy trembled so that he could not speak.

'Well, now, my man,' added the fellow, 'I think we understand each other. What do you want?'

'Oh, let me go,' said Tobias, 'let me go. I will tell nothing. Say to Mr Todd that I will do what he pleases, and tell nothing, only let me go out of this dreadful place. Have mercy upon me—I'm not at all mad—indeed I am not.'

The man closed the door, as he whistled a lively tune.

## 28

## *The Mad-House Yard, and Tobias's New Friend*

THIS sudden retreat of the man was unexpected by Tobias, who at least thought it was the practice to feed people, even if they were confined to such a place; but the unceremonious departure of the keeper, without so much as mentioning anything about breakfast, began to make Tobias think that the plan by which he was to be got rid of was starvation; and yet that was impossible, for how easy it was to kill him if they felt so disposed! 'Oh, no, no,' he repeated to himself, 'surely they will not starve me to death.'

As he uttered these words, he heard the plaintive singing commence again; and he could not help thinking that it sounded like some requiem for the dead, and that it was a sort of signal that his hours were numbered.

Despair again began to take possession of him, and despite the savage threats of the keeper, he would again have called loudly for help, had he not become conscious that there were footsteps close at hand.

By dint of listening most intently he heard a number of doors opened and shut, and sometimes when one was opened, there was a shriek, and the lashing of the whips, which very soon succeeded in drowning all other noises. It occurred to Tobias, and correctly too, for such was the fact, that the inmates of that most horrible abode were living like so many wild beasts, in cages fed. Then he thought how strange it was that even for any amount of money human beings could be got to do the work of such an establishment. And by the time Tobias had made this reflection to himself, his own door was once more opened upon its rusty hinges.

There was the flash of a light, and then a man came in with a water-can in his hand, to which there was a long spout, and this he placed to the mouth of Tobias, who fearing that if he did not drink then he might be a long time without, swallowed some not over-savoury ditch-water, as it seemed to him, which was thus brought to him.

A coarse, brown-looking hard loaf was then thrown at his feet, and the party was about to leave his cell, but he could not forbear speaking, and, in a voice of the most supplicating earnestness, he said, —

'Oh, do not keep me here. Let me go, and I will say nothing of Todd. I will go to sea at once if you will let me out of this place, indeed I will, but I shall go really mad here.'

'Good, that, Watson, ain't it?' said Mr Fogg, who was of the party.

'Very good, sir. Lord bless you, the cunning of 'em is beyond anything in the world, sir; you'd be surprised at what they say to me sometimes.'

'But I am not mad, indeed I am not mad,' cried Tobias.

'Oh,' said Fogg, 'it's a bad case, I'm afraid; the strongest proof of insanity, in my opinion, Watson, is the constant reiteration of the statement that he is not mad on the part of a lunatic. Don't you think it is so, Mr Watson?'

'Oh, of course, sir, of course.'

'Ah! I thought you would be of that opinion; but I suppose as this is a mere lad we may do without chaining him up; besides, you know that to-day is inspection-day, when we get an old fool of a superannuated physician to make us a visit.'

'Yes, sir,' said Watson, with a grin, 'and a report that all is well conducted.'

'Exactly. Who shall we have this time, do you think? I always give a ten guinea fee.'

'Why, sir, there's old Dr Popplejoy, he's 84 years old, they say, and sand-blind;* he'll take it as a great compliment, he will, and no doubt we can humbug him easily.'

'I dare say we may! I'll see to it; and we will have him at twelve o'clock, Watson. You will take care to have everything ready, of course, you know; make all the usual preparations.'

Tobias was astonished that before him they chose thus to speak so freely, but despairing as he was, he little knew how completely he was in the power of Mr Fogg, and how utterly he was shut out from all human sympathy.

Tobias said nothing; but he could not help thinking that however old and stupid the physician whom they mentioned might be, surely there was a hope that he would be able to discover Tobias's perfect sanity.

But the wily Mr Fogg knew perfectly well what he was about, and when he retired to his own room, he wrote the following note to Dr Popplejoy, who was a retired physician, who had purchased a country house in the neighbourhood. The note will speak for itself, being as fine a specimen of hypocrisy as we can ever expect to lay before our readers:—

The Asylum, Peckham

SIR—Probably you may recognise my name as that of the keeper of a lunatic asylum in this neighbourhood. Consistent with a due regard for the safety of that most unhappy class of the community submitted to my care, I am most anxious, with the blessing of Divine Providence, to ameliorate as far as possible, by kindness, that most shocking of all calamities—insanity. Once a year it is my custom to call in some experienced, able, and enlightened physician to see my patients (I enclose a fee)—a physician who has nothing to do with the establishment, and therefore cannot be biased.

If you, sir, would do me the favour, at about twelve o'clock to-day, to make a short visit of inspection, I shall esteem it a great honour, as well as a great favour.

Believe me to be, sir, with the most profound respect, your most obedient and humble servant,

*To Dr Popplejoy, &c.*                                              O. D. Fogg

This note, as might be expected, brought old, purblind, super-annuated Dr Popplejoy to the asylum, and Mr Fogg received him in due form, and with great gravity, saying, almost with tears in his eyes,—

'My dear sir, the whole aim of my existence now is to endeavour to soften the rigours of the necessary confinement of the insane, and I wish this inspection of my establishment to be made by you in order that I may thus for a time stand clear with the world   with my own conscience I am of course always clear, and if your report be satisfactory about the treatment of the unhappy persons I have here, not the slightest breath of slander can touch me.'

'Oh, yes, yes,' said the garrulous old physician; 'I—I—very good—oh yes—cugh, cugh—I have a slight cough.'

'A very slight one, sir. Will you, first of all, take a look at one of the sleeping chambers of the insane?'

The doctor agreed, and Mr Fogg led him into a very comfortable sleeping-room, which the old gentleman declared was very satis-factory indeed, and when they returned to the apartment in which they had already been, Mr Fogg said,—

'Well then, sir, all we have to do is bring in the patients, one by one, to you as fast as we can, so as not to occupy more of your valu-able time than necessary; and any questions you may ask will, no doubt, be answered and I, being by, can give you the heads of any case that may excite your especial notice.'

'Exactly, exactly. I—I—quite correct. Eugh—Eugh!'

The old man was placed in a chair of state, reposing on some very comfortable cushions; and, take him altogether, he was so pleased with the ten guineas and the flattery of Mr Fogg, for nobody had given him a fee for the last fifteen years, that he was quite ready to be the foolish tool of the mad-house keeper in almost any way that he chose to dictate to him.

We need not pursue the examination of the various unfortunates who were brought before old Dr Popplejoy; it will suffice for us if we carry the reader through the examination of Tobias, who is our principal care, without, at the same time, detracting from the genial sympathy we must feel for all who, at that time, were subject to the tender mercies of Mr Fogg.

At about half-past twelve the door of Tobias's cell was opened by Mr Watson, who, walking in, laid hold of the boy by the collar, and said, —

'Hark you, my lad! you are going before a physician, and the less you say the better. I speak to you for your own sake; you can do yourself no good, but you can do yourself a great deal of harm. You know we keep a cart-whip here. Come along.'

Tobias said not a word in answer to this piece of gratuitous advice, but he made up his mind that if the physician was not absolutely deaf, he should hear him.

Before, however, the unhappy boy was taken into the room where old Dr Popplejoy was waiting, he was washed and brushed down generally, so that he presented a much more respectable appearance than he would have done had he been ushered in in his soiled state, as he was taken from the dirty mad-house cell.

'Surely, surely,' thought Tobias, 'the extent of cool impudence can go no further than this; but I will speak to the physician, if my life should be sacrificed in so doing. Yes, of that I am determined.'

In another minute he was in the room, face to face with Mr Fogg and Dr Popplejoy.

'What—what? eugh! eugh!' coughed the old doctor; 'a boy, Mr Fogg, a mere boy. Dear me! I—I—eugh! eugh! eugh! My cough is a little troublesome, I think, today—eugh! eugh!'

'Yes, sir,' said Mr Fogg with a deep sigh, and making a pretence to dash a tear from his eye; 'here you have a mere boy. I am always affected when I look upon him, doctor. We were boys ourselves once, you know, and to think that the divine spark of intelligence has gone out in one so young, is enough to make any feeling heart throb with agony. This lad, though, sir, is only a monomaniac. He has a fancy that someone named Sweeney Todd is a murderer, and that he has discovered his bad practices. On all other subjects he is sane enough; but upon that, and upon his presumed freedom from mental derangement, he is furious.'

'It is false, sir, it is false!' said Tobias, stepping up. 'Oh, sir, if you are not one of the creatures of this horrible place, I beg that you will hear me, and let justice be done.'

'Oh, yes—I—I—eugh! Of course—I—eugh!'

'Sir, I am not mad, but I am placed here because I have become dangerous to the safety of criminal persons.'

'Oh, indeed! Ah—oh—yes.'

'I am a poor lad, sir, but I hate wickedness, and because I found out that Sweeney Todd is a murderer, I am placed here.'

'You hear him, sir,' said Fogg; 'just as I said.'

'Oh, yes, yes. Who is Sweeney Todd, Mr Fogg?'

'Oh, sir, there is no such person in the world.'

'Ah, I thought as much—I thought as much—a sad case, a very sad case indeed. Be calm, my little lad, and Mr Fogg will do all that can be done for you, I'm sure.'

'Oh, how can you be as foolish, sir,' cried Tobias, 'as to be deceived by that man, who is making a mere instrument of you to cover his own villainy? What I say to you is true, and I am not mad!'

'I think, Dr Popplejoy,' said Fogg, with a smile, 'it would take rather a cleverer fellow than I am to make a fool of you; but you perceive, sir, that in a little while the boy would get quite furious, that he would. Shall I take him away?'

'Yes, yes—poor fellow.'

'Hear me—oh, hear me,' shrieked Tobias. 'Sir, on your deathbed you may repent this day's work—I am not mad—Sweeney Todd is a murderer—he is a barber in Fleet-street—I am not mad!'

'It's melancholy, sir, is it not?' said Fogg, as he again made an effort to wipe away a tear from his eye. 'It's very melancholy.'

'Oh! very, very.'

---

'Watson, take away poor Tobias Ragg, but take him very gently and stay with him a little in his nice comfortable room, and try to soothe him; speak to him of his mother, Watson, and get him round if you can. Alas, poor child! my heart quite bleeds to see him. I am not fit exactly for this life, doctor, I ought to be made of sterner stuff, indeed I ought.'

\*     \*     \*     \*     \*

'Well,' said Mr Watson, as he saluted poor Tobias with a furious kick outside the door, 'what a deal of good you have done!'

The boy's patience was exhausted; he had borne all that he could bear, and this last insult maddened him. He turned with the quickness of thought, and sprang at Mr Watson's throat.

So sudden was that attack, and so completely unprepared for it was that gentleman, that down he fell in the passage, with such a blow of his head against the stone floor that he was nearly insensible; and before anybody could get to his assistance, Tobias had pummelled and clawed his face, that there was scarcely a feature discernible, and one of his eyes seemed to be in fearful jeopardy.

The noise of this assault soon brought Mr Fogg to the spot, as well as old Dr Popplejoy, and the former tore Tobias from his victim, whom he seemed intent upon murdering.

## 29

## *The Consultation of Colonel Jeffery with the Magistrate*

THE advice which his friend had given to Colonel Jeffery was certainly the very best that could have been tendered to him; and, under the whole of these circumstances, it would have been something little short of absolute folly to have ventured into the shop of Sweeney Todd without previously taking every possible precaution to ensure the safety of so doing.

Sir Richard was within when they reached his house, and, with the acuteness of a man of business, he at once entered into the affair.

As the colonel, who was the spokesman in it, proceeded, it was evident that the magistrate became deeply interested, and when Jeffery concluded by saying, —

'You will thus, at all events, perceive that there is great mystery somewhere,' he replied, —

'And guilt, I should say.'

'You are of that opinion, Sir Richard?'

'I am, most decidedly.'

'Then what would you propose to do? Believe me, I do not ask out of any idle curiosity, but from a firm faith, that what you set about will be accomplished in a satisfactory manner.'

'Why, in the first place, I shall certainly go and get shaved at Todd's shop.'

'You will venture that?'

'Oh, yes; but do not fancy that I am so headstrong and foolish as to run any unnecessary risks in the matter—I shall do no such thing: you may be assured that I will do all in my power to provide for my own safety; and if I did not think I could do that most effectually, I should not be at all in love with the adventure, but, on the contrary, carefully avoid it to the best of my ability. We have before heard something of Mr Todd.'

'Indeed! and of a criminal character?'

'Yes; a lady once in the street took a fancy to a pair of shoe-buckles in imitation diamonds that Todd had on, when he was going to some city entertainment; she screamed out, and declared that they had belonged to her husband, who had gone out one morning, from his house in Fetter-lane,* to get himself shaved. The case came before me, but the buckles were of too common a kind to enable the lady to persevere in her statement; and Todd, who preserved the most imperturbable coolness throughout the affair, was of course discharged.'

'But the matter left a suspicion upon your mind?'

'It did, and more than once I have resolved in my own mind what means could be adopted of coming at the truth; other affairs, however, of more immediate urgency, have occupied me, but the circumstances you detail revive all my former feelings upon the subject; and I shall now feel that the matter has come before me in a shape to merit immediate attention.'

This was gratifying to Colonel Jeffery, because it not only took a great weight off his shoulders, but it led him to think, from the well-known tact of the magistrate, that something would be accomplished, and that very shortly too, towards unravelling the secret that had as yet only appeared to be more complicated and intricate the more it was enquired into. He made the warmest acknowledgements to the magistrate for the courtesy of his reception, and then took his leave.

As soon as the magistrate was alone, he rang a small hand-bell that was upon the table, and the summons was answered by a man, to whom he said,—

'Is Crotchet here?'

'Yes, your worship.'

'Then tell him I want him at once, will you?'

The messenger retired, but he presently returned, bringing with him about as rough a specimen of humanity as the world could have produced. He was tall and stout, and his face looked as if, by repeated injuries, it had been knocked out of all shape, for the features were most strangely jumbled together indeed, and an obliquity of vision, which rendered it always a matter of doubt who and what he was looking at, by no means added to his personal charms.

'Sit down, Crotchet,' said the magistrate, 'and listen to me without a word of interruption.'

If Mr Crotchet had no other good quality on earth, he still had that of listening most attentively, and he never opened his mouth while the magistrate related to him what had just formed the subject matter of Mr Jeffery's communication; indeed, Crotchet seemed to be looking out of the window all the while; but then Sir Richard knew the little peculiarities of his visual organs.

When he had concluded his statement, Sir Richard said,—

'Well, Crotchet, what do you think of all that? What does Sweeney Todd do with his customers?'

Mr Crotchet gave a singular and peculiar kind of grin as he said, still looking apparently out of the window, although his eyes were really fixed upon the magistrate,—

'He *smugs* 'em.'*

'What?'

'Uses 'em up, yer worship: it's as clear to me as mud in a wine-glass, that it is. Lor' bless you! I've been thinking he does that 'ere sort of thing a deuce of a while, but I didn't like to interfere too soon, you see.'

'What do you advise, Crotchet? I know I can trust to your saga-city in such a case.'

'Why, your worship, I'll think it over a bit in the course of the day, and let your worship know what I think . . . It's an awkward job, rather, for a wariety of reasons, but howsomdever, there's always a something to be done, and if we don't do it, I'll be hung if I know who can, that's all!'

'True, true, you are right there, and perhaps, before you see me again, you will walk down Fleet-street, and see if you can make any observations that will be of advantage in the matter. It is an affair which requires great caution indeed.'

'Trust me, yer worship: I'll do it, and no mistake. Lor' bless you, it's easy for anybody now to go lounging about Fleet-street, without being taken much notice of; for the fact is, the whole place is agog about the horrid smell, as has been for never so long in the old church of St Dunstan.'

'Smell, smell, in St Dunstan's church! I never heard of that before, Crotchet.'

'O Lor' yes, it's enough to pison the devil himself, Sir Richard; and t'other day, when the blessed bishop went to '*firm* a lot of people, he as good as told 'em they might all be damned first, afore he 'firm nobody in such a place.'

The magistrate was in deep thought for a few minutes, and then he said suddenly, —

'Well, well, Crotchet, you turn the matter over in your mind and see what you can make of it; I will think it over, likewise. Do you hear? mind you are with me at six this evening punctually; I do not intend to let the matter rest, you may depend, but from that moment will give it my greatest attention.'

'Wery good, yer worship, wery good indeed. I'll be here, and something seems to strike me uncommon forcible that we shall unearth this very soon, yer worship.'

'I sincerely hope so.'

Mr Crotchet took his leave, and when he was alone the magistrate rose and paced his apartment for some time with rapid strides, as if he were much agitated by the reflections that were passing through his mind. At length he flung himself into a chair with something like a groan, as he said, —

'A horrible idea forces itself upon my consideration, most horrible! most horrible! most horrible! Well, well, we shall see, we shall see. It may not be so; and yet what a hideous probability stares me in the face! I will go down at once to St Dunstan's and see what they are really about. Yes, yes, I shall not get much sleep, I think now, until some of these mysteries are developed. A most horrible idea, truly!'

The magistrate left some directions at home concerning some business calls which he fully expected in the course of the next two hours, and then he put on a plain, sad-coloured cloak and a hat destitute of all ornament, and left his house with a rapid step.

He took the most direct route towards St Dunstan's church, and finding the door of the sacred edifice yielded to the touch, he at once entered it; but he had not advanced many steps before he was met and accosted by the beadle, who said, in a tone of great dignity and authority, —

'This ain't Sunday, sir; there ain't no service here today.'

'I don't suppose there is,' replied the magistrate; 'but I see you have workmen here. What is it you are about?'

'Well, of all the impudence that ever I came near this is the *worstest*—to ask a beadle what he is about. I beg to say, sir, this here is quite private, and there's the door.'

'Yes, I see it, and you may go out at it just as soon as you think proper.'

'Oh, *conwulsions*! oh, *conwulsions*! This to a beadle.'

'What is all this about?' said a gentlemanly-looking man, stepping forward from a part of the church where several masons were employed in raising some of the huge flag-stones with which it was paved. 'What disturbance is this?'

'I believe, Mr Antrobus, you know me,' said the magistrate.

'Oh, Sir Richard, certainly. How do you do?'

'Gracious!' said the beadle, 'I've put my blessed foot in it. Lor' bless us, sir, how should I know as you was Sir Richard? I begs as you won't think nothing o' what I said. If I had a knowed you, in course I shouldn't have said it, you may depend, Sir Richard—I humbly begs your pardon.'

'It's of no consequence, I ought to have announced myself; and you are perfectly justified in keeping strangers out of the church, my friend.'

The magistrate walked up the aisle with Mr Antrobus, who was one of the churchwardens; and as he did so, he said, in a low, confidential tone of voice, —

'I have heard some strange reports about a terrible stench in the church. What does it mean? I suppose you know all about it, and what it arises from?'

'Indeed I do not. If you have heard that there is a horrible smell in the church after it has been shut up some time, and upon the least change in the weather, from dry to wet, or cold to warm, you know as much as we know upon the subject. It is a most serious nuisance, and, in fact, my presence here today is to try and make some discovery of the cause of the stench; and you see we are going to work our way into some of the old vaults that have not been opened for some time, with a hope of finding out the cause of this disagreeable odour.'

'Have you any objection to my being a spectator?'

'None in the least.'

'I thank you. Let us now join the workmen, and I can only now tell you that I feel the strongest possible curiosity to ascertain what can be the meaning of all this, and shall watch the proceedings with the greatest amount of interest.'

'Come along, then; I can only say, for my part, that, as an individual, I am glad you are here, and as a magistrate, likewise, it gives me great satisfaction to have you.'

## *30*

## *Tobias's Escape from Mr Fogg's Establishment*

THE rage into which Mr Fogg was thrown by the attack which the desperate Tobias had made upon his representative Mr Watson, was so great that, had it not been for the presence of stupid old Dr Popplejoy in the house, no doubt he would have taken some most exemplary revenge upon him. As it was, however, Tobias was thrown into his cell with a promise of vengeance as soon as the coast was clear.

These were the kind of promises which Mr Fogg was pretty sure to keep, and when the first impulse of his passion had passed away, poor Tobias, as well indeed he might, gave himself up to despair.

'Now all is over,' he said; 'I shall be half murdered! Oh, why do they not kill me at once? There would be some mercy in that.

Come and murder me at once, you wretches! You villains, murder me at once!'

In his new excitement, he rushed to the door of the cell, and banged it with his fists, when to his surprise it opened, and he found himself nearly falling into the stone corridor from which the various cell doors opened. It was evident that Mr Watson thought he had locked him in, for the bolt of the lock was shot back but had missed its hold—a circumstance probably arising from the state of rage and confusion Mr Watson was in, as a consequence of Tobias's daring attack upon him.

It almost seemed to the boy as if he had already made some advance towards his freedom, when he found himself in the narrow passage beyond his cell-door, but his heart for some minutes beat so tumultuously with the throng of blissful associations connected with freedom that it was quite impossible for him to proceed.

A slight noise, however, in another part of the building roused him again, and he felt that it was only now by great coolness and self-possession, as well as great courage, that he could at all hope to turn to account the fortunate incident which had enabled him, at all events, to make that first step towards liberty.

'Oh, if I could but get out of this dreadful place,' he thought; 'if I could but once again breathe the pure fresh air of heaven, and see the deep blue sky, I think I should ask for no other blessings.'

Never do the charms of nature present themselves to the imagination in more lovely guise than when someone with an imagination full of such beauties and a mind to appreciate the glories of the world is shut up from real, actual contemplation. To Tobias now the thought of green fields, sunshine and flowers, was at once rapture and agony.

'I must,' he said, 'I must—I will be free.'

A thorough determination to do anything, we are well convinced, always goes a long way towards its accomplishment; and certainly Tobias now would cheerfully have faced death in any shape, rather than he would again have been condemned to the solitary horrors of the cell, from which he had by such a chance got free.

He conjectured the stupid old Dr Popplejoy had not left the house by the unusual quiet that reigned in it, and he began to wonder if, while that quiet subsisted, there was the remotest chance of his getting into the garden, and then scaling the wall, and so reaching the open common.

While this thought was establishing itself in his mind, and he was thinking that he would pursue the passage in which he was until he saw where it led to, he heard the sound of footsteps, and he shrank back.

For a few seconds they appeared as if they were approaching where he was; and he began to dread that the cell would be searched, and his absence discovered, in which there would be no chance for him but death. Suddenly, however, the approaching footsteps paused, and then he heard a door banged shut.

It was still, even now, some minutes before Tobias could bring himself to traverse the passage again, and when he did, it was with a slow and stealthy step.

He had not, however, gone above thirty paces, when he heard the indistinct murmur of voices, and being guided by the sound, he paused at a door on his right hand, which he thought must be the one he had heard closed but a few minutes previously.

It was from the interior of the room which that was the door of, that the sound of voices came, and as it was a matter of the very first importance to Tobias to ascertain in what part of the house his enemies were, he placed his ear against the panel, and listened attentively.

He recognised both the voices: they were those of Watson and Fogg.

It was a very doubtful and ticklish situation that poor Tobias was now in, but it was wonderful how, by dint of strong resolution, he had stilled the beating of his heart, and the general nervousness of his disposition. There was but a frail door between him and his enemies, and yet he stood profoundly still and listened.

Mr Fogg was speaking.

'You quite understand me, Watson: I think,' he said, 'as concerns that little viper Tobias Ragg, he is too cunning, and much too dangerous, to live long. He almost staggered old superannuated Popplejoy.'

'Oh, confound him!' replied Watson, 'and he quite staggered me.'

'Why, certainly your face is rather scratched.'

'Yes, the little devil! but it's all in the way of business that, Mr Fogg, and you never heard me grumble at such little matters yet; and I'll be bound never will, that's more.'

'I give you credit for that, Watson; but between you and I, I think the disease of that boy is of a nature that will carry him off very suddenly.'

'I think so too,' said Watson, with a chuckle.

'It strikes me forcibly that he will be found dead in his bed some morning, and I should not in the least wonder if that was tomorrow morning: what's your opinion, Watson?'

'Oh, damn it, what's the use of all this round-about nonsense between us? the boy is to die, and there's an end of it, and die he shall, during the night—I owe him a personal grudge of course now.'

'Of course you do—he has disfigured you.'

'Has he? Well, I can return the compliment, and I say, Mr Fogg, my opinion is, that it's very dangerous having these medical inspections you have such a fancy for.'

'My dear fellow, it is dangerous, that I know as well as you can tell me, but it is from that danger we gather safety. If anything in the shape of a disturbance should arise about any patient, you don't know of what vast importance a report from such a man as old Dr Popplejoy might be.'

'Well, well, have it your own way. I shall not go near Master Tobias for the whole day, and shall see what starvation and solitude does towards taming him down a bit.'

'As you please; but it is time you went your regular rounds.'

'Yes, of course.'

Tobias heard Watson rise. The crisis was a serious one. His eye fell upon a bolt that was outside the door, and, with the quickness of thought, he shot it into its socket, and then made his way down the passage towards his cell, the door of which he shut close.

His next movement was to run to the end of the passage and descend some stairs. A door opposed him, but a push opened it, and he found himself in a small, dimly-lighted room, in one corner of which, upon a heap of straw, lay a woman, apparently sleeping.

The noise which Tobias made in entering the cell, for such it was, roused her up, and she said,—

'Oh! no, no, not the lash! not the lash! If am quiet. God, how quiet I am, although the heart within is breaking. Have mercy upon me!'

'Have mercy upon me,' said Tobias, 'and hide me if you can.'

'Hide you! hide you! God of Heavens, who are you?'

'A poor victim, who has escaped from one of the cells, and I—'

'Hush!' said the woman; and she made Tobias shrink down in the corner of the cell, cleverly covering him up with the straw, and then lying down herself in such a position that he was completely screened. The precaution was not taken a moment too soon, for by the time it was completed, Watson had burst open the door of the room which Tobias had bolted, and stood in the narrow passage.

'How the devil,' he said, 'came that door shut, I wonder?'

'Oh! save me,' whispered Tobias.

'Hush! hush! He will only look in,' was the answer. 'You are safe. I have been only waiting for someone who could assist me, in order to attempt an escape. You must remain here until night, and then I will show you how it may be done. Hush!—he comes.' Watson did come, and looked into the cell, muttering an oath, as he said,—

'Oh, you have enough bread and water till tomorrow morning, I should say; so you need not expect to see me again till then.'

'Oh! we are saved! we shall escape,' said the poor creature, after Watson had been gone some minutes.

'Do you think so?'

'Yes, yes! Oh, boy, I do not know what brought you here, but if you have suffered one-tenth part of the cruelty and oppression I have suffered, you are indeed to be pitied.'

'If we are to stay here,' said Tobias, 'till night, before making any attempt to escape, it will, perhaps, ease your mind, and beguile the time, if you were to tell me how you came here.'

'God knows! it might—it might!'

Tobias was very urgent upon the poor creature to tell her story, to beguile the tedium of the time of waiting, and after some amount of persuasion she consented to do so.

### The Mad Woman's Tale*

You shall now hear (she said to Tobias), if you will listen, such a catalogue of wrongs, unredressed and still enduring, that would indeed drive any human being mad; but I have been able to preserve so much of my mental faculties as will enable me to recollect and understand the many acts of cruelty and injustice I have endured here for many a long and weary day.

My persecutions began when I was very young—so young that I could not comprehend their cause, and used to wonder why I should be treated with greater rigour or with greater cruelty than people used to treat those who were really disobedient and way-ward children.

I was scarcely seven years old when a maiden aunt died; she was the only person whom I remember as being uniformly kind to me, though I can only remember her indistinctly, yet I know she was kind to me. I know also I used to visit her, and she used to look upon me as her favourite, for I used to sit at her feet upon a stool, watching her as she sat amusing herself by embroidering, silent and motionless sometimes, and then I asked her some questions which she answered.

This is the chief feature of my recollection of my aunt: she soon after died, but while she lived, I had no unkindness from anybody; it was only after that that I felt the cruelty and coldness of my family.

It appeared that I was a favourite with my aunt above all others whether in our family or any other; she loved me, and promised that, when she died, she would leave me provided for, and that I should not be dependent upon any one.

Well, I was, from the day after the funeral, an altered being. I was neglected, and no one paid any attention to me whatsoever; I was thrust about, and nobody appeared to care even if I had the neces-saries of life.

Such a change I could not understand. I could not believe the evi-dence of my own senses; I thought it must be something that I did not understand; perhaps my poor aunt's death had caused this dis-tress and alteration in people's demeanour to me.

However, I was a child, and though I was quick enough at noting all this, yet I was too young to feel acutely the conduct of my friends.

My father and mother were careless of me, and let me run where I would; they cared not when I was hurt, they cared not when I was in danger. Come what would, I was left to take my chance.

I recollect one day when I had fallen from the top to the bottom of some stairs and hurt myself very much; but no one comforted me; I was thrust out of the drawing-room, because I cried. I then went to the top of the stairs, where I sat weeping bitterly for some time.

At length, an old servant came out of one of the attics, and said, 'Oh! Miss Mary, what has happened to you, that you sit crying so bitterly on the stair-head? Come in here!'

I arose and went into the attic with her, when she set me on a chair, and busied herself with my bruises, and said to me, 'Now, tell me what you are crying about, and why did they turn you out of the drawing-room, tell me now?'

'Ay,' said I, 'they turned me out because I cried when I was hurt. I fell all the way down stairs, but they don't mind.'

'No, they do not, and yet in many families they would have taken more care of you than they do here!'

'And why do you think they would have done so?' I inquired.

---

'Don't you know what good fortune has lately fallen into your lap? I thought you knew all about it.'

'I don't know anything, save they are very unkind to me lately!'

'They have been very unkind to you, child, and I am sure I don't know why, nor can I tell you why they have not told you of your fortune.'

'My fortune,' said I; 'what fortune?'

'Why, don't you know that when your poor aunt died you were her favourite?'

'I know my aunt loved me,' I said; 'she loved me, and was kind to me; but since she has been dead, nobody cares for me.'

'Well, my child, she has left a will behind her which says that all her fortune shall be yours: when you are old enough you shall have all her fine things; you shall have all her money and her house.'

'Indeed!' said I; 'who told you so?'

'Oh, I have heard of it from those who were present at the reading of the will that you were, when you are old enough, to have all. Think what a great lady you will be then! You will have servants of your own.'

'I don't think I shall live till then.'

'Oh yes, you will—or, at least, I hope so.'

'And if I should not, what will become of all those fine things that you have told me of? Who'll have them?'

'Why, if you do not live till you are of age, your fortune will go to your father and mother, who take all.'

'Then they would sooner I die than live.'

'What makes you think so?' she inquired.

'Why,' said I, 'they don't care anything for me now, and they would have my fortune if I were dead—so they don't want me.'

'Ah, my child,' said the old woman, 'I have thought of that more than once; and now you can see it. I believe that it will be so. There has many a word been spoken truly enough by a child before now, and I am sure you are right—but do you be a good child, and be careful of yourself, and you will always find that Providence will keep you out of any trouble.'

'I hope so,' I said.

'And be sure you don't say who told you about this.'

'Why not?' I inquired; 'why may I not tell who told me about it?'

'Because,' she replied, 'if it were known that I told you anything about it, as you have not been told by them they might discharge me, and I should be turned out.'

'I will not do that,' I replied; 'they shall not learn who told me, though I should like to hear them say the same thing.'

'You may hear them do so one of these days,' she replied, 'if you are not impatient: it will come out one of these days—two may know of it.'

'More than my father and mother?'

'Yes, more—several.'

No more was said then about the matter; but I treasured it up in my mind. I resolved that I would act differently, and not have anything to do with them—that is, I would not be more in their sight than I could help—I would not be in their sight at all, save at meal times—and when there was any company there I always appeared.

I cannot tell why; but I think it was because I sometimes attracted the attention of others, and I hoped to be able to hear something respecting my fortune; and in the end I succeeded in doing so, and then I was satisfied—not that it made any alteration in my conduct, but I felt I was entitled to a fortune.

How such an impression became imprinted upon a girl of eight years old, I know not; but it took hold of me, and I had some kind of notion that I was entitled to more consideration than I was treated to.

'Mother,' said I one day to her.

'Well, Mary, what do you want to tease me about now?'

'Didn't Mrs Carter the other day say my aunt left me a fortune?'

'What is the child dreaming about?' said my mother. 'Do you know what you are talking about, child?—you can't comprehend.'

'I don't know, mother, but you said it was so to Mrs Carter.'

'Well, then, what if I did, child?'

'Why, you must have told the truth or a falsehood.'

'Well, Miss Impudence!—I told the truth, what then?'

'Why, then, I am to have a fortune when I grow up, that's all I mean, mother, and then people will take care of me. I shall not be forgotten, but everything will be done for me, and I shall be thought of first.'

My mother looked at me very hard for a moment or two, and then, as if she was actuated by remorse, she made an attempt to speak, but checked herself, and then anger came to her aid, and she said,—

'Upon my word, miss! what thoughts have you taken into your fancy now? I suppose we shall be compelled to be so many servants to you! I am sure you ought to be ashamed of yourself—you ought, indeed!'

'I didn't know I had done wrong,' I said.

'Hold your tongue, will you, or I shall be obliged to flog you!' said my mother, giving me a sound box on the ears that threw me down. 'Now hold your tongue and go upstairs, and give me no more insolence.'

I arose and went upstairs, sobbing as if my heart would break. I can recollect how many bitter hours I spent there, crying by myself—how many tears I shed upon this matter, and how I compared myself to other children, and how much my situation was worse than theirs by a great deal.

They, I thought, had their companions—they had their hours of play. But what companions had I—and what had I in the way of relaxation? What had I to do save to pine over the past, and present, and the future?

My infantile thoughts and hours were alike occupied by the sad reflections that belonged to a more mature age than mine; and yet I was so.

Days, weeks, and months passed on—there was no change, and I grew apace; but I was always regarded by my family with dislike, and always neglected. I could not account for it in any way than they wished me dead.

It may appear dreadful—very dreadful indeed—but what else was I to think? The old servant's words came upon my mind full of their meaning—if I died before I was one-and-twenty, they would have all my aunt's money.

'They wish me to die,' I thought, 'They wish me to die; and I shall die—I am sure I shall die! But they will kill me–they have tried it by neglecting me, and making me sad. What can I do—what can I do?'

These thoughts were the current matter of my mind, and how often do they recur to my recollection now I am in this dull, dreadful place! I can never forget the past. I am here because I have rights elsewhere, which others can enjoy, and do enjoy.

However, that is an old evil. I have thus suffered long. But to return.

After a year had gone by—two, I think, must have passed over my head—before I met with anything that was at all calculated to injure me. I must have been nearly ten years old, when, one evening, I had no sooner got into bed, than I found I had been put into damp—I may say wet sheets.

They were so damp that I could not doubt but this was done on purpose. I am sure no negligence ever came to anything so positive, and so abominable in all my life. I got out of bed, and took them off, and then wrapped myself up in the blankets, and slept till morning, without wakening any one.

When morning came, I inquired who put the sheets there?

'What do you mean, minx?' said my mother.

'Only that somebody was bad and wicked enough to put positively wet sheets in the bed; it could not have been done through carelessness—it must have been done though sheer wilfulness. I'm quite convinced of that.'

'You will get yourself well thrashed if you talk like that,' said my mother. 'The sheets are not damp; there are none in the house that are damp.'

'These are wet.'

This reply brought her hand down heavily upon my shoulder, and I was forced upon my knees. I could not help myself, so violent was the blow.

'There,' added my mother, 'take that, and that, and answer me if you dare.'

As she said this she struck me to the ground, and my head came into violent contact with the table, and I was rendered insensible.

How long I continued so I cannot tell. What I first saw when I awoke was the dreariness of the attics into which I had been thrust, and thrown upon a small bed without any furniture. I looked around and saw nothing that indicated comfort, and upon looking at my clothes, there were traces of blood. This, I had no doubt, came from myself.

I was hurt, and upon putting my hand to my head found that I was much hurt, as my head was bound up.

At that moment the door was opened, and the old servant came in.

'Well, Miss Mary,' she said, 'and so you have come round again? I really began to be afraid you were killed. What a fall you must have had!'

'Fall,' said I; 'who said it was a fall?'

'They told me so.'

'I was struck down.'

'Struck, Miss Mary? Who could strike you? And what did you do to deserve such a severe chastisement? Who did it?'

'I spoke to my mother about the wet sheets.'

'Ah! what a mercy you were not killed! If you had slept in them, your life would not have been worth a farthing. You would have caught cold, and you would have died of inflammation, I am sure of it. If anybody wants to commit murder without being found out, they have only to put them into damp sheets.'

'So I thought, and I took them out.'

'You did quite right—quite right.'

'What have you heard about them?' said I.

'Oh! I only went into the room in which you sleep, and I at once found how damp they were, and how dangerous it was; and I was going to tell your mamma, when I met her, and she told me to hold my tongue, but to go down and take you away, as you had fallen down in a fit, and she could not bear to see you lying there.'

'And she didn't do anything for me?'

'Oh, no, not as I know of, because you were lying on the floor bleeding. I picked you up, and brought you here.'

'And she has not enquired after me since?'

'Not once.'

'And don't know whether I am yet sensible or not?'

'She does not know that yet.'

'Well,' I replied, 'I think they don't care much for me, I think not at all, but the time may come when they will act differently.'

'No, Miss, they think, or affect to think, that you have injured them; but that cannot be, because you could not be cunning enough to dispose your aunt to leave you all, and so deprive them of what they think they are entitled to.'

'I never could have believed half so much.'

'Such, however, is the case.'

'What can I do?'

'Nothing, my dear, but lie still till you get better, and don't say any more; but sleep, if you can sleep, will do you more good than anything else now for an hour or so, so lie down and sleep.'

\*     \*     \*     \*     \*

The old woman left the room, and I endeavoured to compose myself to sleep; but could not do so for some time, my mind being too actively engaged in considering what I had better do, and I determined upon a course of conduct by which I thought I should escape much of my present persecution.

It was some days, however, before I could put it in practice, and one day I found my father and mother together, and said to her,—

'Mother, why do you not send me to school?'

'You—send you to school! did you mean you, Miss?'

'Yes, I meant myself, because other people go to school to learn something, but I have not been sent at all.'

'Are you not contented?'

'I am not,' I answered, 'because other people learn something; but at the same time, I should be more out of your way, since I am more trouble to you, as you complain of me; it would not cost more than living at home.'

'What is the matter with the child?' asked my father.

'I cannot tell,' said my mother.

'The better way will be to take care of her, and confine her to some part of the house, if she does not behave better.'

'The little minx will be very troublesome.'

'Do you think so?'

'Yes, decidedly.'

'Then we must adopt some more active measures, or we shall have to do what we do not wish. I am amused at her asking to be sent to school! Was ever there heard such wickedness? Well, I could not have believed such ingratitude could have existed in human nature.'

'Get out of the room, you huzzy,' said my mother; 'go out of the room, and don't let me hear a word from you more.'

I left the room terrified at the storm I had raised up against me. I knew not that I had done wrong, and went up crying to my attic alone, and found the old servant, who asked what was the matter. I told her all I had said, and what had been the result, and how I had been abused.

'Why, you should let things take their own course, my dear.'

'Yes, but I can learn nothing.'

'Never mind; you will have plenty of money when you grow older, and that will cure many defects; people who have money never want for friends.'

'But I have them not, and yet I have money.'

'Most certainly—most certainly, but you have it not in your power, and you are not old enough to make use of it, if you had it.'

'Who has it?' I inquired.

'Your father and mother.'

No more was said at that time, and the old woman left me to myself, and I recollect I long and deeply pondered over this matter, and yet I could see no way out of it, and resolved that I would take things as easily as I could; but I feared that I was not likely to have a very quiet life; indeed, active cruelty was exercised against me.

They would lock me up in a room a whole day at a time, so that I was debarred the use of my limbs. I was even kept without food, and on every occasion I was knocked about, from one to the other, without remorse—everyone took a delight in tormenting me, and in showing me how much they dared to do.

Of course servants and all would not treat me with neglect and harshness if they did not see it was agreeable to my parents.

This was shocking cruelty; but yet I found that this was not all. Many were the little contrivances made and invented to cause me to fall down stairs—to slip—to trip, to do anything that might have ended in some fatal accident, which would have left them at liberty to enjoy my legacy, and no blame would be attached to them for the accident, and I should most likely get blamed for what was done, and from which I had been the sufferer—indeed, I should have been deemed to have suffered justly.

On one occasion, after I had been in bed some time, I found it was very damp, and upon examination I found the bed itself had been made quite wet, with the sheet put over it to hide it.

This I did not discover until it was too late, for I caught a violent cold, and it took me some weeks to get over it, and yet I escaped eventually, though after some months' illness. I recovered, and it evidently made them angry because I did live.

They must have believed me to be very obstinate; they thought me obdurate in the extreme—they called me all the names they could imagine, and treated me with every indignity they could heap upon me.

Well, time ran on, and in my twelfth year I obtained the notice of one or two of our friends, who made some enquiries about me.

I always remarked that my parents disliked anyone to speak to, or take any notice of me. They did not permit me to say much—they did not like my speaking; and on one occasion, when I made some remark respecting school, she replied, —

'Her health is so bad that I have not yet sent her, but shall do so by and by, when she grows stronger.'

There was a look bent upon me that told me at once what I must expect if I persisted in my half-formed resolve of contradicting all that had been said.

When the visitor went I was well aware of what kind of a life I should have had, if I did not absolutely receive some serious injury. I was terrified, and held my tongue.

Soon after that I was seized with violent pains and vomiting. I was very ill, and the servant being at home only, a doctor was sent for, who at once said I had been poisoned, and ordered me to be taken care of.

I know how it was done; I had taken some cake given me—it was left out for me; and that was the only thing I had eaten, and it astonished me, for I had not had such a thing given me for years, and that is why I believe the poison was put in the cake, and I think others thought so too.

However, I got over that after a time, though I was a long while before I did so; but at the same time I was very weak, and the surgeon said that had I been a little longer without assistance, or had I not thrown it up, I must have sunk beneath the effects of a violent poison.

He advised my parents to take some measures to ascertain who it was that had administered the poison to me; but though they promised compliance, they never troubled themselves about it— but I was for a long time very cautious of what I took, and was in great fear of the food that was given to me.

However, nothing more of that character took place, and at length I quite recovered, and began to think in my own mind that I ought to take some active steps in the matter, and that I ought to seek an asylum elsewhere.

I was now nearly fifteen years of age, and could well see how inveterate was the dislike with which I was regarded by my family: I thought that they ought to use me better, for I could remember no cause for it. I had given no deadly offence, nor was there any motive why I should be treated thus with neglect and disdain.

It was, then, a matter of serious consideration with me as to whether I should not go and throw myself upon the protection of some friend, and beg their interference in my behalf; but then there was no one whom I felt would do so much for me—no one from whom I expected so great an act of friendship.

It was hardly to be expected from anyone that they should inter-fere between me and my parents; they would have had their first say, and I should have contradicted all said, and should have appeared in a very bad light indeed.

I could not say they had neglected my education—I could not say that, because there I had been careful myself, and I had assidu-ously striven when alone to remedy this defect, and had actually succeeded; so that, if I were examined, I should have denied my own assertions by contrary facts, which would injure me. Then again, if I were neglected, I could not prove any injury, because I had all the means of existence; and all I could say would be either attrib-uted to some evil source, or it was entirely false—but at the same time I felt I had great cause of complaint, and none of gratitude.

I could hold no communion with any one—all alike deserted me, and I knew none who could say aught for me if I requested their good-will.

I had serious thoughts of possessing myself of some money, and then leaving home, and staying away until I had arrived at age; but this I deferred doing, seeing that there was no means, and I could not do more than I did then—that is, to live on without any mischief happening, and wait for a few years more.

I contracted an acquaintance with a young man who came to visit my father—he came several times, and paid me more civility and attention than anyone else ever did, and I felt that he was the only friend I possessed.

It is no wonder I looked upon him as being my best and my only friend. I thought him the best and the handsomest man I ever beheld.

This put other thoughts into my head. I did not dress as others did, much less had I the opportunity of becoming possessed of many of those little trinkets that most young women of my age had.

But this made no alteration in the good opinion of the young gentleman, who took no notice of that, but made me several pretty presents.

These were treasures to me, and I must say I gloated over them, and often, when alone, I have spent hours in admiring them; trifling as they were, they made me happier. I knew now one person who cared for me, and a delightful feeling it was too. I shall never know it again—it is quite impossible.

Here among the dark walls and unwholesome cells we have no cheering ray of life or hope—all is dreary and cold; a long and horrible imprisonment takes place, to which there is no end save with life, and in which there is not one mitigating circumstance—all is bad and dark. God help me!

\*     \*     \*     \*     \*

However, my dream of happiness was soon disturbed. By some means my parents had got an idea of this, and the young man was dismissed the house, and forbidden to come to it again. This he determined to do, and more than once we met, and then in secret I told him all my woes.

When he had heard all I had said, he expressed the deepest commiseration, and declared I had been most unjustly and harshly treated, and thought that there was not a harder or harsher treatment than that which I had received.

He then advised me to leave home.

'Leave home,' I said; 'where shall I fly? I have no friend.'

'Come to me, I will protect you, I will stand between you and all the world; they shall not stir hand or foot to your injury.'

'But I cannot, dare not do that; if they found me out, they would force me back with all the ignominy and shame that could be felt from having done a bad act; not any pity would they show me.'

'Nor need you; you would be my wife, I mean to make you my wife.'

'You?'

'Yes! I dreamed not of anything else. You shall be my wife; we will hide ourselves, and remain unknown to all until the time shall have arrived when you are of age—when you can claim all your property, and run no risk of being poisoned or killed by any other means.'

'This is a matter,' said I, 'that ought to be considered well before adopting anything as violent or so sudden.'

'It is; and it is not one that I think will injure by being reflected upon by those who are the principal actors; for my own part my mind is made up, and I am ready to perform my share of the engagement.'

I resolved to consider the matter well in my own mind, and felt every inclination to do what he proposed, because it took me away from home, and because it would give me one of my own.

My parents had become utterly estranged from me; they did not act as parents, they did not act as friends, they had steeled my heart against them; they never could have borne any love to me, I am sure of it, who could have committed such great crimes against me.

As the hour drew near, that in which I was likely to become an object of still greater hatred and dislike to them, I thought I was often the subject of their private thoughts, and often when I entered the room my mother, and father, and the rest, would suddenly leave off speaking, and look at me, as if to ascertain if I had ever heard them say anything. On one occasion I remember very well I heard them conversing in a low tone. The door happened to have opened of itself, the hasp not having been allowed to enter the mortice; I heard my name mentioned: I paused and listened.

'We must soon get rid of her,' said my mother.

'Undoubtedly,' he replied; 'if we do not, we shall have her about our ears: she'll get married, or some infernal thing, and then we shall have to refund.'

'We could prevent that.'

'Not if her husband was to insist upon it, we could not; but the only plan I can now form is what I told you of already.'

'Putting her in a mad-house?'

'Yes: there, you see, she will be secured, and cannot get away. Besides, those who go there die in a natural way before many years.'

'But she can speak.'

'So she may; but who attends to the ravings of a mad woman? No, no; depend upon it that is the best plan: send her to a lunatic asylum—a private mad-house. I can obtain all that is requisite in a day or two.'

'Then we will consider that settled.'

'Certainly.'

'In a few days, then?'

'Before next Sunday; because we can enjoy ourselves on that day without any restraint, or without any uncomfortable feelings of uncertainty about us.'

*        *        *        *        *

I waited to hear no more: I had heard enough to tell me what I had to expect. I went back to my own room, and having put on my bonnet and shawl I went out to see the individual to whom I have alluded, and saw him.

I then informed him of all that had taken place, and heard him exclaim against them in terms of rising indignation.

'Come to me,' he said; 'come to me at once.'

'Not at once.'

'Don't stop a day.'

'Hush!' said I; 'there's no danger: I will come the day after tomorrow; and then I will bid adieu to all these unhappy moments, to all these persecutions; and in three years' time I shall be able to demand my fortune, which will be yours.'

*        *        *        *        *

We were to meet the next day but one, early in the morning—there were not, in fact, to be more than thirty hours elapse before I was to leave home—if home I could call it—however there was no time to be lost. I made up a small bundle and had all in readiness, before I went to bed, and placed in security, intending to rise early and let myself out and leave the house.

That, however, was never to happen. While I slept, at a late hour of the night, I was awakened by two men standing by my bedside, who desired me to get up and follow them. I refused, and they pulled me rudely out of bed.

I called out for aid, and exclaimed against the barbarity of their proceedings.

'It is useless to listen to her,' said my father, 'you know what a mad woman will say!'

'Ay, we do,' replied the men, 'they are the cunningest devils we ever heard. We have seen enough of them to know that.'

To make the matter plain, I was seized, gagged, and thrust into a coach, and brought here, where I have remained ever since.

## 31

## *The Rapid Journey to London of Tobias*

THERE was something extremely touching in the tone, and apparently in the manner, in which the poor persecuted one detailed the story of her wrongs, and she had the tribute of a willing tear from Tobias.

'After the generous confidence you have had in me,' he said, 'I ought to tell you something of myself.'

'Do so,' she replied, 'we are companions in misfortune.'

'We are indeed.'

Tobias then related to her at large all about Sweeney Todd's villainies, and how at length he, Tobias, had been placed where he was, for the purpose of silencing his testimony of the evil and desperate practices of the barber. After that, he related to her what he had overheard about the intention to murder him that night, and he concluded by saying, —

'If you have any plan of escape from this horrible place, let me implore you to tell it to me, and let us put it into practice tonight, and if we fail, death is at any time preferable to continued existence here.'

'It is—it is—listen to me.'

'I will indeed,' said Tobias; 'you will say you never had such attention as I will now pay to you.'

'You must know, then, that this cell is paved with flag-stones, as you see, and that the wall here at the back forms likewise part of the wall of an old wood-house in the garden, which is never visited.'

'Yes, I understand.'

'Well, as I have been here so long, I managed to get up one of the flag-stones that forms the flooring here, and to work under the wall with my hands—a slow labour, and one of pain, until I managed to render a kind of excavation, one end of which is here, and the other in the wood-house.'

'Glorious!' said Tobias, 'I see—I see—go on.'

'I should have made my escape if I could, but the height of the garden wall has always been the obstacle. I thought of tearing this miserable quilt into strips, and making a sort of rope of it; but then how was I to get it on the wall? You, perhaps, will, with your activity and youth, be able to accomplish that.'

'Oh, yes, yes! you're right enough there; it is not a wall that shall stop me.'

They waited until, from a church clock in the vicinity, they heard ten strike, and then they began operations. Tobias assisted his new friend to raise the stone in the cell, and there, immediately beneath, appeared the excavation leading to the wood-house, just sufficiently wide for one person to creep through.

It did not take long to do that, and Tobias took with him a piece of work, upon which he had been occupied for the last two hours, namely, the quilt torn up into long pieces, twisted and tied together, so that it formed a very tolerable rope, which Tobias thought would sustain the weight of his companion.

The wood-house was a miserable-looking hole enough, and Tobias at first thought that the door of it was fastened, but by a little pressure it came open; it had only stuck through the dampness of the woodwork at that low point of the garden.

And now they were certainly both of them at liberty, with the exception of surmounting the wall, which rose frowningly before them in all its terrors.

There was a fine cool fresh air in the garden, which was indeed most grateful to the senses of Tobias, and he seemed doubly nerved for anything that might be required of him after inhaling that delicious cool, fresh breeze.

There grew close to the wall one of those beautiful mountain-ash trees, which bend over into such graceful foliage, and which are so useful in the formation of pretty summerhouses. Tobias saw that if he ascended to the top of this tree, there would not be much trouble in getting from there to the wall.

'We shall do it,' he said, 'we shall succeed.'

'Thank God, that I hear you say so,' replied his companion.

Tobias tied one end of the long rope they had made of the quilt to his waist, so that he might carry it up with him, and yet leave him free use of hands and feet, and then he commenced, with great activity, ascending the tree. In three minutes he was on the wall.

The moon shone sweetly. There was not a tree or house in the vicinity that was not made beautiful now, in some portions of it, by the sweet, soft light that poured down upon them.

Tobias could not resist pausing a moment to look around him upon the glorious scene. but the voice of her for whom he was bound to do all that was possible, aroused him.

'Oh, Tobias!' she said, 'quick, quick—lower the rope; oh, quick!'

'In a moment—in a moment,' he cried.

The top of the wall was here and there armed with iron spikes, and some of these formed an excellent grappling place for the torn quilt. In the course of another minute Tobias had his end of it secure.

'Now,' he said, 'can you climb up by it, do you think? Don't hurry about it. Remember, there is no alarm, and for all we know we have hours to ourselves yet.'

'Yes, yes—oh, yes—thank God!' he heard her say.

Tobias was not where he could, by any exertion of strength, render her now the least assistance, and he watched the tightening of the frail support by which she was gradually climbing to the top of the wall with the most intense and painful interest that can be imagined.

'I come—I come,' she said, 'I am saved.'

'Come slowly—for God's sake do not hurry.'

'No, no.'

At this moment Tobias heard the frail rope giving way: there was a tearing sound—it broke, and she fell.

Lights, too, at that unlucky moment, flashed from the house, and it was now evident an alarm had been given. What could he do? if two could not be saved, one could be saved.

He turned, and flung his feet over the wall, he hung by his hands, as low as he could, and then he dropped the remainder of the distance.

He was hurt, but in a moment he sprang to his feet, for he felt that safety could only lie in instant and rapid flight.

The terror of pursuit was so strong upon him that he forgot his bruises.

\*     \*     \*     \*     \*

'Thank Heaven,' exclaimed Tobias, 'I am at last free from that horrible place. Oh, if I can but reach London now, I shall be safe; and as for Sweeney Todd, let him beware, for a day of retribution for him cannot be far off.'

So saying, Tobias turned his steps towards the city, and at a hard trot, soon left Peckham Rye far behind him as he pursued his route.

---

## 32

## *The Announcement in Sweeney Todd's Window. Johanna Oakley's Adventure*

HAVING thus far traced Tobias's career, we are the better enabled to turn now our exclusive attention to the proceedings of Johanna Oakley, who, we cannot help thinking, is about to commence a most dangerous adventure.

The advice which had been given to her by her romantic young friend, Arabella Wilmot, had from the first taken a strong hold upon her imagination; and the more she had thought it over, and the more she found the others failed, in procuring any tidings of her lost lover, the more intent she was upon carrying it out.

'Yes,' she said, 'yes, true love will accomplish very great wonders; and what force or ability will fail at, confident affection even of a mere girl may succeed in. 'Tis true I risk my life; but what is life to

me without what made it desirable? What is continued existence
to me, embittered with the constant thought that such a dreadful
mystery hangs over the fate of Mark Ingestrie?'

So it will be seen it was partly despair, and partly a kind of presentiment she had that success would attend her enterprise, that
induced her to go to Sweeney Todd's.

There was a placard in Todd's window, which bore the following
announcement:

> *'Wanted: a lad, one of strict religious principles preferred.*
> *Apply within.'*

The fact is, as we have said, although Sweeney Todd now, from
the sale of the string of pearls, had the means of retiring from his
avocations, and fully meant to do so, he did not think it prudent to
hurry over such a step, and was resolved to wait until all noise and
enquiry, if any were made, about the pearls had subsided; and
therefore was it that he found it necessary to provide himself with
a new boy, who, for all he cared, might share the fate of poor Tobias—
that fate which Sweeney Todd considered certain, but concerning
which the reader is better informed.

'Ah,' muttered Todd to himself, 'I like boys of a religious turn.
They are much easier managed, for the imagination in such cases
has been cultivated at the expense of the understanding. Hilloa,
who have we here?'

Todd was stropping a razor, and peering out into the street while
he spoke, and he saw a decent-looking young lad of remarkably
handsome exterior, stop at the window, and read the tempting
announcement. The lad advanced a step towards the door, hesitated, retreated, and then advanced again, as if he wished to apply
for the vacant situation, and yet dreaded to do so.

'Who can he be?' said Todd, as he looked curiously at him. 'He
don't seem the likely sort to apply for the situation of barber's boy.'

Todd was right enough there, for this seeming lad was no other
than Johanna Oakley; and little, indeed, did she seem as if she
belonged to the rough class from whom Sweeney Todd, the barber,
might be supposed to find a lad for his shop.

In another moment she entered the shop, and was face to face
with the man whom she might fairly consider to be the bane of her
young existence, if what was suspected of him were true.

Todd fixed his strange glance upon her; but he was silent, for it was no rule of his to speak first, and Johanna felt constrained to commence the rather embarrassing conversation.

'You are in want of a lad, sir,' she said, 'to mind your shop, I suppose?'

'Yes.'

Johanna had certainly hoped for a longer answer; but as Todd was silent, she had now no recourse but to go on.

'I shall be glad to take the situation.'

'Who are you? You don't seem likely to want such a place. Who and what are you?'

Johanna had her story ready, for of course she had anticipated questions being asked of her; so she replied, with a readiness that did not seem at all forced, —

'I am an orphan, I was left in the care of a mother-in-law;* I don't like her, she was cruel to me, and I ran away.'

'Where from?'

'Oxford.'

'Oxford, Oxford,' muttered Todd; 'then nobody knows you in London, I suppose, my little lad?'

'No one. I have come to town comfortably enough, in a wagon; but, if I don't get something to do, I shall have to go back, which I don't like the idea of at all. I'd rather be anything in London, than go back to Mrs Green.'

'Green, and what's your name?'

'Charley Green, of course; you sees my name's the same as hers, because she married my father.'

'Oh, you won't suit me; you ain't the sort of boy I want.'

'Sorry I troubled you, sir,' said Johanna, as she turned carelessly and left the shop without making the least attempt to move the barber's determination, or even looking behind her.

'Pshaw!' exclaimed Todd, as he flung down the razor he had commenced sharpening again, 'how foolishly suspicious I am. I shall wait a while, I think, before I get anyone to suit me as this lad will. In London alone, without friends, an orphan, nobody to enquire after him—the very thing.'

Sweeney Todd was at his door in an instant. 'Hoi! hoi!' he called. Johanna looked back, and saw him beckon to her; with new hope she returned, and was again in the shop.

'Hark ye, my lad,' said Todd; 'I feel disposed to take you on account of your friendless condition. I feel for you, I'm an orphan myself, that's a fact.' Here he made one of those hideous grimaces he was in the habit of indulging in when he thought he said anything particularly racy. 'Yes, I'm a poor orphan myself, with nothing but my strong sense of religion to support me. I'll take you on trial.'

'I am much beholden to you, sir.'

'Oh, don't mention that; your duties will consist of minding the shop if I happen to be absent. You will have sixpence a day, but nothing else from me; for out of that, you provide yourself with food; and the cheapest and the best thing you can do is, to go always to Lovett's, in Bell-yard, and have a pie for your dinner; you will sleep at night here in the shop, run messages, see and hear much, but if you gossip about me and my affairs, I'll cut your throat.'

'You may depend upon me, sir: I'm only too happy in being taken into the service of such a respectable gentleman.'

'Respectable gentleman!' repeated Todd, as he finished stropping the razor. 'Respectable'; and then he gave one of his hideous laughs, which thrilled through the very heart of Johanna, as she thought that it might have been the last noise that sounded in the ears of Mark Ingestrie in this world. Todd turned very suddenly round, and said, —

'Did you groan?'

'I groan!' replied Johanna; 'what for?'

'Oh, I only thought you did, Master Charley, that's all. See if that water on the fire is hot, and if so, bring it to me. Ha! a customer.'

As Todd uttered these words, two persons entered the shop; they looked like substantial countrymen, farmers perhaps, in a good way of business; and one of them said, —

'Now, Mr Barber, for a clean shave, if you please,' while the other stood at the door, as if to wait for his companion.

'Certainly, sir,' said Todd. 'Pray sit down here if you please, sir; a nice day for the time of year; come from the country, sir, I suppose?'

'Yes, me and my cousin; we don't know much of London, yet.'

'Indeed, sir, you ought not to leave it soon, then, I'm sure, for there is much to see, and that can't be seen quickly; and if you live far off, it's better to take the opportunity while you are here. Give me that soap dish, Charley.'

'Yes, sir.'

'Ah, to be sure,' replied the countryman, 'it is; but we have brought up to the London market a number of beasts, which having sold well, we have too much money about us to risk in going to see sights.'

'Indeed! you are prudent. Would you like your whiskers trimmed?'

'A little, but not quite off.'

There was now a pause of some moments' duration, after which Sweeney Todd said, in a very offhand manner—'I suppose you have seen the two figures at St Dunstan's church strike the hour?'

'Two figures?' said the one who was not being shaved, for the other would have had a mouthful of lather if he had spoken; 'two figures? No;—what may they be all about?'

'Well,' resumed Todd, with the most indifferent air and manner in the world, 'if you have not seen them, it's quite a shame that you should not; and while I am shaving your friend, as it now only wants about five minutes to eleven, you have a good opportunity of going and getting back in time when your friend is—disposed of— what do you say to that? Charley, go with the gentleman, and show him the figures striking the hour at St Dunstan's. You must cross over to the other side of the way, you know, to see them properly and effectually. Don't hurry, sir.'

'Very much obliged,' said the disengaged grazier, for such he seemed to be; 'but I would rather go with my friend here, when he is shaven. You can't think what cynical remarks he makes at any-thing he has not seen before, so that to go with him is really always to me half the treat.'

'Very good and very right,' said Todd; 'I shall soon be done. I have just about finished you off, now, sir. That will do.'

There was no disappointment at all visible in Todd's manner, and the grazier rose and wiped his face on the jack-towel,* that hung from a roller for the use of those whom it might concern, paid his money, and with a civil good-day to the barber, left the shop along with his friend.

An awfully diabolical look came across the countenance of Sweeney Todd, as he muttered to himself,—

'Curses on them both! I may yet have one of them though.'

'What did you say, sir?' asked Johanna.

'What is that to you, you young imp?' roared Todd. 'Curse you! I'll pull out your teeth by degrees, with red-hot pincers, if you pre-sume to listen to what I say! I'll be the death of you, you devil's cub.'

Johanna shrank back, alarmed, and then Todd walked across his shop to the back-parlour, the door of which he carefully double-locked, after which, turning to Johanna, he said, —

'You will mind the shop till I return, and if anybody comes, you can tell them that they need not wait, for I shall probably be some time gone. All you have to do is mind the place, and, hark you, no peeping nor prying about; sit still, and touch nothing, for if you do, I shall most assuredly discover it, and your punishment will be certain and perhaps terrible.'

'I will be careful, sir.'

'Do so, and you will be rewarded. Why, the last lad I had served me so well that I have had him taken care of for life, in a fine handsome country house, with grounds attached, a perfect villa, where he is waited upon by attendants, in the most attentive manner.'

'How kind,' said Johanna, 'and is he happy?'

'Very, very—notwithstanding the general discontent of human nature, he is quite happy, as a matter of course. Mind my instructions, and in due time you will no doubt yourself share as amiable a fate.'

Todd put on his hat, and with a horrible and strange leer upon his countenance, left the shop, and Johanna found herself in the situation she had coveted, namely, to be alone in the shop of Sweeney Todd, and able to make what examination of it she pleased, without the probability of much interruption.

'Heaven be my aid,' she cried, 'for the sake of truth.'

## 33

## *The Discoveries in the Vaults of St Dunstan's*

'WELL, Sir Richard,' remarked the beadle of St Dunstan's to the magistrate, after the ponderous stone was raised in the centre of the church, upon which the workmen had been busy, 'don't you smell nothink now?'

The magistrate, churchwardens, and, indeed, everyone present, shrank back from the horrible stench that saluted them, now that the stone was fairly removed.

'Why, good God!' exclaimed the senior churchwarden; 'have we been sitting and hearing sermons with such a charnel-house under? I always understood that none of the vaults exactly underneath the church had been used for many years past.'

'Hush!' said the magistrate. 'The enquiry we are upon is, perhaps, a more important one than you imagine, sir.'

'More important! How can that be? Didn't the bishop smell it when he came to confirm the people, and didn't he say in the vestry that he could not confirm anybody while such a smell was in the church, and didn't we tell him that it would be a sad thing if he didn't? and then he did confirm the people in such a twinkling, that they didn't know what they were confirmed in at all.'

'Hush! my good sir, hush, and hear me. Will you, now that you have got up this great stone, and opened, as I see, the top of a stone staircase, by so doing, send away the workmen, and, indeed, all persons but yourself and me?'

'Well, but—but you don't mean us to go down, sir, do you?'

'I mean to go, you may depend. Send away the men at once, if you please. I have ample warrant for all I am about to do, I assure you. I suspect I shall be well able to free St Dunstan's church from the horrible stench that has been infesting it for some time past.'

'You think so, sir? Bless you, then, I'll do just whatever you like.'

The workmen were not sorry to be dismissed from the uncomfortable employment, but the beadle who was holding his nose, and who having overheard what Sir Richard had said, was extremely anxious upon the subject, put in his claim to stay, on the ground of being one of the officials of the church; and he was accordingly permitted to remain.

'This seems to lead to the vaults,' remarked Sir Richard, as he looked down the chasm, which the removal of the stone had left.

'Yes,' replied the churchwarden, 'it does, and they have, as I say, been unused for a long time; but how that dreadful smell can come from bodies that have been forty or fifty years there, I can't think.'

'We must be careful of the foul air,' remarked the magistrate. 'Get a torch, Mr Beadle, if you please, and we will lower it into the vault. If that lives, we can: and if you please go first to the door of the church, and take this silk handkerchief with you, and hold it up in your hand; and upon that signal, four persons will come to you. They are officers of mine, and you will bring them to me.'

'Oh, dear, yes, certainly,' said the beadle, who was quite happy at the thoughts of such a reinforcement. 'I'll do it, sir, and as for a torch, there is some famous links in the vestry cupboard, as I'll get in a minute. Well, I do think the smell is a little better already; don't you, sir? I'm a going. Don't be impatient, sir. I'm going like a shot, I am.'

To give the beadle his due, he certainly executed his orders quickly. The four officers, sure enough, obeyed the signal of the handkerchief, and in a few minutes more, a torchlight was lowered by a rope down the gloomy aperture. All watched the light with great interest as it descended; but, although it certainly burnt dimmer than before, yet it showed no signs of going out, and the magistrate said, —

'We may safely descend. The air that will support flame will likewise support animal life; therefore we need be under no sort of apprehension. Follow me.'

He commenced a careful descent of the stone steps, and was promptly followed by his four men, and much more slowly by the beadle and the churchwarden, neither of whom seemed much to relish the adventure, although their curiosity prompted them to continue it.

The stone steps consisted of about twenty, and when the bottom was gained, it was found to be covered with flag-stones of considerable size, upon which sawdust was strewn, but not sufficiently thickly to cover them in all places completely.

There was a death-like stillness in the place, and the few crumbling coffins which were in niches in the walls were, with their tenants, evidently too old to give forth that frightful odour of animal decomposition which pervaded the place.

'You will see, Sir Richard,' said the churchwarden, producing a piece of paper, 'that, according to the plans of the vault I have here, this one opens into a passage that runs halfway round the church, and from that passage opens a number of vaults, not one of which has been used for years past.'

'I see the door is open.'

'Yes, it is as you say. That's odd, Sir Richard, ain't it? Oh! gracious!—just put your head out into the passage, and won't you smell it then!'

They all tried the experiment, and found, indeed, that the smell was horrible. Sir Richard took a torch from one of the constables, and advanced into the passage. He could see nothing but the doors of some of the vaults open: he crossed the threshold of one of them, and was away about a minute; after which he came back, saying,—

'I think we will all retire now: we have seen enough to convince us all about it.'

'All about it, sir!' said the churchwarden, 'what about it?'

'Exactly, that will do—follow me, my men.'

The officers, without the slightest questions or remarks, followed Sir Richard, and he began rapidly, with them at his heels, to ascend the stone staircase into the church again.

'Hilloa!' cried the beadle—'I say, stop. O lord! don't let me be lost—Oh, don't! I shall think something horrible is coming up after me, and going to lay hold of my heels: don't let me be lost! oh dear!'

'You can't be lost,' said one of the officers; 'you know if anything is going to lay hold of your heels. Take it easy; it's only a ghost at the most, you know.'

By the time the beadle got fairly into the church, he was in that state of perspiration and fright, that he was obliged to sit down upon a tomb to recover himself; and the magistrate took that opportunity of whispering to the churchwarden,—

'I want to speak to you alone; come out with me—order the church to be locked up, as if we meditated no further search in the vaults.'

'Yes, oh, yes! I knew there was some secret.'

'There is a horrible one!—such a one as all London will ring with in twenty-four hours more—such a secret as will never be forgotten in connection with old St Dunstan's church, while it is in existence.'

There was a solemnity about the manner in which the magistrate spoke, which quite alarmed the churchwarden, and he turned rather pale as they stood upon the church threshold.

'Do you know one Sweeney Todd?' asked the magistrate.

'Oh, yes—a barber.'

'Good. Incline your ear to me while we walk down to Downing-street. I am going to call upon the Secretary of State for the Home Department, and before we get there, I shall be able to tell you why and what sort of assistance I want of you.'

The churchwarden did incline his ear most eagerly, but before they had got half way down the Strand, he was compelled to go into a public-house to get some brandy, such an overpowering effect had the horrible communication of the magistrate upon him. What that communication was we shall very soon discover; but it is necessary that we follow Mr Todd a little in his proceedings after he left Johanna in charge of his shop.

Todd walked briskly on, till he came nearly to Pickett-street, in the Strand, and then he went into a chemist's shop that was there, in which only a lad was serving.

'You recollect,' said Todd, 'serving me with some rat poison?'

'Oh, yes, yes—Mr Todd, I believe.'

'The same. I want some more; for the fact is, that owing to the ointments I have in my shop for the hair, the vermin are attracted, and I have now as many as ever. It was only last night I awakened, and saw one actually lapping up hair-oil, and another drinking some rose-water, that they had upset, and broken a bottle of, so I will thank you to give me some liquid poison, if you please, as they seem so fond of drink.'

'Exactly, sir, exactly,' said the lad, as he took down a bottle, and made up a potion; 'exactly, sir. If you put a few drops only of this in half a pint of liquid, it will do.'

'A couple of drops? This must be powerful.'

'It is—a dozen drops, or about half a teaspoonful, would kill a man to a certainty, so you will be careful of it, Mr Todd. Of course, we don't sell such things to strangers, you know, but you being a neighbour alters the case.'

'True enough. Thank you. Good day. I think we shall have rain shortly, do you know.'

Todd walked away with the poison in his pocket, and when he had got a few yards from the chemist's door, he gave such a hideous chuckle that an old gentleman, who was close before him, ran like a lamp-lighter* in his fright, and put himself quite out of breath.

'This will do,' muttered Todd; 'I must smooth the path to my retirement from business. I know well that if I were to hint at such a thing in a certain quarter, it would be considered a certain proof that I had made enough to be worth dividing, and that is a process I don't intend exactly to go through. No, no, Mrs Lovett, no, no.'

Todd marched slowly towards his own house, but when he got to the corner of Bell-yard, and heard St Dunstan's strike twelve, he paused a moment, and then muttered, —

'I'll call and see her—yes, I'll call, and see her. The evening will answer better my present purpose.'

He then walked up Bell-yard, until he came to the fascinating Mrs Lovett's pie-shop. He paused a moment at the window, and leered in at two lawyer's clerks who were eating some of yesterday's pies. The warm day batch had not yet come up. 'Happy youths!' he chuckled, and walked into the shop.

Mrs Lovett received him graciously as an acquaintance, and invited him into the parlour, while the two limbs of the law continued eating and praising the pies.

'Delicious, ain't they?' said one.

'Oh, I believe you,' replied the other; 'and such jolly lots of gravy, too, ain't there? I wonder how she does make 'em. Lor' bless you, I almost live upon 'em. You know, I used to take all my meals with my fat old uncle, Marsh, but since he disappeared one day, I live on Lovett's pies, instead of the old buffer.'

## 34

### *Johanna Alone.—The Secret.— Mr Todd's Suspicions.—The Mysterious Letter*

FOR some time after Todd had left the shop, Johanna could scarcely believe that she was sufficiently alone to dare to look about her; but as minute after minute passed away, and no sound indicative of his speedy return fell upon her ears, she gathered more courage.

'Yes,' she said, 'I am at last alone, in the place where my suspicions have always pointed as the death place of poor Mark. O Heavens, grant that it may not be so, and that, in unravelling the evident mystery of this man's life, I may hail you living, my dear Mark, and not have to mourn you dead! And yet, how can I, even for a moment, delude myself with such false hopes? No, no, he has fallen a victim to this ruthless man.'

For a few minutes, as Johanna gave way to this violent burst of grief, she wrung her hands and wept; but then, as a thought of the danger she would be in should Todd return and see signs of emotion crossed her mind, she controlled her tears, and managed to bear the outward semblance of composure.

She then began to look about her in the same way that poor Tobias had done; but she could find nothing of an explanatory character, although her suspicions made almost everything into grounds of suspicion. She looked into the cupboard, and there she saw several costly sticks and some umbrellas, and then she narrowly examined all the walls, but could see nothing indicative of another opening, save the door, visible and apparent. As she moved backwards, she came against the shaving chair, which she found was a fixture, as, upon examination, she saw that the legs of it were firmly secured to the floor. What there could be suspicious in such a circumstance she hardly knew, and yet it did strike her as such.

'If I had but time,' she thought, 'I would make an attempt to go into that parlour; but I dare not yet. No, no, I must be more sure of the continued absence of Todd, before I dare make any such attempt.'

As she uttered these words, someone opened the door cautiously, and, peeping in, said, 'Is Mr Todd at home?'

'No,' replied Johanna.

'Oh, very good. Then you are to take this letter, if you please, and read it. You will find, I dare say, whom it's from, when you open it. Keep it to yourself though, and if Mr Todd should come in, hide it, mind, whatever you do.'

Before Johanna could make any reply, the man disappeared, and great was her astonishment to read upon the outside of the letter that had been put into her hands, her own proper name. With trembling fingers she opened it, and read as follows:—

*From Sir Richard Blunt, magistrate, to Miss Oakley*:—

Miss Johanna Oakley, you have with great chivalry of spirit embarked in a very dangerous enterprise—an enterprise which, considering your youth and your sex, should have been left to others; and it is well that others are in a position to watch over you and ensure your safety.

Your young friend, Arabella Wilmot, after giving so much romantic advice, and finding that you followed it, became herself alarmed at its possible consequences, and very prudently informed one who brought the intelligence to me, so that you are now well looked after; and should any danger present itself to you, you have but to seize any article that comes within your reach and throw it through a pane of glass in the shop window, when assistance will immediately come to you. I tell you this in order that you should feel quite at ease.

———————

As, however, you have placed yourself in your present position in Todd's shop, it is more than likely you will be able to do good service in aiding to unmask that villain. You will, therefore, be good enough, towards the dusk of the evening, to hold yourself in readiness to do anything required of you by anyone who shall pronounce to you the password of 'St Dunstan'.

From your Friend (mentioned above)

Johanna read this letter, certainly, with most unmitigated surprise, and yet there was a glow of satisfaction in her mind as she perused it, and the difference in her feelings, now that she was assured of protection, was certainly something wonderful and striking. To think that she had but to seize any one of the numerous stray articles that lay about and fling it through the window, in order to get assistance, was a most consolatory idea, and she felt nerved for almost any adventure.

She had just hidden the letter, when Sweeney Todd made his appearance.

'Anybody been?' he asked.

'Yes, one man, but he would not wait.'

'Ah, wanted to be shaved, I suppose; but no matter—no matter; and I hope you have been quiet, and not been attempting to indulge your curiosity in any way, since I have been gone. Hush! there's somebody coming. Why, it's old Mr Wrankley, the tobacconist, I declare. Good-day to you, sir—shaved, I suppose; I'm glad you have come, sir, for I have been out till this moment. Hot water, Charley, directly, and hand me that razor.'

Johanna, in handing Todd the razor, knocked the edge of it against the chair, and it being uncommonly sharp, cut a great slice of the wood off one of the arms of it.

'What shameful carelessness,' said Todd; 'I have half a mind to lay the strop over your back, sir; here, you have spoilt a capital razor—not a bit of edge left upon it.'

'Oh, excuse him, Mr Todd—excuse him,' said the old gentleman; 'he's only a little lad, after all. Let me intercede for him.'

'Very good, sir; if you wish me to look over it, of course I will, and, thank God, we have a stock of razors, of course, always at hand. Is there any news stirring, sir?'

'Nothing that I know of, Mr Todd, except it's the illness of Mr Cummings, the overseer. They say he got home about twelve to his own house, in Chancery-lane, and ever since then he has been sick as a dog, and all they can get him to say is, "Oh, those pies—oh, those pies!" '

'Very odd, sir.'

'Very. I think Mr Cummings must be touched in the upper storey, do you know, Mr Todd. He's a very respectable man, but, between you and I, was never very bright.'

'Certainly not—certainly not. But it's a very odd case. What pies can he possibly mean, sir? Did you call when you came from home?'

'No. Ha, ha! I can't help laughing; but ha, ha! I have come away from home on the sly, you see. The fact is, my wife's cousin, Mr Mundel—hilloa!—I think you have cut me.'

'No, no; we can't cut anybody for three-halfpence, sir.'

'Oh, very good—very good. Well, as I was saying, my wife's cousin, Mr Mundel, came to our house last night, and brought with him a string of pearls, you see. He wanted me to go to the City, this morning, with them, to Round and Bridget, the court jewellers', and ask them if they had ever seen them before.'

'Were they beauties?'

'Yes, they are brilliant ones. You see, Mundel lends money, and he didn't like to go himself, so he asked me to go, as Mr Round knows me very well; for between you and me, Mr Todd, my wife's cousin, Mr Mundel, thinks they belonged, once upon a time, to some lady.'

'Oh, indeed!'

'Yes; and as it won't do to say too much to women, I told my wife I was going over the water, you see, and just popped out. Ha, ha, ha! and I've got the pearls in my pocket. Mundel says they are worth £12,000 at the least, ha, ha!'

'Indeed, sir, £12,000? A pretty sum that, sir—a very pretty sum. No doubt Mr Mundel lent £7,000 or £8,000 upon the pearls. I think I will just give you another lather, sir, before I polish you off; and so you have the pearls with you, well, how odd things come round, to be sure.'

'What do you mean?'

'This shaving-brush is just in a good state now. Always as a shaving-brush is on the point of wearing out, it's the best. Charley, you will go at once to Mr Cummings's, and ask if he is any better; you need not hurry, that's a good lad, I am not at all angry with you now; and so, sir, they think at home that you have gone after some business over the water, do they, and have not the least idea that you have come here to be shaved—there, be off, Charley—shut the door, that's a good lad, bless you.'

\*     \*     \*     \*     \*

When Johanna came back, the tobacconist was gone.

'Well,' said Sweeney Todd, as he sharpened a razor, very leisurely; 'how is Mr Cummings?'

'I found out his house, sir, with some difficulty, and they say he is better, having gone to sleep.'

'Oh, very good! I am going to look over some accounts in the parlour, so don't choose to be disturbed, you understand; and for the next ten minutes, if anybody comes, you will say I am out.'

Sweeney Todd walked quite coolly into the parlour, and Johanna heard him lock the door on the inside; a strange, undefined sensation of terror crept over her, she knew not why, and she shuddered, as she looked around her. The cupboard door was not close shut, and she knew not what prompted her to approach and peep in. On the first shelf was the hat of the tobacconist: it was a rather remarkable one, and recognised in a moment.

'What has happened? Good God! what can have happened?' thought Johanna, as she staggered back, until she reached the shaving-chair, into which she cast herself for support. Her eyes fell upon the arm which she had taken such a shaving off with the razor, but all was perfectly whole and correct; there was not the least mark of the cut that so recently had been given to it; and, lost in wonder, Johanna, for more than a minute, continued looking for the mark of the injury she knew could not have been, by any possibility, effaced.

And yet she found it not, although there was the chair, just as usual, with its wide spreading arms and its worn, tarnished paint and gilding. No wonder that Johanna rubbed her eyes, and asked herself if she were really awake.

What could account for such a phenomenon? The chair was a fixture too, and the others in the shop were of a widely different make and construction, so it could not have been changed.

'Alas, alas!' mourned Johanna, 'my mind is full of horrible surmise, and yet I can form no rational conjecture. I suspect everything, and know nothing. What can I do? What ought I to do, to relieve myself from this state of horrible suspense? Am I really in a place where, by some frightful ingenuity, murder has become bold and familiar, or can it all be a delusion?'

She covered her face with her hands for a time, and when she uncovered them, she saw that Sweeney Todd was staring at her with looks of suspicion from the inner room.

The necessity of acting her part came over Johanna, and she gave a loud scream.

'What the devil is all this about?' said Todd, advancing with a sinister expression. 'What's the meaning of it? I suspect—'

'Yes, sir,' said Johanna, 'and so do I; I must tomorrow have it out.'

'Have what out?'

'My tooth, sir, it's been aching for some hours; did you ever have the toothache? If you did, you can feel for me, and not wonder that I lean my head upon my hands and groan.'

## 35

## *Sweeney Todd Commences Clearing the Road to Retirement*

TODD was but half satisfied with this excuse of Master Charley's, and yet it was one he could not very well object to, and might be true; so, after looking at Johanna for some moments suspiciously, he thought he might take it upon trust.

'Well, well,' he said, 'no doubt you will be better tomorrow. There's your sixpence for today; go and get yourself some dinner; and the cheapest thing you can do is to go to Lovett's pie-shop with it.'

'Thank you, sir.'

Johanna was aware as she walked out of the shop, that the eyes of Sweeney Todd were fixed upon her, and that if she betrayed, by even the remotest gesture, that she had suspicions of him, probably he would yet prevent her exit; so she kept herself seemingly calm, and went out very slowly; but it was a great relief to gain the street, and feel that she was not under the same roof with that dreadful and dreaded man.

Instead of going to Lovett's pie-shop, Johanna turned into a pastry-cook's near at hand, and partook of some refreshments; and while she is doing so, we will go back again, and take a glance at Sweeney Todd as he sat in his shop alone.

There was a look of great triumph upon his face, and his eyes sparkled with an unwonted brilliance. It was quite clear that Sweeney Todd was deeply congratulating himself upon something; and, at length, diving his hand into the depths of a huge pocket, he produced the identical string of pearls for which he had already received so large a sum from Mr Mundel.

'Truly,' he said, 'I must be one of Fortune's prime favourites, indeed. Why, this string of pearls to me is a continued fortune; who could have for one moment dreamed of such a piece of rare fortune? I need not now be at all suspicious or troubled concerning John Mundel. He has lost his pearls, and lost his money. Ha, ha, ha! That is glorious; I will shut up shop sooner than I intended by far, and be off to the Continent. Yes, my next sale of the string of pearls shall be in Holland.'

With the pearls in his hand, Todd now appeared to fall into a very distracted train of thought, which lasted him about ten minutes, and then some accidental noise in the street, or the next house, jarred upon his nerves, and he sprang to his feet, exclaiming, —

'What's that—what's that?'

All was still again, and he became reassured.

'What a fool I get,' he muttered to himself, 'That every casual sound disturbs me, and causes this tremor. It is time, now that I am getting nervous, that I should leave England. But first, I must dispose of one whose implacable disposition I know well, and who would hunt me to the farthest corner of the earth, if she were not at peace in the grave. Yes, the peace of the grave must do for her. I can think of no other mode of silencing so large a claim.'

As he spoke those words, he took from his pocket the small packet of poison that he had purchased, and held it up between him and the light with a self-satisfied expression. Then he rose hastily, for he had again seated himself, and walked to the window, as if he were anxious for the return of Johanna, in order that he might leave the place. As he waited, he saw a young girl approach the shop, and having entered it, she said, —

'Mrs Lovett's compliments, Mr Todd, and she has sent you this note, and will be glad to see you at eight o'clock this evening.'

'Oh, very well, very well. Why, Lucy, you look prettier than ever.'

'It's more than you do, Mr Todd,' said the girl, as she left, apparently in high indignation that so ugly a specimen of humanity as Sweeney Todd should have taken it upon himself to pay her a compliment.

Todd only gave a hideous sort of a grin, and then he opened the letter which had been brought to him. It was without signature, and contained the following words: —

The new cook is already tired of his place, and you must tonight make another vacancy. He is the most troublesome one I have had, because the most educated. He must be got rid of—you know how. I am certain mischief will come of it.

'Indeed!' said Todd, when he finished this epistle, 'this is quick; well, well, we shall see, we shall see. Perhaps we shall get rid of more than one person, who otherwise would be troublesome tonight. But here comes my new boy; he suspects nothing.'

Johanna returned, and Todd asked somewhat curiously about the toothache; however, she made him so apparently calm and cool a reply, that he was completely foiled, and fancied that his former suspicions must surely have had no real foundation, but had been provoked merely by his fears.

'Charley,' he said, 'you will keep an eye on the door, and when anyone wants me, you will pull that spring, which communicates with a bell that will make me hear. I am merely going to my bedroom.'

'Very well, sir.'

Todd gave another suspicious glance at her, and then left the shop. She had hoped that he would have gone out, so that there would have been another opportunity, and a better one than the last, of searching the place, but in that she was disappointed; and there was no recourse but to wait with patience.

The day was on the decline, and a strong impression came over Johanna's mind, that something in particular would happen before it wholly passed away into darkness. She almost trembled to think what that something could be, and that she might be compelled to be a witness to violence, from which her gentle spirit revolted; and had it not been that she had determined nothing should stop her from investigating the fate of poor Mark Ingestrie, she could even then have rushed into the street in despair.

But as the soft daylight deepened into the dim shadows of evening, she grew more composed, and was better able, with a calmer spirit, to await the progress of events.

Objects were but faintly discernible in the shop when Sweeney Todd came downstairs again; and he ordered Johanna to light a small oil lamp which shed but a very faint and sickly ray around it, and by no means facilitated the curiosity of anyone who might wish to peep in at the window.

'I am going out,' he said, 'I shall be gone an hour, but not longer. You may say so to anyone who calls.'

'I will, sir.'

'Be vigilant, Charley, and your reward is certain.'

'I pray to Heaven it may be,' said Johanna, when she was again alone; but scarcely had the words passed her lips, when a hackney coach drove up to the door; and then alighted someone who came direct into the shop. He was a tall, gentlemanly-looking man, and before Johanna could utter a word, he said, —

'The watchword, Miss Oakley, is St Dunstan; I am a friend.'

Oh, how delightful it was to Johanna, to hear such words, oppressed as she was by the fearful solitude of that house; she sprang eagerly forward, saying, —

'Yes, yes; oh, yes! I had the letter.'

'Hush! there is no time to lose. Is there any hiding-place here at all?'

'Oh yes! a large cupboard.'

'That will do; wait here a moment while I bring in a friend of mine, if you please, Miss Oakley. We have got some work to do to-night.'

The tall man, who was as cool and collected as anyone might be, went to the door, and presently returned with two persons, both of whom, it was found, might with very little trouble be hidden in the cupboard. Then there was a whispered consultation for a few minutes, after which the first comer turned to Johanna, and said, —

'Miss Oakley, when do you expect Todd to return?'

'In an hour.'

'Very well. As soon as he does return, I shall come in to be shaved, and no doubt you will be sent away; but do not go further than the door, whatever you do, as we may possibly want you. You can easily linger about the window.'

'Yes, yes! But why is all this mystery? Tell me what it is that you mean by all this. Is there any necessity for keeping me in the dark about it?'

'Miss Oakley, there is nothing exactly to tell you yet, but it is hoped that this night will remove some mysteries, and open your eyes to many circumstances that at present you cannot see. The villainy of Sweeney Todd will be espied, and if there be any hope of your restoration to one in whom you feel a great interest, it will be by such means.'

'You mean Mark Ingestrie?'

'I do. Your history has been related to me.'

'And who are you—why keep up to me a disguise if you are a friend?'

'I am a magistrate, and my name is Blunt; so you may be assured that all that can be done shall be done.'

'But, hold! you spoke of coming here to be shaved. If you do, let me implore you not to sit in that chair. There is some horrible mystery connected with it, but what it is, I cannot tell. Do not sit in it.'

'I thank you for your caution, but it is to be shaved in that very chair that I came. I know there is a mystery connected with it, and it is in order that it should be no longer a mystery that I have resolved upon running what, perhaps, may be considered a little risk. But our further stay here would be imprudent. Now, if you please.'

These last words were uttered to the two officers that the magistrate had brought with him, and it was quite wonderful to see with what tact and precision they managed to wedge themselves into the cupboard, the door of which they desired Johanna to close upon them, and when she had done so and turned round, she found that the magistrate was gone.

Johanna was in a great state of agitation, but still it was some comfort to her now to know that she was not alone, and that there.

were two strong and no doubt well-armed men ready to take her part, should anything occur amiss; she was much more assured of her own safety, and yet she was much more nervous than she had been.

She waited for Sweeney Todd, and strove to catch the sound of his returning footstep, but she heard it not; and, as that gentleman went about some rather important business, we cannot do better than follow him, and see how he progressed with it.

When he left his shop, he went direct to Bell-yard, although it was a little before the time named for his visit to Mrs Lovett.

## 36

## *The Last Batch of the Delicious Pies*

I T would have been quite clear to anyone, who looked at Sweeney Todd as he took his route from his own shop in Fleet-street to Bell-yard, Temple-bar, that it was not to eat pies he went there.

No; he was on very different thoughts indeed intent, and as he neared the shop of Mrs Lovett, where those delicacies were vended, there was such a diabolical expression upon his face that, had he not stooped like grim War to 'Smooth his wrinkled form',* ere he made his way into the shop, he would, most unquestionably, have excited the violent suspicions of Mrs Lovett, that all was not exactly as it should be, and that the mysterious bond of union that held her and the barber together was not in that blooming state that it had been.

When he actually did enter the shop, he was all sweetness and placidity.

Mrs Lovett was behind the counter, for it seldom happened that the shop was free of customers, for when the batches of hot pies were all over, there usually remained some which were devoured cold with avidity by the lawyers' clerks, from the offices and chambers in the neighbourhood.

But at nine o'clock, there was a batch of hot pies coming up, for of late Mrs Lovett had fancied that between half-past eight and nine, there was a great turn-out of clerks from Lincoln's-inn, and a pie became a very desirable and comfortable prelude to half-price at the theatre, or any other amusements of the three hours before midnight.

Many people, too, liked them as a relish for supper, and took them home quite carefully. Indeed, in Lincoln's-inn, it may be said, that the affections of the clerks oscillated between Lovett's pies and sheep's heads; and it frequently so nicely balanced in their minds, that the two attractions depended upon the toss-up of a halfpenny, whether to choose 'sang amary Jameses'* from Clare Market, or pies from Lovett's.

Half-and-half washed both down equally well.

Mrs Lovett, then, may be supposed to be waiting for the nine o'clock batch of pies, when Sweeney Todd, on this most eventful evening, made his appearance.

Todd and Mrs Lovett met now with all the familiarity of old acquaintance.

'Ah, Mr Todd,' said the lady, 'how do you do? Why, we have not seen you for a long time.'

'It has been some time; and how are you, Mrs Lovett?'

'Quite well, thank you. Of course, you will take a pie?'

Todd made a horrible face, as he replied, —

'No, thank you; it's very foolish, when I knew I was going to make a call here, but I have just had a pork chop.'

'Had it the kidney in it, sir?' asked one of the lads who were eating cold pies.

'Yes, it had.'

'Oh, that's what I like! Lor' bless you, I'd eat my mother, if she was a pork chop, done brown and crisp, and the kidney in it; just fancy it, grilling hot, you know, and just popped on a slice of bread, when you are cold and hungry.'

'Will you walk in, Mr Todd?' said Mrs Lovett, raising a portion of the counter, by which an opening was made, that enabled Mr Todd to pass into the sacred precincts of the parlour.

The invitation was complied with by Todd, who remarked that he hadn't above a minute to spare, but that he would sit down while he could stay, since Mrs Lovett was so kind as to ask him.

This extreme suavity of manner, however, left Sweeney Todd when he was in the parlour, and there was nobody to take notice of him but Mrs Lovett; nor did she think it necessary to wreathe her face in smiles, but with something of both anger and agitation in her manner, she said, 'And when is all this to have an end, Sweeney Todd? you have been now for these six months providing me such a division of spoil as shall enable me, with an ample independence, once again to appear in the salons of Paris. I ask you now when is this to be?'

'You are very impatient!'

'Impatient, impatient? May I not well be impatient? do I not run a frightful risk, while you must have the best of the profits? It is useless your pretending to tell me that you do not get much. I know you better, Sweeney Todd; you never strike, unless for profit or revenge.'

'Well?'

'Is it well, then, that I should have no account? O God! if you had the dreams I sometimes have!'

'Dreams?'

She did not answer him, but sank into a chair, and trembled so violently that he became alarmed, thinking she was very, very unwell. His hand was upon a bell rope, when she motioned him to be still, and then she managed to say in a very faint and nearly inarticulate voice, —

'You will go to that cupboard. You will see a bottle. I am forced to drink, or I should kill myself, or go mad, or denounce you; give it to me quick—quick, give it to me: it is brandy. Give it to me, I say: do not stand gazing at it there, I must, and I will have it. Yes, yes, I am better now, much better now. It is horrible, very horrible, but I am better; and I say, I must, and I will have an account at once. Oh. Todd, what an enemy you have been to me!'

'You wrong me. The worst enemy you ever had is in your head.'

'No, no, no! I must have that to drown thought!'

'Indeed! can you be so superstitious? I presume you are afraid of your reception in another world.'

'No, no—oh no! you and I do not believe in a hereafter, Sweeney Todd; if we did, we should go raving mad, to think what we had sacrificed. Oh, no—no, we dare not, we dare not!'

'Enough of this,' said Todd, somewhat violently, 'enough of this; you shall have an account tomorrow evening; and when you find yourself in possession of £20,000, you will not accuse me of having been unmindful of your interests; but now, there is someone in the shop who seems to be enquiring for you.'

Mrs Lovett rose, and went into the shop. The moment her back was turned, Todd produced the little bottle of poison he had got from the chemist's boy, and emptied it into the brandy decanter. He had just succeeded in this manoeuvre, and concealed the bottle again, when she returned, and flung herself into a chair.

'Did I hear you aright,' she said, 'or is this promise but a mere mockery; £20,000—is it possible that you have so much? oh, why was not all this dreadful trade left off sooner? Much less would have been done. But when shall I have it—when shall I be enabled to fly from here for ever? Todd, we must live in different countries; I could never bear the chance of seeing you.'

'As you please. It don't matter to me at all; you may be off tomorrow night, if you like. I tell you your share of the last eight years' work shall be £20,000. You shall have the sum tomorrow, and then you are free to go where you please; it matters not to me one straw where you spend your money. But tell me now, what immediate danger do you apprehend from your new cook?'

'Great and immediate; he has refused to work—a sign that he has got desperate, hopeless and impatient; and then only a few hours ago, I heard him call to me, and he said he had thought better of it, and would bake the nine o'clock batch, which, to my mind, was saying, that he had made up his mind to some course which gave him hope, and made it worth his while to temporise with me for a time, to lull suspicion.'

'You are a clever woman. Something must and shall be done. I will be here at midnight, and we shall see if a vacancy cannot be made in your establishment.'

'It will be necessary, and it is but one more.'

'That's all—that's all, and I must say you have a very perfect and philosophic mode of settling the question; avoid the brandy as much as you can, but I suppose you are sure to take some between now and the morning?'

'Quite sure. It is not in this house that I can wean myself of such a habit. I may do so abroad, but not here.'

'Oh, well, it can't matter; but, as regards the fellow downstairs, I will, of course, come and rid you of him. You must keep a good lookout now for the short time you will be here, and a good countenance. There, you are wanted again, and I may as well go likewise.'

Mrs Lovett and Todd walked from the parlour to the shop together, and when they got there, they found a respectable-looking woman and a boy, the latter of whom carried a bundle of printed papers with him; the woman was evidently in great distress of mind.

'Cold pie, ma'am?' said Mrs Lovett.

'Oh dear no, Mrs Lovett,' said the woman; 'I know you by sight, mem, though you don't know me. I am Mrs Wrankley, mem, the wife of Mr Wrankley, the tobacconist, and I've come to ask a favour of you, Mrs Lovett, to allow one of these bills to be put in your window?'

'Dear me,' said Mrs Lovett, 'what's it about?'

Mrs Wrankley handed her one of the bills and then seemed so overcome with grief, that she was forced to sink into a chair while it was read, which was done aloud by Mrs Lovett, who, as she did so, now and then stole a glance at Sweeney Todd, who looked as impenetrable and destitute of all emotion as a block of wood.

'Missing!—Mr John Wrankley, tobacconist, of 92 Fleet-street. The above gentleman left his home to go over the water, on business, and has not since been heard of. He is supposed to have had some valuable property with him, in the shape of a string of pearls. The said Mr John Wrankley is five feet four inches high, full face, short thick nose, black whiskers, and what is commonly called a bullet-head; thickset and skittle-made, not very well upon his feet; and whoever will give any information of him at 92 Fleet-street, shall be amply rewarded.'

'Yes, yes,' said Mrs Wrankley, when the reading of the bill was finished, 'that's him to a T, my poor, dear, handsome Wrankley! oh, I shall never be myself again; I have not eaten anything since he went out.'

'Then buy a pie, madam,' said Todd, as he held one close to her. 'Look up, Mrs Wrankley, lift off the top crust, madam, and you may take my word for it you will soon see *something* of Mr Wrankley.'

The hideous face that Todd made during the utterance of these words quite alarmed the disconsolate widow, but she did partake of the pie for all that. It was very tempting—a veal one, full of coagulated gravy—who could resist it? Not she, certainly, and besides, did not Todd say she would see something of Wrankley? There was hope in his words, at all events, if nothing else.

'Well,' she said, 'I will hope for the best; he may have been taken ill, and not have had his address in his pocket, poor dear soul! at the time.'

'And at all events, madam,' said Todd, 'you need not be cut up about it, you know; I dare say you will know what has become of him some-day, soon.'

## 37

## *The Prisoner's Plan of Escape from the Pies*

Mrs Lovett was a woman of judgement, and when she told Sweeney Todd that the prisoner was getting impatient in the lower regions of that house which was devoted to the manufacture of the delicious pies, she had guessed rightly his sensations with regard to his present state and future prospects.

We last left that unfortunate young man lying upon the floor of the place where the steaming and tempting manufacture was carried on; and for a time, as a very natural consequence of exhaustion, he slept profoundly.

That sleep, however, if it rested him bodily, likewise rested him mentally; and when he again awoke it was but to feel more acutely the agony of his most singular and cruel situation. There was a clock in the place by which he had been enabled to accurately regulate the time that the various batches of pies should take in cooking, and upon looking up to that he saw that it was upon the hour of six, and consequently it would be three hours more before a batch of pies was wanted.

He looked about him very mournfully for some time, and then he spoke.

'What evil destiny,' he said, 'has placed me here? Oh, how much better it would have been if I had perished, as I have been near perishing several times during the period of my eventful life, than that I should be shut up in this horrible den and starved to death, as in all human probability I shall be, for I loathe the pies. Damn the pies!'

There was a slight noise, and upon his raising his eyes to that part of the place near the roof where there were some iron bars and between which Mrs Lovett was wont to give him some directions, he saw her now detested face.

'Attend,' she said; 'you will bake an extra batch to-night, at nine precisely.'

'What?'

'An extra batch, two hundred at least; do you understand me?'

'Hark ye, Mrs Lovett. You are carrying this sort of thing too far; it won't do, I tell you, Mrs Lovett; I don't know how soon I may be numbered with the dead, but, as I am a living man now, I will make no more of your detestable pies.'

'Beware!'

'Beware yourself! I am not one to be frightened at shadows. I say I will leave this place, whether you like it or not; I will leave it; and perhaps you will find your power insufficient to keep me here. That there is some frightful mystery at the bottom of all the proceedings here, I am certain, but you shall not make me the victim of it!'

'Rash fool!'

'Very well, say what you like, but remember I defy you.'

'Then you are tired of your life, and you will find, when too late, what are the consequences of your defiance. But listen to me: when I first engaged you, I told you you might leave when you were tired of the employment.'

'You did, and yet you keep me a prisoner here. God knows I'm tired enough of it. Besides, I shall starve, for I cannot eat pies eternally; I hate them.'

'And they so admired!'

'Yes, when one ain't surfeited with them. I am now only subsisting upon baked flour. I cannot eat the pies.'

---

'You are strangely fantastical.'

'Perhaps I am. Do you live upon pies, I should like to know, Mrs Lovett?'

'That is altogether beside the question. You shall, if you like, leave this place tomorrow morning, by which time I hope to have got someone else to take over your situation, but I cannot be left without anyone to make the pies.'

'I don't care for that, I won't make another one.'

'We shall see,' said Mrs Lovett. 'I will come to you in an hour, and see if you persevere in that determination. I advise you as a friend to change, for you will most bitterly repent standing in the way of your own enfranchisement.'

'Well, but—she is gone, and what can I do? I am in her power, but shall I tamely submit? No, no, not while I have my arms at liberty, and strength enough to wield one of these long pokers that stir the coals in the ovens. How foolish of me not to think before that I had such desperate weapons, with which perchance to work my way to freedom.'

As he spoke, he poised in his hand one of the long pokers he spoke of, and, after some few minutes spent in consideration, he said to himself, with something of the cheerfulness of hope, —

'I am in Bell-yard, and there are houses right and left of this accursed pie-shop, and those houses must have cellars. Now surely with such a weapon as this, a willing heart, and an arm that has not yet quite lost all its powers, I may make my way from this abominable abode.'

The very thought of thus achieving his liberty lent him new strength and resolution, so that he felt himself to be quite a different man to what he had been, and he only paused to consider in which direction it would be best to begin his work.

After some reflection upon that head, he considered that it would be better to commence where the meat was kept that meat of which he always found abundance, and which came from—he knew not where; since, if he went to sleep with little or none of it upon the shelves where it was placed for use, he always found plenty when he awoke.

'Yes,' he said, 'I will begin there, and work my way to freedom.'

Before, however, he commenced operations, he glanced at the clock, and found that it wanted very little now to seven, so that he thought it would be but common prudence to wait until Mrs Lovett had paid him her promised visit, as then, if he said he would make the pies she required, he would, in all probability, be left to himself for two hours, and, he thought, if he did not make good progress in that time towards his liberty, it would be strange indeed.

He sat down, and patiently waited until seven o'clock.

Scarcely had the hour sounded, when he heard the voice of his tormentor and mistress at the grating.

'Well,' she said, 'have you considered?'

'Oh, yes, I have. Needs must, you know, Mrs Lovett, when a certain person drives. But I have a great favour to ask of you, madam.'

'What is it?'

'Why, I feel faint, and if you could let me have a pot of porter, I would undertake to make a batch of pies superior to any you have ever had, and without any grumbling either.'

Mrs Lovett was silent for a few moments, and then said, —

'If you are supplied with porter, will you continue in your situation?'

'Well, I don't know that; but perhaps I may. At all events, I will make you the nine o'clock batch, you may depend.'

'Very well. You shall have it.'

She disappeared at these words, and in about ten minutes, a small trap-door opened in the roof, and there was let down by a cord a foaming pot of porter.

'This is capital,' cried the victim of the pies, as he took half of it at a draught. 'This is nectar for the gods. Oh, what a relief, to be sure. It puts new life into me.'

And so it really seemed, for shouldering the poker, which was more like a javelin than anything else, he at once rushed into the vault where the meat was kept.

'Now,' he said, 'for a grand effort at freedom, and if I succeed I promise you, Mrs Lovett, that I will come round to the shop, and rather surprise you, madam. Damn the pies!'

We have before described the place in which the meat was kept, and we need now only say that the shelves were very well stocked indeed, and that our friend, in whose progress we have a great interest, shovelled off the large pieces with celerity from one of the shelves, and commenced operations with the poker.

He was not slow in discovering that his work would not be the most easy in the world, for every now and then he kept encountering what felt very much like a plate of iron; but he fagged away with right good will, and succeeded after a time in getting down one of the shelves, which was one point gained at all events.

'Now for it,' he said. 'Now for it; I shall be able to act—to work upon the wall itself, and it must be something unusually strong to prevent me making a breach through it soon.'

In order to refresh himself, he finished the porter, and then using his javelin-like poker as a battering ram, he banged the wall with the end of it for some moments, without producing any effect, until suddenly a portion of it swung open just like a door, and he paused to wonder how that came about.

All was darkness through the aperture, and yet he saw that it was actually a little square door that he had knocked open; and the idea then recurred to him that he had found how the shelves were supplied with meat, and he had no doubt that there was such a little square door opening at the back of every one of them.

'So,' he said, 'that mystery is solved; but what part of Mrs Lovett's premises have I got upon now? We shall soon see.'

He went boldly into the large cellar, and procured a light—a flaming torch, made of a piece of dry wood, and returning to the opening he had made in the wall, he thrust his head through it, and projected the torch before him.

With a cry of horror he fell backwards, extinguishing the torch in his fall, and he lay for a full quarter of an hour insensible upon the floor. What dreadful sight had he seen that had so chilled his young blood, and frozen up the springs of life?

When he recovered, he looked around him in the dim, borrowed light that came from the other vault, and he shuddered as he said, —

'Was it a dream?'

Soon, however, as he rose, he gave up the idea of having been the victim of any delusion of the imagination, for there was the broken shelf, and there the little square opening, through which he had looked and seen what had so transfixed him with horror.

Keeping his face in that direction, as if it would be dreadful to turn his back for a moment upon some frightful object, he made his way into the larger cellar where the ovens were, and then he sat down with a deep groan.

'What shall I do? Oh, what shall I do?' he muttered. 'I am doomed—doomed.'

'Are the pies doing?' said the voice of Mrs Lovett. 'It's eight o'clock.'

'Eight, is it?'

'Yes, to be sure, and I want to know if you are bent upon your own destruction or not? I don't hear the furnaces going, and I'm quite sure you have not made the pies.'

'Oh, I will keep my word, madam, you may depend. You want two hundred pies at nine o'clock, and you will see that they shall come up quite punctually to the minute.'

'Very good. I am glad you are better satisfied than you were.'

'I am quite satisfied now, Mrs Lovett. I am quite in a different mood of mind to what I was before. I can assure you, madam, that I have no complaints to make, and I think the place has done me some good; and if at nine o'clock you let down the platform, you shall have two hundred pies up, as sure as fate, and something else, too,' he added to himself, 'or I shall be of a very different mind to what I now am.'

We have already seen that Mrs Lovett was not deceived by this seeming submission on the part of the cook, for she used that as an argument with Todd, when she was expatiating upon the necessity of getting rid of him that night.

But the cleverest people make mistakes at times, and probably, when the nine o'clock batch of pies makes its appearance, something may occur at the same time which will surprise a great many more persons than Mrs Lovett and the reader.

But we must not anticipate, merely saying with the eastern sage, what will be will be, and what's impossible don't often come to pass; certain it is that the nine o'clock batch of two hundred pies were made and put in the ovens; and equally certain is it that the cook remarked, as he did so,—

'Yes, I'll do it—it may succeed; nay, it must succeed; and if so, woe be to you, Mrs Lovett, and all who are joined with you in this horrible speculation, at which I sicken.'

## 38

### *Sweeney Todd Shaves a Good Customer.—The Arrest*

J OHANNA is alone still in the barber's shop. Her head is resting upon her hands, and she is thinking of times gone past, when she had hoped for happiness with Mark Ingestrie. When we say alone, we must not be presumed to have forgotten the two officers who were so snugly packed in the cupboard. But Johanna, as her mind wandered back to her last interview with him whom she had loved so well, and clung to so fondly, and so constantly, almost for a time forgot where she was and that there was such a person as Sweeney Todd in existence.

'Alas, alas!' she said, 'it seems likely enough that by the adoption of this disguise, so unsuited to me, I may achieve vengeance, but nothing more. Where are you, Mark Ingestrie? Oh, horror! something seems to tell me that no mortal voice can answer me.'

Tears came trickling to her relief; and as she felt them trickling through her fingers, she started as she thought that the hour which Todd had said would expire before he returned must have nearly gone.

'I must control these thoughts,' she said, 'and this emotion. I must seem that which I am not.'

She rose, and ceased weeping; she trimmed the little miserable lamp, and then she was about to go to the door to look for the return of Todd, when that individual, with a slow and sneaking footstep, made his appearance, as if he had been hiding just within the door-way.

Todd hung his hat upon a peg, and then turning his eyes enquiringly upon Johanna, he said, —

'Well, has anyone been?'

'Yes.'

'Who? Speak, speak out. Confound you, you mumble so, I can hardly hear you.'

'A gentleman to be shaved, and he went away again. I don't know what puts you in such a passion, Mr Todd; I'm sure nothing—'

'What is it to you? Get out of my way, will you, and you may begin to think of shutting up, I think, for we shall have no more customers tonight. I am tired and weary. You are to sleep under the counter, you know.'

'Yes, sir, you told me so. I dare say I shall be very comfortable there.'

'And you have not been peeping and prying about, have you?'

'Not at all.'

'Not looking even into that cupboard, I suppose, eh? It's not locked, but that's no reason why you should look into it—not that there is any secret in it, but I object to peeping and prying upon principle.'

Todd, as he spoke, advanced towards the cupboard, and Johanna thought that in another moment a discovery would undoubtedly take place of the two officers who were there concealed; and probably that would have been the case had not the handle of the shop-door been turned at that moment and a man presented himself, at which Todd turned quickly, and saw that he was a substantial-looking farmer with dirty top boots, as if he had just come off a journey.

'Well, master,' said the visitor, 'I wants a clean shave.'

'Oh,' said Todd, not in the best of humours, 'it's rather late. I suppose you would not like to wait till morning, for I don't know if I have any hot water?'

'Oh, cold will do.'

'Cold, oh dear, no; we never shave in cold water; but if you must, you must; so sit down, sir, and we will soon settle the business.'

'Thank you, thank you, I can't go to bed comfortable without a clean shave, do you see? I have come up from Braintree with beasts on commission, and I'm staying at the Bull's Head,* you see.'

'Oh, indeed,' said Todd, as he adjusted the shaving cloth, 'the Bull's Head.'

'Yes, master; why I brought up a matter o' 220 beasts, I did, do you see, and was on my *pooney*, as good a stepper as you'd wish to see; and I sold 'em all, do you see, for 550 *pun*. Ho, ho! good work, that, do you see, and only forty-two on 'em was my beasts, do you see; I've got a missus at home, and a daughter; my girl's called Johanna—ahem!'

Up to this point, Johanna had not suspected that the game had begun, and that this was the magistrate who had come to put an end to the malpractices of Sweeney Todd; but his marked pronunciation of her name at once opened her eyes to the fact, and she knew that something interesting must soon happen.

'And so you sold them all,' said Todd.

'Yes, master, I did, and I've got the money in my pocket now, in bank-notes; I never leaves my money about at inns, do you see, master; safe bind, safe find, you see; I carries it about with me.'

'A good plan, too,' said Todd; 'Charley, some hot water; that's a good lad—and—and, Charley.'

'Yes, sir.'

'While I am just finishing off this gentleman, you may as well just run to the Temple to Mr Serjeant Toldrunis and ask for his wig;

we shall have to do it in the morning, and may as well have it the first thing in the day to begin upon, and you need not hurry, Charley, as we shall shut up when you come back.'

'Yes, sir.'

Johanna walked out, but went no further than the shop window, close to which she placed her eyes so that, between a pomatum jar and a lot of hair brushes, she could clearly see what was going on.

'A nice-looking, little lad, that,' said Todd's customer.

'Very, sir; an orphan boy; I took him out of charity, poor little fellow; but there, we ought to try to do all the good we can.'

'Just so; I'm glad I have come to be shaved here. Mine's a rather strong beard, I think, do you see.'

'Why, sir, in a manner of speaking,' replied Todd, 'it is a strong beard. I suppose you didn't come to London alone, sir?'

'Oh, yes, quite alone; except the drovers, I had no company with me; why do you ask?'

'Why, sir, I thought if you had any gentleman with you who might be waiting at the Bull's Head, you would recommend him to me if anything was wanting in my way, you know, sir; you might have just left him, saying you were going to Todd, the barber's, to have a clean shave, sir.'

'No, not at all; the fact is, I did not come out to have a shave, but a walk, and it wasn't till I gave my chin a stroke, and found what a beard I had, that I thought of it, and then passing your shop, in I popped, do you see.'

'Exactly, sir, I comprehend; you are quite alone in London?'

'Oh, quite, but when I come again, I'll come to you to be shaved, you may depend, and I'll recommend you too.'

'I'm very much obliged to you,' said Todd, as he passed his hand over the chin of his customer. 'I'm very much obliged; I find I must give you another lather, sir, and I'll get another razor with a keener edge, now that I have taken off all the rough as one may say in a manner of speaking.'

'Oh, I shall do.'

'No, no, don't move, sir, I shall not detain you a moment; I have my other razors in the next room, and will polish you off now, sir, before you will know where you are; you know, sir, you have promised to recommend me, so I must do the best I can with you.'

'Well, well, a clean shave is a comfort, but don't be long, for I want to get back, do you see.'

'Not a moment, not a moment.'

Sweeney Todd walked into his back-parlour, conveying with him the only light that was in the shop, so that the dim glimpse that, up to this time, Johanna from the outside had contrived to get of what was going on, was denied to her; and all that met her eyes was impenetrable darkness.

Oh, what a world of anxious agonising sensations crossed the mind of the young and beautiful girl at that moment. She felt as if some great crisis in her history had arrived, and that she was condemned to look in vain into the darkness to see of what it consisted.

We must not, however, allow the reader to remain in the same state of mystification, which came over the perceptive faculties of Johanna Oakley; but we shall proceed to state clearly and distinctly what did happen in the barber's shop, while he went to get an uncommonly keen razor in his back-parlour.

The moment his back was turned, the seeming farmer who had made such a good thing of his beasts, sprang from the shaving-chair, as if he had been electrified; and yet he did not do it with any appearance of fright, nor did he make any noise. It was only astonishingly quick, and then he placed himself close to the window, and waited patiently with his eyes fixed upon the chair, to see what would happen next.

In the space of about a quarter of a minute, there came from the next room a sound like the rapid drawing of a heavy bolt, and then in an instant the shaving-chair disappeared beneath the floor; and the circumstances by which Sweeney Todd's customers disappeared was evident.

There was a piece of the flooring turning upon a centre, and the weight of the chair when a bolt was withdrawn, by means of a simple leverage from the inner room, weighed down upon one end of the top, which, by a little apparatus, was to swing completely round, there being another chair on the under surface, which thus became the upper, exactly resembling the one in which the unhappy customer was supposed to be 'polished off'.

Hence was it that in one moment, as if by magic, Sweeney Todd's visitors disappeared, and there was the empty chair. No doubt, he trusted to a fall of about twenty feet below, on to a stone floor, to be the death of them, or, at all events, to stun them until he could go down to finish the murder, and—*to cut them up for Mrs Lovett's pies!* after robbing them of all money and valuables they might have about them.

In another moment, the sound as of a bolt was again heard, and Sir Richard Blunt, who had played the part of the wealthy farmer, feeling that the trap was closed again, seated himself in the new chair that had made its appearance with all the nonchalance in life, as if nothing had happened.

It was a full minute before Todd ventured to look from the parlour into the darkened shop, and then he shook so that he had to hold by the door to steady himself.

'That's done,' he said. 'That's the last, I hope. It is time I finished; I never felt so nervous since the first time. Then I did quake a little. How quiet he went; I have sometimes had a shriek ringing in my ears for a whole week.'

It was a large high-backed piece of furniture, that shaving-chair, so that, when Todd crept into the shop with the light in his hand, he had not the remotest idea it was tenanted; but when he got round it, and saw his customer calmly waiting with the lather upon his face, the cry of horror that came gurgling and gushing from his throat was horrible to hear.

'Why, what's the matter?' said Sir Richard.

'O God, the dead! the dead! O God!' cried Todd, 'this is the beginning of my punishment. Have mercy, Heaven! oh, do not look upon me with those dead eyes!'

'Murderer!' shouted Sir Richard, in a voice that rang like the blast of a trumpet through the house.

In an instant he sprang upon Sweeney Todd, and grappled him by the throat. There was a short struggle, and they were down upon the floor together, but Todd's wrists were suddenly laid hold of, and a pair of handcuffs were scientifically put upon him by the officers, who, at the word 'murderer', that being a preconcerted signal, came from the cupboard where they had been concealed.

'Secure him well, my men,' said the magistrate, 'and don't let him lay violent hands upon himself. Ah! Miss Oakley, you are in time. This man is a murderer. I found out all the secret about the chair last night, after twelve, by exploring the vaults under the old church. Thank God, we have stopped his career.'

# 39

## *The Conclusion*

I<small>T</small> wants five minutes to nine, and Mrs Lovett's shop is filling with persons anxious to devour or to carry away one or more of the nine o'clock batch of savoury, delightful, gushing gravy pies.

Many of Mrs Lovett's customers paid her in advance for the pies, in order that they might be quite sure of getting their orders fulfilled when the first batch should make its gracious appearance from the depths below.

'Well, Jiggs,' said one of the legal fraternity to another. 'How are you to-day, old fellow? What do you bring it in?'

'Oh! I ain't very blooming. The fact is the count and I, and a few others, made a night of it last evening, and, somehow or another, I don't think whiskey and water, half-and-half, and tripe go together.'

'I should wonder if they did.'

'And so I've come for a pie just to settle my stomach; you see, I'm rather delicate.'

'Ah! you are just like me, young man, there,' said an elderly personage; 'I have a delicate stomach, and the slightest thing disagrees with me. A mere idea will make me quite ill.'

'Will it, really?'

'Yes; and my wife, she—'

'Oh! bother your wife. It's only five minutes to nine, don't you see? What a crowd there is, to be sure. Mrs Lovett, you charmer, I hope you have ordered enough pies to be made to-night. You see what a lot of customers you have.'

'Oh! there will be plenty.'

'That's right. I say, don't push so; you'll be in time, I tell you; don't be pushing and shoving in that sort of way—I've got ribs.'

'And so have I. Last night, I didn't get to bed at all, and my old woman is in a certain condition, you see, gentlemen, and won't fancy anything but one of Lovett's veal pies, so I've come all the way from Newington to get one for—'

'Hold your row, will you? and don't push.'

'For to have the child marked as a pie\* as its—'

'Behind there, I say; don't be pushing a fellow as if it was half-price at a theatre.'

Each moment added some new comers to the throng, and at last any strangers who had known nothing of the attractions of Mrs Lovett's pie-shop, and had walked down Bell-yard, would have been astonished at the throng of persons there assembled—a throng, that was each moment increasing in density, and becoming more and more urgent and clamorous.

\*     \*     \*     \*     \*

One, two, three, four, five, six, seven, eight, nine! Yes, it is nine at last. It strikes by old St Dunstan's church clock, and in weaker strains the chronometrical machine at the pie-shop echoes the sound. What excitement there is now to get at the pies when they shall come! Mrs Lovett lets down the square, moveable platform that goes upon pulleys into the cellar; some machinery, which only requires a handle to be turned, brings up a hundred pies in a tray. These are eagerly seized by parties who have previously paid, and such a smacking of lips ensues as never was known.

Down goes the platform for the next hundred, and a gentlemanly man says,—

'Let me work the handle, Mrs Lovett, if you please; it's too much for you, I'm sure.'

'Sir, you are very kind, but I never allow anybody on this side of the counter but my own people, sir; I can turn the handle myself, sir, if you please, with the assistance of this girl. Keep your distance, sir, nobody wants your help.'

How the waggish young lawyers' clerks laughed as they smacked their lips, and sucked in the golopshious gravy of the pies, which, by-the-by, appeared to be all delicious veal this time, and Mrs Lovett worked the handle of the machine all the more vigorously, that she was a little angry with the officious stranger. What an unusual trouble it seemed to be to wind up those forthcoming hundred pies! How she toiled, and how the people waited; but at length there came up the savoury steam, and then the tops of the pies were visible.

They came up upon a large tray, about six feet square, and the moment Mrs Lovett ceased turning the handle, and let a catch fall that prevented the platform receding again, to the astonishment and terror of everyone, away flew all the pies, tray and all, across the counter, and a man, who was lying crouched down in an exceedingly flat state under the tray, sprang to his feet.

Mrs Lovett shrieked, as well she might, and then she stood trembling, and looking as pale as death itself. It was the doomed cook from the cellars, who had adopted this mode of escape.

The throngs of persons in the shop looked petrified, and after Mrs Lovett's shriek, there was an awful stillness for about a minute, and then the young man who officiated as cook spoke.

'Ladies and Gentlemen—I fear that what I am going to say will spoil your appetites; but the truth is beautiful at all times, and I have to state that Mrs Lovett's pies are made of *human flesh!*'

\* \* \* \* \*

How the throng of persons recoiled—what a roar of agony and dismay there was! How frightfully sick about forty lawyers' clerks became all at once, and how they spat out the gelatinous clinging portions of the rich pies they had been devouring. 'Good gracious!—oh, the pies!—confound it!'

' 'Tis false!' screamed Mrs Lovett.

'You are my prisoner, madam,' said the man who had obligingly offered to turn the handle of the machine that wound up the pies, at the same time producing a constable's staff.

'Prisoner!'

'Yes, on a charge of aiding and abetting Sweeney Todd, now in custody, in the commission of many murders.'

Mrs Lovett staggered back, and her complexion turned a livid colour.

'I am poisoned,' she said. 'Good God! I am poisoned,' and she sank insensible to the floor.

There was now some confusion at the door of the shop, for several people were effecting an entrance. These consisted of Sir Richard Blunt, Colonel Jeffery, Johanna Oakley, and Tobias Ragg, who, when he escaped from the mad-house at Peckham Rye, went direct to a gentleman in the Temple, who took him to the magistrate.

'Miss Oakley,' said Sir Richard, 'you objected to coming here, but I told you I had a particular reason for bringing you. This night, about half an hour since, I made an acquaintance I want to introduce you to.'

'Who—oh, who?'

"There's an underground communication all the way from Sweeney Todd's cellar to the ovens of this pie-shop; and I found there Mrs Lovett's cook, with whom I arranged this little surprise for his mistress. Look at him, Miss Oakley, do you know him? Look up, Master Cook.'

'Mark—Mark Ingestrie!' shrieked Johanna, the moment she glanced at the person alluded to.

'Johanna!'

In another moment she was in his arms, and clasped to his heart.

'Oh, Mark, Mark—you are not dead.'

'No, no—I never was. And you, Johanna, are not in love with a fellow, in military undress, you met in the Temple.'

'No, no, I never was.'

When Mrs Lovett was picked up by the officers, she was found to be dead. The poison which Sweeney Todd had put into the brandy she was accustomed to solace herself with, when the pangs of conscience troubled her, and of which she always took some before the evening batch of pies came up, had done its work.

That night Todd passed in Newgate, and in due time a swinging corpse was all that remained of the barber of Fleet-street. Mr Fogg's establishment, at Peckham Rye, was broken up, and that gentleman persuaded to emigrate, for which the government kindly paid all expenses. Tobias went into the service of Mark Ingestrie, and, at the marriage of Mark with his beautiful bride, Big Ben, the beef-eater, did some extraordinary things, which space and opportunity will not permit us to chronicle in these pages.

The youths who visited Lovett's pie-shop, and there luxuriated upon those delicacies, are youths no longer. Indeed, the grave has closed over all but one, and he is very, very old, but even now, as he thinks of how he enjoyed the flavour of the 'veal', he shudders, and has to take a drop of brandy.

Beneath the old church of St Dunstan were found the heads and bones of Todd's victims. As little as possible was said by the authorities about it; but it was supposed that some hundreds of persons must have perished in the frightful manner we have detailed.

\*     \*     \*     \*     \*

Our tale is over, and the only seeming mystery that has to be explained consists in settling the point with regard to who Thornhill was, and what became of him.

He was just what he represented himself to be, the friend of Mark Ingestrie, to whom had been, by Mark, entrusted the care of the string of pearls; but he fell a victim to the awful criminality of Sweeney Todd, who was in league with Mrs Lovett, and who robbed his murdered customers, while she sold them for pies.

Mark Ingestrie, after many dangers and hardships, had reached London; but he did so, unfortunately, only just in time to follow Johanna to the Temple-gardens, in one of her innocent ramblings with Colonel Jeffery, but believing from that circumstance that she was false to him, and hearing nothing of his friend Thornhill, he, in a moment of despair, took the desperate situation of cook at Mrs Lovett's far-famed pie-shop, from where he so narrowly escaped with his life.

*       *       *       *       *

Johanna and Mark Ingestrie lived long and happily together, enjoying all the comforts of an independent existence; but they never forgot the strange and eventful circumstances connected with the String of Pearls.

# Explanatory Notes

I would like here to acknowledge several reference works that have been invaluable in the general preparation of the notes that follow.

*The A to Z of Georgian London* (Lympne Castle, Kent: Harry Margary, in association with Guildhall Library, London, 1981), Introductory Notes by Ralph Hyde.

*Britain in the Hanoverian Age, 1714–1837: An Encyclopedia*, ed. Gerald Newman (New York and London: Garland Publishing, 1997).

*Johnson's England: An Account of the Life & Manners of his Age*, ed. A. S. Turberville, 2 vols. (Oxford: Clarendon Press, 1933).

*Lexicon Balatronicum: A Dictionary of Buckish Slang, University Wit, and Pickpocket Eloquence*, 'compiled by Captain Francis Grose' (London: C. Chappel, 1811).

*The London Encyclopedia*, ed. Ben Weinreb and Christopher Hibbert (London: Macmillan Ltd., 1983; 1993).

3 BEFORE *Fleet-street had reached its present importance . . . a man of the name of Sweeney Todd*: Fleet Street is the central artery extending eastwards from Temple Bar (which marks the official western limits of the city of London) as far as Ludgate Circus (at which point Fleet Bridge had once crossed the Fleet River, long since channelled underground). Fleet Street was the main thoroughfare of medieval London and—even as early as the beginning of the sixteenth century—was associated with the nation's emergent publishing industry. Most of the country's earliest printers and booksellers maintained shops and premises either on Fleet Street itself, or in the many alleys and side streets that snaked their way both north and south of its broad expanse. The area within which the action of the novel takes place is relatively tightly delimited to a specific stretch extending roughly along Fleet Street from just beyond Chancery Lane in the west, to Fetter Lane in the east, and encompassing Temple Bar, Bell-yard, and the Precincts of the Inner Temple to Temple Stairs on the river Thames.

The reference here to 'the two figures who used to strike the chimes at old St Dunstan's church' places the building—more properly known as St Dunstan's in the West (demolished 1830; rebuilt 1831–3)—at the epicentre of the narrative. The reader is constantly returned, both in fact and recollection, to St Dunstan's, and the image of the church is itself most frequently fixed in the reader's imagination by a return to its best-known feature—the famous bracket clock, with its giants (supposed to represent the ancient figures of Gog and Magog) striking the hours with their clubs. The clock, as the author notes, remained a matter of 'gaping curiosity' to country visitors to the capital well into the nineteenth century (it is mentioned as a prominent tourist attraction in, among other works, Goldsmith's *The Vicar of Wakefield* (1766), Scott's *The Fortunes of Nigel* (1822), and also in Dickens's *Barnaby Rudge* (1841) and *David Copperfield* (1850) ).

Finally, the opening sentence notes that the story takes place 'in the days when George the Third was young', although just a few paragraphs later the reader is informed that the year is 'AD 1785', and the conversation between Johanna Oakley and her father in the next chapter tells us even more specifically that the date on which the novel's action begins is 20 August. George III, who came to the throne in 1760, had just turned 47 in the summer of 1785.

*How it was that he came by the name of Sweeney . . . there to look for it*: the name is indeed an unusual one. The surname Todd or 'tod' [*sic*], a northern word of unknown origin from Middle English, means, literally, 'fox'; metaphorically it was used to refer to 'a person likened to a fox; a crafty person' (*OED*). Sweeney or 'sweeny' [*sic*], although referring literally to atrophy in the shoulder-muscles of a horse, was also more commonly and figuratively used to connote 'the stiffness of "pride" or self-conceit' (*OED*). Alternatively, Sweeney's name may have recalled for some readers the Irish name and figure of the mad king 'Sweeney' of the *Buile Suibhne* of Celtic legend. Louis James, in his *Fiction for the Working Man* (Oxford, 1963), first noted with reference to the story's original title that 'an interesting process of association of ideas is suggested by the fact that the London Directories record an "S. Todd, pearl-stringer", who lived at Clerkenwell at this time' (191). Finally, the name may simply be an unconsciously reversed recollection and slightly jumbled reformulation, in its assonance, of the character of 'Poll Sweedlepipe' in Dickens's *Martin Chuzzlewit* (see Introduction, xvii). Sweedlepipe, whose services as 'an easy shaver . . . and a fashionable hairdresser, also' were advertised to his clients in his shop-window at Kingsgate Street, High Holborn, would still have been fresh in the public's imagination.

*Barbers by that time . . . without the aid of that unctuous auxiliary*: by the time of the serial's publication in 1846–7 (as opposed to the period in which the narrative is ostensibly set) it had become increasingly fashionable for gentlemen to wear their natural hair groomed and fashioned with the help of 'pomatums' or pomades of various sorts; these scented greases and oils (as the author notes here) were indeed typically compounded either of various sorts of animal fat, or (later) from coconut, almond, or macassar oils. Some basic knowledge of the changing fashions with regard to wigs, hair, and hairdressing from the late-eighteenth to the mid-nineteenth centuries is necessary to understand just how Sweeney Todd manages to run 'a most thriving business' despite his distinctly unsavoury appearance and disconcerting, barking laugh. Throughout the eighteenth century, all men who could afford to do so wore wigs. The styles of these wigs became more elaborate as the century wore on; in 1727 there were only a handful of hairdressers in London, yet by 1795 there were close to 50,000 employed in England. Much of Todd's business

would have consisted not in the cutting of hair, but in tending and main-
taining those gentlemen's wigs that were sent, independently of their
owners, to his shop. Beards, moustaches, or, indeed, any other display of
natural hair would have been extremely rare; hence the 'thriving business' Todd would likewise have gained through shaving. Only after 1810
would all classes of men, generally, begin slowly to sport whiskers of
any kind, or to wear their natural head of hair to such a length as to show
full curls.

4 *A long pole painted white . . . into the street from his doorway*: on
contemporary notions regarding the possible symbolism of the traditional barber's pole, see, for example, the following passage included in
*The Gentleman's Magazine* in 1818: 'It has been said that the original dis-
tinction of our barber's shops, was the figure of a human head or *poll* (a
name now almost obsolete except in poll-text), and that from cheapness
or convenience it was changed into a long thick stick, because that too is
called a *pole*. But surgery and shaving were formerly practised by the
same person . . . and the original intention of the parti-coloured staff on
their doors was, to show that the master of the shop could breathe a vein
as well as mow a beard' (*The Gentleman's Magazine*, 27/1 (1818), 228).
Many associate the red of the pole with the blood possibly shed in such
procedures, and the white with the gauze or bandages used to staunch
any wounds. It is rather more likely that the staff that stands outside the
shop exterior was itself a symbol of the actual, physical staff the barber-
surgeon would have had his patient grasp whilst being bled; red, black,
and blue bands may well have marked the colour of the actual covering
with which the wound was 'patched' or bandaged, or might otherwise
have represented an attempt to distinguish the perceived colours of
arterial and venous blood, etc.

*some young Templer*: i.e. a young lawyer, a member of the Temple,
London. A 'Templer' or Templar was the term applied to 'a barrister or
other person who occupies chambers in the Inner or Middle Temple'
(*OED*); by the mid-1800s, to refer to the 'Temple', generally, was to refer
to the area occupied by these two (of the four) Inns of Court. See also text
and notes to pages 3 and 6.

*cacchinatory*: i.e. cachinnatory; 'of, pertaining to, or connected with loud
or immoderate laughter' (*OED*).

5 *in city phraseology, warm*: 'comfortably off, well to do; rich, affluent'
(*OED*).

*Tobias Ragg . . . you are now my apprentice*: Todd's seemingly harsh stipu
lations with regard to the terms of Tobias Ragg's apprenticeship were in
fact standard features that would also have applied to boys and young
men apprenticed to a master of comparable standing, particularly in
most of the older trades and urban crafts. Apprentices typically lived in
their masters' houses, where they were often provided with food and
clothes as well; masters usually had a responsibility (one that the barber

rather obviously both neglects and abuses) to instruct the young artisans entrusted to their care not only in the 'mysteries' of their particular craft, but in manners and professional demeanour, generally. The Statute of Artificers and Apprentices of 1563 entailed an indentured apprenticeship of seven years, although it was common for the terms of the statutes not to be strictly enforced, and many masters made use of their apprentices as a source of cheap labour.

*laundress*: i.e. office cleaner.

6 *Lovett's in Bell-yard*: there were no fewer than twelve 'Bell-yards' in Georgian London, although Mrs Lovett's pie-shop is obviously located in the narrow passage of that name that stretched north of Fleet Street in the City, just past Temple Bar. The traditional topography of the story thus suggests that Todd's barber shop, which is described in this earliest text simply as '[standing] close to the sacred edifice' of St Dunstan's (3), and the cellar of which is understood to be connected to the lower 'vaults' of Mrs Lovett's bake house (see Chapter 23), is itself situated either directly in front of (186 Fleet Street) or directly behind the church. The only other significant thoroughfare that would have separated the two establishments on the level of the streets would be Chancery Lane, which ran parallel and immediately to the east of Bell-yard.

8 *the young bloods*: a 'blood' was 'a hot spark, a man of fire' . . . a 'buck', a 'fast' or foppish man, rake, roisterer (*OED*).

*Fore-street*: central City street just to the north of the Guildhall and London Wall, extending from Bethlehem Hospital and Finsbury, Moorfields, in the east, towards Redcross Street and Aldersgate. The chief shopping thoroughfare in the northern part of the City well into the nineteenth century, the street was almost entirely destroyed by bombing in the Second World War.

*the Courier*: Todd suggests later in the novel (Chapter 10) that he takes in at least one of the 'morning papers' for the amusement of those customers who are compelled to wait in his shop to be shaved. Although there was a ministerial newspaper named the *Courier* published in the early decades of the nineteenth century, the chief London papers that were published on a daily basis at the time in which the novel is actually supposed to be set more typically included titles such as *The Public Advertiser*, *The Morning Post*, and *The London Chronicle*.

10 *Lord North's*: Frederick North, eighth Lord North and second earl of Guilford (1732–92). North served as prime minister from 1770 to 1782. Although North's administration commanded the loyalty and approval of the electors even until 1780, his ministry was to be remembered most for disastrously mismanaging the war with the American colonies, and achieving little if anything in home affairs. Todd's quip regarding the king's appropriation of North's hat, implying that the subservience of North and his allies (the so-called King's Friends) still had a role to play in government policy and decision-making in 1785, suggests a rather inaccurate

view of the political scene at the time. The younger Pitt, having shattered the Opposition in the general election of 1784, was to be firmly installed as first minister for the next nine years. The barber is likely also to have in mind the fact that it was George III who, when he acceded the throne in 1760, made a point of wearing his own hair rather than (as the fashion would then have dictated) a wig, thereby causing no small degree of anxiety amongst men of Todd's profession, much of whose income came from tending the wigs of men of all stations.

12 *Alderman Judd's house in Cripplegate*: in London, an Alderman was the chief officer of a ward or parish. Cripplegate, one of the gates in the old London wall, had been demolished in 1760, but the term still referred generally to the area at the eastern end of Fore Street, the site of the Oakleys' shop and residence.

13 *his month is up to-day, and I must get rid of him*: Oakley has obviously engaged Sam to work in his shop as a mere employee, and for a trial period.

*his aunt belongs to Mr Lupin's congregation*: the unctuous 'Rev Mr Lupin' is a Nonconformist minister—probably perceived by many readers to be a Methodist—whose 'congregation' worshipped outside the communion of the established Church of England. He is dismissed with contempt by all the characters in the novel (with the sole exception of Mrs Oakley) as a fawning hypocrite whose pretences to strict devotion, 'psalm-singing', and 'tea-drinking' serve only inadequately to mask his real character as a licentious and opportunistic alcoholic. The discord that results from Mrs Oakley's devotion to Lupin in the Fore Street household would appear to be deliberately redolent of the similar disruption prompted by the religious megrims of Mrs Varden's devotion to *The Protestant Manual* in Dickens's *Barnaby Rudge*.

*this is the 20th day of August* : a seemingly precise date, although in 1785, 20 August was not, in fact, a Sunday, but a Wednesday. The author therefore suggests that the action of the novel begins at precisely 6.45 on the evening of Tuesday, 19 August 1785, when Lieutenant Thornhill pauses to observe the 'three-quarters . . . struck by the figures' (p. 6) on the clock of St Dunstan's church. Even more obviously detracting from the supposedly careful verisimilitude of the narrative, however, is the fact that August would have been a month in which the courts would not have been in session; the long vacation extended from the end of Trinity term in June, to the beginning of Michaelmas term, in October. There would consequently have been very little activity indeed in and around Inns of Court in the Temple, and in Chancery Lane.

14 *City train-bands*: i.e., trained companies of citizen soldiery. Mr Oakley's suggestion that his status as a local watchman would particularly qualify him to assist his daughter in her romantic difficulties is perhaps touching but entirely quaint; the City 'train bands' had a reputation for being notoriously inept and ineffective.

14 *the Temple-gardens*: see text and note to p. 3, above; the Temple-gardens are situated between Fountain Court and Middle Temple Hall and the Thames; they are today separated from the river by the road that forms the Embankment.

19 *Sam Bolt*: the comic, narrative strand that suggests Sam Bolt's unrequited affection for Johanna Oakley is closely based on the similar infatuation of 'Sim' Tappertit with Dolly Varden in *Barnaby Rudge* (it also recalls the similar aspirations of the apprentice Leonard Holt for his master's daughter in W. H. Ainsworth's *Old St. Paul's* (1841)). Although picked up and treated with some variation in subsequent prose versions of the story, the sub-plot is not pursued beyond Sam's appearance in Mrs Lovett's pie-shop in chapter 4 of the original serial.

*Sheerness*: flourishing Kentish dockyard at the mouth of the Medway (since the time of Charles II) with view across the Thames estuary, and occupying much of the north-west tip of the Isle of Sheppey.

20 *it was a time of war*: peculiarly, the period in which the novel is set was actually one of the few extended stretches of peace in the eighteenth century, bracketed as it was by the end of the American War (from the end of 1783 to the beginning of 1784), and the war with the French Republic, commencing in 1793.

*Walk'd the waters like a thing of life*: the quotation is from canto I, stanza 3 of Byron's *The Corsair*: 'She walks the waters like a thing of life, | And seems to dare the elements to strife'.

*taffrail*: 'the aftermost portion of the poop-rail of a ship' (*OED*).

21 *cashiered*: 'to dismiss from a position of command or authority; to depose. (In the army and navy involving disgrace and permanent exclusion from the service)' (*OED*).

*the Temple-stairs*: see text and note to p. 3, above; Temple Stairs was a Thames landing place, leading via Middle Temple Lane to Fleet Street just beyond Temple Bar.

22 *Colonel Jeffery, of the Indian Army*: i.e. meaning he was serving in the British Army, and stationed in India.

23 *watch-house*: 'a house used as a station for municipal night-watchmen, in which the chief constable of the night sits to receive and detain in custody till the morning any disorderly persons brought in by the watchmen' (*OED*).

*the Temple in Fleet-street, opposite Chancery-lane*: see text and note to p. 3, above.

28 *Bell-yard, Temple-bar*: see text and note to p. 3, above. Bell-yard was the second street on the north side of Fleet Street past Temple Bar. Some later versions of the narrative would also note that Mrs Lovett's pie-shop was 'on the left hand side of Bell-yard, going down from Carey-street'; consequently, the shop would have been on the east side of Bell-yard.

29 *Lincoln's-inn*: one of the four Inns of Court, situated on the western side of Chancery Lane.

*Gray's-inn*: the last of the four Inns of Court, referred to here as 'distant' due to its location north of Holborn, slightly apart from the other central legal institutions in London.

31 *'a lurking devil in her eye'*: in all likelihood a recollection or allusion to the opening lines of Henry Carey's 'An Extempore Thought on Flattery', included in his 1720 *Poems on Several Occasions* ('Flattery's a base, unmanly, coward Vice, | A lurking Devil in a fair Disguise . . .'). The phrase 'a lurking devil in her eye' was to become a favourite description of writers of later Gothic fiction.

*Mr Snow's in Paper-buildings*: legal chambers in the Temple, the backs of which overlooked Temple Gardens. The chambers figure prominently in *Barnaby Rudge* (chapter 15), in which they are featured as the residence of Sir John Chester.

32 *cut*: i.e. ran away from; quit.

34 *'they would take her life!'*: the theft of private property such as a silver candlestick would have been based upon the particular properties of the item(s) stolen, and the prosecutor's estimation of the value of the goods in actual monetary terms. If the silver candlestick that Todd alleges Mrs Ragg to have stolen was estimated in court even to be of modest value (the theft of anything valued above a shilling—a silk handkerchief, for example—was considered to be a capital crime, and so punishable by death), she would indeed be likely, if convicted, to be sentenced to hanging. Depending upon the whim of the judge or the intervention of a patron or protector, such a death sentence could be commuted or reduced to transportation overseas.

38 *like the dog in the manger*: proverbial phrase to refer to those who would still begrudge others something for which they themselves had no use.

45 *a river which deposited an enormous quantity of gold dust in its progress to the ocean*: the rumour of such a bountiful source of wealth recalls the Pactolus, a river in ancient Lydia, the sands of which contained gold.

52 *The course of true love never yet ran smooth*: a reference to Shakespeare's *A Midsummer Night's Dream*, I. i. 134.

53 *one of the most celebrated lapidaries*: i.e. jeweller and dealer in precious stones; in this instance, a practised fence for stolen goods as well.

*Moorfields*: area to the north of the city, considered earlier in the eighteenth century to be disreputable, and a favourite haunt of highwaymen and other thieves; Moorfields had continued to grow throughout the period, however. In the novel it is the area in which the Oakleys' shop and residence are situated (see p. 8 and note).

*brilliants*: diamonds of the finest cut and brilliancy.

55 *chaffing*: bantering, chatting inconsequentially.

58 *The Thieves' Home*: the setting of the thieves' den and the secretive and ritualistic nature of its habitués appears to be based to some extent on the account of Sim Tappertit's presiding over a meeting of the ' 'Prentice Knights' in chapter 8 of *Barnaby Rudge*.

59 *tell us what you are, cutpurse, footpad, or what not?*: 'cutpurse' was the general term for a pickpocket or thief (noted in Samuel Johnson's 1755 *Dictionary* to have designated 'one who steals by the method of cutting purses, a common practice when men wore their purses at their girdles'); 'footpads' were highwaymen who robbed on foot, as distinguished from those who did so on horseback.

63 *the north-road*: i.e., the old Great North Road, stretching towards York; traditionally rumoured to be a favourite haunt of thieves and highwaymen.

*the best I have had has been two sixties*: throughout the period banknotes—which served as receipts for money on deposit—were made out to the bearer of the note, and were treated as a general form of currency. The speaker appears to imply that he has recently robbed his victims of two such banknotes to the value of sixty pounds each. Alternatively, 'sixty per-cents' was sometimes used as a colloquial synonym to refer to usurers (who asked for a return of 'sixty i'th'hundred'), so the thief may be suggesting that he has profited from the possessions of two usurers, which could very well have been considerable.

*looby*: ignorant-looking.

*like a don*: like a real, first-class gentleman.

*tip-top*: excellent.

*your swell cove*: a well-dressed gentleman; a rogue to be outwitted.

*bouncing my victim out of a good swag of tin*: (thieves' slang) menacing him out of a nice quantity of money.

73 *Big Ben, the beef-eater from the Tower*: Johanna's uncle has in all likelihood been dubbed 'Big Ben' in recollection of the famous pugilist 'Big Ben' Brain, who from 1791 claimed the title 'Champion of Britain'; he serves as one of the famous Yeomen of the Guard and Warders of the Tower of London.

*guttling*: one that guttles; 'gormandizing, guzzling' (*OED*).

*go and mind your lions and elephants in the Tower*: much like the bracket clock of St Dunstan's (see p. 3 and note), the menagerie traditionally housed within the precincts of the Tower of London was one of the most popular of the city's attractions for country visitors. The menagerie had been founded in 1235 when the Holy Roman Emperor made a gift of three leopards to King Henry III; the animals were open to public viewing, and the popular expression 'going to see the lions' in the sense of 'seeing the sights' appears to date from this period. The royal menagerie soon expanded to include elephants and even polar bears. The animals were moved to the Zoological Gardens, in Regent's

Park, in 1835, after one of the lions attacked several members of the garrison stationed at the Tower.

76 *I am a wolf that stole sheep's clothing*: a recollection of Matthew 7: 15: 'Beware of false prophets, which come to you in sheep's clothing, but inwardly they are ravening wolves'.

77 *If you and I are to live together . . . what you have to expect*: the advice of Oakley's Lawyer Hutchins is in fact generous. The property of both married women and their minor children remained under the legal control of their partners; Oakley need not necessarily have provided his wife with a maintenance should he have turned her out-of-doors.

*the British colony, at the Cape of Good Hope*: within the historical frame in which the story is set, an anachronism. The colony around the Cape of Good Hope, near the southernmost tip of the African continent, was first occupied by the British only in 1795; control of the territory was relinquished temporarily in 1803, although British forces would again occupy the Cape Colony in 1806. It was formally ceded to the British by the Dutch in 1814.

78 *the eastern coast of Madagascar*: island located off the south-eastern coast of Africa, in the Indian Ocean. Its position having made it an important link in the Spice Trade between Europe and the Middle East and India, the island had witnessed attempts by both the French and the English to establish permanent settlements in Madagascar since as early as the seventeenth century.

*a lee shore*: shore sheltered from the wind.

87 *smalls*: knee breeches.

93 *By the earliest dawn of the day . . . call at their residences*: more traditional, itinerant street-dealers still plied their ancient and thriving trade selling hot pies from Greenwich, in the east, as far as Hyde Park Corner, the traditional entrance to London from the west (see p. 134 and note, below). Permanently situated retail pie-shops had begun to flourish in the city only throughout the late eighteenth and early nineteenth centuries.

96 *My poverty and my destitution consent, if my will be adverse*: another recollection of Shakespeare, from *Romeo and Juliet* (v. ii. 75).

106 *take him for all in all as the man in the play says . . . look upon his like again*: again a reference to Shakespeare, *Hamlet* (i. ii. 187–8).

111 *like the ignis-fatuus of the swamp*: more popularly known as a 'will-o'-the wisp'; 'a phosphorescent light seen hovering or flitting over marshy ground, and supposed to be due to the spontaneous combustion of an inflammable gas . . . derived from decaying organic matter' (*OED*).

134 *At that time Hyde Park Corner was very nearly out of town*: Hyde Park Corner was in fact, until the very end of the eighteenth century, the site only of a turnpike or toll gate on the roads leading towards the villages of Kensington and Knightsbridge, and was considered not only 'very nearly

out of town', as the author writes, but marked the western entrance to the metropolis.

135 *At that period . . . enormous rates of interest*: as the subsequent paragraphs make clear, Mundel is not merely a moneylender, but a usurer who charges excessive and illegal rates of interest and exchange, and lends money upon security. The official limit on the rate of interest had—since the earliest decades of the eighteenth century—been set at 5 per cent; the normal rate of interest in the period for money placed in a bank would typically have been 3 per cent. The author's comment that 'the follies and vices of the nobility [had been] somewhat as great' in 1785 as they were when he was writing in 1846–7 is to some extent confirmed by the depiction of characters such as 'Moses' in Richard Brinsley Sheridan's *The School for Scandal* (1777).

*the Uxbridge Road*: in 1785, a journey of two miles along the Uxbridge Road would have brought Todd to a rural area that was still little more than a tiny village surrounded by market gardens and small private estates, like John Mundel's own.

137 *'I wonder . . . if he is a duke . . . I'll call him your grace next time and see if he objects to it'*: 'Your Grace' was the proper form of address to a duke or duchess; 'My Lord' was the proper form of address to a peer below the rank of duke. 'Lord' was used when addressing an earl, marquis, or viscount. Mundel later in the novel (p. 202) is stated more clearly to be under the assumption that Todd is a 'nobleman who came from the Queen to borrow £8,000 upon a string of pearls'.

146 *there were thirty or forty swords . . . richly ornamented*: gentlemen in the eighteenth century still typically carried swords about with them as a sign of their birth and status.

148 *Whitefriars*: area just east of the Temple.

*Hamlet's grave-digger*: a reference to Hamlet's exchange with the grave-digger in *Hamlet*, v. i.

150 *atymonspheric . . . stinkifications*: like many characters in Dickens's novels—most memorably Sam and Tony Weller (in *Pickwick Papers* (1837)) and Mrs Gamp (in *Martin Chuzzlewit*)—the beadle is prone to comic malapropisms.

*some mechanics' institution of those days . . . some service to him*: Mechanics' Institutes (the first of which was established in 1823) aimed at the improvement of the working classes, and looked to provide education and political self-betterment both for manual workers and for tradesmen who had risen in the world.

151 *At last there was a confirmation to be held at St Dunstan's church . . . nobody knew what*: in ecclesiastical terms, a confirmation normally referred specifically to the formal ratification of the election or other appointment of a bishop.

152 *Moreover the beadle . . . on any account*: like so many other portraits of this parish functionary in the period, the author's characterization of the beadle owes an enormous amount to some of the most memorable passages in Dickens's early work, including that novelist's devastating caricature of the local beadle in *Our Parish* (when yet writing under the pseudonym 'Boz') collected in the *Sketches by Boz* in 1836, and of course Bumble in *Oliver Twist* (1837–9).

*a poor, miserable charity boy . . . muffin cap in his hand*: 'muffin caps' were the characteristic flat, woollen caps, typically worn by such 'charity boys'. The so-called charity schools of the city provided education to the poorest Londoners, who were distinguished from other children by their distinctive and pointedly conspicuous uniforms, often adorned with some sort of benefactor's badge.

161 *no inept representation of the Mephistopheles of the German drama*: the traditional tale of the German physician and alchemist Faust, who sells his soul to the demon Mephistopheles, is likely already to have been familiar to English readers from plays such as Marlowe's *The Tragical History of Doctor Faustus* (pub. *c*.1600). The author's specific reference here to 'the Mephistopheles of the German drama' is altogether more likely to refer to a native drama such as H. P. Gratin's *Faust; or, the Demon of the Drachenfels*, which had been staged at Sadler's Wells in September 1842, with the actor Henry Marston featured in the role of Mephistopheles. The character was destined to enjoy a relatively prosperous career in the late-nineteenth- and early-twentieth-century English theatre as a fixture of Christmas pantomimes, featuring in pieces with titles such as *Faust, or Merry Mephistopheles and his Mysterious Mysteries*, etc.

163 *old Fleet Market*: the meat and vegetable market on this site was actually built on the bridge that had been arched to cover the old Fleet Ditch—the filthy and polluted sewer that had once been the Fleet River—between Fleet Street and Holborn in 1733. The notoriously dilapidated market had consisted of two rows of one-storey shops connected by a covered walkway; it had slowly been demolished (in 1826–30) some fifteen to twenty years prior to the publication of *The String of Pearls*, to make way for Farringdon Street. The author's justly contemptuous dismissal of Fleet Market as one of the features of 'Old' London, the primary 'glory' of which had 'consisted in all sorts of filth enough to produce a pestilence within the city of London' offers some indication of the extent to which the readers of the period perceived themselves to be living in generally progressive and meliorating times.

*'Jarvey'*: i.e. 'Jarvis', slang for a hackney coachman or cab-driver.

*Peckham Rye*: even until as late as the mid-nineteenth century, Peckham—south of the bustling dockland of Rotherhithe, and north of 'the Forest' (or Forest Hill)—remained a predominantly rural area; its fields were dotted with market gardens, or otherwise provided pasturage for cattle being driven to the London markets by drovers from the south.

In the course of the eighteenth century several large houses were built, and the area had also gained something of a reputation for its literary and philosophical societies and its educational institutions and boarding schools (the novelist and playwright Oliver Goldsmith lived and taught at the Peckham academy of Dr Milner in 1756–7, and the poet Robert Browning attended a similar establishment run by the Revd Thomas Ready in the 1820s); it was also increasingly well-known as a centre and meeting place for Methodists, Quakers, and other Nonconformists. The construction of the Grand Surry Canal in the first decade of the nineteenth century and the arrival of the South Metropolitan Gas Company near the Old Kent Road in the early 1840s signalled the earliest beginnings of the rapid industrial transformations that would change the area for ever. In representing Fogg's asylum as a 'lonely, large, rambling old-looking house' situated in a remote, isolated, and generally uncultivated and 'wild spot, on which now and then a serious robbery had been committed' (165), the author is once again creating a purposefully 'nostalgic' feel for his readers, for whom the area had become increasingly suburban, and would—within only a few years—be easily accessible by omnibus and (eventually) railway.

164 *a distance of about a mile and a half*: after crossing Blackfriars-bridge (built 1760–9), Todd travels a short distance on Great Surry Street before making for the Old Kent Road, which passes through Peckham on its way towards Dover.

167 *further proof of his mental disorder*: although the eighteenth century had witnessed some genuine improvements with regard to the manner in which madness and perceived mental illnesses were treated by the medical establishment, for a long time London's Bethlehem Hospital remained the only institution dedicated exclusively to the care of the mentally infirm or the insane, and the hospital was of course open to sightseers until the 1770s. The move away from regarding mental illness itself as some form of demonic possession at least facilitated the development of more humane forms of therapy, many of which advocated that patients be sequestered in rural asylums far removed from the hectic activity of the city. The period also witnessed considerable concern, however, regarding reports of systematic abuse in some of the new, private asylums that had been established in the London suburbs.

172 *Banbury cakes*: cakes traditionally made in the town of Banbury, in Oxfordshire.

185 *a large Whitney riding-coat with a cape that would have thrown off a deluge*: i.e. a riding coat made of Whitney or 'Witney', a heavy, loose woollen material with a nap manufactured in the Oxfordshire town of the same name.

189 *Grosvenor-street, near Park-lane*: a location still—in the period in which the action of the novel is set—almost at the very edge of the north-west boundary of London. The junction of Tyburn Lane (Park Lane) and

Tyburn Road (modern Oxford Street) still led only to a 'Marybone Lane' bordered almost entirely by open fields.

191 *a small dose of laudanum*: a solution of opium in alcohol, and easily available for purchase at an apothecary's shop in the eighteenth century.

193 *a wooden surtout*: a surtout was a man's double-breasted, full-length, and close-bodied coat; a wooden 'overcoat' is consequently a euphemism for a coffin.

199 *reconnaissance, as they called it*: the author calls attention to (strictly speaking) a term of military strategy that would yet have been unknown to many of his readers; i.e. 'an examination or survey of a tract of country, made with a view to ascertain the position or strength of an enemy' (*OED*).

203 *yeoman*: meaning, here, simply a 'countryman of respectable standing'.

212 *sand-blind*: dim-sighted, but also meaning dull-witted.

217 *Fetter-lane*: major street, just to the east of St Dunstan's church, stretching north from Fleet-street to Holborn.

218 *'He smugs 'om'*: i.e. does away with them, as Crotchet makes clear, although also a pun; more commonly, to 'smug' meant 'to smarten up (oneself or another, one's appearance)' (*OED*). Like Blathers and Duff, the two Bow Street Runners in Dickens's *Oliver Twist*, Crotchet employs a peculiar, cant dialect of criminal or underworld language.

225 *The Mud Woman's Tale*: not subtitled as such in the original 1846–7 serial. The fate of the woman in this inset narrative, following her participation in Tobias's escape from Fogg's asylum in the next chapter, is not pursued in this original version of the story. In the much-expanded version of the narrative published by Charles Fox in 1880, she is recaptured by Fogg and his assistant, Watson, and brutally murdered by being thrown into a well, a procedure they casually refer to as placing her 'in number ten'. See *Sweeney Todd, The Demon Barber of Fleet Street* (London: Charles Fox, 1880): 91–3.

244 *mother-in-law*: i.e. stepmother.

246 *jack-towel*: 'a long towel with the ends sewed together, suspended from a roller' (*OED*).

251 *ran like a lamp-lighter*: 'said with allusion to the rapidity with which the lamplighter ran on his rounds, or climbed the ladders formerly used to reach the street lamps' (*OED*).

262 *like grim War to 'Smooth his wrinkled form'*: cf. Shakespeare, *Richard III*, I. i. 9: 'Grim-visag'd War hath smooth'd his wrinkled front'.

263 *'sang amary Jameses'*: a 'James' or 'jemmy' was a sheep's head, when served as a dish; hence, slang expression here for 'bloody sheep's heads' ('sang amary = sanguinary'). Henry Mayhew, in his *London Labour and the London Poor* (London, 1851–61), writes of street vendors having a

'prime hot jemmy' apiece (ii. 48). Clare Market was a venue for the stalls of butchers and greengrocers not far from Fleet-street and Bell-yard.

274 *come up from Braintree . . . staying at the Bull's Head*: the Braintree district, in Essex, about ten miles from Chelmsford, was then still a small farming community; the Bull's Head was an inn in nearby Clare Market (see p. 263 and note).

279 *to have the child marked as a pie*: i.e., the man has travelled from Newington with his wife, who 'won't fancy anything but one of Lovett's veal pies', in accordance with the popular belief that the particular cravings of pregnant women would 'mark' their child's character in life (although there is also a slight pun on 'marking' in the sense of scoring pastry or pie dough in cookery). The couple obviously believe the particular craving to be a promising sign for their future child.

# Suggestions for Further Reading

All of the items listed below contain information relating either to the story of Sweeney Todd itself, or to specific circumstances under which the tale was first published, and the more general commercial, theatrical, and cultural contexts within which it was later popularized. Readers should be warned, however, that not all of these sources are entirely to be relied upon when it comes to matters of historical fact; a great many journalists and popular authors writing on Todd remain to this day eager to believe that the barber's story is a true one.

## The History of 'Sweeney Todd', The String of Pearls, and the Literature of Crime

Haining, Peter (ed.), *Dead of Night: Thirteen Stories by the Masters of the Macabre* (New York: Dorset Press, 1989).

——(ed.), *The Penny Dreadful, Or, Strange, Horrid & Sensational Tales!* (London: Victor Gollancz, 1975).

——*The Mystery and Horrible Murders of Sweeney Todd, the Demon Barber of Fleet Street* (London: Frederick Muller Ltd., 1979).

——*Sweeney Todd: The Real Story of the Demon Barber of Fleet Street* (London: Boxtree Ltd., 1993).

Hibbert, H. G., *A Playgoer's Memories* (London: Grant Richards, 1920).

Kent, William, *London Mystery and Mythology* (London and New York: Staples Press, 1952).

Kilburn, Matthew, 'Sweeney Todd [*called* the Demon Barber of Fleet Street] (supp. *fl.*1784)', in the *Oxford Dictionary of National Biography*, 54: 887–8.

Smith, Helen R., *New Light on Sweeney Todd, Thomas Peckett Prest, James Malcolm Rymer and Elizabeth Caroline Grey* (London: Jarndyce, 2002).

## Victorian Popular Literature, 'Penny Bloods', and Melodrama

Booth, Michael, *English Melodrama* (London: Herbert Jenkins, 1965).

—— 'The Social and Literary Context: The Theatre and Its Audience', in Clifford Leech and T. W. Craik (eds.), *The Revels History of Drama in English (1750–1880)* (London: Methuen, 1975), 1–58.

Cross, Gilbert, *Next Week—East Lynne: Domestic Drama in Performance 1820–1874* (London: Associated University Presses, 1977).

Davis, Jim, and Emeljanow, Victor, *Reflecting the Audience: London Theatregoing, 1840–1880* (Iowa City: University of Iowa Press, 2001).

Disher, Maurice Willson, *Blood and Thunder: Mid-Victorian Melodrama and its Origins* (London: Frederick Muller Ltd., 1949).

James, Louis (ed.), *Print and People: 1819–1859* (London: Peregrine Books, 1978).

—— 'James Malcolm Rymer [*pseuds*. M. J. Merry, Malcolm J. Merry] (1803/4–1884)', in the *Oxford Dictionary of National Biography*, 48: 494–5.

—— 'Thomas Peckett Prest (1809/10–1859)', in the *Oxford Dictionary of National Biography*, 45: 251–2.

Kalikoff, Beth, *Murder and Moral Decay in Victorian Popular Literature* (Ann Arbor: UMI Research, 1986).

Kilgariff, Michael (ed.), *The Golden Age of Melodrama: Twelve 19th-Century Melodramas* (London: Wolfe Publishing Ltd., 1974).

McWilliam, Rohan, 'Edward Lloyd (1815–1890)', in the *Oxford Dictionary of National Biography* (2004), 34: 118–19.

Springhall, John, '"Disseminating Impure Literature": The "Penny Dreadful" Publishing Business since 1860', in *Economic History Review*, NS, 47/3 (Aug. 1994), 567–84.

Summers, Montague, *A Gothic Bibliography* (London: Fortune Press, 1940).

—— *The Gothic Quest: A History of the Gothic Novel* (London: Fortune Press, 1938).

Turner, E. S., *Boys Will Be Boys: The Story of Sweeney Todd, Deadwood Dick, Sexton Blake, Billy Bunter et. al.* (London: Michael Joseph, 1948).

Waite, A. E., *The Quest for Bloods* (London: Ferret, 1997).

### *Modern Versions, Editions, and Adaptations of 'Sweeney Todd', and Related Criticism*

Bond, Christopher G., *Sweeney Todd, The Demon Barber of Fleet Street, A Melodrama* (London: Samuel French, 1974).

Charmoy, Cozette de, *The True Life of Sweeney Todd: (A Collage Novel)* (London: Gaberbocchus, 1973).

Collins, Dick, 'Introduction' to *The String of Pearls: The Original Tale of Sweeney Todd* (Ware, Hertfordshire: Wordsworth Editions, 2005), v–xii.

Cross, Gillian, *The Dark Behind the Curtain* (Oxford: Oxford University Press, 1982).

Pate, Janet, *The Black Book of Villains* (London: David & Charles, 1975).

Richards, Jeffrey (ed.), *The Unknown 1930s: An Alternative History of the British Cinema 1929–1939* (London: I. B. Tauris, Publishers, 1998).

Rosser, Austin, *Sweeney Todd: The Demon Barber of Fleet Street, A Victorian Melodrama*. Based on the original by George Dibdin Pitt (London: Samuel French, 1971).

*Sweeney Todd*. Producer Harry Rowson, Perf. Moore Marriott, Zoe Palmer, Charles Ashton. Stoll Films, 1928.

*Sweeney Todd. The Demon Barber*. Celebrated Crime Series (London: Mellifont Press, 1936).

*Sweeney Todd, The Demon Barber of Fleet Street*. Dir. George King. Perf. Tod Slaughter, Stella Rho, Johnny Singer, Eve Lister. Ambassador Pictures, 1936.

*Sweeney Todd*. Dir. David Moore. Perf. Roy Winstone, Essie Davis, and David Warner. BBC One Film Productions, 2006.

*The Tale of Sweeney Todd*. Dir. John Schlesinger. Perf. Ben Kingsley, Joanna Lumley, and Campbell Scott. Showtime/Third Row Center Films, 1998.

### *Stephen Sondheim's* Sweeney Todd, The Demon Barber of Fleet Street *and Related Criticism*

Banfield, Stephen, *Sondheim's Broadway Musicals* (Ann Arbor: Michigan Press, 1993).

Bordman, Gerald Martin, *American Operetta from H.M.S. Pinafore to Sweeney Todd* (New York: Oxford University Press, 1981).

Gordon, Joanne, *Art Isn't Easy* (Carbondale, Ill.: Southern Illinois University Press, 1990).

Gottfried, Martin, *Sondheim* (New York: Harry N. Abrams, 1993).

Hurrell, Christopher, 'The Time They Did *Sweeney* in Chicago', *Sondheim Review*, 9/4 (Spring 2003), 31–3.

Keller, James, Booklet, 'Notes on *Sweeney Todd*', in *Sweeney Todd: Live In Concert*, by Stephen Sondheim and Hugh Wheeler (New York Philharmonic, 2000), 14–23.

Olsen, John, 'Terfel Stars in a Rich and Eerie *Sweeney*', *Sondheim Review*, 9/3 (Winter 2003), 12.

—— 'Sondheim Wanted *Sweeney* to be Very Scary', *Sondheim Review*, 9/3 (Winter 2003), 13.

Secrest, Meryle, *Stephen Sondheim: A Life* (New York: Alfred E. Knopf, 1998).

Sondheim, Stephen, and Wheeler, Hugh, *Sweeney Todd, The Demon Barber of Fleet Street. A Musical Thriller* (New York: Dodd, Mead & Company, 1979).

—— *Sweeney Todd: The Demon Barber of Fleet Street. A Musical Thriller*. Orch. Sarah Travis. Perf. Patti LuPone, Michael Cerveris. Nonesuch, 2005.

—— *Sweeney Todd: The Demon Barber of Fleet Street. A Musical Thriller*. Orch. Jonathan Tunick. Perf. Angela Lansbury, Len Cariou, and Victor Garber. Cond. Paul Gemignani. RCA Red Seal, 1979.

Zadan, Craig, *Sondheim & Company* (New York: HarperCollins, 1974; 2nd edn., updated, De Capo Press, 1994).

### Online Information and Internet Resources

*BloodsandDimeNovels*: *a forum for collectors to discuss Bloods, Penny Dreadfuls, and Dime Novels*. Yahoo Groups. Founded August 2000. Owner and Manager: Justin Gilbert. <http://groups.yahoo.com/group/BloodsandDimeNovels>

*Crime Library: Criminal Minds and Methods*. Serial Killers: Truly Weird or Shocking: Sweeney Todd. Mark Gribben. Courtroom Television Network. 2005. <http://www.crimelibrary.com/serial_killers/weird/todd/index_1.html>

*Dime Novels and Penny Dreadfuls*. Project Managers: Connie Brooks, Jim Coleman, and Eleanore Stewart. Stanford University Dept. of Special Collections. December 2006. <http://www-sul.stanford.edu/depts/dp/pennies/home.html>

*Sweeney Todd, The Demon Barber of Fleet Street in Concert*. Ellen M. Krass Productions and KQED. Public Broadcasting Service. October 2001. <http://www.pbs.org/kqed/demonbarber/index.html>